"I WANT YOU."

Together they sank down among the violets, upon the silken sheets. He leaned to taste the nipple of her breast, tested the pulse on the side of her neck, and allowed his hand to settle upon the small mound at the apex of her thighs.

In an instant she was glowing with internal heat. Pleasure rippled through her in waves. He held her, his fingers tirelessly, gently moving until her stomach muscles contracted in spasms, his mouth teasing her nipples into tight buds of anticipation. He began to enter her, then he went still.

"DON'T STOP," SHE WHISPERED, "OH, DON'T, PLEASE."

He eased deeper, soothing, stretching, applying exquisite pressure until she moaned. She was melting, her body and spirit as liquid as hot candle wax. The need to take him inside her was beginning to feel like desperation. He began to move within her in a rhythm as measureless as it was ancient. She rose against him, clinging, surrendering to the rapture. Boundless, gilded with firelight, it caught them and sent them striving together into the darkness.

Also by Jennifer Blake

LOVE'S WILD DESIRE

TENDER BETRAYAL

THE STORM AND THE SPLENDOR

GOLDEN FANCY

EMBRACE AND CONQUER

ROYAL SEDUCTION

SURRENDER IN MOONLIGHT

MIDNIGHT WALTZ

FIERCE EDEN

Royal Passion

JENNIFER BLAKE

FAWCETT COLUMBINE • NEW YORK

A Fawcett Columbine Book
Published by Ballantine Books
 Published in the United States by Ballantine Books, a division of Random House, Inc., New York, and simultaneously in Canada by Random House of Canada Limited, Toronto.

Library of Congress Catalog Card Number: 85-90597

ISBN: 0-449-90101-7

Cover painting by James Griffin
Designed by Ann Gold
Manufactured in the United States of America

First Edition: February 1986

10 9 8 7 6 5 4 3 2 1

Royal Passion

CHAPTER

1

The fire leaped high, its resinous wood crackling and snapping so that orange sparks swirled with the smoke up into the dark branches of the overhanging trees. The glow of the flames was reflected in the paint of the gypsy caravans, highlighting their chipped red and blue glaze and their tarnished gilt. It shone on the bracelets and belts of polished coins worn by the gypsy women and on the earrings that hung from the ears of the lounging men. Polished brass uniform buttons and shining boots also refracted the blaze, glinting in the dimness as the men of the cadre of Prince Roderic of Ruthenia shifted on the piled rugs that formed their couches. They talked among themselves in low voices, laughing, lifting cups to drink.

The prince himself sat with his blond head bent over a mandolin. His strong, nimble fingers drew from it a wild rhapsody, a heart-quickening song that seemed to throb with gaiety and reckless passion in the cool night air. An old gypsy with a bent back kept pace with him on a violin. Roderic looked up, his face alight with laughter as together the two played point and counterpoint; the music blending, clashing, swelling with the fierce pleasure of the players. The fire's glow gleamed on the high cheekbones of the prince and shone bright in the vivid blue of his eyes while leaving the triangular hollows of his jaw in shadow. It caught the straight line of his nose and the square jut of his chin. It turned his hair to molten gold and made a pale blur of his open-necked shirt and white uniform trousers. He appeared relaxed there among his friends, without care, and yet there was about him a guarded awareness, a tension that could be released instantly into explosive action. Virile, broad of shoulder, he seemed like some hero of the ancient legends, sure of his power, without peer, frighteningly invincible.

Marie Angeline Rachel Delacroix stood watching from the shadows of an oak thicket, her wide gray gaze fixed upon the prince. Her head ached, and there was a burning wetness at her temple where a deep graze spread blood into the dark waves of her hair. She could hardly lift her right arm for the stiffness of her shoulder. Her cloak was stained with mud, her gown of white silk was torn loose at the waist, and she thought that only the thickness of her petticoats with their horsehair padding had saved her from a broken knee.

None of these things was surprising, considering that she had been pushed from a moving carriage not more than a half hour before. But it was not the pain of her injuries, or even the shock of what had happened, that caused the shudders rippling over her body and the feeling of sick fear in the pit of her stomach. It was the man she saw before her in the gypsy camp.

It was Prince Roderic of the Balkan country of Ruthenia; the man she must seduce. And betray.

She had never seduced a man in her life. Oh, she had flirted a little, had practiced the art of attracting members of the opposite sex at the various balls and picnics and pink teas arranged for the entertainment of young ladies making their first appearance in New Orleans society. But never had she set out to entice a man, to enthrall him so that he would willingly do her bidding. Never. No matter what others might say.

Or perhaps she had. She did not know, could not be sure. Still, whatever she may have done in the past, she did not deserve to be set such an impossible task.

The music of violin and mandolin rose to a crescendo, hovering, then with sweet resonance died away. The gypsies leaped to their feet, shouting, beating their hands and rattling tambourines in applause. The prince tilted his head in brief acknowledgment, smiling, and slapped the old gypsy on the shoulder. Then, with a smooth flexing of muscles, he rose to his feet and swung away from the fire. His long strides carried him across the clearing with incredible swiftness. He was moving toward where Mara stood, his movements sure, as if he knew precisely where he was going, had known of her presence for some time.

She took a hasty step backward, but it was too late. He was before her, reaching to take her hand and draw her into the light. She swayed a little, and his grip, warm and firm on her fingers, tightened in instant support.

"Welcome, fair wraith," he said, his voice gentle but cool, though a moment later it held the quiet scrape of drawn steel as he turned toward his men. "Fair or not, it is without doubt a wraith, else how could she get through the sentries?"

"The fault is mine, Your Highness."

From the darkness behind her stepped a young man. He was dark and handsome in a raffish fashion, with liquid brown eyes, a gold ring in his ear, and a cowrie-shell amulet on a leather thong around his neck. He held himself well, with no sign of submissiveness or guilt.

"Well, Luca?"

The gypsy Luca swept a hand in Mara's direction. "Look at her. Do you see a threat? I saw her thrown from a carriage. When she came this way, I followed."

"Graceless," said Prince Roderic, "you might have offered aid." The words were offhand, but he was frowning as his gaze rested on Mara's pale face.

"It seemed best to see what she would do."

Mara, hearing the note of lingering curiosity in the gypsy's voice, thought back to the moment when she had picked herself up and started toward the encampment. Had it seemed too obvious that she had known where she was going? She had been told in which direction to look, but after her jarring fall she had been stunned, disoriented. In the end, she had simply followed the sound of the music. Her progress had been slow, erratic. It could not have appeared otherwise. Her relief was weakening; her fingers trembled in the prince's grasp.

"Come," he said abruptly, and led her toward the pile of rugs he had left.

She sank down upon them. As she felt the warmth of the fire, she shivered, and the graze on her forehead began to throb. She reached up to touch the skin near it. The prince snapped his fingers, giving a low-voiced order, and immediately a pair of gypsy women came forward. They bathed her injuries and used a scarf of red cotton shot with gold silk thread to tie a bandage pad to her temple over the loosened waves of her dark hair, which fell to her waist. Pressing a cup of red wine into her hand, they moved silently back to their places.

The wine was new and harsh, but it gave her strength. She sipped at it, trying to clear her mind, to subdue the trembling inside her by force of will. Through her lashes, she could see the prince's men gathered around her. Their faces mirrored a disturbing sympathy combined with judicial patience. Near her on the rugs sat the prince, with one elbow resting on a drawn-up knee and his cupped palm supporting his chin. His gaze upon her was lucid, steady, assessing.

Roderic shifted his position, rubbing his finger along his nose. This woman was not the kind a man would use and discard; she was too fine, too fresh. Despite the shadow of fear that she sought to hide in the depths of her clear gray eyes, she appeared untouched, so untutored in the ways of men that he would swear it had not yet occurred to her how vulnerable her position was, there among them. More, she was beautiful, her skin soft and translucent, her mouth tenderly shaped, infinitely kissable. The line of her cheek, the curve of her neck, the firm molding of her chin were perfection. She had capable hands with long fingers, but so slim and white were they that it was plain she did no labor. The silk of her gown was finely woven, far from cheap, and the style, though fairly restrained, was easily recognizable as coming from one of the most fashionable modistes in Paris. No, she was not the kind of woman a man would take out into the French countryside and fling from him like some useless thing.

He leaned toward her. "Gypsy hospitality does not require that a guest give a name; still, I ask it. Dark angel, who are you?"

Mara lifted her gaze to meet his hard blue stare. She moistened her lips, remembering her instructions. They had seemed easy, at least when compared to the enormity of what she must do, but now she could not seem to bring herself to follow them. Once she had spoken the words, once the lies had begun, there would be no drawing back.

"What?" Roderic said softly. "Is it guile that restrains you or conscience?"

The trap had been sprung so suddenly, and was so blatant, that Mara felt the stir of anger. It gave her courage. Allowing the distress she had been hiding to seep into her eyes, she shook her head. "I don't—I can't—remember my name."

"Ah, the misfortune of Ulysses, another waylaid traveler. A loss of memory can be most inconvenient—or entirely otherwise. Have you a purse about you?"

A purse, with some means of identification. Mara made a show of searching through the pockets of her cloak. "No. Apparently not."

"Robbed? Then the culprit was either inept or stupid, for he discarded what was of most value."

"You mean—"

"Holding you to ransom would have made much more sense."

There was a low rumble of comment among the uniformed men. For the first time, Mara allowed herself to look at them as individuals rather than as simply members of the prince's entourage. They were only five in number, though they seemed more.

Roderic, following the line of her gaze with a swift turn of his head, came to his feet. "Does my *garde du corps* disturb you? Perhaps a presentation in form would allay your fears? Michael, come forward and make your bow to our lady-guest."

The young man so named stepped near the rug and, with a click of his heels, inclined his head. Tall and slim, with dark hair, he had the same blue eyes as the prince, though they were more somber. He appeared to be a few years younger than Roderic, perhaps in his midtwenties. The impression he gave was one of earnest dependability.

"I give you my cousin Michael, the Baron von Brasov, son of Leopold the Steadfast," the prince said.

As Michael stepped aside, another of the *garde du corps* took his place. This one was also above average height, though his hair was silver-white and his eyes hazel. But as he bowed, Mara, blinking, saw that the hair was worn in braids wrapped close to the head and the uniform, impeccably tailored for fit, covered the form of a woman.

"Trude, our spear maiden."

The woman, straightening with all the pride and hauteur of a Valkyrie, gave Mara a stare that was as level and searching as a man's. Satisfied, she wheeled with precision and dropped back.

Advancing next came a matched pair. Their curling sandy hair was the same, their green eyes were the same, and so was the laughter in their faces, the level of their heads, and the set of their shoulders. They saluted her in unison, their swords held at the exact same angle behind them, and their smiles as they stood erect again were warm, almost caressing.

Roderic's tone was resigned as he made the introduction. "Jacques and Jared, the brothers Maniu, skirt chasers par excellence, twin crosses."

"But, my prince!" they said together in protest.

"My personal crosses," Roderic said firmly, and waved them aside.

As they moved, they revealed a short, slender man with thinning dark hair and merry eyes above a magnificent set of whiskers and mustache. Despite the cut of his uniform, he managed to appear rather seedy, and his bearing was less than military. At his side was a ragged mongrel with a scruffy coat of mixed black and brown, and drooping whiskers about his nose gave him a ludicrous resemblance to his master.

"Estes, the Count Ciano."

"And this," said the count, indicating his pet with a flourish, "is Demon, the very valuable guardian dog of the cadre." The dog, hearing his name, lolled out his tongue and wagged his tail in a complete circle.

The prince gave the animal a skeptical look. "A veritable Cerberus, one who makes up in valor what he lacks in discipline, manners, size, and appearance, or at least that's the claim."

The prince himself had not been introduced. She could not be expected to know who he was. Greatly daring, Mara said, "And you, sir?"

"I am Roderic."

The Italian count lifted a brow. "His Royal Highness, Prince Roderic son of King Rolfe of Ruthenia, my lady."

There was a silence. They were waiting, Mara knew, for some acknowledgment and for her to give her own name in return. She could not bring herself to meet their eyes. Stretching out a hand that trembled toward the dog, she said, "I am pleased to know all of you. I would tell you who I am, if I could."

Demon capered forward to lick her fingers, wriggling in delight as she scratched behind his ear.

"Disloyal brute," Michael said.

"Ugly, too," Jacques offered without heat.

"But lucky." Estes sighed as Demon tried to climb into Mara's lap.

Roderic transferred his gaze from the dog to the men before him. He did not speak; still, so forbidding was his glance that smiles faded and spines stiffened. The dog was removed at once. The cadre drifted away. The old gypsy began to play a quick tune, and a woman with loose, dusky black hair and high cheekbones got up to dance, capturing the attention of the others.

"Even the enigma of the Sphinx can pall. How is it that we may serve you?"

The tone of the prince was abrupt, dismissive. He meant, it seemed, to have done with her. That was not at all what Mara wished or needed. She looked up at him with panic rising in her eyes. "I don't know. I—I can't seem to remember where I came from, where I live."

"Your accent is not Parisian, but interesting, with the cadence of an old song. Is it typical of your province?"

Another trap. "I couldn't say."

But she could, of course. Hers was the accent of the

Louisiana French and was closer to that used by Parisians of the past century than of the present year of 1847. Oh, she knew the idiom; there was enough travel, enough commerce between Paris and New Orleans to keep it current, but the rhythm was different, slower, more musical, with now and then a word or a twist of phrase that had once been heard at the court of the Sun King.

Mara had lived much in New Orleans, journeying from her father's plantation near St. Martinville to enjoy the *saison des visites* in the city each winter with her widowed grandmother, Helene Delacroix. She had made her debut at the opera house dressed in the purest white, wearing white roses in her hair as she received the visits of friends, relatives, and the numerous eligible suitors who had ensured that the night was a success. How long ago that seemed.

Her father, André, had always accompanied her to New Orleans, but seldom stayed longer than a week or two. He had no heart for the amusements and entertainments that Mara and her grandmother had so enjoyed, preferring the quiet of his plantation with its waving acres of sugarcane. It had been different once, or so Helene said, when André Delacroix was a young man, before his marriage.

His wife, Mara's mother, had been Irish, a quiet woman with eyes the color of the fog on Galway Bay and the gift of second sight. The marriage had been considered a misalliance; the Irish were looked on as little more than uncouth savages by the French Creoles, those of French blood born on American soil. No one knew precisely what André Delacroix felt for the Irishwoman, but he had taken her to his plantation and always treated her with kindness and honor.

It had not been enough. Mara's mother had soon discovered that her husband's deepest affections had been given, years before, to another woman. Angeline Fortin had been her name, and she had been taken from him under peculiar circumstances by a Balkan prince, Rolfe of Ruthenia, who had been visiting in Louisiana. When Mara was born, André, with unusual stubbornness, had insisted that Angeline in far-off Ruthenia be named as godmother to the child. Mara's mother had protested. The connection with Ruthenia would bring sorrow, she had insisted. André had remained adamant. In due course there had been the usual gifts of silver and lace from the woman who, by that time, ruled as queen of Ruthenia. There had also been unfailing gifts on Mara's birthdays through the years, with sometimes a note of great warmth and friendliness. But there had been no other contact.

Little by little, Maureen O'Connor Delacroix had retreated. She refused to come down when there were guests, never attended social occasions. She called her daughter Mara, instead of Marie Angeline, and because it was easier the servants and even her husband did the same. Gradually the lullabies she sang in Gaelic to her daughter ceased. She no longer intruded on the meals shared by father and daughter but ate in her room with a priest sometimes in attendence. She died quietly of a fever when Mara was ten, and she had hardly been missed.

Mara had grown up secure in the open adoration of her father and with the affection, guidance, and common sense of her grandmother. She rode on the plantation with André, trotting behind him on a cream-colored pony, and followed behind Grandmère Helene in New Orleans, wearing a gown just like her grandmother's and a veil to protect her fair complexion, while buying for the household at the stalls of the French market. She had been installed in a convent school during a portion of each year until she was twelve so that though she was sometimes spoiled and willful, she also understood the value of self-discipline.

By the time she was fifteen, she had received three

offers of marriage. André was in no hurry to see her wed, however, so had sent her to a finishing school in Mobile. There she had learned a thousand rules of etiquette, but also many arts, among them the agreeable one of flirtation. Until then she had not taken much notice of her effect upon the young men of her acquaintance, but, in practicing on the brothers, cousins, and friends who came to visit her fellow students, had found a heady sense of power in her own attraction. With lighthearted pleasure and a comfortable familiarity with men that she had learned in dealing with her own father, she had tried her hand at captivating the males who brought themselves to her notice.

When she returned to St. Martinville in the summer of 1844, the men swarmed around her like wasps to a ripening apple. Proud and indulgent, André placed no curb upon her. She did not pass the bounds of good behavior, but still she embarked on a constant round of rides, carriage drives, picnics, teas, and balls.

Before many weeks had passed she had collected a garden of bouquets, enough sonnets to her beauty to fill a volume, and so many cones and boxes of candy that her maid had gained pounds. There were any number of young men who had possessed themselves of one of her gloves, handkerchiefs, ribbons, or flowers from her hair, and it was rumored that at least two duels had been fought over her. One man emerged with his arm supported, most romantically, in a black silk sling. She never allowed a man to do more than kiss her fingers or put his hands on her waist when she dismounted from horse or carriage; still, the whispers began to circulate that she was far too at ease with gentlemen for her own welfare, that she was running wild and would come to no good end.

It made little difference. Even if Mara had known what was being said, she was having too much fun to consider the consequences. A year passed, two, and still she showed no indication of settling down. Finally, there came a reckoning.

Dennis Mulholland was one of her most persistent suitors. He was something of a firebrand, a touchy young man always spoiling for a fight. He had attended Jefferson Military College in Mississippi and spoke often of going off to join the army, which was involved in the border skirmishes taking place more and more often between the United States and Mexico. That was when he was not proposing marriage. He wanted to be possessive, but Mara, uncertain that he would make a suitable husband and mistrusting his ardor, kept him at arm's length. Though he danced well and rode better, he had a tendency to bring up the subject of the duels he had fought far too often, and to brag about his progress up and down notorious Gallatin Street in New Orleans when not among his elders.

It was a hot night in late May. Mara had planned a ball with a gold and blue color theme in the flowers and decorations, the favors, the programs, and the trimming of the ladies' ball gowns. It was a great success, with carriages lining the drive and extending into the road. The night was sultry and hot, however, with thunder in the air. The press of people made the ballroom stifling, airless. The musicians had played a set of fast dances ending with a polka. Mara whirled through them all, and could scarcely breathe due to the exertion and the tight lacing of her corsets. She was gasping, fanning herself near a window, when Dennis suggested a stroll.

His progress was not slow, however. He practically pulled her down the path to the summerhouse that sat wreathed in roses some distance from the main house. Once inside, he proposed yet again, though this time with greater force. The die was cast; he had joined the army and must report for duty, but before he went he wanted to make her his wife.

She tried to distract him by making some playful rejoinder. Incensed by her failure to take him seriously, he caught her in his arms and covered her face with kisses as he held her tightly to him. Her first reaction had been surprise, but it was quickly followed by real distress as she could not catch her breath. She pushed at him, but he would not release her, only muttering thickly about her damned coquettish ways that led a man on. A moment later she lost consciousness, fainting from lack of air in exactly the same boneless manner of the whey-faced females she had always despised.

The swoon had lasted no more than a minute or two, but when she opened her eyes she was lying on the floor and Dennis Mulholland's hand was under her skirts, groping at her thighs. He had been trying to loosen her stays, he claimed, but she did not believe him. Neither did her father, who came upon them before she could straighten her gown.

André Delacroix had been enraged, not the least reason being because he felt himself to blame. Most girls of Mara's age were already married with families, but he had kept her near him, discouraging any man who seemed too determined. Now he swore that the scoundrel who had dared to touch his daughter, who had compromised her with such impunity, would marry her or face his pistol at twenty paces.

Dennis was more than willing to be married; it was Mara who refused, who paced up and down alternately raging and pleading. In the end, she had her way, at least in part. There would be no wedding for the moment, but there would be a betrothal, and when Dennis returned from the war in Mexico they would be wed. She must make her mind up to it, for that was the way it would be.

Dennis had rode away, and though he had kissed Mara good-bye, his eyes had been hollow with the knowledge that she cared not at all for him. He had been killed in his first battle.

Everyone had been amazed at how her betrothal had subdued Mara's high spirits. Later they had watched with raised brows as she donned black for the death of her fiancé. There were those who said she was well paid for her flightiness, that she deserved to lose the man she loved, though others spoke of her Irish mother whom everyone knew had been unstable by both breeding and temperament. But as the weeks and months passed, and she grew daily paler and more withdrawn, their interest had turned to concern.

Mara had taken little notice. Day after day she sat staring out the window, often holding in her hand the letter she had received from Dennis saying that he cared not whether he lived or died if she did not love him. Guilt and remorse were weights she carried with her, dragging her down. She accused herself of being careless and self-centered. Her own emotions had been so little involved that she had not fully understood how deeply others could feel for her, how easily they could be aroused to commit acts of which they were bitterly ashamed. If she had realized, she would have been more careful, more restrained. Such thoughts were well enough, but they had come too late.

André, becoming alarmed at his daughter's state of mind, had sent for Mara's grandmother. Grandmère Helene had taken charge. A spritely and warmhearted woman with little regard for her increasing years, she had declared that Mara must accompany her to France. It had been ages since she had last made the voyage, and she longed to see Paris again. Too much for her? Nonsense! She was far from her dotage. They would visit relatives, attend the opera, absorb a bit of culture, but most of all they would patronize the modistes in order to banish the black and purple from Mara's wardrobe. The period of mourning was over; Mara must begin to live again.

Roderic, watching the flicker of emotion playing with the firelight over Mara's face, made an abrupt gesture. "There is a husband who will be anxious for your return? A lover?"

"No," she answered, her voice tight, then added, "at least, I don't think so."

"Ah, you don't think, but can virginity, like pregnancy, legitimacy, fidelity, prosperity, security, or liberty be in doubt? Do you know if there is mother, father, or child waiting? Sister? Brother? Priest? Faithful maid? Lap dog? Is there no one who will mourn you if you don't return?"

"I can't say."

Her grandmother would not know where she was, what she was doing. Her grandmother who had brought her to Europe.

Paris had been everything Helene had promised, a place of grace and beauty and unbounded fascination. They had stayed with a distant cousin, an elderly woman of aristocratic habits and connections if rather reduced circumstances. When Helene was not tracing exhaustively the relationship of some elusive branch of the Delacroix family with their cousin, she and Mara had walked the streets of the city, crossing and recrossing the many bridges over the Seine. They had sampled the confections at the pastry shops, sipped cups of tea or coffee at the sidewalk cafés, stared at the antiques in the shops on the Left Bank, and searched out the houses where the famous and infamous had lived. They had duly visited the Louvre, strolling its endless galleries, admiring the paintings and sculpture they had only read about before, and promenaded in the gardens of the Tuileries, which were open to the public despite the fact that the Tuileries Palace was the official residence of King Louis Philippe.

These agreeable promenades had come to a halt following a visit to the fashionable modiste, Madame Palmyre. There had been time afterward for nothing except fittings and more fittings, or else shopping excursions for bonnets and shawls, gloves and whisper-light silk corsets and stockings from the shops on the rue de Richelieu. One of Mara's favorite purchases had been made at the Maison Gagelin where an assistant with a heavy English accent and the unlikely name of Worth had taken one look at her and brought out a shawl of a clear gray wool so finely woven it could be pulled through a wedding ring. It had been made for her alone, he had declared with fervor, and in truth it had made her skin appear as fine and delicate as porcelain and turned her eyes into pools of soft mystery.

With her wardrobe replenished, Mara and her grandmother had embarked on a round of entertainments: attending the opera, the Comédie Française; being fêted at dinners and balls kindly arranged by their hostess. It was at one of the latter that they had met Nicholas de Landes.

De Landes was an official of the court, serving in a minor capacity in the ministry of foreign affairs, though Mara had never discovered exactly what it was that he did. Slim and dark, with a close-trimmed mustache and beard, he had had the manners and breeding of a courtier of the *ancien régime,* and the same meaningless smile. He had declared himself enchanted to make the acquaintance of the ladies from Louisiana, once a much valued colony of France, and offered to do everything in his power to make their stay in Paris memorable.

Their Parisian cousin had warned them against him, saying that for all his airs he was merely of the petty bourgeoisie; his parents, the son of a notary and the daughter of a small landowner. He very much wished to rise higher; this was a known fact. Such obvious class consciousness had not impressed Mara and her grandmother. If anything, it had caused them to treat him with greater warmth, as if in compensation.

It would have been better if they had listened to their cousin. De Landes had introduced Mara's grandmother to one or two of the discreet gaming houses hidden away in the less fashionable districts of the city. Gaming was illegal within thirty miles of the city, but there were always those who would cater to so intriguing a pastime. At first the play had been exciting because it was forbidden and Helene had won small amounts, but by degrees it became an obsession. She lost more and more. De Landes acted as her banker, extending the loan of various sums and accepting her scribbled notes of hand in lieu of payment. Each morning after a disastrous night at the card tables Helene had vowed she would never return, but when night fell she could not seem to stay away. Mara, watching her, had been anxious, but had considered Grandmère Helene a reasonable woman, one with a firm grasp on the worth of money.

The morning had come when Nicholas de Landes had paid them a call. Though he was devastated to be forced to say such a thing to a lady, he could no longer support the gambling losses of Madame Helene Delacroix. She must repay what was owed to him with interest. He was sure there would be no difficulty since it was well known that the sugar planters of Louisiana commanded enormous wealth, and he knew that Madame's son would not fail to extend her the money, should she be temporarily embarrassed. The only question was how it was to be arranged.

Helene had been aghast at the total of her losses. How the sum could have mounted so high without her being aware of it, she was at a loss to explain. But there it was, neatly totaled day by day, an accumulated debt in excess of one hundred thousand francs. She did not have that much, or anything near it. Nor, she knew, did André.

The years of 1847 had seen a financial panic in the United States, and in the world, for that matter. The previous fall, a potato blight had destroyed one of the major food crops all over Europe, and unseasonably cold and wet weather had made the wheat harvest scanty. Now food was so scarce that prices had soared out of sight, and the French were calling it the Year of Dear Bread. André had been affected along with everyone else; he had, in fact, been forced to borrow against his next crop in order to find the cash to send them to Europe and to see Mara properly outfitted. With his finances already under such a strain, he would be forced to sell some portion of his holdings to meet this new debt, and that would take time.

De Landes was in no mood to wait. He required payment immediately. If it was not forthcoming, he would take drastic action. Madame would certainly not enjoy that, he promised.

Helene had been shocked at the ruthless mien that had been hidden under the façade of the courtier, but that was nothing compared to her agitation when he suggested in tones of implacable reason that if Helen could not find the money, her charming granddaughter might redeem her notes by doing a service for him. If Madame would permit, he would take Mademoiselle Delacroix for a short drive while he explained the matter to her.

The suggestion that de Landes had to make was so incredible, so insulting, that Mara had stared at him in disbelief. There was a Balkan prince who was being obstructive, he said. It would benefit de Landes and those with whom he was associated if this royal gentleman were to become susceptible to influence. In order to redeem her grandmother's notes, Mara would be required to seduce the troublesome prince, to become his mistress.

There had been a moment when she had not been able to speak, could not trust her voice, so great was her rage and indignation.

"Stop the carriage! Set me down at once!" When he did not comply, she reached for the handle of the carriage door.

He caught her wrist in a hard grasp, his fingers biting into her flesh. His tone smooth, but carrying a malicious undercurrent, he said, "To refuse is your prerogative, of course."

"I do refuse!"

"A hasty decision, and one far from wise. Before you give me your final answer, you should consider that accidents sometimes befall those who fail to pay their just gambling debts. The bones of elderly women such as your Grandmère Helene are so very fragile. Even a small mishap can have extremely painful—possibly even fatal—consequences."

Cold fear struck Mara, taking her breath. She sank slowly back against the seat. Her heart thudded in her chest as she gazed with sick comprehension into the narrow black eyes of the man beside her. He was, she thought, taking a peculiar pleasure in her apprehension. She moistened her suddenly dry lips.

"You are saying that if I don't do as you ask, you will harm Grandmère?"

"Crudely put but accurate. Her safety and comfort rests in your hands, my dear Mara. You must consider well."

It was blackmail, an ugly and sordid coercion, but it could not be fought. The authorities, as de Landes pointed out so reasonably, were unlikely to be interested in the difficulties of two American women, especially since illegal gambling was involved. And that was even if they could be brought to believe that he, in his official capacity, would offer so bizarre a proposal to a young female. She could apply to her elderly, aristocratic cousin for aid, but that lady would be no more able to prevent any accident that might happen than they were. Mara's father was far away, and she had no other male relatives who might come to her defense. It would be best if she resigned herself to the task, however unpleasant she might find it.

After two days of agonizing indecision, Mara had been forced to concede that he was right. She had no choice except to agree to de Landes's debasing demand.

It had not been possible to tell her grandmother what de Landes had proposed; Grandmère would have insisted on defying him and taking the risk. That could not be. The elderly woman, well past seventy, had aged years since her confrontation with de Landes. She had never seemed old to Mara, but now, almost before her eyes, she became frail and distracted, in need of care. Mara gave her grandmother to understand that she was expected to do no more than initiate a flirtation with the prince at some public function, then lead him to a rendezvous with de Landes's superior, François Guizot, the minister of foreign affairs and a favorite of King Louis Philippe.

Helene had fretted over the supposed assignment, but accepted the explanation at last. Affairs of state were often complicated, nearly impossible to untangle, and perhaps the favor was not so small as it seemed; indeed, it could not be since de Landes was willing to sacrific such a sum to arrange it. She, Helene Delacroix, had little doubt that de Landes had known all along of their connection to the prince. She strongly suspected that he had enticed her into the gambling dens for exactly the end he had achieved.

Watching the clever way de Landes had persuaded her grandmother to act as his hostess for a house party at his château while leaving Mara behind to complete her mission, seeing the maneuvering and changing of carriages that had led the elderly cousin with whom she and Helene were staying to believe that Mara was going to the Loire Valley with her grandmother, Mara could only agree. The detailed instructions as to what she must say and do, which she had received on the long ride to the gypsy camp, and the violent way that ride had ended, had served to reinforce the impression.

There was no time to dwell upon what was done, however, for questions, as swift and lethal as an ambuscade of arrows, were hurtling around her.

"From whence did your carriage come? What was its color? How many horses, outriders? What folly caused you to be expelled? Was it lack of cooperation or too much? How came such beauty to be scorned? And where then is the fury? And the hell?"

The questions were directed with suspicion. That it was well founded did not prevent the rise of a feeling of ill-usage in Mara. "Doubtless," she said, sending the prince a flashing glance as she acknowledged the quote that had become a saw and traced it to its source, "in the same place as the rage of heaven."

"There are things, then, that you remember," Roderic said, his tone soft.

Mara stared into his bright blue gaze, refusing to look away. "So it would seem."

"How fortunate, otherwise you would be as a child again, wet, wiggling, and beguiling, as well as quite helpless . . ."

"Fortunate for you that I am not."

"Oh, I don't know. I might have enjoyed jogging you on my knee."

"A perilous undertaking, under the conditions you describe."

"You mean if you were wet?"

She had, of course, but it was disconcerting to be taken so literally, and with such an open and engaging, therefore dangerous, smile. She had been warned about the prince's penchant for games with words. He meant her to be disconcerted.

"It would be a natural condition," she said, her tone even.

The voice of the prince softened, lowered. "The man was a fool."

"What?"

"To discard you."

Mara felt something tighten inside her chest, but she refused to follow so obvious a lead. "It might have been a woman."

"Do you think so? An abbess, perhaps? But none would wish to be rid of such tender and easily sold merchandise. A jealous rival? She could have cut your throat as easily or else splashed vitriol here and there where it would do the most harm. A relative, perhaps, bent on discrediting you? But why? To destroy your good name and make you unfit for a proper bridegroom? Men can be such idiots about such things, as if a night in the dew mattered. Will it matter?"

"Oh, don't!" she exlaimed, swaying a little, frowning as tension caused her head to pound. "There is no need to mock me."

"I was thinking, instead, of sending you to your repose. It seems, above all, what you need."

Was that compassion she heard in his voice? She could not be sure. Repose, composure. No doubt he was right. She could not seem to think any longer. If she weren't careful, some unguarded remark would give her away. Her gaze shifted to the caravans drawn up around the fire, particularly to the one painted blue and white and decorated with scrolls of gold; one newer, neater, than the others.

"Where shall I sleep?" she asked, and began wearily to gather her cloak around her.

Roderic, hearing that simple question, caught his breath. The temptation to direct her to his caravan, his bed, was so great that he was startled into silence. Where had it come from, this sudden wave of desire for a bedraggled, injured female without a name? She was beautiful, but he had seen beautiful women before, had had more than his share of them. She intrigued him—not the least because the lilt of her voice and her choice of words were the same as those of his mother, easily recognizable as being of Louisiana—but women with mysterious pasts were ten per centime in Paris. No, it was something more, something indefinable, something of which he must be wary. Still, his caravan was the safest place.

Mara looked up and, seeing the blank, suspended expression on his face, felt her heart begin to pound. Inside her rose a terrible hope, and, just as wracking, a fear, that this seduction was going to be made easy. She felt a great need to reach out, to touch him, and knew with an instinctive certainty that it would be the right thing to do. The urge grew, burgeoning until she could not tell whether it was a mental and calculated desire or a real physical need. It made no difference. She could not force herself to move.

He surged to his feet, swinging away from her with the powerful grace of well-used muscles. His order sliced the night air with the feral quietness of a rapier blow. The music stopped. Men and women moved, gathering up rugs and pots and bowls and weapons, melting away from the fire, slipping away into the caravans or the encircling darkness. A young girl came and curtsied to Mara, taking her hand to lead her toward the blue and white caravan. Stiffly, Mara got to her feet to follow and would not turn her head to look back.

The prince stood alone beside the leaping flames, his expression grim. Then, with controlled movements, he lowered himself once more to the pile of rugs that were left. He picked up the mandolin and began to pluck out a tune.

Mara, catching the melody as she stepped into the caravan, stopped still. Torn between amusement, anger, and a strange feeling of being near tears, she had to force herself to move again. Mocking in its sweetness, haunting and delicate, the song the prince played was a lullaby.

CHAPTER 2

The caravan of the prince was little different from the others on the outside, except perhaps that the paint was brighter. The interior, however, was furnished in what appeared to Mara to be royal, rather than gypsy, fashion. The appointments had been chosen for richness and quality, but also with a care and variety that seemed an indication of the man.

Two walls of the caravan were lined with books in five languages, volumes on philosophy and the arts, religion and history, music and the theory of war. The other two walls were richly paneled and set with brass whale-oil lamps in gimbals. In one corner was a table with folios of music strewn across it, half hiding a chased sword of steel and brass, while underneath were cases holding musical instruments. Nudging the table for room was a desk. On its surface was an inkstand of gold and glass with a gold pen in its holder and several sheets of foolscap in a precise pile. A straight-back chair was behind the desk, but for comfort there was also an armchair with a winged back and a matching footstool, both covered in dark blue velvet. The floor was of polished wood parquet centered with a Turkish rug in cream, gold, and blue. Built-in armoires flanked an alcove at one end that held the bed in a lengthwise position. The bed curtains fell from a gilded rod that was shaped like a giant's spear and were looped back on either side with tasseled cords. On the mattress was a bolster and pillows encased in cream linen piped with dark blue, cream sheets discreetly monogrammed, and a coverlet of white fox fur. The impression was one of utility and aestheticism, with more than a touch of opulence.

The girl who had led Mara into the caravan lighted the lamps, brought a can of hot water, and then laid out linen toweling and a block of soap with the fragrance of sandalwood. She offered her services as maid to aid Mara in preparing for bed. Mara allowed her to release her from her gown and stays, then dismissed her. A moment later, she wished she had not been so hasty. She had no nightgown, nothing to sleep in other than her camisole and pantalettes.

It hardly mattered. All she really needed was to be left alone, to lie down and close her eyes in some dark place away from the questions, the scrutiny, and the suspicion. It was a pity she couldn't also hide from her own thoughts.

She had passed the first test. The realization was slow in coming. It was only after the creep of minutes into hours that she allowed herself to believe it. She was here with the prince, here, in the gypsy camp among the people who claimed him as their own. She was in his caravan, even sleeping in his bed. De Landes had been right in thinking that this was the best approach to him, here where he was relaxed and at ease away from the city, here where there were no authorities to take charge of her and few distractions to turn the attention of the prince from her. She had, she thought, aroused Roderic's curiosity, and perhaps his sympathy.

That was not enough, not nearly enough. There had been an opportunity, she was almost certain, to do more, and she had failed to seize it. Her resolution had wavered when faced with the man himself. She must not let it happen again, she could not, for her grandmother's sake. Oh, but could she force herself to smile and be enticing? Could she take the final, irrevocable step of inviting the man into her bed?

With a sudden convulsive wrench, she turned onto her back, staring up into the darkness lit only by the orange flicker of firelight reflected into the caravan from outside. She must take that step. She must become intimate with the prince, must persuade him to take her with him when he returned to Paris. There was no other choice.

She thought of her grandmother in the hands of de Landes. Was there truly a house party at his château, or had that merely been an excuse? Was she being ill-treated? Was she warm? Was she being given enough to eat? Was the place she was being held a comfortable country house, or was it some crumbling stone fortress with dungeons, bare cells with barred doors, and straw on the floor for a bed? Was it some former nobleman's seat that de Landes had taken as the spoils of his office?

There were many such places in France, landed estates that had changed hands dozens of times with every shift of government since the revolution. The rich lands and great houses of the Loire Valley were particularly coveted by the new rich of each administration. Every tumbledown house with its neighboring village became an excuse to add the ennobling "de" to a surname, purloining the old glory. Few cared to live in such places, however. The lure of Paris and the court of Louis Philippe, staid though it might be, was far greater; besides, the great, drafty houses were bitterly cold and uncomfortable in winter.

A shiver ran through Mara there in the prince's bed. The chill came from within, however, and could not be banished, not even by the covering of thick, soft fur. She lay staring with burning eyes into the dimness.

She was awakened by a sound so slight that she could not tell what it was. After a moment, she discovered that rain had begun to fall. It pattered overhead on the roof of the caravan, neither heavy nor light but relentless, though there came an occasional splattering of windblown drops. It was a moment before she recognized that, persistent though the sound was, it had not roused her. She raised herself on one elbow.

"Don't be alarmed," the prince said from the darkness. "All I seek is shelter."

She was supposed to have lost her memory, not her common sense or her courage. She answered with some asperity, "I'm not alarmed."

"Aren't you? I had not looked for such sangfroid."

The words were accompanied by a soft rustling. It took no great effort of imagination to understand that he was undressing there in the darkness. Mara felt her heart begin to beat with quick, throbbing strokes. A suffocating feeling rose in her chest as she realized that another opportunity was upon her. All too aware of the stretching silence, she searched her mind for something to say.

"Did—did you get wet?'

There was laughter in his voice as he answered, "As a puling brat with no one to change or to dandle the darling child."

It was a reference to their earlier conversation. She let it pass. "Not, I hope, from a reluctance to disturb me."

" 'A very, parfit gentil knight,' suffering rather than intrude upon a lady's sanctity? Nothing so gallant. The horses were restless."

"And you acted as the groom?" She could not keep the surprise from her voice.

"Not alone. Horses are the livelihood, the transportation, and the wealth of the *Tziganes,* the gypsies, and particularly this group, who are breeders and traders of fine stock. But I, myself, have an aversion to being left afoot when there is something I can do to prevent it."

Mara did not doubt that there were servants in plenty he could have called to see to the matter. That he had gone himself gave her pause. She had thought of him as the consummate aristocrat, with the carelessness of that breed for the welfare of underlings and animals, and for anything that did not directly affect his own comfort and consequence. This was no time, however, for explorations of personality. What the prince was like as a man had no bearing on what she had to do.

"You must be . . . cold."

"Are you by chance offering to warm me?"

All she had to do was to say yes, and yet the very boldness of the question shook her resolve. She said in haste, "Only to share the covers."

The air wafted in a faint draft, then his voice came from just above her as if he had moved to kneel beside the low bed. "No soft pillow on your breast, no sweet sucklings and bouncing joy before I drift into sated sleep?"

"I am not—not your nurse!" The catch in her voice was caused not by panic, but by the warm curling of some odd pain in her chest.

"An excellent thing," he said, then, rising in one swift movement, lifted the fur coverlet and slid in beside her.

She flung herself away from him with a sharp exclamation, then, as she realized what she was doing, abruptly stopped. She was a fool. She could have wept with pent-up nerves and self-castigation. Somehow she must learn to control herself, to force her body to accept the dictates of her will. If the prince made another advance, if he reached out to touch her, she must not, would not, retreat. She would accept it and, pray God, respond.

He did not move. She might have been alone in the bed, so scant was the evidence of his presence. If he was breathing, she could not tell it, so quiet was he. The lack of strain in the coverlet over them both was an indication of his complete relaxation. It seemed after a time that he must have the facility for instant sleep, for he made no restless shifts of position. By degreees the tension left her own muscles and she allowed her eyelids to close. The rain drummed on the caravan roof with a soothing, unfaltering rhythm. Her shoulder, which was uncovered, grew cool, and she eased the fur higher, snuggling under its warmth.

The gray creep of daylight into the caravan brought Mara awake once more. She lifted her lashes with reluctance. She tried to stretch and stifled a small sound of distress. She was sore in every muscle, and her shoulder was so stiff that she was not sure she would be able to move it. It was not memory, however, but some tingling sense of awareness that reminded her that she was not alone in the bed. She swung her head to one side and stared into the eyes of the prince.

He lay on his side watching her, with his head propped on one hand. The cover had slipped from him so that his torso was bare. The soft light of morning gleamed bronze across the sculptured muscles of his wide shoulders and caught glints of gold in the soft mat of hair on his chest. The appreciation in his gaze was bright, but underlying it was concentrated and cogent thought.

Her dark hair lay in shining serpentine waves around her head on the pillow. The pure oval of her face grew slowly flushed with delicate shell-pink color that also extended along the graceful turn of her neck to the curves of her breasts beneath the low neckline of her silk camisole. Her lips, parted in surprise, were sweetly molded, soft and moist. But her hand, which lay on the coverlet, was clenched into a fist, and the smudged gray of her Irish eyes was slowly darkening with apprehension.

Roderic leaned toward her. Her lashes, like black silk fringes, fluttered downward to hide her expression. She made no move to draw away. It seemed ignoble then to press his mouth to hers, but he was not driven by simple desire. The slight physical contact was a test. He was curious to see what she would do about it, whether she would accept it or repulse him.

Mara lay still, her lips cool, and yet so heightened was their sensitivity that she registered the warmth and smoothness, the firmness and pressure of his mouth in some deep recess of her being. Her fear receded, to be replaced by an intimation of pleasure. Minutely, she moved, molding her mouth to his. The pressure increased, and she felt the subtle touch of his tongue.

Dennis had kissed her like that on the night of the ball, thrusting his tongue wet and hot into her mouth. With remembrance came welling panic, and she wrenched her mouth away, lifting her hand to push at Roderic's shoulder.

He released her at once, but still he lay studying her: the livid bruise on her temple revealed where her bandage had been dislodged in the night; the smudged shadows under her eyes; the fine transparency of her skin that now glowed with a flush from some emotion, the origin of which he could only surmise. She was a beautiful enigma, this woman who had come to them out of the night. He scented a mystery, something more than a mere lady in distress who had misplaced her identity.

The schemes and plotting of the courts and political factions of half the countries of Europe were as familiar to him as the patterns of his own thoughts. He had developed an instinct for dangerous undercurrents, one he had learned to trust. He knew now that the best thing he could do would be to leave her to the gypsies. And yet she was beginning to fascinate him with her tentative advances and swift retreats. There was something in her eyes that disturbed him, like a doe he had once seen turn at bay after being hunted by hounds.

"Forgive me," he said, the words abrupt. "It was wrong of me to take advantage of your injuries."

How much easier it would be if he would just take advantage of her completely so that the thing was over and done. A wry smile for the desperation of that thought tugged at Mara's mouth, then disappeared. "I suppose you are used to—to waking with a woman in your bed."

"Not one for which I have no name, professional or otherwise."

"I told you—"

"I remember vividly. It creates a problem, does it not? I could snap my fingers or whistle when your attention is required, but it seems awkward. Every new soul needs a name, and like a child born last night, you have the opportunity to be freshly christened, created anew, this morning. What then shall you be called? *Chère* is too common, and *chère amie* somewhat premature."

"Yes," she said, sending him a look both incensed and frightened. She was not his mistress, his *chèrie amie,* yet, and though she thought his words were meant to be teasing, a way of easing the tension between them, she could not be sure he had not guessed her purpose. He was said to be extremely acute.

"Shall you be Claire or Caroline then, Candance or Chloe? It isn't everyone who is permitted to choose."

The urge to say her own name was strong. She could not afford the gesture, however. "I don't know. Call me what you will."

"You tempt me. Circe, from the pagan sorceress who turned men into swine? Daphne, who became a laurel tree for the sake of love? Or perhaps after the beautiful and faithless Helen?"

"Nothing so classical, I think. But need there be anything? I may recall my own name shortly."

"And may not."

How despicable was this falseness. She lowered her

lashes. "Then common though it may be, perhaps Chère would be best."

"As you like. Are you hungry?"

"Not very."

"Yet you ate nothing last evening, unless it was before you reached us. Have you a fever?"

He reached out to touch her forehead, and it was only by an immense effort of will that she prevented herself from flinching. "I believe not."

"No," he agreed, lifting his hand. "What then will it take to tempt your appetite? Lark's tongues? The locusts of the Mediterranean and the wine of Bacchus that opens the gates of the heart?"

"No," she said, shuddering.

"Can you stomach a roll, then, and chocolate with goat's milk?"

If he had meant to make the plain fare acceptable, he had succeeded. At her nod he smiled and, with smooth grace, slid from the bed and began to dress. Mara stared fixedly at her hands, all too aware of the hot flush suffusing her face. He had been naked. She had suspected as much, but that had not been like knowing. Strong and vital and virile, wrapped in the powerful aura of his noble title, this man had shared her bed for a night and left her untouched. It was deflating. It was also the source of guilt twice over. She should have done something, anything, to arouse him. But what a terrible thing it would be to use a man, as she must, who was so considerate in his relationships with females.

The depression of her spirits caused by his forebearance remained with her when he had left the caravan. She tried to tell herself that he had desired her; she had been forced to refuse him in the early-morning hours, hadn't she? But he had taken her refusal so well. In a man used to having his way, as he must be, she would have expected some attempt at persuasion, some sign of temper or affront at the very least. These were the reactions of wounded pride, of course. Perhaps it was simply that his consequence was so great that he could not conceive of a woman refusing him except for the most extreme of reasons.

She smiled a little at the idea. No, it could only be that his interest had been momentary, because she was conveniently at hand. His desire being no more than a passing fancy, he had not been upset at her withdrawal. That was all there was to it. She had failed to take the chance that fortune had thrown into her lap, and it was unlikely it would come again.

The day was cold and damp. Mara had her rolls and chocolate in bed, brought in by the same girl who had acted as her maid the night before. While she ate, the girl brought needle and thread and made sketchy repairs to Mara's gown. The needlework was less than expert, but the result was wearable and the impulse had been generous. The warmth of her praise drew a fugitive smile from the berry-brown gypsy girl and opened the way to a few bits of information. The cadre of the prince and most of the gypsies had left the camp that morning, ordered out to search for some sign of the carriage that had brought Mara and to question anyone who might have seen it.

The gypsy Luca had been subjected to a rigorous interrogation as to what he had seen and heard. The carriage had been pulled by four matched grays, without postilions, he said; it was new enough for the paint to shine even on a dark night and constructed in the latest shape. The carriage lanterns had not been lighted, so it had been impossible to tell the color. The voice of a man, not rough but raised in anger, had rung out as Mara was thrown to the ground. Immediately afterward, the carriage door had slammed shut and the vehicle had bowled away at high speed. At first Luca had thought it was a body that had been dumped upon the roadside. There had seemed no hurry to investigate. When she had moaned and staggered to her feet, he had seen the sheen of her white dress and had realized it was a woman. She had moved off in the direction of the camp, and he had let her go. She was a problem he thought it best that the prince handle himself.

Movement, the effort of getting dressed, seemed to ease some of the stiffness of Mara's shoulder. She was relieved, for she had begun to fear that it might have been dislocated. She could not lift her arms enough to put up her hair, however, and so allowed the gypsy girl to braid it for her and wrap it in a coronet around her head.

When she was presentable, she wandered about the caravan, watching the girl make the bed and put away the discarded clothing of the prince. She did not know what to do with herself, whether it would be best to go outside and try to talk to Roderic or to stay where she was and hope that he would seek her out. For herself, she would have preferred that his men be present; someone else to help carry the conversation. She had been taught the art of saying nothing for hours, of asking the questions that would put another person at ease, but she seemed to have lost her facility at it in the last year. And there was so much that she could not talk about because of her supposed loss of memory, so many pitfalls that she could fall into with such ease. Her brain felt numb, incapable of the task of being witty and entertaining. If she could not pretend to that capability, what was the point in engaging the attention of the prince, or of any man for that matter?

The rain had stopped, but the morning was cloudy and gray. The low area where the gypsies had camped was a morass of mud and rocks. The dampness made the cold penetrating. It was necessary to move about, to be active in some way, to keep the chill from the bones. Inside the caravan, Mara huddled into her cloak, wondering if she dared to build a fire in the small ceramic stove that sat in one corner. In the end, it seemed easiest to leave her shelter for the warmth of the fire in the center of the camp.

Demon, leaping about, wriggling, wagging his whole body as well as his tail, welcomed her with ecstasy. He licked the hand that she held out to him and jumped up to claw at her skirts. So violent was his greeting that she could hardly walk without him under her feet.

The prince, standing near the fire, turned and snapped his fingers. "Down, Demon."

The dog looked at him and dropped his tail, but an instant later had leaped up to lean on Mara once more, his mouth open and his tongue lolling out in his frantic affection.

"He obeys so well," Roderic said, his tones laced with irony.

Mara glanced up with a smile from where she stood, rubbing the dog's head. "I don't mind."

"It's bad for discipline."

"Oh? Whose?"

"His. He'll run to the wrong person one day and get his throat cut."

She looked up, startled. "Surely not?"

"Not everyone holds life dear, whether animal or human."

"Yes," Mara said, her tone subdued as she thought of Dennis Mulholland riding, careless of his life, into battle.

"What, a bad memory?"

At the soft query, Mara caught her breath, then forced a smile. "I—I'm not sure. Something close, perhaps."

Prince Roderic watched her, his features closed in. He made no answer, however, for the twins, Jacques and Jared, with Trude between them, rode in then. Gypsy children, playing in the mud, squealed and ran to escape the dirty water thrown up by the horses' hooves. Demon barked and ran in a circle, which roused the hounds of the *Tziganes,* and in turn set the donkeys to braying and the geese and chickens in their crates slung under the caravans to squawking and cackling.

The two young men and the woman dismounted and walked forward to report. The carriage, insofar as they could tell, had headed straight for Paris at high speed immediately after depositing Mara at the gypsy camp. There was nothing to distinguish its track from a thousand others. It was a pity they had not set out after the vehicle the night before when there might have been some chance of catching it, if news of it and its occupant was of such interest.

Roderic, frowning, made no return to that last sally other than a brief nod of acknowledgment. It was Trude, magnificent in her white uniform, who turned to stare with quelling force at the twins, as if she considered them impertinent even if Roderic did not. There was something very nearly protective in her manner. It caught Mara's attention. The presence of the woman had seemed odd the night before, but she had been too upset to consider it. Now she could not help wondering how she had come to be one of the prince's trusted band and just what her position was among them.

The cadre itself, the small group of followers with the prince, did not seem odd at all. She had heard so much from Grandmère Helene about Prince Rolfe, Roderic's father, and the men who had come with him to Louisiana all those years ago that it might have seemed strange if Roderic had not had a bodyguard, his own *garde du corps,* around him.

There had been five members in Rolfe's cadre also. Grandmère had enjoyed telling her of how they had arrived at the ball she was giving in the country near St. Martinville, of how they had entered the room with their dress uniforms flashing with gilt braid and the gems of military orders, their movements precisely coordinated as if they were on parade. So brilliant had they appeared in such country society, so stunning had been their attendance there, that it had been as if a phalanx of peacocks had seen fit to invade a dovecote.

The ball had been disrupted. Prince Rolfe had singled out Angeline Fortin for his attention. His cousin Leopold, his half brother Meyer, the veteran with one eye, Gustave, and the twins Oscar and Oswald had also found partners. They had danced one dance, then, at the signal of the prince, departed, leaving behind ladies drooping and sighing—those who had been disappointed, and ladies sighing with ecstasy—those who had been honored. The night had been one of triumph for Grandmère Helene: Her house had been honored by a prince! She had not known then that the same prince would steal away the woman her son loved.

Prince Roderic had identified the first of his cadre that he introducted to her as his cousin Michael, son of Leopold. This must be the same Leopold who had been in Louisiana with Rolfe. Were the others also the children of some of that original loyal band? Mara wished that she could ask, but so long as she had to keep her name and background secret, so long as she must pretend to have no memory of her own past, she could not. It was frustrating.

Despite her handicap, however, there came an opportunity to discover some few details later that day. The others, Michael and the Italian count, Estes, had returned. A noon meal of stew and hard-crusted bread washed down with wine was eaten. The camp was nearly empty; many of the gypsies had been gone since before daybreak, dispersed throughout the country on various errands and schemes. Roderic had ridden out with Michael and the twins, leaving Estes and Trude behind, ostensibly to watch the camp, but actually to keep an eye on her, or so Mara thought.

The blond amazon busied herself currying her horse. Finished at last, she came to drop down on the rug beside the fire. Mara looked up from where she had been pulling the burrs from the long hair around Demon's muzzle. Estes had been with her, entertaining her with tales of droll happenings while the cadre had been on campaign in Italy, but had excused himself to make a circuit of the camp. She gave the other woman a tentative smile, well aware that Trude was less than pleased at her guard duty.

"Estes tells me that the cadre has been in many battles all over Europe. Were you—that is, do you fight with the others?"

"Estes talks too much." The voice of the other woman was grim, but far from masculine.

"He was bearing my company, a kindly impulse."

"He was ingratiating himself. He likes the company of women, any woman."

The scathing tone touched Mara on the raw. "And you, I suppose, have little use for your own kind?"

"I would as soon not listen to their giggling and constant talk of clothing and conquests."

"You care not at all for such things, in fact?"

"No."

"You like killing instead." The woman's attitude made it impossible not to press her.

"I don't like it, but I can do it."

"Then you should be well suited with your place."

"I am, indeed," Trude said, her voice flat.

"Strange," Mara said, tilting her head, "you don't sound happy."

Trude did not answer directly. After a moment she said, "I would give you some advice if I thought you would heed it."

"Yes?"

"You have attracted Roderic's attention. He is curious about you, and there is nothing he likes so well as a mental puzzle. But his interest will last no longer than it takes to penetrate your mystery. If you expect more, you will be hurt."

"It is . . . kind of you to tell me." The choice of words was suggestive. Had it been deliberate?

"I do it for your own good."

It might have been true. Mara did not think so. Since she had no personal interest in the prince, however, it seemed unnecessary to say it. Her voice soothing, she said, "You seem to know Prince Roderic well."

"We have been together since we were in our cradles."

"You are related, perhaps?"

"Not at all. My father was the King Rolfe's, Roderic's father's, good right arm."

"I only asked because of your coloring. You said *was*; may I assume that your father is no longer—"

"He is dead, a soldier's death in battle."

"I'm sorry. You must be proud of him. He was a handsome man, I should think?"

The other girl was visibly startled. "I wouldn't say so. He was a bull of a man, with only one eye."

That piece of information identified the man who had sired Trude. She was the daughter of Gustave, the oldest member of the original cadre then, a man who, in the memory of Grandmère Helene, had been a veteran well past first youth when in Louisiana. It seemed fitting somehow.

"Are you like your mother then? Was she as attractive as you?"

"Are you trying to flatter me? My mother was a German milkmaid, big and blond and rather simple. She died while I was still at the breast, which is why I was brought to Ruthenia by my father to be raised by the queen."

The woman was so serious, so lacking in grace and humor, that it was impossible to resist the impulse to tease her. "I see. You were raised as a sister to Roderic then."

"He has a sister, Princess Juliana."

The reply was flat with displeasure. Mara set her teeth on the flesh inside her lip to prevent a smile. It was so obvious that Trude had a tendre for the prince. She was surprised that the other members of the cadre seemed unaware of it. As for Juliana, a girl near her own age, Mara had known about her, though she had nearly forgotten her existence. Still, it was Trude, who must be nearly twenty-seven years old to Roderic's twenty-eight, who held her interest at the moment.

"You must forgive my prying," Mara said. "It's only that I am fascinated by the idea of a woman in uniform."

"Why? I am as capable as a man with sword or musket."

"But surely in hand-to-hand fighting you are at a disadvantage?"

"Perhaps," Trude said coldly, "then perhaps not. It has never come to that."

"You haven't been in battle."

"I didn't say that. No man has gotten close enough to grapple with me."

There was something about the bald statement that made it believable. "You have proven yourself then. Not many women have had the chance."

"No," Trude said, then went on as if the words had been dragged out of her. "It is because Roderic is a fair man that I had mine."

"Fair?"

"Ah, fair indeed!" Estes cried, approaching them in time to hear the question. "Two ladies, one dark and mysterious, one blond and glorious, both beautiful. Lucky,

lucky man that I am to be here alone with the pair of you. I am tempted to spirit you both away. What say you? Shall we leave this gray climate and seek the sun on Capri, the three of us?"

"Conceited popinjay," Trude said, and, rising to her feet, walked away.

"She doesn't love me," Estes mourned, "while I am besotted, puny worm that I am, with every magnificent inch of her!"

It should have been funny since Trude topped him by half a foot at least. But listening to the strain in the mock outrage of the Italian, Mara thought there was too much truth in it for amusement.

The gypsies straggled back into camp as darkness began to fall. They came in ones and twos, some of those returning alone no older than four or five years. It was not uncommon, according to Estes, for children of that age to forage for themselves, begging at farm doors or stealing chickens and geese by "fishing" for them with a baited hook on a piece of line. They seldom became lost. There were trail markers left by the gypsies for each other, small arrangements of stones or twigs called *patterans* that always pointed the way toward reunion with the band, whether it was stationary or traveling. Because no one paid much attention to them, these youngsters were highly efficient at gathering information useful to the tribe.

The gypsy men tended the horses and did odd repair jobs around the camp before throwing themselves on the rugs around the central fire. The women cleaned the turkeys brought by several of the children, throwing the refuse to the waiting dogs. They stuffed the birds with herbs and onions and set them to roast over the coals of a separate cookfire. The children played, chasing each other around the caravans or knocking a ball about with a stick. The old violinist began to play. A man picked up the mandolin, strumming it, and they were joined by someone else on a concertina. A young woman, stirred by the music, pushed away from where she leaned on a caravan and began to dance. Her hair, held only by a fillet around her forehead, spilled in a wild black tangle down her back. Her eyes were dark and lustrous with pleasure. Her blouse of soft cotton hugged her body, while her skirt swirled around her in its bright-colored fullness, now outlining her hips, now lifting to show her knees and thighs. She swayed as if in a trance, whirling; her legs and arms, feet and hands, moving in smooth, natural rhythm, a pure interpretation of the night and the moment and the sweet passion of the music.

The evening advanced, but none seemed to care about the hour or even to notice it. Food would be forthcoming when it was ready. Babies who cried were given the breast at once or fed bread soaked in wine or goat's milk or bits of meat before being put to bed. The elderly nodded, half asleep. In the meantime, life was life and meant to be lived. Who knew what the next hour might bring? Let the music play. Dance. Sing. To Mara, watching, it seemed a beguiling philosophy.

She did not hear the arrival of the prince. Whether it was truly as silent as it seemed or if it was just that she was lost in the music and the dance, she could not tell, but one moment she was alone, the next he was beside her.

No particular welcome greeted him. His presence was accepted as natural, as if he were one of them. It was surprising to Mara. She had expected some acknowledgment, some form of honor. There came an opportunity to ask him about it later, when the turkeys had been carved and handed around and the camp, intent on eating, was quiet.

"I am the son of the *boyar,*" he said. "What honor should there be for that?"

"I don't know since I have no idea what you mean by *boyar*."

"In my part of the world, the *boyar* is the owner, the ruler. It's the title my father holds over these people."

"He owns them?"

"No one ever really owns a gypsy; the old *boyars* only thought they did. But because my father's father, and his father before him, cared for their ancestors, fed and clothed them and gave them work while letting them come and go at will, this band still gives our line the right to the title. It means little except for the remembrance of ancient privilege, ancient loyalty."

"But if this band comes, as I suppose they must, from your country, what are they doing here in France?"

The glance he sent her was opaque. "Wanderers, outlaws, victims with hungry hearts, they come and go. Must there be a reason?"

"I thought perhaps it was because you are here."

"Why? Is that what brought you?"

With deadly astuteness, he had found his mark. She felt the words like a rapier thrust to the chest, but she had learned enough of this man to know to expect an attack. Quite suddenly she had no appetite, however. She leaned forward to place the turkey wing she held in front of Demon, who was lying at her feet. The dog looked from the wing to her, as if in doubt, then, barking at a slinking gypsy dog that was encroaching, began to gnaw on the wing.

Straightening again, Mara drew her brows together in a frown. "What makes you say that? I did not come of my own will so far as I know. Or have you learned something to my discredit? Am I the kind of woman who would be likely to pay a clandestine visit to a man?"

"A courtesan, all satin smiles and silken guile? A strumpet with outstretched hand? I think not. But they are not always easily identified, such women, and those who hide behind respectability are the worst of their kind."

"How very like a man to condemn women who—who only do what they must."

He tilted his head. "You would defend them?"

She felt herself floundering in verbal quicksand, but could not discover a way to extricate herself. "Not—not exactly. I only question the right of any man to censure females who must live in accordance with the rules laid down by men."

"Another advocate of suffrage for women. Our George will be delighted."

"What?"

"George Sand, known otherwise, and much against her will, as Madame Dudevant. You must meet her."

He rose to his feet without giving her time to answer. His voice quiet and yet carrying, he gave terse orders. The cadre looked up, most with food in their hands or mouths. No one moved. The gypsies watched motionless also. "You heard me correctly," the prince said, his tone gentle, "unless there has been an epidemic of deafness?"

Instantly, food and drink was abandoned. Men scrambled to their feet and moved purposely in every direction, gypsies as well as the prince's men. Mara, seeing what appeared to be preparation for a full-scale departure rather than a sortie, felt a terrible fear move through her. Was the prince leaving the camp? If so, when would he return?

"Where are you going?" she asked, her lips dry.

"That must be obvious."

"Not—not to me."

"The tracks of the carriage that brought you came from Paris and returned there. Nothing more can be learned of you here. We must also return to Paris."

"You and your men—your followers."

"Of course. And you."

"You want me to come?" The sickness inside her should have disappeared. It did not.

The glow of the fire turned the prince's face into an inscrutable mask with blue enamel for eyes. His voice was deep, with a chilling caress, as he answered.

"I want you."

CHAPTER 3

The pace Roderic set on the road to Paris was swift, with no concession to a weak rider. At first Mara had been exhilarated by the thunder of the horses' hooves, the whip of the wind in her face, the racing of the blood in her veins. She had enjoyed, in some strange way, the feeling that she was a part of the group around the prince, as if she belonged. More, she had had the satisfaction of achieving a part of her goal without effort, that of being taken into the prince's household and of going back to Paris with him. Neither of these were enough to sustain her.

Mara's mount was a large roan, built to carry the weight of a man. His strength was tireless, but it took much of hers to hold him in. Though a good rider, she was used to a sidesaddle; her muscles were not conditioned to riding astride, the only method available. As the hours passed with only infrequent pauses to rest the horses, her bruised shoulder began to ache, spreading to the small of her back. A throbbing began in her injured temple and grew until it pulsed with every stride of her mount. Her entire body began to feel as if she were being beaten, a methodical punishment. The need to stop became an agony.

She refused to cry quarter. It was easy to see that the men with the prince felt no fatigue, nor did Trude. Roderic himself rode with the ease of a man accustomed to unending days in the saddle, so used to moving with his horse that he did it effortlessly, bending his thoughts to other problems. To ask to stop and rest for what remained of the night would be to become an encumbrance. The others would resent her weakness that held them back, even if they were too polite to show it. The prince might also decide that bringing her with him had been a mistake, one he could not risk. In any case, after a time it was too late. She had the distinct feeling that if she ever stopped, ever got down, she might be violently ill. The prospect of that humiliation kept her upright.

The gray light of dawn crept into the sky. Slowly, the forms of the other riders became visible. The prince rode in the lead with Michael beside him. Next came Trude and one of the twins, while Estes rode alongside Mara and the other twin brought up the rear. The Italian, catching her glance, gave her a broad smile and a salute. From a basket attached to his saddle, Demon, blinking sleepily, yawned and wagged his tail in greeting. As the pale light increased, the dark pall that was the smoke rising from the chimney pots of Paris could be seen ahead of them.

They were nearing a side lane. A cart, piled high with cabbage and driven by a stolid French peasant as broad as he was tall, was coming along the lane. An ancient horse plodded between the shafts, his back so thick with scars that he was immune to the cracking of the whip at his ears. The peasant saw them advancing, for they caught the look he sent from under thick brows in their direction, saw the unpleasant curl of his thick lips. Yet he made no effort to halt or give way. Instead, he began to pull across the main road, turning into it.

There was no order given, not the exchange of so much

as a word, but suddenly the pace of the cadre quickened to a gallop. Grins appeared. Horses were urged as the members of the cadre leaned forward and reins were gathered close. Under her, Mara's own mount, responding to the charge of his fellows, picked up speed. Hooves began to thunder. Clods of dirt were thrown up. They were sweeping down on a collision course with the cart.

The peasant, his mouth open, began to saw on his reins, trying too late to back up his vehicle. Closer, they came. Closer. Soft murmurs were heard as men spoke to their horses. Demon made a sound that was half whimper, half growl, then retreated into his basket. The swift wind of their passage stung the eyes. Roderic's face was alight with exuberance and joy and steely purpose.

They were going to jump the cart. It was to be a lesson in manners and a pointed reminder of the perils of stubbornness for the surly peasant. Mara saw the course and her own choice. She could wrench her mount around, if she had the strength, if she did not crowd into the man behind her so that they both came down. Or she could give the roan his head and pray that she had not held him back too long. There was no time for the careful weighing of alternatives, only for the pulse of instinct. She loosened her reins.

The peasant shouted and flung himself from the cart. The cart horse reared once, twice. Michael's mount gathered himself, then soared. In that moment, Roderic, even as his own white stallion began the jump, looked back. He saw Mara's loose reins, saw her hand clenched in her horse's mane. His features hardened, then horse and man made a clean white arch above the cart, landing on the other side. Mara's roan gave a last tremendous stride, bunched his muscles and took flight.

She was surging upward, sailing as if on some winged steed. The cart and the gaping peasant and the hard ground seemed far below. She saw Roderic clinging to the back of his stallion, which was rearing with the suddenness of the halt, the horse's neck arched as his head was dragged around. Then the downward plunge began. The forefeet of the roan hit the ground with an earth-shaking thud. She waited for the jolting pain of it to strike through her. It did not come, for she was still airborne, her feet free of the stirrups, her cloak and skirts flying in the wind.

Abruptly, she collided with something white and hard. It seared her forehead, ramming her neck into her shoulders, and whipped around her waist to constrict her breathing. She cried out, a sound that was echoed by a hoarse yell nearby and a soft and fluent cursing above her. She felt the rush of a heavy body, heard the muffled thumping and pounding as the rest of the cadre cleared the barrier of the cart.

She was shifted. She drew air into her lungs, then wondered as sickness rushed in upon her if that deep breath had been a mistake. She swallowed hard, then opened her eyes.

She was lying in the arms of the prince, held across his saddlebow. He had swung his mount to view the damage, and she could see the others milling around, soothing their horses, though Michael and one of the twins was helping Estes to his feet. The Italian grimaced at their rough dusting-off of his person and, limping a little, came at once toward Mara and the prince.

"The lady," he asked, his tone anxious as he stared upward, "she is all right?"

Mara managed a nod. "And . . . you, sir?"

"I have in my time been an acrobat. Falling is of no importance, but for you— It was madness for you to try this jump."

"I had no choice." She closed her eyes, swallowing again as a shudder rippled through her.

"See to your mount," Roderic said, his voice rough as he spoke to the count.

Then came a clamor behind them as the peasant, recovering, came shouting and blundering among them. They had upset his cart with their aristocratic antics, spilled his cabbages into the mud. He demanded repayment at once.

"Unlettered, unmannered, unwashed, and proud with it," Roderic said, staring down at him. "The right of way, my friend, does not belong to him who takes it. You are the agent of your own misfortune and that of this lady. Will you press it?"

The threat in the softly spoken words was palpable. The peasant blanched and began to back away muttering excuses. With hands that jerked, he unhooked the horse from the cart, then scrambled onto his back. His fat haunches bounced on the swayback of the animal as he galloped away.

Mara lay still with her eyes tightly shut throughout the exchange. She heard the stirring of the others, the report as her roan was brought back unharmed from where it had stopped running. She knew when Roderic loosened his grasp to look down at her.

"And how are you, in truth?"

She lifted her lashes, gazing up at him. "I am not," she said as distinctly as she could through set teeth, "going to be sick."

Roderic saw the determination in her eyes and the jut of her pointed chin, saw, too, the shadow of panic that was not for her pain or the danger she had just passed through, but for the fear of humiliation. It caused a tightness in his chest, a peculiar feeling he had never had before, though the full sensation in another part of his body, brought about by her warm and slender form against him, was familiar enough. The glib spate of words that he used so often for weapon and shield deserted him.

"No, you are not."

Mara heard the iron-hard assurance in his voice, and her tension eased. The threat of physical illness receded. She grew aware of the hard strength of the arms that held her, of the ridged muscles in the thigh across which she lay. His eyes, she discovered, were a deep sea-blue, dark with fleeting concern. In confusion, she lowered her lashes, fixing her gaze on a red smear on his white tunic.

"I—I seem to have gotten blood on you. I'm sorry."

"Don't apologize. You hit the graze on your forehead again. But for my negligence it would not have happened."

A faint smile curved her lips. "That sounds strange coming from you."

"Why? Have I given the impression that I am too proud to acknowledge a fault?"

"No, no. Only that you have none."

His silence was complete, abrupt. For long moments he did not even breathe. She opened her eyes again. In his face as he watched her was such virulent doubt that she put out her hand, struggling to sit up.

His hold tightened. "Trude! Cognac?"

The woman, her face stern, twisted in the saddle and brought out a flat silver flask. She removed the cap and passed it across. Roderic took it and held it to Mara's lips.

She turned her head. "I don't need reviving."

"It will help the pain and other discomforts. Think of it as medicine."

The rim of the container was against her mouth once more. She took a cautious sip, and immediately the prince tipped the bottle so that she was forced to swallow several times. The liquor took her breath with its fire, burning its way into her stomach. When she could speak, she gasped, "You will make me drunk."

"Would that be bad?" he asked softly, and lifted the flask again.

It wasn't. She floated into Paris on cognac fumes made more potent by exhaustion and enforced forgetfulness. She hardly knew when they reached the dwelling place of the prince, when they entered the courtyard entrance, or when she was carried inside. But as the prince placed her on the resilient surface of a bed and began to unlace her arms from around his neck, she surfaced enough to smile sleepily up at him.

"Mine is a bachelor household, but there should be a maid about somewhere. I will send her to you or, failing that, Trude will come."

"You are very kind," she murmured.

"Take care. Just as you would not credit me with faults, it would be wrong to ascribe to me unwarranted virtues."

"Have you none? Then could I seduce you?"

Laughter leaped brightly into his eyes. "Is it permission you seek or an opinion? If the first, I give it without reservation; if the second, the answer is yes, without doubt."

"You might not like it."

"How should I not?"

His lashes, she discovered, were tipped with gold, a radiant barrier to screen his thoughts. Something she saw behind them, however, carried a warning to her muddled senses, bringing the rush of returning caution. The candid light died out of her face. She released her hold and drew back. "Men, so I've been told, prefer being the hunter."

"As some women enjoy being prey?"

"Not I," she said quickly.

"Do you expect me to curb my instincts for that reason and sit dulcet and smug, waiting to be enraptured?"

"You couldn't."

"Could I not? It would be a novelty."

It seemed he was issuing a challenge, though with the dullness of her mind caused by the cognac she could not be sure. But if he was, it was not one she felt capable of meeting at that moment. She permitted a yawn to overtake her and smothered it with the back of her hand. "Very well. Tomorrow."

"The sun is rising. This is tomorrow."

"You will have to wait."

He eased her back against the pillow and reached to draw up the linen sheet and coverlet. There was a quiver in his voice that might have been amusement as he answered, "But how shall I bear it?"

The section of Paris where the house owned by the royal family of Ruthenia was located was called La Marais. Once a swamp, the area had been filled in and gradually built up as the city was enlarged. Due to its convenience to the old Louvre Palace and the Tuileries, over the years it had become a most elite and aristocratic district with many fine homes that were themselves like small palaces. Decay had set in when the nobles were required by Louis XIV to move en masse with him to Versailles, and the revolution had hastened the process. With the occupation of the Tuileries by Napoleon as emperor, however, the great houses had been occupied once more and had remained so during the return of the Bourbons and the Orléans to the throne. The section was then a curious mixture of slum dwellings and elite residences where the nobility rubbed shoulders with the descendents of sansculottes, and all were entertained by the activities of the artists and writers who lived in the garrets of the district.

Known simply as Ruthenia House, the residence of the prince was constructed of the same pale gold stone used for so many buildings in the city. That stone had been overlaid with years of drifting soot from chimney pots so that it was now a dull and streaked gray in color, as was the rest of Paris. The massive front gate of wrought iron set with the crest of Ruthenia guarded a cobblestoned entrance court, the largest of four such courtyards that were incorporated in the rectangular building.

The rooms were built one-deep around the four sides of the court areas, which for convenience were named for the cardinal points of the compass, with the larger entrance area being designated the south court. The arrangement allowed for a feeling of openness within the solid façade presented to the outside world, as well as ample light and the free flow of air from tall, leaded and stained-glass windows. Though the entrance court was fairly utilitarian, paved with cobblestones and containing only a statue of Diana and bas-reliefs over the entrance doorway representing Grecian women of the four seasons, the other enclosures were planted with clipped evergreen shrubbery set in intricate geometric designs. As one passed from room to room, it was always possible to see greenery and open space. In the summer, blooming plants and herbs would add color, but now in late November there was nothing but dark green shrubs, turned earth, and a few empty urns.

To Mara, the house was a palace, nothing less. There were, she had been reliably told, some seventy rooms under the various angles of its roofline. Above the south court, the entrance court, was the main gallery, a long hall holding the grand staircase that mounted from the entrance and led to the public reception rooms that occupied the wing on the left. To the right were the apartments of the prince, including various antechambers, salons, and other rooms, and beyond them the state apartments for King Rolfe and Queen Angeline, all grouped around the east court. Around the north and west courts were private salons built whimsically in oval and circular shapes, a long gallery sometimes used for exercise and for dancing, plus various other salons, antechambers, bedchambers, and dressing rooms. Near Mara's own suite, which included a salon, bedchamber, and small dressing room, was a back stair that led down to the kitchens on the ground floor. Also on that lower level were the servants' quarters, the storage rooms, the carriage house, and stables.

It was without doubt an emormous and splendid residence, and yet the furniture and draperies, the paintings and enamelware, the faience, crystal chandeliers, and chinaware, though once of superb quality, were now of a uniform shabbiness. There had been little effort to update the great, rambling place; though many houses in Paris had installed gas lighting, here there was only accommodation for candlelight. There was treasures hidden in the dark recesses of the various rooms, but also ancient dirt and bits of broken furnishings. The windows needed washing, the floors polishing, the ceilings cleaning of the accumulated soot and grime of decades. Not one of the cavernous chimneys in the place drew as it should, nor was the service from the kitchens efficient enough to assure hot food delivered to any room. There were piles of horse manure in the entrance court and noisome heaps of refuse that would not bear investigating on the street outside the kitchen door. In some wings the stench of chamber pots was pervasive; in others the odor was unidentifiable and indescribable, but just as overpowering.

Mara had been ordered to keep to her bed. She had obeyed from necessity for two days, from choice for another, but on the fourth she had rebelled. The food that had been brought to her was inedible; the girl who brought it a slattern. The sheets on her bed had been musty to begin with and had remained unchanged. There was ancient dust in the folds of the bed curtains and on the speckled, gilt picture frames on the walls, and enough dirt in the rug beside the bed to sprout seed. Visitors had apparently been forbidden to see her, for she had had none. It was disgust, no less than the boredom and the feeling that valuable time was passing while she did nothing, that had driven her finally from her chamber.

She had not seen Roderic since that first morning. In the back of her mind was a vague memory of a conversation with him on the day they had reached Paris. She was afraid that cognac on a virtually empty stomach, coupled with exhaustion and pain, had made her indiscreet. She could not quite recall what had been said, however, a true loss of memory. She could not think that she had been too confiding or surely she would not still be in the household of the prince. And yet it was possible that something she had said had caused him to isolate her, to suspect her convenient amnesia.

She had wondered more than once if the prince had not deliberately made her intoxicated. Such a tactic, she thought, would not be beyond him. Oh, she absolved him of using any such means to force himself upon a woman—a man with his appearance and title would have little need of it. Regardless, there was a ruthlessness about him that suggested that he would not be too scrupulous about his methods of gaining information if he thought the situation called for it. The idea gave her a feeling of unpleasant vulnerability.

Roderic also, Mara suspected, used more conventional methods of gathering information. In the few short hours she had been up and about, there had been a steady stream of visitors to see the prince. To this the official embassy of Ruthenia had come men with the stern and pompous look of statesmen and financiers and ladies wrapped in furs who trailed silk skirts and clouds of expensive perfume. These were to be expected, and were received in the public salon that overlooked the main entrance court. But what of the authors with ink-stained fingers, artists with flowing ties in the romantic style, street cleaners, fish vendors, drivers of cabriolets, black-coated waiters, and little seamstresses in their cheap gray dresses that had given them the name of *grisettes*? What purpose could such people serve except for what they might be able to tell Roderic? What reason could he have for gathering such knowledge except to find answers to the riddle she represented?

Perhaps she was giving herself too much importance. It seemed doubtful that a man such as the prince would go to so much trouble to discover the identity of a woman. She could not flatter herself that he was that taken with her charms. Certainly she had seen little sign of anything more than curiosity. There might have been a moment of brief attraction, but it had been quickly submerged by irritation and annoyance. She could not feel that an undying passion for her had been kindled out of such minor reactions.

She was no longer certain, of course, that such passion was to be desired. Her instructions had been to persuade Roderic to bring her with him on his return to Paris, to install herself in his home. It had been expected that she would be forced to share his bed in order to accomplish that object. She had not. It had not been explained to her what the purpose of her presence was, except that she would be instrumental in involving the prince in some scheme de Landes had in mind. She might well be able to do what was necessary without going so far as actual intimacy with the prince.

But did it matter? Mara, for all the indulgence of her upbringing, was a realist. She was not foolish enough to think that she could emerge unscathed from this escapade. It was true that she was not well known in Paris; still, there were people whom she had met, people who would recognize her. Sooner or later, if she stayed long enough with Roderic, there would be someone who would see her and draw the inescapable conclusion.

It was possible it would not happen until she had done what she must—she prayed that it would not for the sake of her grandmother. But if it did, if it was discovered that she was in Paris rather than in the country with her grandmother, as her cousin belived, the scandal would be great. Paris, for all its cosmopolitan outlook, was provincial about some things. The appearance of virtue must be maintained. Some railed against such a bourgeois attitude, one that had emerged with the advance of the middle class after the revolution and steadily increased in strictness with every year since. But it did no good. A woman who cared for her good name did not live under the same roof with a man, especially one such as the prince.

Once the tale was out, it would reach New Orleans without delay. What her father would say and do, Mara did not like to think. What she herself would do afterward, how and where she would live when her task was complete, she preferred not to consider. Her grandmother would be safe, and that was all that mattered.

Mara was traversing the main gallery above the south entrance court after inspecting the public rooms when she heard the faint sound of barking. It was Demon, she was sure, though the sound seemed to be coming from some distance away. The acoustics in the house, as in all houses of any size, were peculiar. A person could yell herself hoarse in one spot and not be heard beyond the next room, while a whisper in another place would reverberate through the entire upper floor.

She thought at first that the dog might be in Roderic's apartments. She had not penetrated into that section of the building, but knew that the rooms occupied by the cadre were located in the same wing, along one side of the east court, with the exception of Trude's, which was near to her own. The dog was surely with his master,

Estes, since he was seldom far from the count's side. Estes would, in all likelihood, be with the other men of the cadre.

She had not spoken to them since her arrival. They seemed to have a constant round of duties to carry out for Roderic, duties that took them to all parts of the city, moving back and forth in a steady stream. Their relaxation was pursued with the same intensity; they were always setting out for a cockfight or a prizefight, the theater or a drinking bout in the rooms above some restaurant. They must rest sometime, she knew, but she had not yet discovered where or when.

She had not looked for Roderic's cadre, of course. She had been intent on her inspection of the building, on learning her way around it and discovering why it was in such disorder.

She had come to the conclusion that it was one of two possible reasons. Either there was no money to hire the necessary number of servants to keep things as they should be or else there was no one to direct them and hold them responsible for keeping their jobs done. She thought it the latter, for she had come upon any number of men and women in livery and aprons standing gossiping in the corridors, drinking and arguing in the kitchens, or playing slap and tickle behind the doors of the guest bedchambers. It would be an enormous undertaking to bring order to the great house, but just the sight of all the grit and filth, to say nothing of slacking servants, made her itch to try it.

The barking sounded again. She turned her head, listening. Combined with sharp, excited yelping were dull thumps and thuds, with now and then a shout. The noise was not coming from the east wing after all, but from the north court wing. Lifting her skirts, she hurried along the gallery, turning left into an antechamber, moving from it into an extra bedchamber with a dressing room beyond, then right into a long salon, which she crossed before turning right again into another long gallery.

The room, lined with windows on both sides and heated by a fireplace at each end, was as warm and bright as it was possible to be on such a cold and gray day. Candles burned in the chandeliers overhead so that their grime-coated luster appeared silver. A long, woven rug, thread-bare but beautiful still in a design of classical figures on a cream background in dark blue, red, and gold lay on the intricate parquet floor, the only item of furnishing in the room. The high ceiling was groined, with heavy moldings and cornices covered with gold leaf, leaving a series of open squares down the room. These squares were painted with scenes depicting the life of Diana and were of the same colors in the rug beneath them. The paintings were dim beneath layers of dirt, but the colors were still warm and rich. In the center of the room, directly under a scene of Diana with Cupid, was a pyramid of people.

The bottom tier was made up of Michael, Jacques, and Jared on their hands and knees. Braced on top of them, also on hands and knees, were Trude and the gypsy Luca. On the top of these two was Estes, who was balancing precariously as the others swayed back and forth in an apparent effort to dislodge him, while doing his best to persuade Demon to scramble up to crown their pile. The dog, his mough hanging open in a canine grin between sharp barks, was keeping well away from them.

There were complaints about sharp knees, bony shoulders, and great behemoths who overeat; groans, moans, and muttered curses. But there was also breathless laughter and a feeling of fun and ready camaraderie. Mara, putting her hands on her hips, could not keep from smiling.

"What are you doing?" she demanded.

Michael turned his head sharply. His face flushed as he saw her and, instinctively, he started to rise. Luca gave a yell as he lost his balance. Trude slipped and said something under her breath. Then in a tangle of legs and arms the pyramid dissolved. Estes sprang to his feet, raised his arms, and flipped into the air. Trude and Luca made a diving roll forward. Michael, Jared, and Jacques somersaulted. And suddenly there they were, all six, on their feet in front of her with their arms spread wide. As one, they bent double in a bow. Demon, not to be outdone, capered forward and stood on his hind legs, dancing in a circle.

"Oh, well done!" Mara exclaimed, applauding.

Estes bounced upright. With his arms still spread, he turned to the others. "Shall we do it again?"

"No!" they chorused.

Estes turned back with a shrug. "*Eh bien,* the show is over."

"Show, my eye," Jared said, flexing his shoulder and back muscles.

"A demonstration of the art of falling then, a useful skill."

"Yes," Mara said, her tone rueful, "I seem to remember you mentioning it before. Do you think I could learn?"

"Nothing easier, when you are recovered."

"I'm perfectly well."

"No more *mal de tête*?"

"No headache."

"Your shoulder?"

"A bit stiff, but it might be as well if I used it."

"Well, then!" the Italian count exclaimed, then as he glanced down at her slender form, his face fell.

"What is it?"

"Ah, there is the matter of . . . you see—"

"What he is trying to say," Trude interrupted, stepping forward, "is that it will be difficult for you in your skirts."

Mara gave a slow nod. "I see."

"You have the trousers?" Estes asked, his tone hopeful.

"No. Nothing except this gown."

"Ah."

They looked at one another, then back to Mara. They looked at Trude, who shook her head. "Mine are too large."

"And mine too small," Estes said regretfully.

"Mine are too long," Michael said.

Luca flashed a grin that showed white teeth. "I have only one pair of a quality fit for a lady, and I have them on as I came today to Paris to see Roderic. Of course, if they are required, I will gladly—"

"That will not be necessary." Trude gave him a repressive look.

"Ours are too big," the twins said.

Trude pursed her lips as she looked at them. "Perhaps not. Size in the lower body of a woman is deceiving; our pelves are larger than they may appear, for natural reasons."

"Still, I think not," Estes said.

"Roderic's?" Michael asked.

Sadly, Estes shook his head. "Too large."

As one, they turned toward Michael. "Scissors. Who has scissors?"

Mara did not cut the trousers that they brought for her, however; she only rolled them to her knees. The shirt she had also been loaned hung upon her with the sleeves in rolls around her elbows where she had turned them up. There were no studs to hold the shirt closed, so she used a piece of ribbon from her camisole to tie it at the top and tucked the remainder into her trousers. She removed her waist-heeled shoes, but retained her stockings of opaque white silk, bedraggled though they were, since they gave her some feeling of semirespectability. Still, it was rather embarrassing to emerge from the salon where she had changed wearing them, a little like appearing in public in her pantalettes and camisole.

They began with simple somersaults down the length of the rug, rolling over and over like so many garden bugs tucked into balls. Agile as a monkey and twice as droll, Estes showed her how to relax as she fell. It was tight muscles and joints that caused injury, he claimed; she must relax and move in the direction of the fall, continuing the motion so that it was dispelled, instead of trying to stop it and having it come to a jarring halt against the hard ground with her body in the way. They progressed from somersaults to gentle tumbles and cartwheels for Mara, while the others bounded down the length of the gallery in a series of quick, head-over-heels springs. So fast did they move, and so vigorously, that it was as if they were made of coiled steel.

Time passed, and Mara began to lose a sense of self, to feel that her muscles could and would respond to the dictates of her brain on an instant's command. At first there had been some soreness in her shoulder, but it seeped away. Her hair came down from the loose knot she had put it up in that morning. It spilled around her, clinging to her flushed face with its dew of perspiration from the exertion. They were moving so quickly, however, that there was no time to see to it.

"Now we will teach you to land on your feet like the cat," Estes declared. "We make the standing pyramid, all seven!"

Once again, Michael and the twins took the load on the bottom row. Estes, talking all the time about footholds and handholds and the art of climbing a human body, clambered up to stand on Michael's shoulders on one side. Trude made her way up to balance on Jared's shoulders on the other, and Luca climbed up onto those of Jacques in the middle. Those on bottom held the ankles of those in the second row, who in turn linked arms, gently swaying for balance.

"Come, *Chère,* now you on the very top. Up you go!"

She could not do it, she told herself as she stared up at the place she was meant to be, so near the painting on the top of the high ceiling. At the same time, she took a few running steps and began to climb, bracing on a knee, the crook of an arm, a shoulder, pushing, pulling, gasping with the effort to draw herself higher. At last she knelt on Luca's shoulders, her fingers clutching his hair.

"Ouch!" the gypsy yelled.

"Steady, my angel," Estes called as she released her grasp and had to fling her arm out abruptly, wobbling back and forth to maintain her place on the wavering, shifting column of bodies.

"I'm going to break my neck and be an angel indeed," she said with resignation.

"Indeed not!"

There was more gaiety than she thought seemly in the Italian's tone. "Yes!"

"Trust me, my cabbage. Put your hand on Luca's head. Now push, fast, fast, up, and get your foot on his shoulder. Good. Steady. Now take your fingers from his hair—"

"Thank you," Luca said.

"Quiet. Rise, little one, rise. Turn. Place your other foot on his other shoulder. Easy. Hands on hips. *Voilà!*"

The muscles in her legs were on fire, trembling with the effort. Her heart was beating with hammer strokes, thudding against her rib cage. Her breathing was a sharp pain in her chest. Her hands were balled into fists for self-control, and her toes were tightly curled. But she was there. She had made it.

They cheered, a lusty roar that held a note of admiration for her pluckiness, plus warm male appreciation for the fact that she was a woman and attractive. So vital and loud was the sound that they did not hear the opening of the door.

"A fine carouse and an edifying spectacle, but not a proper greeting for a guest—or treatment for an injured lady."

It was Roderic, standing straight and tall in the doorway with a large gentleman at his side and the sharp chill of ice shards in his voice.

"Hoopla!" Estes called. Demon barked once, then sat with his tongue lolling out and tail wagging expectantly.

The pyramid disintegrated. One moment it stood firm and steady beneath her; the next there was only air between her and the hard parquet floor. She exhaled as she had been taught and relaxed, beginning to curl forward as she fell. Abruptly, she was caught in a net of arms. The cadre, grinning hugely, held her a moment until she had caught her breath. Then they bounced her gently and tipped her up forward onto her feet.

Estes turned to Roderic with a flourish. "You see, my prince! The lady was as safe with us as a babe in arms, safer than she knew, this you may believe."

The prince was displeased. He said nothing, but it was there in the set of his shoulders, the bronze implacability of his face. He transferred his gaze to Mara, missing nothing of her dishevelment and odd costume, her flushed and moist cheeks, and the flustered concern for her dignity that was dawning behind the bright triumph and merriment in her eyes.

"Magnifique!" The man beside Roderic stepped up to catch Estes's hand, giving it a hearty shake. "A fantastic thing; such control, such strength and agility! I wish I might try it, but, alas, I have partaken too well of the good things of life for such acrobatics."

"Monsieur exaggerates." Estes inclined his head in acknowledgment of the compliment, his tone polite.

"No, no, I assure you I wouldn't try," the man said, patting his bulging waistline. "But it's said that my father, when he was an officer in the army of Napoleon, was able to sit in the saddle holding on to a stable beam and pick up his horse with his thighs."

"Formidable," Estes said, his eyes wide.

"Yes."

"Forgive me, Alex," Roderic said, "I did not mean to neglect you. You know my *garde du corps,* but permit me to present to you this lady whom you wished to meet, Mademoiselle Incognito. Chère, the well-known writer Alexandre Dumas."

"My appreciation for those kind words, Roderic. Mademoiselle, I am enchanted. The prince has told me something of your story. What a delicious mystery, the very stuff of a novel—I must consider it."

"It would make a short and sorry tale, I fear."

"Not," he said superbly, "when I had finished with it."

"Perhaps so," she agreed, her lips curving in a smile for the courtesy and simple ego of the man. He was tall as well as large, in his midforties, handsome in a florid fashion. He was well dressed in a frock coat and trousers of the latest cut, though the waistcoat that covered his expansive chest was of a blindingly bright red brocade embroidered with gold thread. His hair was dark blond and wildly curling, with traces of white over his ears. His eyes were blue and his complexion the color of the *café au lait* commonly given to children, more milky cream than coffee. It was common knowledge that his grandmother had been a Negro slave from the West Indies plantation of his grandfather when the two had begun to live together, a relationship that may or may not have been legalized. In New Orleans it would have been cause for shame; here in Paris it merely made him interesting. She added, "It is a great pleasure to meet you. I have enjoyed your historical romances so very much, particularly *The Three Musketeers.*"

"You remember my book, you who have forgotten so

much else of importance? How delightful. The brain is a strange thing, is it not, picking and choosing among its memories?"

"So it seems. But I am happy to be able to tell you that of all you have written, I think this book and also *The Count of Monte Cristo* are surely masterpieces." She had always spent much time during the long Louisiana summers reading, but books had been an especially valued retreat during her period of mourning for Dennis.

"Of all I have written! Apt words. I wish the Académie Française might agree with you. Due to my prolific output, they consider me negligible, me and my dear friend Balzac, who suffers from the same problem, a too great facility with words."

Estes stepped forward and snapped his fingers. "That for the Académie. You will be remembered, Monsieur, when the ones who refuse you admittance are forgotten."

"But what of Monsieur Hugo who has also written great reams?" Mara asked with a smile. "He is a member of the Académie, I believe."

Dumas shrugged. "Ah, yes, Victor's output of words is prodigious, though not so great as mine, naturally. But the great Hugo had to apply four times—four!—before he was admitted, and even then it was only the influence of the late duc d'Orléans that made the difference."

"A political victory then?"

"Exactly, mademoiselle. But then Victor considers himself a politician. He has been supreme in the realms of poetry, drama, novels, finance, and in the boudoir. For him, politics is one of the last fields left unconquered."

He seemed in his wry self-depreciation and openness to invite familiarity. "And what of you, Monsieur? Have you no ambitions in that direction?"

He gave a great laugh. "I have still many fields to conquer. But all I truly want is to be wealthy enough to write what pleases me—and to finish my house. You have been so amiable, all of you. You are good for me. It would please me greatly if you would all come to my house when it is completed. We will eat and drink and talk, and celebrate my beautiful monstrosity."

"You are building a house?"

"Rather a monument," the prince said.

"Yes, to history and to melodrama, and to all the things I find beautiful. It will be unique and stupendous, perhaps ugly to some, but with many fascinating parts."

"In imitation of its builder?" Roderic suggested.

Alexandre Dumas fixed a sorrowful gaze on the prince. "Someday, my dear friend, someone is going to slip a large knife between your shoulder blades or else cut out your clever tongue."

"And someday you will spend more on your follies than can be made with your facile pen, and you will be hounded out of Paris for debt. But it won't happen this afternoon." Roderic swept the bare room with a comprehensive glance. "I would offer you a chair, Alex, but it appears there are none in here. Shall we all move to the salon?"

The prince stood aside to allow his guest to go before him. At a gesture from him, the others began filing from the room. Roderic touched the arm of the gypsy, detaining him. There was no surprise in the gaze that rested upon him, however. It was as if the prince had marked the man's presence earlier and was only now at leisure to give it a portion of his attention.

When there were only the dark-haired gypsy, Mara, and himself left in the long gallery, he said, "Joining the cadre, Luca?"

"If it pleases you," the gypsy answered, though there was a suggestion of hauteur in his manner, as if he expected to be refused and was ready to retreat into stiff unconcern.

"The choice isn't mine alone. You will have to please the others."

"You mean, your men?"

"It is a requirement. They are not easily satisfied." The tone of the prince was quiet, incisive with warning.

"I will try to be worthy, Your Highness."

"You had something to report?"

The gypsy hesitated, as if he would say something more. Finally, he inclined his dark head in acceptance. "My people are encamped at Montreuil outside the gates of Paris, as you instructed. They await your bidding."

"Drink, eat, sing, dance, but stay out of the city. You comprehend?"

"No begging, no picking of pockets, no enticements of the women, no trading of unsound horses. I comprehend."

"To admiration. Will you join us?"

Moisture sprang into the eyes of the gypsy. He made no answer beyond a tight, short bow, but squared his shoulders and lifted his head before he moved after the cadre.

"And you, Chère?"

Mara had been hanging back, hoping to escape unnoticed. She had no idea if she was to be included in this gathering of men, but she did not intend to join them. It was one thing to tumble about on the floor with the cadre dressed in trousers and a baggy shirt, but quite another to enter a salon with such a distinguished visitor, to sip wine and eat cakes there in formal hospitality. "I think not. I—I really should get dressed."

"Unnecessary. We have seen you as you are and can bear the sight for some time longer."

"I prefer not to sit among you looking like a boy dressed up in his father's clothes."

A smile curved his mouth, rising into his eyes. "There is little danger of that."

A peculiar doubt struck her. She glanced down at her shirtfront, following the direction of his warm gaze. The ribbon holding the edges of the voluminous garment together in lieu of studs had come untied, allowing it to fall open to her waist. Through the gap could be seen her camisole with the soft, white curves of her breasts rising above the lace-trimmed neckline. She turned away quickly, clutching at the shirt with one hand.

"Regardless, you must hold me excused. Perhaps I will join you later."

"Chère?"

The word was soft, but no less commanding for that. She paused in her retreat to glance back over her shoulder.

"Be certain that you do. Or expect to explain in detail of exacting plausibility why you failed."

"Why? I have not been with you for some days; surely there is no need for my presence now."

"I wish it. What other need should there be?"

"An arrogant attitude, I must say!"

"But my own. Is there a reason why you would avoid us?"

"Perhaps I am tired."

"It would not be a surpassing surprise. Are you?"

She was beginning to feel the ominous return of her old headache, but refused to give him the satisfaction of admitting it. It was not from her exertions, she thought, but purely from the strain of this exchange with him.

"The truth is, I . . . my wardrobe is somewhat scanty. It doesn't lend itself to appearing at formal entertainments."

"One subject for discussion between us."

Did he mean there were others? The possibility was dismaying. She concentrated on the subject he had broached. "I require nothing of that nature from you."

"Do you not? But I require that so long as you are under my roof you will not appear like a waif, bedraggled and spattered with cinders. It doesn't suit my consequence to have anyone think I would keep a woman in such a state."

"You are not keeping me!" she said, her voice hard.

"No? You are here and, by ancient law, any woman who shares the rooftree of a hereditary lord of Ruthenia enjoys his protection."

"It was not my choice!"

Swift and hard came his reply. "Is it against your will?"

"What—what has that to do with the matter? I have no memory, so have no way of knowing where I belong, where I wish to be."

"Exactly. But my guest is waiting. I will expect you shortly, and later we will talk."

Mara stared after him when he and the others had gone. In her mind was a niggling disquiet. Could it be that he had deliberately played on her fears and her anger, hoping for some unguarded reaction, some revealing remark? She did not like to think so, and yet there had been something odd in his manner, some hint of a carefully directed testing of her defenses. He was capable of it, she knew. It could well be that he had left her alone until now out of consideration for her weak state, but that on finding her so nearly returned to health he had decided that she was able to withstand such means of interrogation.

But what of it? He was a forbidding man, armored in intelligence and vital strength, sufficient within himself, possessed of that silvery and trenchant turn of phrase that Helene had described so often in his father, and yet he was only a man, an unimportant princeling from a powerless Balkan state at the outer edges of central Europe. It was ridiculous the way everyone jumped at his merest whisper, cringed at the lift of his brow.

She would not do so. She might have no moral right to be where she was, might be a source of some form of danger to him, but that did not give him the right to order her life or to treat her with condescension. She was required at the moment to live as near to him as she could, but she did not have to accept any treatment he cared to mete out. Nor would she.

CHAPTER 4

By the time Mara reached the salon an hour later, there was no sign of the cadre or Monsieur Dumas. The prince sat alone before the fire under the great marble mantel. He lounged in a chair, his golden head bright against the dark blue silk brocade. He stared at the flames, with one long leg and booted foot thrust out before him and a glass of wine in his hand.

Beyond the windows, the afternoon had advanced to early evening and was made darker by the overcast sky. A branch of candles burned with a smoky and unsteady light on the table that was centered in the large room. It made a pool of brightness, leaving the corners in shadow. In the gloom could be seen the tapestries by Gobelin that covered the walls, the frieze of classical figures carved into the marble around the top of the fireplace, the Persian carpet with its riot of flowers in gold and blue, and several commode chests, settees, and chairs from the Louis XV period. Mercifully, the dust and grime was concealed by the dimness.

Mara had thought Roderic unaware of her presence, but as she paused halfway into the room, he rose to his feet and turned to face her. His glance flicked over the crumpled gown of white silk she had of necessity put on once more, but he made no comment. Moving to a commode where a wine tray with glasses sat, he refilled his own glass, then poured one for her and stepped over to offer it to her.

"Sit down, please."

She could not object to his tone. It was not warm, but neither was it imperious. She came forward to take the wine. There was a fauteuil chair to match the one he had occupied on the other side of the great fireplace, and she sank down upon the edge of it.

He did not immediately return to his seat, but stood with his back to the fireplace. He stared down at her, and his eyes were dark, as if he were weighing alternatives. Stretching out his hand, he touched the rough and scabbed area on her temple. When she drew back at once, he frowned and lowered his hand.

"A paragon of healing. You have recovered quickly from your ordeal."

"There was nothing of any importance wrong with me."

"Except for a small matter of memory. I can't think that you would still be with us if that had returned, so I assume it has not?"

Was there a trace of derision in his voice? She could not be sure. "No."

"There has not, apparently, been a report filed with the authorities concerning the disappearance of a woman of your description. Nor is there word in the streets of such an occurrence."

"I see." The wine in her glass was ruby red. She watched the shift of its rich color as she turned the glass in her fingers.

"It appears that you must stay with us."

"Must?"

"Unless you have somewhere else you would prefer to go."

She gave a slow shake of her head. "I . . . am sorry for the imposition."

"There will be no imposition. I had in mind that you might—earn your keep."

He had deliberately used the word she had objected to earlier, she was sure of it. She looked up at him, steeling her features in the effort to prevent the alarm she felt coursing in her veins from showing on her face. "What do you mean?"

Roderic watched the flush slowly stain her cheekbones and wished he knew what she was thinking, what she expected from him. Did she remember their conversation on the night they had arrived in Paris? If so, he saw no consciousness of it, no coquettish side glances, no embarrassment other than for her state of dress, or undress, earlier. That she could forget was almost enough to convince him that her amnesia was authentic. Almost.

"My majordomo is a fine man; there could not be one more loyal or devoted. Sarus has been with me all my life, and was my father's valet and majordomo years before. His own father, grandfather, and great-grandfather served mine as both serfs and free men. I tell you this so that you will understand why I cannot simply discharge him for neglect of his duties, the results of which you must have seen. In fact, it isn't neglect: it's age. Sarus no longer sees well, nor is he able to work as he once did or even to move much beyond his room in my apartments. And yet, because his life has been the service of my father and me, to replace him with a younger man would be to kill him."

Roderic paused a moment, then went on deliberately, "The only arrangement he might accept without feeling that his place was usurped would be for me to give the household affairs into the hands of a woman."

"You mean hire a housekeeper?"

"A middle-aged harridan all bustling efficiency and

contempt for Sarus's poor efforts? Hardly. I mean a woman he will accept because he can feel she is attached to me. The rights of my wife he would acknowledge without question, or, if I insisted and she was tactful, my mistress."

That suggestion, coinciding so neatly with her need, raised her protective instincts. "You mean—"

He raised a brow, a wicked smile curving his mouth as she floundered for the right words. "Not at all. Only the appearance, unless you prefer the actuality?"

It wasn't necessary, surely it wasn't necessary, not now. In addition, Mara had the feeling that it would be dangerous to agree to any part of this peculiar proposal. "No, but—"

"I understood that you objected to being kept by me, that you would rather earn your own way in some fashion. If I am wrong, only say so and it will be forgotten."

His voice was silken. Her mistrust grew, though she could see no way to avoid the answer he expected. She must stay here in this house with him. "I don't care to be dependent on you, but this is so—so unusual."

"There are many women directing the households of men in Paris. No few such arrangements are irregular."

"I don't quite see how you are to convince your majordomo that I am—that I have the proper authority."

"You may leave that to me."

That hint of arrogance was in his voice once more. Or was it quite fair to call it that? It might just as easily be no more than total self-confidence.

"I will admit that you are in need of someone to direct your servants," she said slowly, "but what makes you think that I can do it? You know nothing about my capabilities."

"You couldn't be worse than Sarus."

"The people in your employ may not take orders from me."

"They will or you may discharge them and hire others more amenable."

She stared at him, at the strong lines of his face and the calm and intent expression in the depths of his eyes. With asperity brought on by his annoying assurance and her own sense of helplessness, she said, "Since you have demolished my every objection, I suppose I must agree."

"Only if you wish. I am not coercing you, merely requesting your assistance with a problem."

"I did not mean that you—" she began, then stopped as she realized the impossibility of explaining the constraint upon her. "I will be happy to help you in any way I can."

"A generous offer, but I will not explore it. The next problem is one of outfitting you for your position."

"That is simply done," she said with resignation. "I am sure you must have a regular supplier of the usual gray stuff, plus aprons and caps."

"No." The word was hard, uncompromising.

"It should be easy enough to discover one. You have only to ask among the maids."

"You misunderstand me, and with purpose, or so it seems. Let me make myself plain. I do not require that you dress as a servant."

"Then how," she asked, her voice hard, "do you require that I dress?"

"In furbelows and frills and clinging gauzes, in satins and ribbons and discreet veilings of lace? Like a whore, in fact?" He smiled, and his voice was caressing. "What a lurid imagination you have, *my chère.* But no. We will call in Madame Palmyre."

"No!"

"Now why should you object to the attendance of Paris's most celebrated modiste?"

Here was the snare, sprung when she had least expected it. And she had blundered into it with open eyes. It had been Madame Palmyre who had made the gown she had on and a dozen others. The modiste would recognize her on sight.

"Her—her prices are certain to be far too dear for the outfitting of a mere housekeeper."

"Mere? Remember my position if you will—and recall that you must appear something more to Sarus, who knows a great deal about such things, having escorted ladies to modistes in the past."

"I don't care what your other women wore, I can manage well enough with something less fashionable."

"Petulant and peevish. Now I wonder why? You will not be one among many. It is some time since I was willing to be entertained by the expensive antics of courtesans."

"I am not jealous if that is what you are implying!"

There was a glint of appreciation for the swiftness of her uptake in his eyes. "You might have pretended. It will be Madame Palmyre then."

She lifted her chin in defiance. "I prefer to make my own."

"As you did the once charming creation you are wearing?"

His tone was faintly mocking, but without other inflection. She was beginning to know him, however, and her senses signaled a warning. She summoned a frown as she glanced down at her gown. "I don't think so. But I feel sure that I am good with needle and thread."

Roderic studied her, allowing his gaze to move over her hair drawn back into a soft knot from a center part made touchingly inexact in her hurry, and down the pure line of her cheek. She had made a good recovery, but she had been shaken; he knew it. "You will have very little time for plying such a skill. Besides, it might be adequate for day gowns, but what of ensembles for more formal occasions?"

"There will be no need for me to appear at events of that sort."

"You will stay hidden away, cowering in your room in shame and disguise? How do you ever expect to discover who you are?"

"Suppose I am someone best not discovered under your protection? No, I prefer to hope that I will remember, given enough time."

"How much will be enough? A few weeks, a month, a year? You can't stay hidden forever."

"But I can for—for a little while."

He was disappointed. He recognized that the irritation he felt sprang from that source and so refused to give it rein; still, he felt it. He had thought that he might come to some understanding with this woman he thought of only as Chère, that she might trust him. Or failing that, if her lack of memory was real, he might with sheer force of will bring her to remembrance. Neither had happened. The puzzle of her was beginning to haunt him. The thought of her lying abed under his roof had been a constant distraction in the last few days as he caught up with the paperwork and contacts neglected during his absence. He had kept himself informed about her progress in anticipation of the day when she would be well enough for further questioning. That she still eluded him left him restless, dissatisfied. He recognized all the symptoms within himself, in fact, of a towering, royal pet and was grimly amused.

"Do as you will then. It is only my wish that you be properly attired, and since you have no apparent means of seeing to it, the responsibility is mine. For the supplies of the household, food, wine, and other goods, you may select what you will, where you please, and have the bills sent here to me; the same arrangement will suffice for your clothing. But I reserve the right to decide what is, or is not, suitable as to quality of material or cut."

"I will try not to disgrace you."

"It will be better if you seek to please me."

The interview, if such if could be termed, appeared to be at an end. Her smile was icy as she set her untasted wine aside and stood up. "Better for whom?"

"Oh, for me, of course," he said gently. "Who else?"

"*Bonjour,* mademoiselle. I am Worth. How may I be of service?"

She was taking a chance in returning to Maison Gagelin, the draper's establishment on the rue de Richelieu that she had visited with her grandmother. It seemed unlikely that anyone would remember a single customer out of all those who must have been in and out of the shop since. She had bought only a shawl on that visit, not placed an order for something important such as a trousseau or funeral vestments. There was no reason at all that she should stand out in the mind of the sales staff, and she knew that here she would be certain of a quality of cloth with which the prince could not find fault.

It was ill luck, nothing less, that brought the same young Englishman who had sold her the shawl to serve her. She was tempted to turn and walk out at once, but not only would it be rudeness to one who had been of great help to her before, it might well appear strange to Luca, who was acting as her escort.

She had thought at first that purest altruism had prompted the gypsy to accompany her, that perhaps he had felt it was unsafe for her to be on the streets alone. But as the morning had worn on and he had followed her in and out of *boucheries* searching for the freshest meat, through innumerable *pâtisseries* testing for the best small cakes and jellies, and even marching past the stalls at the open market of Les Halles looking for the freshest vegetables, she could see his boredom. He would much have preferred being with the other members of the cadre who were off on some expedition near Montmartre, the purpose of which had not been explained to her. The only thing that had kept him from it, she strongly suspected, was orders to the contrary. He enjoyed her company, but what she was doing was the province of women, not of men. He was more uncomfortable in some of the places than others, she knew, and was particularly so here at the draper's where one of the clerks eyed the way he was dressed, his dark skin, the earring in his ear, and the cowrie amulet, and had audibly sniffed before turning away.

Luca gave no sign that he had noticed. He only stood leaning against a marble column, surveying with weary disdain the red Persian carpet, the damask-covered walls, the crystal chandeliers on chains reflected in tall looking glasses, the hothouse flowers, and the mahogany serving counters.

"Bonjour," she said, returning the polite greeting before stating her need for cloth for a few day gowns. She had decided that four would suffice to make her presentable. She would sew one together quickly to show her skill and to give her something to wear other than the white silk now concealed under her cloak. The silk, with the addition of a bit of lace or ribbon trim at the waist and clever needlework to hide the tears, would be adequate for evening wear, should she need such a thing.

Worth inclined his head in understanding. "Will you come this way, mademoiselle? But I know you, do I not? Ah, you are the lady with the gray shawl. So pleasant to see you again."

Had Luca heard? She could not be sure he had not, though they had moved some distance from him. Who would have thought the shop assistant would remember her? At least he had not blurted out her name, probably because he did not know it. She had been just another customer, one who took her purchase with her rather than having it delivered.

From under a counter the Englishman began to pull out bolts of cloth. He worked with a will, this young man in his early twenties who handled the materials as if they were precious stuffs, nearly alive, in his hands.

As Mara saw the jewellike colors he had selected from the stock, she said, "No, no, I should have told you. My need is for something quite practical, perhaps in gray or brown."

"As you wish, mademoiselle," he answered, his English accent suddenly pronounced. He was frowning as he placed a bolt or two in the colors she had indicated on the counter.

Mara had no time to concern herself with the approval of a shop assistant. She picked up the corner of each piece of cloth in turn. The material was fine wool challis, tightly woven and with a silky texture to the fibers. She hesitated over it, however, touching first one bolt, then another in the attempt to make a choice. She had worn such drab colors for so long before coming to France. They had little appeal now.

"If I may be permitted to make a suggestion, mademoiselle?"

She sighed as she nodded agreement.

"The tan will extinguish you, draining your face of vitality. The gray is better. But best of all would be this." He picked up a bolt of rich, deep red with a hint of purple in the folds and sent it flowing over the counter.

"It's beautiful, but hardly the thing for supervising the cleaning."

"Why not? One should look just as *soignée* for such a task as for attending the theater or pouring tea. And the color is no more likely to show stains, perhaps even less so. Besides, in it your skin will appear with its true clarity and perfection."

His words were said with such earnestness that it robbed them of any hint of flattery. "You are very persuasive."

"I am right," he said simply.

She consented to the garnet red, also to a clear deep blue and a rich green in addition to the gray. With that out of the way, she stood considering how the dresses should be made up in order to decide on the amount of each color needed. It would not do to scrimp on trim, but there was so much of it added to gowns these days, so much draping and swathing, so many bows and rosettes and flounces, that such things often took as much cloth as the gown itself. She said as much aloud.

"True, mademoiselle, and a great waste it is, for this excessive decoration inclines one to look at the gown, not the wearer. For you, it would be a mistake in any event. You have the look of a Raphael madonna, pure, natural, but with a hint of the sensual. You need no great adornment."

This was a most unusual shop assistant. She came very near to asking him if he had some idea of designing women's apparel, but dismissed the idea. It was far more likely that he wanted only to increase his sales to the point that he would be made head manager with nothing to do but wear a tailcoat and direct the other assistants.

"I require also a few lengths of white lawn or cambric," she said.

"Certainly, mademoiselle. A shipment of exceptional quality arrived this morning. I will show it to you."

It was obvious that such a request could only be for undergarments. Worth's agreement was polite without a sign of consciousness, however. It might well be that he would become head manager in no great length of time, perhaps before he was thirty.

The lighter-weight materials were in a different section of the establishment. As the young Englishman went away to fetch them, a man who had been standing somewhere behind Mara moved to her side.

"You are looking well, Mademoiselle Delacroix."

She whirled, her eyes widening as she faced a tall, thin, satanic-looking man dressed in black. It was de Landes, the man who had thrown her out of a carriage less than a week before. Even as she registered that fact, she was aware of Lucas staring in their direction. The gypsy straightened, pushing away from the marble column as he waited to see if she required help with the man who was accosting her.

"I see you have a bodyguard," de Landes murmured. "Send him away."

"How?"

"You are an intelligent young woman. Think of some excuse."

He did not tarry to see if she would obey, but strolled away a short distance, pretending an interest in a stand of umbrellas.

Mara turned back to the cloth still on the counter, fingering it as if still trying to come to a decision. She set her teeth into her bottom lip as she sought in her mind for a subterfuge. It crossed her mind to cry out, to allow Luca to overpower de Landes, then seek Roderic's help in finding and freeing her grandmother. But she could not. The risk was too great. Abruptly, an idea came to her and she turned, walking to where the gypsy stood.

"Shopping is such a wearying business, isn't it?" she said with a forced smile. "I don't think I can face the walk back to Ruthenia House. Could you please summon a cabriolet?"

"At once." Luca inclined his head, but as he went he cast a dark look at the man by the umbrellas.

"What a fine conspirator you make," de Landes said from close beside her a moment later. "I chose well."

She turned on him. "What do you want?"

"How fierce you are! You would do well to remember your position and that of your beloved grandmother." The man touched his mustache, smoothing it into the thin black line that led on each side of his red, moist mouth to a narrow, pointed beard. His smile was cold.

Mara stared at him. Inside her rose a virulent hatred allied with a chill fear. De Landes was handsome in a dark and diabolical fashion, an image he deliberately heightened with his black clothing and the pointed shape of his beard and mustache. During the short time of their acquaintance, she had come to the conclusion that he enjoyed his scheming and considered himself another Machiavelli. That egotism made him no less dangerous.

He gave a brief nod of satisfaction at her silent acceptance of his rebuke. "Quickly then. I congratulate you on your swift conquest of the prince. I had not thought you would find it so easy."

"Your congratulations are premature. I am living under his roof, nothing more."

"How disappointing. It must be remedied."

His voice was cold, the words precise. There could be no misunderstanding. She raised her chin. "I see no need."

"Don't you? I will explain once again. In a short time you are going to have to exert influence over this man, this prince. Your greatest hope of being heeded is for you to be on the most intimate terms possible with him."

"It's madness," she cried in low tones, her hands clenched at her sides. "He isn't a man to be influenced by a woman, no matter how close his relationship with her."

"All men listen to their mistresses, especially if the affair is new and the woman is clever."

"You don't understand. The prince is suspicious. He doesn't believe in the loss of memory, I know he doesn't. I'm afraid he may have brought me with him to Paris only to watch me. It won't work!"

"You must see that it does. You can, if you will put aside your maidenly shrinking and foolish excuses. I assure you it's so, for even I feel your attraction."

She sent him a look of revulsion. "I can't do this, I can't !"

"You had best steel yourself to it." His voice was sibilant, and there was a red tint to his white skin for her lack of response to his compliment. "In two weeks' time the prince must attend a ball given by the Vicomtesse Beausire. It is your job to be certain that he is present. The consequences for failure you well know."

"But how—I can't—"

"An invitation will come. You will see that he accepts it."

"He may accept it regardless. There might be no need at all for my interference."

"And he could just as easily disregard it. Prince Roderic is known for being discriminating and also most politically astute when it comes to obliging a hostess with his presence. But this is an occasion he must attend. I depend on you."

"This is a political matter then?" Mara inquired.

De Landes ignored the question. "You will also see that the prince arrives at the proper time and that he is in the proper place. I will contact you later to tell you when and where."

"But how am I to do that without attending?"

"You will attend. The occasion will be such that a man may bring his mistress if it pleases him."

"What if I am recognized?"

"By then it won't matter."

"Not to you and your plans, but to me—"

"That is of no importance. There is much more at stake here than your good name, my dear."

"What is it? What are you doing? Why must I bring the prince to this ball?"

"It isn't necessary or advisable that you know these things, only that you realize what will happen to Madame

Helene and to you if you do not comply exactly with my instructions."

"But I—"

"That will do. Remember what I have said. You have only two weeks. Use them well."

The shop assistant Worth was returning. De Landes bowed, smiling politely as if he had been doing no more than passing the time of day, before he turned and walked away.

Her hands were trembling, her whole body jerking. It was only by a great effort of will that she was able to turn back and complete her purchase. By the time she had given directions for where it should be sent, Luca had returned and the hired cabriolet was waiting. She thought Worth looked at her in some surprise as he wrote down the name of Ruthenia House, but she could not help it. Turning away, she allowed the gypsy to escort her from the shop.

There was a river of carriages of every make and description, wagons, carts, and handbarrows moving in jerking stops and starts along the narrow streets of the city. Drivers cursed, whips cracked, horses neighed, people shouted out the windows at other drivers and occupants of passing vehicles. Iron-rimmed wheels rang as they thudded over the uneven cobblestones. Inside the cabriolet, the ride was so rough that Mara had to cling to the inside strap and so slow that people on foot continually passed around the vehicle, threading with insouciance through the traffic.

Luca, rather than sit inside with Mara, had swung up beside the driver. Alone and unobserved, Mara frowned in thought. What possible reason could de Landes have for wanting the prince to appear at a ball given by a woman of the petty nobility such as the Vicomtesse Beausire? The only thing that sprang to mind was a vendetta of some kind. Nothing else made any sense. De Landes had mentioned politics, but as a cause it seemed doubtful. The Frenchman was entrenched in the government of Louis Philippe of the house of Orléans and must therefore be assumed to be an Orleanist with personal reasons for supporting the monarchy. The prince was the heir apparent to the throne of Ruthenia, and it was obvious he would favor the same form of government.

Mara had little real interest in political matters, particularly those in France. It was her grandmother who had for years kept abreast of the various revolutions and factions, and particularly the delicious scandals that often erupted. It was as fascinating as a play, the things men got up to, Helene had said; sometimes the poses and attitudes they struck and their reasons for espousing certain ideas were just as ridiculous as the most popular farce. Because her grandmother had often read bits and pieces from the newssheets and journals to her, interspersed with her own sharp comments, Mara had a fair grasp of the situation.

With the fall of the empire of Napoleon some thirty years before, the Bourbons had returned to power in the person of Louis XVIII, brother of Louis XVI who had been beheaded in 1793, and uncle of the young Louis XVII who had died in the Temple. In the words of Napoleon, the Bourbons had forgotten nothing and learned nothing. Though Louis XVIII was a prudent king who gave the people a constitution, he was also a cold and calculating one who in later years considered that his divine right to rule took precedent over the rights of the people. He was succeeded by his brother, Charles X, who was a kind man and an honest one, but even more inclined to rule absolutely. After a reign of just six years, King Charles's inability to compromise or to comprehend the nature of the changes in France had brought about a revolution that had resulted in his abdication in favor of his grandson, the comte de Chambord.

The country had, at the time, been in the hands of a provisional government that had had enough of the Bourbons, however. The throne was declared vacant, and the duc d'Orléans, a member of a minor branch of the Bourbon family, was handed the crown in a coup that was called the July Revolution. Rather than being styled the king of France, he had been given the title of "king of the French by the grace of god and the will of the people." So he had remained until the present.

The seventeen years of Louis Philippe's reign had not been easy. The legitimist party, dedicated to returning a true Bourbon to the throne, considered Louis Philippe a usurper and despised him for being the son of the regicide Philippe Égalité. The socialists wanted a new republic, a government more representative of the people without the trappings of royalty. The reformists wanted changes wrought in the assembly that would deprive Louis Philippe of some of his powers, leaving him more like the figurehead monarchs of England. There were also the Bonapartists who felt that never had there been a more glorious and progressive era for France than during the time of the Napoleonic empire. The return of the hero Napoleon Bonaparte's body to France from St. Helena in 1840, and his internment at Les Invalides in a nest of six coffins, had given rise to a new impetus to bring the nephew of the great man to the throne. This man, Charles Louis Napoleon, was the third child of the emperor's brother Louis, king of the Netherlands, and Hortense de Beauharnais, daughter of Josephine.

Louis Philippe had come into office as a result of the approval of the middle class. He continued to court that support, becoming in fact a bourgeois king who was often seen on the streets, in restaurants, and in cafés in a dark coat and hat with a rolled umbrella under his arm. His habits were frugal, a trait he had acquired in exile when he had often gone hungry. He had also, while on a prolonged visit to Louisiana during that period, taken on the American characteristics of early rising and hard work. It was said that the king rose at dawn each morning, kindled his own fire, and worked at his desk until breakfast. These traits appealed to the bourgeoisie, but could not endear him to those who expected a king to act like a king.

The middle class was the largest and the most influential because of its wealth and the monopoly it held on representation in the assembly. Regardless, the furthering of its rights and prerogatives at the expense of the nobility or the common people was a mistake. Plotting was rife at both upper and lower levels, but particularly among the more radical elements propounding the rights of the working man.

In the past few years there had been numerous attempts on the life of the king, notably one by Giuseppe Fieschi who had constructed an "infernal machine" made of twenty-five guns arranged to fire simultaneously. The king and his sons had been unhurt in the attack, but eighteen people had been killed. Fieschi and the other conspirators had been sent to the guillotine. Bonaparte's nephew, Charles Louis Napoleon, had twice tried to bring about a popular insurrection. On the last attempt he had been tried and sentenced to imprisonment at Ham, but only the year before he had escaped, dressed as a laborer, and taken refuge in England.

Grandmère Helene, in common with most of the older women among the French Creoles of Louisiana, had, from long practice in tracing family relationships, an excellent head for the complicated genealogies of the current principals in the intrigues around the French throne. She had called it a squabble among thieves to steal a stolen throne. Louis Philippe, she had declared, had no right whatever to sit upon it. He was merely the great-great-great grandson of an Austrian princess and an Italian cardinal, no Bourbon at all. Those with an ear for old tales would remember that the second son of Anne of Austria, the queen consort of Louis XIII, was known to have been sired not by the king but by her lover, Cardinal Mazarin. As for Charles Louis Napoleon, his mother, the young Hortense de Beauharnais, had made a great scene over being wedded to a doltish man who was her uncle by marriage and had declared that she would never submit in the nuptial bed. Even if her first son had, perhaps, been born of the union, it was suspected that Charles Louis, her third, was the result of an affair with a famous Dutch admiral. Her lovers had been so numerous at the time, however, that it was possible Hortense herself could not have named the father. As for the older Bourbon line so acclaimed as royally pure by the legitimists, well! There were so many possibilities for dilution of that blue blood that naming them would be tedious beyond words.

What would Grandmère Helene say if she knew what her granddaughter was contemplating at this moment? Would the affair Mara was embroiled in seem as sordidly amusing as those of more prominent personages?

She must seduce the prince. The assignment was inescapable. She had wasted so much time with her reluctance and procrastination. The deed could have been done, she suspected, if she had been more forward.

Two weeks. She had two weeks in which to attach the prince, to gain his bed. It was not enough to merely become his mistress, she must also enthrall him so that he would accede to her requests. A light flirtation, a brief liaison would not do. This formidable man must be captivated by her to the point that he would enjoy pleasing her, bowing to her wishes.

How was it to be done? How?

CHAPTER 5

On the afternoon of the shopping excursion, Mara requested a meeting of the staff of Ruthenia House. Luca, having no set duties, chanced to be idling in the private salon just off the long exercise gallery of the cadre when she sent a maid with the message to the servants' quarters on the lower floor. He made no comment, but when the servants filed into the room, he set aside the piece of wood he was carving and moved to stand behind her chair.

Mara, seated at a desk that she had taken as her own, was grateful for the silent gesture of support. She had managed her father's house for some years, ordering the buying of food and supplies, directing the slaves in the cleaning and repair. But that was different from handling French servants with their ancient notions of the perquisites of having a place in a household, their belief in their own worth that amounted very nearly to a sense of superiority, and their republican notions of equality. She would have to take a high hand if she was not to be overborne.

Twenty household employees had presented themselves. According to the account book listing their names and wages, there was a cook, two assistants, three scullery maids, four housemaids, two under-housemaids, four footmen, a gardener, an under-gardener, a coachman, and two men whose duty it was to dispose of garbage and slop. Mara sat for a long moment surveying the group. They were not impressive. The women wore no caps, and their aprons were grubby and stained. The men looked as if their coats and waistcoats had been hastily donned and in any case were of the kind they might wear in the street. There was a general air of slovenliness, and a sullenness with it, as if they enjoyed their easy positions and preferred to keep them the way they were.

She made a swift mental count of their number, then glanced down at her account book once more. Looking up, she asked, "Where is the woman who is acting as cook?"

They shifted, exchanging looks from the corners of their eyes. Finally a footman spoke up. "Madame Cook says that she is no ordinary servant, but an artist. She refuses to answer a summons from a—from one who is not the lady of the house. She says that anyone wishing to speak to her may come to the kitchens."

"I see," Mara said, her voice quiet and even. "You will go to Madame and say to her that I require her presence here, for a private interview, within the half hour. If she does not come, she may consider herself discharged. Now, is there anyone else who is uncomfortable taking their orders from me?"

Quiet descended. No one spoke or moved. Mara waited a few seconds more, then nodded her dismissal to the footman who was to deliver her message to the kitchens. He bowed and went away.

"From this moment, there will be a number of changes made in the operation of Ruthenia House. The first of these will be in the matter of dress. New livery, aprons, and caps have been ordered for you and will be delivered within the week. These garments will be worn when you are on duty, without exception, as is fitting in a house that is the official residence of the Ruthenian government. It is important that you present a neat and correct appearance and that you can be recognized as a member of the household staff by guests. Is this understood?"

Seeing one or two nods of assent, Mara consulted the list she held in her hand, then went on. She indicated various other changes that must be made in the manner of service, level of cleanliness, and degree of responsibility, then began to outline the tasks that each man and woman would begin on the following morning. She was just finishing when the door was flung open, crashing against the wall.

A stout, square-faced woman with a saucepan in her hand marched into the room. She looked around and, sighting Mara, bore down on her as if she would strike her. Behind Mara, Luca took a step forward. The woman looked at his dark, impassive face and stopped, though when she spoke her voice was shrill with rage.

"By what right do you send me such a message? Never have I been so insulted! Men plead with me, yes, the most exalted of gentlemen, to come into their houses to prepare their food. I am without peer, a great artist! My salary is far in excess of what such a one as you could hope to earn on your back in years!"

Mara rose to her feet. "Indeed. Then you are vastly overpaid."

The cool comment brought the spate of words to a sudden halt. The cook's face turned purple. "I have a mind to walk out of this house! It would serve you right if I did. The prince would very likely throw you out when he discovered you were the cause of losing me!"

"You may do as you wish. I assure you, it is unlikely that your absence will be noted."

"Do you dare to insult my skill?"

"Do you dare to suggest that the meals sent up from the kitchens in this house are fair examples of it?"

The woman opened her mouth, then shut it again. The saucepan that she had been brandishing was lowered to her side. "I was engaged by the majordomo of the prince. No one else can or shall discharge me."

The words were valiant, but the tone was subdued. Mara knew she had won. "There will be no question of discharge so long as the food sent to the table of the prince represents your best efforts. I am sure that for the sake of your own reputation, you would not have it otherwise."

"Of course not."

There was no other answer the woman could have given, but she sounded sincere. "Good. I will depend on you to use your talents to create menus that will make having a meal here at Ruthenia House something to remember. If you will write them out and bring them to me each morning, we will discuss them."

"This household is impossible! People come, people go. How can I do my best when each day I am told only at the last instant whether I will be required to have food ready for four or four dozen?"

"I will undertake to see that you are given notice in good time. You must learn to be generous with your portions, however, to allow room for expansion as the hospitality of the house demands."

The cook pursed her lips, then gave a slow nod. "About the ordering of food—"

"I will leave that in your hands, for the most part," Mara said at once, then added, "though I will sometimes shop for the ingredients that must be bought fresh each day. And we will, naturally, go over the bills together before they are paid."

"Naturally," the woman agreed, and though her tone was hard, it also held a grudging respect.

It was the prerogative of the cook in a great house to

receive remuneration from suppliers for placing orders with them. The practice was ignored so long as it did not result in inferior food being served up to the master at elevated prices. The cook was aware that Mara meant to watch over this aspect of the housekeeping. The quality of the meat and produce, milk, butter, and eggs, would undoubtedly improve.

"The contents of the wine cellar seem adequate. The prince's majordomo has been seeing to this, I believe. He will continue. It should not be necessary for anyone to count the bottles every day, but an inventory will be taken and checked periodically."

The cook threw a look toward the footmen. They avoided her gaze, studying their hands or else staring fixedly ahead. One of the housemaids stifled a nervous giggle, then turned it into a dry cough.

Mara waited a long moment, then went smoothly on to the next item on her list. It seemed they understood one another.

The two days that followed were filled with upheaval. The servants were divided into crews of three or four persons. They set to work early and did not stop until late. Everywhere one went, there were pails and cloths, brushes and ladders, cleansers and polishes. It was impossible to go up or down any staircase, or along any corridor, without passing a man or woman carrying either clean hot water or dirty, soap-scummed water. The heavy draperies at the windows and around the beds were shaken and brushed and beaten until clouds of dust billowed in the rooms. The upholstery of chairs and settees was brushed and wiped, and a careful list drawn up of pieces that needed refurbishing.

They cleaned the stone stairs with carbonate of lime, sprinkled tealeaves on the carpets to help remove the dirt as they were swept, and used a bellows to blow the dust off the painted and frescoed ceilings before gently brushing them down. They washed woodwork with a combination of soft lye soap, sand, and table beer; polished the furniture with vinegar, linseed oil, and spirits of wine; and rubbed brass andirons and other metal pieces with neat's-foot oil and spirits of turpentine. They scrubbed the grime and stains of ages from the parquet and marble floors, and polished them to gleaming with bee's-wax.

The windows were washed and polished until they shone, as well as the looking glasses, clock faces, vases, marble busts; also the sixteen hundred crystal glasses and the thirty-six hundred pieces of the china service. The silver was polished, from the tiniest of demitasse spoons to the large, hollow-handled serving knives, from the knife rests to the great samovar for the serving of tea.

In the rear courtyard, huge kettles were set to boil for the washing of the linens that had grown yellowed and mildewed from long storage: sheets, napkins, tablecloths, toweling, and various other pieces whose use could not be determined. The boiling-hot soapy water was then used to scrub the cobblestones of the courtyards until they steamed, after which the dirty water was sluiced away along with the refuse of decades. The orderly lines and curves of shrubbery were pruned and clipped, and every blade of grass beneath them removed, after which they were carefully manured, then mulched with chopped hay straw.

The work had begun in the public rooms, but soon spread to the apartments of the prince and the nearby bedchambers of the cadre. Roderic and his men were routed, leaving at the first light of dawn and returning only when night, and quiet, descended. They took to carefully testing every chair for dampness before they sat down on it and wiping a quick, furtive finger over tabletops to test for polish residue before putting an arm or uniformed elbow on it. They were inclined to tiptoe gingerly over newly waxed floors, and were seen to polish fingerprints off shining brass and silver with a rub of a sleeve. But despite such initial discomfort, they were loud in their praise of the improvements in progress.

Mara delegated the tasks and checked the different groups now and then, making regular rounds throughout the area where work was in progress. The bulk of her time was spent, however, in sewing. She had commandeered the services of one of the under-housemaids, a girl named Lila, who had admitted to having once been a seamstress. Between the two of them, they had designed a quartet of gowns that were rather medieval in appearance. The garnet red had a square neckline, a pointed basque, and full sleeves that were gathered in three places: at the wrist, just above the elbow, and on the shoulder. Silk braiding banded the neckline and each section of the gathered sleeves. The dark blue gown was similar, with sleeves that were slashed to reveal insets made from the garnet red cloth and a band of the same material just above the hem of the skirt. The gray and green gowns followed the same general pattern. Because of the simplicity, the work went fast; still, Mara and the maid Lila plied their needles far into the night. In addition to the gowns, Mara had cut out from the cambric four sets of camisoles and pantalettes, and from the lawn a nightgown very much like the day gowns except that around the square neckline was an edging of lace that rose to a standing collar to frame her throat and neck.

Finally, the house was clean, at least the more important rooms were; the meals had become more hearty and delicious, with a vastly improved list of courses. The gowns and undergarments were finished, pressed, and hanging in the armoire. The seduction could begin.

A comfortable man was a receptive man. At least that was the theory on which Mara was depending. She thought she had heard Grandmère Helene say much the same before, but could not be certain. Still, it made sense that if Roderic was relaxed in the atmosphere of freshness that she had provided, that if he was filled with the good food that she had arranged, he would be more likely to respond.

It was also likely that the vivid color of her new gowns, their snug fit through the bodice, and the lowness of the décolletage that exposed the tops of her breasts would be beneficial. She had, with the household funds, purchased a small vial of Guerlain perfume that she intended to apply with a liberal touch. She had ordered for that very evening a deep hip bath filled with hot water and had instructed Lila in the way she wanted her hair dressed. All these things should help.

A part of her was aghast at her careful and cynical planning. It seemed too calculating, too much like the machinations of one of the ladies of the night with which Paris abounded. But what else was she to do? Her grandmother's safety was hanging in the balance. She had to act. Now.

She could tell herself that the two days just gone by had been necessary, that they had helped her to lay her plans. It was just as possible that they had been wasted in useless procrastination. She was afraid. She would have liked to race down the stairs and through the courtyard out into the streets, never to return. She would give anything to be able to go to the prince and say, "My name is Mara, Marie Angeline Delacroix. I am deeply sorry for the subterfuge that brought me here and ask that you forgive it, but I want to go home."

What would Roderic say? Would he be angry? Disgusted? Contemptuous? Would he be happy to be rid of her, or would he regret her departure? It did not matter, of course, but she wished she knew.

The early-winter darkness came much too quickly. Mara paid a final visit to the kitchens to check on the progress of the special meal she and Madame Cook had planned together. The skins of the small roasted chickens were golden brown; the veal simmered delicately in its wine sauce; the lobsters in their rich, creamy dressing perfumed the air. Cakes and custards sat in their crystal servers, and a caramel sauce bubbled on the back burner of the huge iron stove that held pride of place in these nether regions. Madame Cook, dressed in a gray gown covered by a crisp white apron and with a tall white hat over her hair, displayed the fare with pride. Mara was profuse in her compliments, but so tight was the knot in her stomach that the dishes might as well have been made of coals and ashes for all they tempted her appetite.

Finally, everything was ready. Her bath was done, her hair dressed, the new undergarments and garnet red gown donned. Lila had laid her new nightgown out on the bed. The air was scented with flowers from the perfume she had touched to her throat, her breasts, the inside of her elbows and wrists. She gave herself a last glance in the looking glass. The gown hung well, draping in graceful folds over her petticoats, and the color reflected a hint of pink up into her face. Even so, she was pale.

"Mademoiselle est très belle."

"Thank you, Lila. You did a marvelous job with your sewing."

Mara swung from the looking glass, then stopped, standing irresolute in the middle of the room. She looked around her, at the canopied bed with its soft rose silk hangings that sat on a platform at one end, at the armoire with its bonnet top and carved scrolls, at the white marble fireplace with gilt-touched classical figures, at the tapestries and the Aubusson rug with its design of flowers underfoot. She felt as if she had never seen it before, as if she were a stranger to it as well as to herself. Perhaps she really did have some form of memory loss. It was almost as if Marie Angeline, the girl who had flirted with Dennis Mulholland and grieved over his death, was another person.

"Is something wrong, mademoiselle?"

Mara started and discovered that she had clasped her hands, squeezing them so tightly that the fingers were waxen. She released them with difficulty and summoned a smile. "No, nothing. What could be wrong?"

She was greeted with cheers and a torrent of compliments from the cadre. They escorted her in to dinner, with Jared and Jacques giving her their arms on either side, Estes leading the way, and Michael and Luca bringing up the rear. Roderic, careless of the rules of precedence, strolled in last beside Trude.

The meal was a great success. The food was perfection, the wines that had been selected for each course delectable. The cook was toasted, as well as Mara for her abilities as a housekeeper, for her competence at organization, and for her beauty. They raised their glasses to the man who had pushed her from the carriage and so brought her to them; to the country of France where they had found her; to its ruler Louis Philippe; and for good measure, and not to show partiality, to their own homeland of Ruthenia and its strong King Rolfe. Mara ate little, but was forced to drink to the many subjects the cadre saw fit to honor with a toast. By degrees, the tightness inside her began to dissolve.

They were not expecting guests that evening. When the last crumb of cake had been eaten and the last spoonful of custard swallowed, they retreated to the private salon in Rolfe's wing, rather than to the public salon, for coffee. It was a smaller room, though still large enough for a fireplace at either end and three different groupings of chairs and settees. The cadre spread out, some gathering to throw dice, which they called knucklebones, others settling down around a chessboard. Roderic sat down at a pianoforte and began to play. Mara, after a moment's hesitation, moved to take a seat before the fire at the far end of the room. She had never joined the men here before, and despite the presence of Trude, who was in the thick of the dice game, she felt conspicuous in the predominantly male company.

The coffee tray containing the silver service, a plate of small cakes, and a fruit bowl was brought in and placed before Mara. When she had poured Roderic's coffee, Luca carried the cup to him where he sat playing a soft melody that Mara thought was one of Mozart's rhapsodies based on a Hungarian folk song. The others walked over to fetch their own coffee, pausing to exchange nonsensical banter and friendly jostling while they drank.

Mara had expected the cadre to disperse when the coffee tray was removed. They did not. Impervious to her desire to be rid of them, they returned to their games. She watched them, trying to think how she was to use her wiles upon their leader before such a large audience, especially one that might find the exercise highly diverting. She could not do it.

She sent a glance toward Roderic. The light from the candelabra on the candle-rest of the pianoforte made a warm golden gleam on his hair. It shone across his high, slavic cheekbones, leaving dark hollows around his eyes. It caught the fine blond hairs on the backs of his fingers and threw the shadows of his fingers themselves across the keys so that they appeared even longer and more supple than they were in fact. He played on, as if oblivious to what was happening around him. Mara had reason to suspect the impression was false. Now and then he looked up, and that brief glance was intent, encompassing.

She cudgeled her brain for some way to see Roderic alone. She could think of an errand for one of the cadre, or even two, but nothing that would keep them away for any length of time. Anything she might suggest that would remove the entire group would most likely take the prince away also. She watched them hopefully for signs of sleepiness, but they appeared as fresh as when they had risen that morning. As a half hour passed, then turned into an hour, she grew desperate.

She rose, moving toward where the dice game progressed. "How very housebound you all are this evening," she said, leaning over Estes's shoulder to peer at the dice as they clattered on the table. "Are there no salons to visit, nothing going on at the opera or the Comédie Française? Surely Monsieur Dumas has a new production opening? Doesn't he always?"

Nearby, Michael looked up from his chess game. "I believe his latest is *Le Chevalier de Maison-Rouge* at his Historical Theater on the boulevard du Temple."

"I was sure there must be one!"

"He's always good for a laugh or two, plus a few bloodcurdling screams." The comment was from Trude, whose broad face registered a certain interest.

"Ah, you know it's the tender love scenes that you like," Jacques told her.

"You, rather," Trude said without rancor. "I like the sword fights. There are never any good opportunities to whip out a sword these days."

"That's because you are living in the wrong neighborhood," Estes told her.

"The wrong century rather. I would have enjoyed being one of Monsieur Dumas's musketeers."

"Don't repine, my goddess; for with us it's still all for one, and one for all!" The Italian count made a flourishing gesture.

"Is it, indeed?"

"Can you doubt it?"

"It seems to me these days that your allegiance, and that of the rest as well, is given to a female of the most useless sort, a *hausfrau,* vain in her new clothes and puffed-up with her puny accomplishment of tearing this barn of a place apart and putting it back together again."

The comment had not been meant for everyone to hear. Trude had spoken for Estes alone, but there had occurred one of those pauses in the conversation when words ring out loud and plain. An uncomfortable silence fell. Trude grew red around the ears.

"If the *hausfrau* does have our allegiance," Estes said deliberately, "it may be because she has better manners."

"I didn't mean—" Trude began.

Roderic spoke then, the words slicing across the strained atmosphere. "Discretion seems in order. I suggest that the possible attraction of Dumas's gentleman of the red house should, nay, must be explored. What say you, my brave, my very brave ones?"

It was, in spite of the wording, an order. Agreement took less than a second.

Estes turned to Mara. "Do you go, mademoiselle?"

"I . . . think not. I'm rather tired."

"What of you, my prince?"

Mara caught her breath, waiting.

"The prospects of screams and sword fights do not, at the moment, enrapture me. Another time."

Estes tipped his head, an audacious expression on his puckish face. "You forget the scenes of love."

"I try."

Within a few moments, they were gone. Only Luca was left behind. The gypsy waited until the door had closed on the cadre and the noise of their boots had died away down the hall. Then he bowed to Roderic. "May I have permission to sleep outside this night, Your Highness?"

The prince finished the last notes of the piece he was playing, then lifted his hands and got to his feet. "The smell of soap is strong, I agree, but is it that overpowering?"

The other man shook his head. "I feel the need for an open sky."

"Need or desire? Some things can and should be conquered."

"I am a gypsy. It is a need."

Roderic gave a brief nod. "As you will."

Luca turned to Mara, saying in grave tones, "I do not insult your hospitality, your house, mademoiselle."

"It isn't mine," she returned quietly.

"You are the woman. For us, woman is like the earth. The earth is our mother, our home, and so is woman. I express it badly, perhaps, but as you are woman, you are the home from which comes food and ease. It has nothing to do with owning, only with being."

"You express it well, Luca, and I thank you. Sleep well."

When he had gone, Mara turned away. The coffee tray still sat before her chair to one side of the fireplace. Moving to the tray, she picked up the pot and touched the side. Over her shoulder, she said, "I believe it's still hot. Would you care for another cup?"

"Thank you, no."

The sound of his voice was closer. In sudden nervousness, she set the silver coffeepot down so clumsily that it clattered on the tray. She picked up one of the tiny, individually iced cakes and bit into it. It was moist enough, but her mouth was so dry that she nearly choked trying to swallow. She put down the other half.

What was she going to do? How was she going to approach the prince? She could not just throw herself into his lap, could she? There were women who were able to walk up to a man and invite him to make love to them, but she was not one of them. There had to be some more subtle course. In the meantime, the silence was stretching.

"Are you certain you didn't care for the theater tonight?" Roderic asked. "Or was it a case of having misplaced, along with your name, your diamonds and opera glasses?"

It seemed that Trude's criticism of her was to be dismissed. She was just as happy to have it so. "Nothing so tiresome. I simply didn't feel like making the effort."

"You have done a great deal in a short time, perhaps too much."

"Are you displeased?"

"How could I be? You have performed miracles of cleanliness. But I have not, as yet, set up as a slave driver."

She turned to look at him where he stood with his back to the fire. How tall he looked in his white uniform and how far above her. "Are you displeased with me for some reason? Did you wish to go the theater? You need not have stayed behind for my sake."

They were mere words, polite mouthings, but she waited, barely breathing, to hear what he might say.

"I am not displeased."

What she had expected she could not have said; still, irritation at his answer welled up inside her. "Luca seems to have escaped your censure on the grounds of being a gypsy. Perhaps I should have said merely that I have a single reason also, that I am a woman."

"Unacceptable. Most women would be on their way at this moment to enjoy the lights and noise and dramatics, reveling in the escort of four attentive men and an amazon."

"I am not most women."

"I have suspected as much for some time."

What did he mean? She did not doubt there was something there, but she could not afford to pursue it. Regardless, it was more comfortable sparring with him with words than trying to find ways to entice him. She knew she was putting off the inevitable, but she could not prevent the impulse to keep the conversation going by any possible means.

"Luca was a little strange tonight, but then the gypsies are strange people."

"Tinkers, traders, and thieves, tarts and tellers of fortunes, all damned? They are perfectly understandable when you recognize that they have been hounded across the face of the earth for centuries. They recognize no home but mother earth, claim no ownership nor admit any for others, have no word for possession or, in fact, for duty. Is that surprising when time after time what they own has been taken from them, and they have been left to wander homeless, naked, and starving? When duty would only bind them to some master or require them to die for some state?"

"Where are they from, where did they start? Do you know?"

"The base of their language, the *calo,* is Indian, possibly a form of Hindu. They were dispossessed of their lands in that country near the time of Alexander the Great. They were not Hindu, however. Their religion was the most ancient known to man, one based on the supremacy of the earth mother, the goddess whose symbol is the cowrie shell, and their society was matrilineal. Their conquerors belonged to a patriarchal society that was threatened by their beliefs. They were turned into nonhumans, lower than an untouchable or an animal, without rights or privileges under the law. They fled into Macedonia where they joined the van of the armies of Alexander during the conquest, spreading over the known world."

"People tend to think of them as romantic nomads," Mara said. "In reality they are to be pitied."

"Yes and no. They find occupation as herdsmen, horse traders and trainers, and workers with metal. They are often despised and killed, always hounded farther and farther onward until they have become consummate thieves and prostitutes and kidnappers of children in order to live. But they also have a passionate love for life, and for the music, the singing and dancing that serve as free expressions of it. They have been in Europe for perhaps eight hundred years, in western Europe almost five hundred. Here they have been looked on as pagans because they have little belief in the Christian religion. They have been called Minions of the Moon and Diana's Foresters and burned as heretics. Never have they had a home. They have now ceased to want one, and so are freer than you or me."

"You are very sympathetic."

"The gypsies have been in my country for as long as there has been a Ruthenia." He smiled, a slow warming of his face. "Besides, my great-grandfather was a Russian, a count they called the Golden Wolf, a title since bestowed on my father. The old count was fond of fighting, drinking, and gypsy women. He married the daughter of the king of Ruthenia, a cold woman, but they do say that it was the son of a gypsy mistress that he smuggled into the nursery to become his heir and the future king."

"It's kinship you feel then?"

"Particularly when the weight of being the latest future king grows heavy."

"You would like to forget duty and become a vagabond?"

"Why not? In a hundred years who will care what I do now?"

"Perhaps your children?"

"Insufferable, snotty-nosed brats, destructive and degenerate? I remember my own childhood too well to feel a concern that they are unlikely to deserve."

His sons would be sturdy and proud, his daughters angelic with golden curls and sweet, self-contained smiles. At this time of night they would come in their long white gowns to be kissed goodnight. Mara banished the mental picture with an effort, and also with the sudden fear that had not plagued her in years, a fear that she might have inherited her mother's second sight.

Involvement with the house of Ruthenia will bring sorrow. Had her mother's words been, perhaps, a prophecy? This memory, too, she pushed from her.

"You have obligations," she said, her voice low. "You are the prince, like it or not. There are things you must do—things we all must do."

"Lamentable but true."

A log in the fire broke, crumbling into flames that leaped higher. Along the wall, a draft stirred the heavy draperies. Outside, the wind whined around the eaves and the gargoyle downspouts. The house was silent; the servants had gone to bed or else retreated to the warmth of the kitchens. Beyond the salon, the long corridors seemed to echo with emptiness.

It was instinct that made Mara pick up an apple from the fruit basket. It was red and firm and cool to the touch. The silver fruit knife lay beside the basket, and she picked it up with the other hand. "Would you care to share an apple with me?"

Roderic stared down at her, at the red globe she held that was so nearly the same rich color as her gown, at the gentle curve of her cheeks and the dark shadows that her lashes cast upon them. The whiteness of her skin above the neckline of her gown, the straightness and the touch of pink in the line of the parting in her black hair affected him with an astonishing feeling of tenderness. He wanted to take the knife from her before she cut herself, to make her look at him without the evasion that he always sensed in her. He spoke almost without thinking, as a screen for his thoughts.

"Among the gypsies, a girl choosing her lover tosses him an apple. It stands as a symbol for the heart."

The apple seemed to fly out of her hand. She had no conscious intention of throwing it to him. One moment it was in her possession, the next in his. His fingers closed on it, gripping hard. The look in his eyes was wary, edged with brightness, but his voice soft as he asked, "Has tomorrow come then?"

She met his gaze, her gray eyes wide with surprise at her own temerity and an odd excitement. The pink of a flush crept under her skin, warming it, routing the paleness. "Tomorrow?"

"A conversation we had once, a promise you made."

"I . . . don't remember."

"But I do."

He stepped toward her and, with the apple in one hand, reached to take the knife in the other. With a quick movement, he sliced the fruit, handing her one half. His voice deep, he said, "I am your nourishment, you are mine. We are the feast."

It had the sound of a ritual or an incantation. Slowly, Mara lifted the apple to her mouth, taking a small bite. The prince bit into his section, chewing slowly as he put the rest aside. He took her hand then, drawing her to her feet and into his arms. She came willingly, easily, her mind giddy with relief that the long waiting was over, and with a lacing of fear for the firm touch and unrelenting intention of the prince. She swallowed convulsively. His throat moved as he did the same.

He brushed her lips with his in a feather-light caress that seemed to burn. His hold was close, but not tight. She could feel the press of his uniform buttons and the hard beat of his heart against her breasts. His thighs were firm ridges through the thickness of her skirts. The urge to move nearer warred inside her with the need to draw back before it was too late. She did neither, only standing still.

Her lips parted, only partially by design. She slid her arms around his neck, enjoying the faint roughness of his uniform and the warmth of his skin under her hands. There was about him the scent of starched linen and soap in combination with his own fresh maleness. He tasted of wine and coffee and apple, a sweet and heady blend. His lips were warm and tender, gently moving, tasting. He explored the soft surface of her lips with the tip of his tongue, making them tingle, and tested the moist and sensitive corners.

With slow sureness, his grasp tightened. The pressure of his mouth increased. She answered it with her own, straining against him. His tongue touched hers with rasping warmth, and she accepted it, returning the minute strokings, feeling her senses expand with the onrush of sensual delight. She had never known such a sensation before. The discovery that she could find pleasure in this enforced seduction was shocking. And yet it seemed very much like a gift, a reward for her endurance.

His lips seared her cheek, her eyes, between her brows; he found the delicate hollow under her ear, and the warm flick of his tongue there sent a shiver along her nerves. She twined her fingers in the short and silky curls that grew low on his neck, her breathing quick and shallow. The blood raced in her veins, and she was flushed with warmth. Her hands seemed to have no strength, and in the lower part of her body was a quickening in the midst of heaviness.

He trailed heated kisses along the turn of her jaw to the tender curve of her neck and the hollow of her throat. He moved lower as she lay in his arms, his mouth searing as he pressed his face to the soft, white curves of her breasts pushed up by her corset. He inhaled the heady scent she wore and her own sweet fragrance, and the sound of his breathing was ragged.

"Chère," he whispered, and, with one hand cupping her breast, took her lips with his once more in a hard, yearning kiss.

There came the tapping of heels outside. The door burst open and a woman swept into the room. Roderic released

Mara, but held her in the curve of his arm as he swung, alert and incensed, to face the intruder.

The woman paused. She wore a traveling costume in luxurious sea-blue velvet that was fitted like a glove to her tall, elegant shape. A dashing hat with a waving cream plume was tipped forward on her high-piled, silver blond hair. She carried a great beaver muff fully the size of a bed pillow, while trotting at her side on a leash was a Pekingese who, on seeing Roderic, immediately took refuge under the skirts of her mistress.

"My dear brother," the lady exclaimed with laughter in her clear voice, "if you must do your wenching in the salon, you might at least have the decency to lock the door!"

CHAPTER 6

The tension went out of Roderic's hold. There was resignation and affection in his voice as he said, "Dear Juliana, tell me you have the gendarmes on your heels; that will make it complete."

"An incensed father and a puffed-up Prussian, nothing more. But what kind of welcome is this when I have come so far?"

"Did you expect bugles and cymbals and dancing bears? I fear we can't accommodate you. Permit me to present the lady at my side. She is called Chère, lacking any other name. My sweet, this is my sister Juliana."

The two women nodded. Juliana lifted a brow. "Lovely, quite lovely. But what will Papa say when he hears you have installed your inamorata here?"

"She is not my inamorata, my mistress, my trull; she is a lady and hears perfectly well, if you would care to address her?"

Juliana moved swiftly forward, a rueful smile on her face as she stretched out her hand to Mara. "Have I been rude? Forgive me, if you please. It was the surprise."

Their banter had given Mara a few moments to regain her composure. "Not at all. Do I understand that you have left your home? Or is it some other father who seeks you?"

A laugh, light and gay, broke from the other girl. "Oh, I like you! No, no, not some irate papa whose son I have wronged! I have run away, creeping out of my locked room in the still of night, eluding all pursuers in order to fly to my brother. Is it not romantic?"

"Bringing a yapping Pekingese and a few dozen trunks, and dressed in your most elegant ensemble," Roderic suggested.

"Not my most elegant," Juliana said, flicking a quick glance down her form, "but acceptable."

"Are you certain our revered parent didn't leave the door unlocked for you?"

Juliana stared at him with wrath dawning in her eyes. "You mean you think he allowed me to leave?"

"You are here, are you not? It seems unlikely you would have escaped the borders of Ruthenia otherwise."

"It would be just like him! Now why? Why?"

"The answer, I suspect, may lie in the Prussian."

"Arvin? But Papa dotes on the man! He has been entertaining him with hunting and hawking, with sweetmeats, the best wine, and showers of guile. He has, in a word, been treating him like a son-in-law, preparing to offer the crown prince his most precious jewel. Me!"

"I take it you wish to decline the honor."

"Precisely."

"Crafty *boyar* that he is, could it be that the king was reluctant to give his, er, jewel but was loathe to offend Prussia?"

"So he shouted me a homily on duty and the joys of being the mother of tiny, bald-headed giants, all the while whipping up my horses?"

Diverted, Roderic asked, "Bald? Your Prussian is bald?"

"Or shaven, I never felt to see which. He is also big," Juliana said absently as she frowned over her problem.

"Damn all men and their playing at statesmanship. Why could Papa not have told me?"

"And offended you by having you suspect that the reason he preferred not to marry his daughter into the Prussian nobility had nothing to do with fatherly affection but was because Prussia has a habit of gobbling up smaller countries? He could not risk you deciding to encourage the bald one out of spite."

"I am not so stupid!"

"No, but deny being regrettably volatile."

"That," his sister told Roderic with satisfaction, "is what Papa says about you."

"Does he, indeed?" he said softly.

Mara, sensing a quarrel of epic proportions in the making, hastily intervened. "Did I understand you to say, Juliana, that your Prussian might be behind you?"

"Arvin is not brilliant, but he has tenacity. If he can discover where I have gone, he will follow."

"Given the state in which you usually travel—" Roderic began.

"I had only two outriders and two footmen, and, of course, my maid and a man to travel with the baggage wagon!"

"Why didn't you tie bells to the carriage or hire a herald to announce your coming?" Roderic said conversationally.

Juliana drew in her breath for a retort, but it was not made. Her attention was caught by a movement in the open doorway. Luca, his expression grim, stepped through. The Pekingese began to bark, backing deeper under Juliana's skirts all the while. The girl swooped down to pick up the dog, scolding, "Hush, Sophie, hush."

The gypsy spoke to Mara, studiously ignoring Juliana. "The baggage of the lady has been unloaded as ordered and moved into the house. But there is some problem with the suite of rooms."

"Yes?" Mara asked.

Luca looked uncomfortable. "It seems that when in Paris she usually stays in the suite of rooms that Mademoiselle—well, the fact is—"

"Oh, I see," Mara said, "then my things must be moved."

At the same time, Juliana spoke up. "There are other suites of rooms in that wing; any of them will do so long as I have a pillow to place my head upon."

Roderic shook his head. "Such nobility. It would be touching if I didn't know the pillow was required to be cased in silk, preferably monogrammed."

Ignoring his comment, Mara said, "I would not take your place."

"Another noble female," Roderic told Luca.

"Nor I yours," Juliana said with firmness.

"I assure you—"

Juliana turned toward Luca. "Tell that foolish woman of mine to stop making a fuss and put my things in the first convenient bedchamber."

Luca sketched a bow. "I will ring for a servant to carry your message."

"Nobility, gypsy fashion," Roderic murmured.

"Oh," Juliana said, staring at the tall, dark-haired man who had defied her for a long moment before turning to her brother. "What an unusual ménage you keep, Roderic. A mistress who is not and a guest who makes his bed in the courtyard!"

"And I appear to be adding to it a relative who must be constantly reminded of her conduct." His tone spritely, he made his sister known to the gypsy.

Juliana gave Luca her hand. "I am stupid from weariness. Will you accept my apology?"

Her smile was warm and engaging, her manner without the least condescension. Luca, raising her hand to his lips, met her bright blue gaze and his expression took on a dazed look, as if he had been struck by a heavy blow. "With all my heart, Your Highness," he answered.

It was only then that Mara realized the young woman who had spoken with such naturalness and familiarity was a princess. No doubt she should have curtsied when she was presented. It was too late now to be concerned.

Juliana went on to the gypsy, "Perhaps I could prevail upon you to escort me to my rooms? Not that I fear footpads in the corridors, but it is extremely dark. This wind has blown out half the candles in the girandoles, and, like all these old houses, there were only half enough to begin with."

"I am yours to command," Luca said, bowing with his best form.

"But not to order?" Juliana sent him a smiling glance from under her lashes.

"No one does that."

"Ah, a strong declaration. I admire strength of will in a man."

They had moved away beyond the doorway. Roderic called after them, "One moment!" To Mara, he said in low tones, "If the Prussian comes, we may count ourselves lucky if we don't have to pluck a gypsy knife from his back."

Mara agreed, but her mind was on Roderic's movements as he lifted her hand to his mouth, pressing a kiss to the palm.

"In any case," he went on, "you seem to have lost your shadow, your *cavaliere servitore*. Are you sorry?"

"He was hardly that." Luca and Juliana stood waiting, talking, laughing, oblivious of anything except each other.

"Near enough. He is susceptible to women, is Luca. He is not alone; I seem to be more susceptible than is wise to you."

"Why is it unwise?" His grip on her hand was warm, firm. The look in his eyes was the same. He was going to dismiss her. She knew it.

"There is an innocence about you that it would be wrong to betray. You would hate me if, when you regain your memory, you found you were a beloved fiancée or a wife."

He would not keep her with him because he thought she did not know who she was, and if she told him otherwise, he would send her away completely. There was a terrible irony in the situation, but she could not appreciate it.

"You are wrong," was all she could think of to say.

"I prefer that to a lifetime of regret for you." She would have protested again, but he lifted his voice. "Chére will go with the two of you. She is ready for her bed."

The cadre was bored. They had the night before, following the visit to the theater, commandeered a pair of cabriolets and raced each other back and forth across the Pont Neuf until the four ladies of the evening who were their passengers had screamed in terror. They had engaged a pair of French guardsmen from the corps that protected King Louis Philippe in a drinking bout, and in the process extracted everything the guardsmen knew about the habits, predilections, and movements of the French king. The presence of Juliana, who had been known to them since she had emerged from the nursery, had enlivened matters for a while, but since she had gone off immediately after breakfast to make a round of the shops, the distraction did not last.

They lay on the floor in the long gallery where they had been practicing tumbling. Even acrobatics had palled, however, mainly because Mara had laughingly refused to be their pupil any longer, pleading that there was too much work to be done. She had ushered in a tray of apple tarts and coffee at midmorning when she had brought in her mending to do by the gallery fire, but she could think of nothing else that might relieve their ennui.

"What we need," Michael said, staring into the flames in the great fireplace with his chin resting on his hands and his thin face serious, "is a good war. Not a large one, just a small one with a nice skirmish or two."

Estes sighed. "Yes, one with a few villages to capture, preferably with plenty of maidens, pretty ones."

"Or even only passably pretty," Jared said.

"Just not quite plain," Jacques agreed.

"Wives. Not maidens, but bored and frustrated wives. I remember once in the lowlands—"

"Ahem," Michael said, clearing his throat with a warning sound. Estes, after a quick glance at Mara, ducked his head, leaving his tale unfinished.

"They are rising in Poland and Parma, rioting in Venice and Vienna, agitating in Berlin, Milan, and Rome," Trude said in disgruntled tones. "Why is it that with all the nice little revolutions in Europe, we have to be stuck in Paris?"

"In Paris!" they groaned as one, and the cry was only half-mocking.

"I've had better sport," Estes said with deliberation, "in a cockpit behind a fourth-rate bawdy house in a two-cart town in the Croatia. Fourth-rate? I am not sure, not at all, that it could be rated so high. The women in this house were so ugly they wore their unmentionables over their heads and their kerchiefs over their—"

"Ahem," Michael said.

"Why don't you throw the dice?" Mara suggested tactfully.

"None of us has anything to be won or to lose," Jared said.

Jacques, rolling over so that he lay on his stomach at Mara's feet, looked up at her. "Of course you could offer a prize, say a kiss . . ."

"Brilliant, brother, brilliant," Jared exclaimed, roused to sudden interest as he raised himself on one elbow.

"Sorry," Mara said, her tone brisk. She knotted her thread at the end of her darn and snapped it off.

Estes said, "I am so tired of playing the knucklebones and watching Michael move his *petits* soldiers around on his chessboard that I could—"

"Ahem," the rest of the cadre said.

"Complaints?" Roderic asked in gentle tones from where he had entered the room with nearly soundless steps. "Such injustice that any man should suffer dull lassitude for my sake. What will it take to return you to pleasure in my service?"

"The gods preserve us," Estes breathed, and it was a true prayer.

"Jared, could I trouble you to move sufficiently to bring the swords?"

"Holy mother of us all," Jacques whispered, and got to his feet, wiping the palms of his hands on his trouser legs as his twin brother sprang up to do Roderic's bidding. The others exchanged glances and pushed themselves slowly erect.

The swords were brought. They had long, slender blades chased in a Far Eastern design and fitted to silver and brass hilts. Supple and lethal, they had no buttons on the tips, which were commonly used for practice at swordplay, nor did the cadre fit them with any. Coats and boots were removed and sleeves rolled to the elbows. Then without the least protection for face or body, they faced each other.

"To first blood only. Strike well but lightly."

The apathy in the room had been most effectively banished. In its place was agitation allied to a curious gleeful apprehension and stark determination. They knew one and all that, in the heat of the fierce striving to win, anything could happen, minor to serious injury, disfigurement, maiming, even death. Mara sat mesmerized, unwilling to appear the coward by leaving, uncertain she would be able to watch.

The most amazing thing to her was the pairing. Roderic's cousin Michael faced Jared, and the other twin, Jacques, stood in front of Estes, leaving Trude, their female member, to face the prince. It had not been at her own choosing, or even by default, but had been the direct order of Roderic.

What was his thinking? As a gentleman, did he intend to allow her to inflict some small injury upon him? It did not seem likely, since at no time had Mara seen the woman treated as anything other than one of the cadre. And even if he did, could Trude bring herself to do it, feeling, as Mara suspected, the way she did about her leader? Could it be perhaps that Trude was swordswoman enough to provide a challenge, one Roderic wished to test? It seemed a possibility since she possessed an unusual agility and strong wrists. It was possible, however, that if Roderic was the superior of them all, as indicated by their comments, he might feel Trude was safer with him. But how would he protect himself without injuring her? How could he allow himself to be defeated and still keep the respect of his cadre? Or how could he defeat Trude without drawing blood?

"Ready?"

"Ready," came the answer in a ragged chorus.

"Salute!" When the swords had swept up and down again in unison, the prince went on, "Our Chère will give the signal."

Surprise held Mara speechless. She had not thought that he had even noticed she was there. Then as she realized they were standing, rigidly waiting, she picked up the heavy white linen table napkin she had just finished mending and held it out, tented, from her fingers. *"En garde,"* she said, and let the napkin fall.

The swords clanged together with a musical dissonance, scraping, grating, springing apart. The movements were as stylized as a ballet and appeared hardly more strenuous. And yet within seconds drops of sweat appeared on their faces and their breathing became loud over the soft shuffle and slide of their footsteps moving back and forth. Still, every person in the deadly contest was fit. Each moved with oiled precision as muscles strained and bent in a thousand difficult exercises and improbable tasks. At no time had Mara been made more aware that they were a unit, trained and directed for fighting in concerted effort, than in this moment when they were striving against each other.

Their concentration was intent, confined to the glinting sword tip and the appraisal of the person facing them. As the minutes ticked past, the apprehension seeped away, to be replaced by a dependence on skills well learned and a growing exultation. Grins appeared at the parrying of a finely aimed thrust and at the counterblow. A comment or two was made, mostly ribald. The swordplay became more daring, more spectacular. The blades tapped together in a peculiarly even rhythm, musically chiming, suddenly clanging, at some swift feint or aborted riposte.

A pale gray light fell through the delicately tinted glass of the high windows. It gave the faces of the contestants a ghostly pallor and colored their clothing with shifting shades of yellow and lavender and rose. It lent a curious sense of unreality to the scene, as if those touched by it were bloodless shades of themselves or else trespassers from some more violent time. In the dimness the sparks as the blades scraped together were bright orange.

Then Jacques lunged, drew back. Estes gave a great and histrionic cry of despair, clasping his arm. "Pinked, and by a child with a child's move. The shame of it, the shame!"

"You let me do it on purpose, you randy old man," Jacques accused, "because you hoped to have Mademoiselle Chère wrap you up in her napkin."

"Wounded in arm and the quick of the heart, too! How could you think such a thing?"

"I know you. Besides, I thought of it myself."

"Insolent puppy. I have half a mind to take up my sword again and thrash you."

"You can't," Jacques returned smugly. "I have first blood. It's over."

But it was not over for the others. They fought on while Mara indeed wrapped the Italian's arm up with her napkin. The wound was fairly deep, but by no means serious. Estes crowed over his opponent about the attention he was getting from Mara, then strutted about with the piece of white linen around his upper arm as if it had been a decoration for valor or a mark of favor. He paced the floor, making pointed comments on the swordplay of the others like a spectator in a theater box, but instead of annoying them, it seemed only to add to their fighting fury and the atmosphere of strained hilarity. At the open doorway a crowd had formed. It was the servants, attracted by the clash of swords. They spoke among themselves, exchanging comments, exclaiming at a particularly cunning thrust. Mara would not have been surprised to learn that they were also contracting a discreet wager or two.

Michael and Jared were closely matched. Their swords winked blue light, slipping, slithering, endlessly tapping. Abruptly, Jared attacked. Michael parried in quinte and drove into a riposte. Jared recoiled, but in the movement Michael's blade tip slashed across his hand. Jared cursed without heat and dropped his sword.

So intent was Mara on the injury to Jared that she did

not see the end of the match between Trude and Roderic. There was a flurry of swirling blades caught from the corner of her eye, then Trude was standing with her sword tip resting on the floor, staring at the prince with one hand held to her face.

Mara moved forward with quick steps as Roderic stepped back. Before she reached Trude, however, the young woman slowly lowered her hand to look at the blood on her fingers. The wound was small, no more than a scratch. It would not even leave a scar, but Trude was white, swaying on her feet. She raised her hazel gaze to Roderic.

"You never do anything without a reason," she said on a choking breath. "Why?"

"Think," he recommended.

Her voice cold and yet bewildered, she answered, "I would rather not."

"That is your prerogative."

At the doorway, the servants scattered as before a tidal wave, scurrying about their business. Juliana entered the room in impetuous style with her rose silk skirts swirling and the plumes in her rose velvet hat floating in the breeze of her passage. "Where, pray, are the brigands? I heard the din the instant I entered the house and flew to the fray. Don't tell me they have been routed already?"

"There were no brigands," Roderic said shortly.

"No brigands? Burglars, stranglers, footpads, then, sneak thieves, assassins? Come, there must have been someone to inflict such carnage!" Her tones were strident, with anger masquerading as irony. It was prompted, Mara thought, by concern that had proven to be needless.

Most unwisely, Michael said, "It was only a cure for boredom."

"One likely to be permanent! I suppose if one of your number complained of headache the rest would cut off his head!"

"You are becoming quite a scold," Roderic said, drawing her fire from his man. "Viragoes are not to the taste of many men. Are you so certain your Prussian is following?"

"Leave Arvin out of this!"

"Gladly, except that we must weigh the effects on your temper of his coming or, alternately, his failing to show himself."

"I am not the only one grown acerbic. If I had know how frustration would affect you, I would have shut the door on you and your ladylove last night and gone quietly away."

"Would that you had," Roderic said, unperturbed, "or that you had never come."

"If you mean to make me feel unwelcome, you have succeeded to admiration, but it won't serve," Juliana declared in magnificent scorn. "Here I am, and here I stay!"

Mara did not wait to hear more. Gathering up her mending, she skirted the group and moved out of the room. She thought Roderic watched her go, but, if so, he made no attempt to detain her.

Roderic's words to his sister seemed to indicate regret that they had been interrupted the night before. Would he have preferred that there had not been an opportunity for the heat of the moment to fade, for a cooler head to counsel caution? Certainly she must feel that way. She had come so close to completing her task, and so painlessly. How strange it seemed. She had known that there was more of the temptress in her than she had imagined after the incident with Dennis Mulholland—there must be or he would never have behaved as he did. Still, she was surprised to think that she had been quite undismayed by the idea of giving herself to the prince in those moments; it had seemed natural, indeed, almost inevitable. The feel of his arms around her, the tenderness of his kiss, the stirring of the blood she had felt, had been a shock to her somehow. She had resigned herself to seducing the man; she had not expected to enjoy it.

It seemed almost depraved then, the degree of disappointment she felt that her object had not been accomplished. It was the fear, the feeling of precious time slipping away, that made her so emotional, or so she tried to tell herself. She only half-believed it. No matter. There were only eleven days left. Eleven days. She must make them count.

Mara had not been in her bedchamber for more than a few minutes when a knock fell on the door. It was Juliana who entered at her call. The blond girl hesitated in the doorway, her teeth set into her bottom lip.

"You may tell me to go away if you like and I wouldn't blame you. I was rude to you just now, but it was not intentional. I am afraid that in our family we have a tendency to speak our minds with unblushing frankness. It can cause difficulties."

"Please come in."

"Thank you." She turned in a whirl of skirts to shut the door carefully behind her.

"I have been thinking this morning," Mara said, "that you will wish to take over the running of your brother's house. Perhaps that is what you wanted to talk to me about?"

"Good heavens, no! I am not at all domestic." Juliana's expression was blank.

"I would not usurp your privileges as well as your rooms."

"Please do. Please. From what I remember of this house from my last excursion here, you have produced wonders of refinement. I would not dream of interfering."

"Then . . . how may I help you?"

The other girl shrugged. "I don't know. It was an impulse to come to you, to tell you that I didn't mean to hurt you just now. I was interested solely in puncturing the conceit of that brother of mine. He is entirely too sure of himself."

"Do you always quarrel?" Mara led the way into the adjoining salon, indicating a chair. Juliana seated herself, sighed, then reached up to take off her hat and cast it on the floor beside her.

"Not invariably, but often."

Mara had wondered many times what it would be like to have a brother or sister. She had thought of them playing together, presenting a united front against the world, not of quarreling. She opened her mouth to say so, but realized in time that it was a dangerous subject for someone who was supposed to have no memory of the past.

"Roderic usually manages to quarrel with everyone except our mother. Maman hates raised voices and so never indulges in tirades with words as weapons like the rest of us. But if she is pushed too far, she will rise up and annihilate you in a single phrase."

"I have noticed Roderic's peculiar speech patterns and also, to some extent, yours," Mara said, her voice dry.

Juliana grimaced. "A trait picked up from our father. I try to curb it; Roderic makes no attempt. You should hear them when they are together. Or perhaps you had better not. When they disagree, bystanders are likely to be dissolved by the acid of their comments. Maman was always caught between them. I think, though I cannot be sure, that it was his concern for the pain such confrontations gave her that made Roderic leave Ruthenia."

Juliana was speaking of Angeline, queen of Ruthenia, Mara's own godmother. Mara resolved to think of some way to discover more about her. "Roderic and his father are estranged then?"

"I wouldn't say that. They are deep men, so it's hard

to tell what passes between them. It could just as easily be that our father forced Roderic from Ruthenia because he thought it best my brother should be on his own, that he should make his way in the world. It was what he was made to do when he was that age."

Mara frowned. "It seems hard."

"Yes, but beneficial. Roderic survived very well, indeed. He and his cadre strike fear into half the courts of Europe."

"Fear?"

"They are called the Death Corps. Didn't you know?"

Mara shook her head. There was a feeling of disquiet inside her, though she was not certain why. "What is it that they do?"

"They fight, or at least so I suppose. They are always found where trouble is brewing. I remember hearing once that they helped to train special units of guards for royal houses, something like that. Assassination is always a threat these days. Everyone must guard against it in the best way they can."

"I don't think I understand why the cadre should be feared if they train others to protect members of the courts."

"It's the way they go about it, not just by honing a fighting force, but by infiltrating, gathering information, becoming friendly with all political elements so as to learn where the greatest threat lies. Some say that with their tactics it would be just as easy for them to overthrow a government as to save it, and on occasion what they have learned has made Roderic decide that the opposition would be best in power. It is a little like letting the wolf in at the back door in order to keep the vultures from the front, and so the title."

"The Death Corps," Mara whispered to herself, and shivered.

In the brief pause there was a scratching on the salon door. Mara looked up sharply. "Come in."

It was Trude who stepped into the room. "I am sorry to trouble you, mademoiselle, but I wondered if—"

As the woman saw Juliana, she stopped abruptly, her tall form stiffening. Juliana lifted a brow, but rose at once. "Don't mind me, I'm just going."

"No, no, don't go," Mara said. There had been no time to ask about Angeline. "Perhaps Trude would care to join us? We could order chocolate and cakes and perhaps chat a little."

"I haven't the time," Trude said, her tone distant. "I only wanted to ask if you had an ointment that I might put on my face. Estes suggested it might prevent scarring."

"I'm afraid I don't," Mara began.

"I do," Juliana said, "and most effective it is. If you will come with me, I'll search it out for you."

"I couldn't allow—"

"Nonsense. We women must stick together. The very idea of Roderic touching your face! He could just as easily have hit your arm if he had wanted. I would not have believed he could be so careless."

"It wasn't carelessness." Trude's voice was harsh, as if the words were forced from her against her will.

"Are you saying it was deliberate?"

"It was a lesson to me, for accusing Mademoiselle Chère of vanity."

"No," Mara whispered, rising to her feet. "He couldn't."

"You don't know him."

The words were a reminder to Mara that she was new among them. They also held a certain bitter derision that might have been directed not only at Mara but at herself.

"If what you say is true, I'm sorry."

"There is no reason for you to be sorry. It was not done because of you, but for—for my own good."

"Well," Juliana said briskly when Mara made no answer, "whatever the reason, we must repair the damage. Come along."

The two women left. Mara took up her mending, but though her needle moved steadily, she could not forget what Trude had said. Had Roderic injured Trude's face as a reprimand? And, if so, had it been done for the reason Trude had implied; as a lesson not to speak of vanity in other women without taking her own into consideration? Or had it been in retaliation for the embarrassment the woman had caused Mara, for an insult that the prince had appeared to dismiss at the time? That any man could act in such a cold-blooded way was disturbing to her. That she must become intimate with one who might have done so made it that much worse.

The Death Corps. What kind of group was the cadre, indeed, and what kind of man was the one who led them? She had thought Roderic a playboy prince, handsome, intelligent, musically gifted, but of minor importance. The more she learned, the less she seemed to know or to understand.

She met Roderic in the long gallery as she was on her way to the public rooms later that evening. He was coming from his apartment while she was making her way from her own through the central corridor rather than going through the rooms taken over by Trude and Juliana in her own wing. She paused as she saw him, unconsciously searching his face for some sign of his humor. He offered his arm. She took it, moving beside him a few steps before she spoke of precisely what was on her mind.

"May I ask you something?"

The glance he sent her was wary, but he inclined his head in silent permission.

"Did you deliberately cut Trude's face?"

"Is that what she is saying?"

"You know that it is."

He exhaled with a soft sound that might have been a sigh. "Trude is too good a soldier. Such devotion has its uses, but she is in danger of forgetting that she is a woman."

"It's hardly surprising since she is seldom treated as one. We tend to see ourselves as others see us."

"When that happens, it would be as well if we were forced to take another look."

"Is that it? You wanted to remind her that she is female and subject to vanity?"

"To remind her that there are other things besides being a member of the cadre."

"I somehow feel that she knows that."

"Buxom and tender of heart she is, or so you think? It also seemed necessary to prevent her from making me into some figure of romance. It's popular at the moment for some men to pose as misunderstood, yearning, poetic souls, but I am none of those things. I am a man with a job to do, and I can do it best without attachments. More, there is room in the cadre only for those who will put the good of all first instead of turning instinctively to see to the welfare of one in particular."

"You fear she will endanger the others for your sake? But where is the threat?" Was there a warning in his words for her? Was he saying in his own peculiar way that he had no time for dalliance with any woman?

"If we knew, it could be neutralized so that it would be no threat for long."

"But why? Why was it necessary for you to—to—"

"To meddle? Trude is my responsibility, as are all the cadre and now you. Anything that happens to any one of you will be laid at my door."

"Who would accuse you?"

"I would."

The timbre of his voice was unrelenting. The question could not be argued. She abandoned it. "Still, it seems a hard lesson for Trude."

"She understands it. Besides, she has her own kind to console her. I don't doubt you soothed and sympathized with her wound and her fears."

"Juliana did."

"The child must have matured behind my back if she can discover pity inside her for one so self-sufficient as our Trude."

"What is it that you were trying to prove; that she was too hard or too soft?"

"Another champion; I thought so. My intent was to make her consider the direction in which she is going. No more."

They had reached the antechamber that led into the public salon with the dining room beyond it. A footman held open the door and they passed through it.

Her voice low, Mara said, "In that case, I suspect that you succeeded."

"Too well, or so it may prove. How shall I contain my joy?"

She sent him a sharp glance and found his blue gaze dark as it rested on her face. There was no time for more, however, for Juliana was there before them, and with her was Trude, wearing a shirtwaist of white silk, with a jabot of fine lace, tucked into her uniform trousers.

What had Roderic meant? Was the regret she had seen reflected in his face for a brief moment because of her disapproval of his action, a disapproval deliberately courted? Was it for what he saw as the necessary lack of closeness between them? Or had it been merely that he had seen Trude in her silk immediately and mourned the corrupting of a good soldier? But if the reason was the last one, hadn't he contributed, with all deliberation, to that excursion into femininity? The possible convolutions of his thinking eluded her, and she gave up the subject in exasperation.

She had planned to try once more to detach the prince from the others that evening. She was given no opportunity to do so, however. Directly after the lengthy dinner, the prince swept them up with him and out of the house. The writer Victor Hugo was holding a literary salon in his home close by at the Place Royale. A card had been received inviting Roderic and as many of his retinue as he cared to bring. They would enjoy the stimulation of the presence of some of the best intellects and most liberal minds in Paris, and if they did not, they could at least be entertained by them.

"Liberal?" Juliana scoffed. "Hugo is a libertine!"

"Prudery, my dear sister, is an affliction that is stifling to the body and the energies of the brain. Would you deny a man greatness merely because he pays expenses for three households, all within walking distance of each other?"

"No man needs two mistresses as well as a wife. And it's indecent that Hugo keeps his collection so close together. What are the women involved thinking of, to live so for the convenience of one man?"

"Not for nothing is his motto 'Ego Hugo.' I call it sublime."

"I call it ridiculous."

"Great men can be forgiven many ridiculous things. Dumas and his waistcoats, for instance."

"Among other things! They say he keeps a menagerie of animals, including a pet vulture named Jugurtha worth fifteen thousand francs and a battalion of mistresses who change places as regularly as a palace guard—and which he shares with his son!"

Roderic refused to be drawn, however. Tucking his sister's hand in one arm and Mara's in the other, he swept them with him, calling over his shoulder. *"En avant, mes enfants!"*

CHAPTER 7

The gathering was not large, but it was loud with talk and laughter. People stood in groups arguing and gesticulating, or else sat here and there with their heads together and expressions of concentration on their faces. Madame Hugo circulated among her guests, making introductions, directing the serving of wine and cheese and small pastries. Victor Hugo held court from a vast armchair near the fire to an audience of men and women seated on the carpet at his feet.

The room was long and commodious, with walls hung with red cloth painted with oriental designs. The furniture was dark and heavy and ornately carved, with a great deal of red plush and a number of fat ottomans, both the latest style in decor, on display. The gaslight overhead sputtered and hissed in a black cast-iron fixture with milky, etched globes. The drapes that shut out the night, and also the skirts on the various tables about the room, dripped with layers of silk fringe.

Mara stood with Estes and Michael in a corner. She was glad of the company of the men and also for their indulgence in pointing out people to her; she felt more than a little intimidated in such unfamiliar and ferociously intellectual surroundings. Everyone seemed so sure of themselves and their ideas, so ready to shout down opposition. They were never at a loss for the meaning of a word or an abstract phrase. Theories and the ramifications of ideologies were tossed about like toys. Books and plays were being discussed that she had never heard of, much less read. There were people there who were no doubt famous in their fields, but she had no idea who they were.

"Not to worry, mademoiselle," Estes reassured her when she said as much to him and Michael, "half the people in this room understand not a tenth of what the other half is saying, but they all—all!—pretend like mad. It is the way of the world."

Mara recognized Alexandre Dumas wearing another of his execrable waistcoats, this one in bilious green and egg-yolk yellow stripes. His round face was beaming with enjoyment and he was eating thick slabs of cheese without bread and talking about his new production of *Hamlet*. Near him, but not of his circle, was a woman in her early forties, dressed conservatively in a gown of black wool with a tight basque and full skirt with organ pleats, and over it a gray-and-black-striped pelerine. This lady had been pointed out to her on the street when she first came to Paris and Roderic had also mentioned her.

"Isn't that Madame Dudevant, who signs her books as George Sand?" she asked in an undertone.

Michael turned to look, then nodded. "She is very drab this evening. Sometimes she enlivens the proceedings by dressing in trousers."

"That can't be a novel sight for you two," Mara said, "after all, you see Trude in trousers all the time."

"Trude is—well, Trude." Michael shrugged.

Perhaps Roderic was right, perhaps it was time Trude was made aware that she was a woman, Mara thought, but Estes spoke then, claiming her attention.

"Madame Dudevant is still mourning her parting with

the composer Chopin, or so I would guess. They had the big quarrel over something to do with the marriage of her daughter, and he walked out. The estrangement, it appears, is to be permanent."

"I hear Chopin is in ill health," Michael said.

"Lung disease," Estes answered. "He blames Madame Dudevant for it, for carrying him with her to Majorca where he caught it several years ago."

"That hardly seems fair," Mara said, "she can't have forced him to go."

"Hers is the stronger personality. She is older by some six or seven years."

"What has that to say to anything?"

"A great deal, as you will see when you meet her! This way." The Italian caught her hand and began to ease through the crowd.

"No, wait!" Mara called, but he paid no attention. A moment later she was being presented to Aurore Dudevant.

"How do you do, my dear." The writer turned with a gracious smile to her companion. "May I make known to you my friend, Balzac?"

The man beside her was, like so many in the room, nearing middle age. Heavy-set, with a large head and thick neck set on bull-like shoulders, he was not particularly tall, but gave an impression of size. His face was red, his nose large and square, and, beneath a ragged mustache, his teeth when he smiled were discolored.

"A pleasure, Monsieur. I have read your books."

"Have you? Which ones?" The words were abrupt, almost eager.

"*Le Père Goirot,* of course, and a few other volumes of *The Human Comedy*, though not all. It is a marvelous endeavor, but such a large undertaking!"

"He is quite as much a glutton for work as for food, is he not?" Madame Dudevant said.

"One must pay one's creditors," Honoré de Balzac said with a sad shake of his head. "Tradesmen have a most uncomfortable habit of expecting a man to have the money to match his desires. It is not possible."

"You and Dumas," Aurore Dudevant said, her voice resigned. "You make money as if it pours from the ends of your pens, and you will both be lucky if you aren't buried in pauper's graves."

"With Hugo beside us."

"Victor is luckier in his women; they not only copy his manuscripts and letters for him as unpaid secretaries, they also manage his money."

"His wife, one hears, certainly holds the purse strings."

"A strong personality, Madame Adele."

"She at least has the good sense not to hold him on too tight a leash."

"Yes. She no longer complains of neglect, I hear. There may have been a lesson for her in the Praslin affair. There was a lesson for many."

Mara, made curious by the significant looks exchanged by the others, interrupted, "The Praslin affair?"

It was George Sand, Madame Dudevant, who explained. Some months before, at the end of August, the duc de Praslin had murdered his wife, stabbing her with a knife and bludgeoning her with a candlestick as she lay sleeping in their house on the rue de Faubourg St. Honoré. There had been whispers of the most virulent sort as to the cause. The duc was rumored to have been in love with his children's governess, Mademoiselle Deluzy; the duchesse was said to have been corrupting the children due to her exposure as a child by her own governess who had, as it was put, sometimes "fled not to the Isle of Cythera, but to that of Lesbos." Some said the duc was a cold and withdrawn man who had lost his sanity, while others declared that he was a quiet man driven to madness by the emotional and sexual domination of his duchesse. The only thing that was known with any degree of accuracy was that the marriage had begun as a love match and continued so for some time, producing nine children in thirteen years. At that point it had disintegrated abruptly into violent quarrels and separate bedrooms—until one hot night in August.

The tragedy had come on top of other indiscretions, other acts of insanity among the highest figures in the country. Not too long before, the comte Mortier had tried to murder his children; the Prince d'Eckmuhl had in a fit of rage stabbed his mistress; the French ambassador to Naples had slit his own throat with a razor; and the Keeper of the Seal, Martin du Nord, had reacted to implication in an affair of morals by taking his own life. The general feeling among the people was that there was poisonous corruption beneath the respectable façade of the reign of Louis Philippe and that it should be destroyed, even if it meant starting at the head.

"Never will I forget the people outside the house where the Praslin murder was committed. They seemed to have no pity for the duchesse lying dead inside, nor any real anger against the duc, who had by then swallowed poison and been taken away by the police. Their rage was against the government. They kept screaming, 'Down with Louis Philippe!' and 'Death to the king!' It was as if it were the Terror all over again."

"It easily could be," Estes said.

"Perhaps we should pray for another such scandal to persuade the king to listen to the cries for reform?" Balzac said.

"Or create one?" Aurore Dudevant suggested.

The seriousness of the group sent a small frisson through Mara. She had listened politely to all that was said, though after the first moments she had remembered hearing of the Praslin case from her grandmother. Now, recalling the beginning of the conversation, she asked, "But what has this to do with Monsieur Hugo?"

"He was fascinated by the details," Balzac answered, "so much so that his good wife became disturbed. I fear that may have been the results he had hoped to achieve, though one cannot be sure. It's difficult to know how much of Hugo's selfishness is a pose and how much is natural to him."

"Ego Hugo," Mara murmured with a smile of remembrance as she glanced toward where Victor Hugo talked to those at his feet without ceasing, waving his arms for emphasis.

"Precisely. He was a great ugly brute of a baby, and now that he has grown into a presentable man, he behaves as if he were still in his swaddling clothes."

"But he is a great man, a great writer," Estes said.

"It goes without saying." Madame Dudevant shrugged. "Who else could write a simple book about a hunchback and a cathedral and singlehandedly change architecture for the century, to say nothing of saving Notre Dame from falling completely into ruins?"

"I do not see Madame Juliette, I think, and I had heard so much of her beauty. I understood she and Madame Hugo were friendly." Estes looked hopefully around him as he spoke.

"It is the other mistress, Madame Leonie, who visits Adele Hugo. Leonie is the one with whom Hugo was caught in flagrante delicto by the husband and for whom he was placed under arrest for the crime of adultery."

"Ah, yes. One has heard of the escapade."

"Who did not? But as Lamartine observed at the time, 'France is elastic: one rises even from a divan.' "

"The French still buy his books," Mara commented.

"More avidly than ever. It is more than one so notorious in his infidelities deserves."

"Now, Aurore," Balzac said placatingly.

Estes lifted a comical brow. "This, from you, my dear lady?"

"Are you suggesting that I have been unfaithful?"

Beads of perspiration broke out on the Italian's head. "I would not dream of it. Still, one has heard . . ."

"Men are such gossips! I have always believed in fidelity; I have preached it, practiced it, demanded it. Others have failed to live up to it and I, too. And yet I have never felt remorse because in my infidelities I have suffered a sort of fatality, an instinctive idealism which impelled me to abandon the imperfect for what seemed to me to be closer to perfection."

"You do not hold the marriage vow sacred?" Mara asked since the woman spoke so openly.

"Hardly, since I have freed myself of a husband to whom I was little more than a chattel. No. It is only common sense and simple humanity that no wife should be forced to remain with a man she despises. Women, as well as men, should be free to love where they will. But it is not love but mere concupiscence to go merrily from house to house as Victor does, making love to three different women on the same day, and likely a few actresses as well."

"In his defense," Balzac said, "I should like to remind you of his wife's notorious affair with Sainte-Beuve. It's my opinion that he has been disillusioned with love from the day he discovered it."

"It's no excuse."

"But to make a cuckold of him with his most virulent literary critic! Men will overlook much, but a betrayal of that magnitude will be neither forgotten nor forgiven."

Betrayal. It was not a subject with which Mara could be comfortable. She had not yet dared think of what Roderic would do when he discovered how she had used him. At one time she had thought it would not matter.

She had been wrong. She permitted her attention to be snared by a man wearing an odd cloak of maroon velvet edged with gold braiding and frogging, with a tasseled hood hanging down in back. He was striking in appearance, tall and dark and saturnine.

"Who is the man in the strange cloak?"

"The burnous? That is Delacroix, the painter. A splendid figure, is he not? He picked up the idea of the burnous on his travels in Algeria. With so many going to that part of the world, it is becoming something of a fashion."

Beyond Delacroix—who was no relation, as far as she knew—was the entrance door. A man was just arriving, giving his hat and cane into the hands of a maidservant. He was also dark and tall, but he had a thin mustache and narrow beard and wore an expression of impatience as he scanned the room. De Landes's gaze found Mara, and he gave a small jerk of his head, summoning her.

Mara felt her nerves tighten like violin strings. That de Landes was here was an indication that her every movement was being watched. Did he know that she had not done what she had been told to do? What would he say?

It would be a wrench to leave the group she was with; still, it must be done. "Excuse me," she said at the first opportunity, "I believe I saw Princess Juliana beckoning."

She moved across the room, pausing to speak to the princess, making a gay comment on the gathering, before threading her way through the crowd to where de Landes stood. He had chosen a spot somewhat shielded by a weeping willow growing in a lacquerware cachepot and a suit of armor complete with visor. She retained her social smile with an effort as she stopped beside him, but spoke without preamble. "What do you want?"

"How charming you look. That sales assistant was right; bright colors become you."

"You did not come here to compliment me."

"No, but I am beginning to wonder if I wasn't a fool

for not giving you some personal instruction in the best way to win a man's—shall we say?—cooperation."

"The prince is most astute. It will not do for him to see us talking together too long since I am supposed to have no remembrance of friends. I repeat, what do you want?"

He looked at her long and hard, then gave an abrupt nod. "The Vicomtesse Beausire will be honored by the presence of the king at her ball. Louis Philippe will be arriving at ten precisely. You will not only make certain that the prince attends, but that he is standing near the entrance through which the king and his guests will pass at that time. Do you understand?"

"Near the entrance? Where? I know nothing about the house or its rooms."

"It doesn't matter. Just have him near the main entrance at the hour of ten o'clock."

"Ten. Main entrance. How is my grandmother?"

"Well enough, for now."

De Landes inclined his head and moved away. It was an instant before Mara realized that it was Roderic's approach that had routed him. The prince was bearing down upon her. He was smiling, but she was not deceived.

"Have I neglected you, have we all, that you must skulk among the greenery talking to strangers?"

Her chin came up. "Skulk?"

"Should I have said hide?"

"I wasn't aware that there was anything clandestine about talking to a gentleman at a literary salon such as this. You might have told me."

"I might have, had I thought it necessary."

"What is it you wished me to do? Stay beside you? But I had the impression earlier that you were trying to warn me away from that course."

His gaze narrowed. "And it rankled?"

She should have known better than to bandy words

with him. It had indeed rankled that he had so easily overcome his desire for her, that he had seen fit, ever so delicately, to repulse her advances. But wasn't it better, for now, to admit to it than to have him press her for an answer concerning de Landes?

She lowered her lashes. "No woman likes to think that she has been obvious."

"Doesn't she?"

She was disturbed by the amusement that lifted slowly into his eyes as if at some pleasing memory. "I can't think a man would care for it either."

"It would depend on the man—and the woman." He raised his hand and opened the visor of the suit of armor, letting it clank shut again.

She had the feeling suddenly that he was ill at ease, that he wished the words unsaid. That could only mean that he regretted them. Why should he, unless they held more truth than he wanted known? Before she could explore the thought, however, he swung back to her.

"Have you met Lamartine? He has the face of an aristocrat and the soul of a butcher, a poet turned politician, the most dangerous kind."

Alphonse de Lamartine had been roundly condemned by Grandmère Helene and her elderly French cousin as a radical, based on his speeches in the Chamber of Deputies and the publication over the past several years of his eight-volume *Histoire des Girondins* celebrating the rights of the proletariat. They called him a traitor to his class, a poltroon who was trying to pull down the most stable and peaceable government they had had in France in a hundred years, and a fool for refusing the ambassadorship that was offered by Louis Philippe in an attempt to seduce him away from his role of reformer.

He was as aristocratic in appearance as Roderic had suggested, with an upright bearing, a slender form, a narrow, intelligent face, and light brown hair going gray at the temples. He was also witty in a soft-spoken manner, Mara discovered. It was a relief to stand chatting with him after the strain of her earlier exchanges with de Landes and Roderic, and the barbed remarks and scandalous tittle-tattle of the others she had met that evening.

Roderic's attention had been snared by a determined woman in a startling gown of chartreuse silk printed with black polka dots and covered with miles of black silk gimp. He only half listened to what she was saying, however. His gaze was on the woman in dark blue he called Chère. The high color was fading from her cheekbones, and her smile now came with ease and naturalness without the overbrightness of fear or guilt. It brought an odd pain to the center of his being to see it; she was always guarded around him. Still, the angles and shadows cast upon the oval of her face by the gaslight, the purity of her skin and the soft gray of her eyes brought out by the deep color of her gown, gave her a haunting beauty. She intrigued him more each day, not only because of her lack of background and the puzzle it presented, but because of something he sensed inside her.

He was almost inclined to allow her to continue as a mystery, to wait until she remembered her past of her own accord or else trusted him with whatever secret it was that she held. It had even crossed his mind once or twice that he might prefer that she do neither. The return of her memory would mean that she must leave him to go back to where she belonged. If, on the other hand, she was withholding information, it could be that she had come to him for a reason, one that he would rather not know.

He *must* know, however. There was too much at stake to indulge in such a quixotic gesture as sheltering a woman under his roof who might betray him.

Luca had pointed out de Landes, had identified him as the man who had spoken to Chère at the draper's shop.

It appeared something less than a coincidence that he had spoken to her again tonight. De Landes was well known, not only as an official in the foreign ministry, but as a man-about-town, a devastating fellow among the little seamstresses known as *grisettes*. An investigation of the man's more recent activities might well yield results. If that was what he himself wanted.

He looked to where Luca was standing. The gypsy tipped his head toward the door, indicating that de Landes had left the salon. Roderic gave a slow nod, his face bleak. Luca, as swift and silent as a shadow, went from the room after the Frenchman.

It was late when the party broke up. As they emerged into the square of the Place Royale, they discovered that it was snowing. The flakes fell with steady persistence, coating the cobblestones an inch deep and forming soft, gold halos around the gas globes of the street lamps. Now and then a gust of wind sent them whirling, dancing, piling against the curb or the bases of the leafless trees of the park in the middle of the square.

"Isn't it beautiful!" Mara cried, holding out her hands to catch the crystal snowflakes. In the lower section of Louisiana where she lived, snow fell perhaps once in five years or more, and even then only a scattering that melted almost before it touched the ground.

Estes snorted, shivering in his uniform jacket. "Beautiful? Bah!"

"Watch your step on the cobblestones," Jared said, taking Mara's arm, then quickly sliding his own about her waist as she slipped.

Juliana looked around them. "Where is Luca?"

"On an errand," Roderic said, the words enveloped in ice.

Jacques bent to scoop up a handful of snow, forming it into a ball in his gloved hands. He looked around him with a gleam in his eye. His gaze caught that of the prince. He dropped the snow and brushed off his gloves with elaborate unconcern.

"Uh-oh," Jared, close to Mara, said under his breath. He looked at his leader, and something he saw in Roderic's face made him remove his arm, leaving Mara only the support of her hand at his elbow.

They moved on in silence toward Ruthenia House.

Had Roderic been jealous? That was the question that plagued Mara as she permitted Lila to unhook her gown and help her prepare for bed. She thought back to the moment when he had walked up to her after her exchange with de Landes, going over every detail of how he had looked and what he had said. Then she did the same with the incident in the Place Royale, and even went so far as to recall the day when he had seen her caught in the arms of the cadre during their acrobatics. Could it be that he truly desired her, that she attracted him, but that he was resisting the attraction? Was the cost of that resistance the reason for his temper this evening?

She was unconvinced. Some small attraction she might allow, some passing fancy, but she had the feeling that there was more to his failure to succumb to her wiles. He might talk of preventing future regret for her or of having no time for females, but the cause, she was sure, went deeper. He was wary of her. That was the long and the short of it.

Lila held out the nightgown of fine cambric, and obediently Mara lifted her arms to permit the maid to slide it over her head. The maid took down her hair and handed her a hairbrush as she held out her hand for it, then moved to the bed and turned it down. Mara tugged the brush through her hair, her gaze blank and unseeing on the maid at her task.

During the incident with Dennis, it had been, she thought, her physical presence, the touch of her body, that had made him forget himself. Roderic, too, once she was in his arms, had not paused to consider the problems inherent in making love to her until they had been interrupted by the arrival of his sister. If Juliana had not come, the seduction would have been completed. She would be the mistress of the prince and need no longer be tormented by these doubts.

As little as she desired the position of female companion to the prince, as little as she wished to entice him into an affair, she wanted desperately for this waiting, this dread of what must be done, to be over. It would be a relief, if the truth were known, when she was installed in his bed.

Mara paused with her hairbrush in her hand and her hair streaming down her back. What if she simply joined him as he slept? Would her presence, her female form and warmth, make him forget his reservations once more?

Her heart jolted in her chest at the thought. Her hands began to tremble, so she quickly put down the hairbrush. Did she dare? After the summary way he had dealt with Trude, after his warning, his temper of the night, could she bring herself to risk it?

"Is something wrong, mademoiselle?"

"No, nothing, Lila," she answered, forcing a smile. "You may go."

The door closed behind the maidservant. Mara waited until the girl's footsteps had faded away through the antechamber and down the back stairway. When there was no longer a sound, she lifted the hem of her nightgown and, without giving herself another moment to think about it and grow more frightened, she left the bedchamber.

The floors of the long and empty rooms that formed the passageway leading to Roderic's wing were cold to her bare feet. Chill drafts wafted under her nightgown, fanning it around her knees and thighs. Most of the candles in their girandoles that lighted the way had burned out so that she walked in darkness lit only by intermittent pools of light. Beyond the tall windows was the deep darkness and the velvet silence of the snowy night. All that could be seen was her own pale form reflected now and then at some odd angle on the leaded window glass.

She passed through the center of the house where the corridors of rooms formed a St. Andrew's cross dividing the four courtyards. Ahead of her was a small antechamber that led into the prince's wing surrounding the east court. To the left was a door that opened into the bedchambers of the cadre, all adjoining. Straight ahead lay the personal salon of the prince, and beyond it his bedchamber and dressing room. On the other side of them lay a small room where he kept a table piled high with books and papers. Beyond these, in the wing at a left angle to the prince's rooms, lay the suite occupied by his mother and father when they were in residence. She hesitated only a moment to be certain that no one was on guard. Seeing no one, hearing nothing, she pressed down the heavy brass door handle and pushed open the door, stepping into Roderic's private salon.

The darkness was total here. She would have to move carefully. During her childhood, there had been a summer when there had been much talk of Indians, of their being moved from the Southern states to lands farther west. She and several of the slave children on the plantation had spent weeks playing at being Indians, hiding among the shrubbery in the garden, creeping about the house to jump out at the adults in mock attacks. She had learned how to walk quietly in bare feet, how to move with care and agility so as to avoid any object that might cause a noise. Now, in the dense quiet of the room, it seemed natural to fall back on those ingrained lessons.

She skirted a table, a settee, a chair, a footstool. She remembered the placement of the bedchamber door from her tours of inspection, and, within a few short moments, her fingertips were brushing the facing and outlining the handle. She pressed it down and eased the heavy door open, slipping inside.

There was not a sound in the room: no soft snore, no regular, whispering breaths of one heavily asleep. Was he that quiet a sleeper, or was he out of the room, perhaps working in the next? But not a glimmer of light could be seen in that direction.

Like her own, the prince's bed sat on a platform. The carved and gilded frame that held it was enormously wide and long. Though nothing of it could be seen, the headboard soared up into the lofty ceiling in a massive half-tester carved with the gilded and painted crown and coat of arms of Ruthenia. From it hung silk draperies that were looped back on each side. She must take care not to stir the draperies, for their movement might awaken a man as alert as Roderic.

The edge of her foot brushed the platform. She stepped up onto it, easing her weight upward before lifting her other foot. Still no sound. She moved closer so that the lawn of her nightgown swept against the bedclothes. She located the draperies with a feather-light touch, then leaned forward with her hand outstretched.

Her wrist was caught in an iron grasp and she was jerked forward. She lost her footing as she was dragged across the bed. A gasp of shock rasped in her throat. Her hair whipped around her like a silken flail, and then she was falling. She struck the mattress on her back, and a weight descended upon her, pressing into her breastbone, holding her immobile. A hard thigh descended across her knees, locking them. Her other wrist was captured in a grip like a manacle and wrenched above her head.

"Sweet-scented and pliable, softer than a Mussulman's dream of paradise: Have you come to take me there or merely to dispatch me?"

"What . . . do you . . . think?" she said, the words panting from the pressure on her chest.

The hard weight was removed, her hands released. "Dare I guess?"

Mara breathed deep, swallowing against the hard knot of apprehension in her throat and a hysterical need to laugh. She was well and truly in his bed. "You . . . could search for weapons, if you like."

Taut stillness held him. He drawled, "An interesting offer."

The throbbing heat of his body against hers was at variance with the blandness of his words. His rigidity spoke of stringent self-control directed by an iron will that ignored bodily discomfort. Drawing on every ounce of her own will, she kept her hand steady as she reached to brush her fingers across his chest. The muscles were knotted and hard beneath the fine mat of hair. Grateful for the covering of darkness that hid her hectic flush, she trailed her fingers downward over the flat surface of his abdomen, following the descending line of hair.

He drew in his breath and snatched her hand away. The next moment he cupped her face in his hand and his mouth descended upon hers. Directed by fury and restrained desire, it was a devouring kiss, a searing, implacable invasion. Slanting, merciless, his lips took possession of the sweetness of hers. His tongue abraded the tender interior of her mouth, twining with her tongue in sinuous initiation, thrusting deep.

Mara's heart jarred in her chest. The blood pounded in her head and poured in a torrent along her veins. She made a small sound that might have been of distress, of anger, or of pleasure.

He drew back abruptly, drawing a single, ragged breath. "You are no houri, no harlot, no dispenser of clandestine joy, sweet Chère. *What are you doing?*"

"Don't—don't you want me?" She felt like a whore,

which was, she saw with anguished clarity, what he had intended.

"Want you? What has that to do with anything?"

She flinched at the quiet savagery of his words. "I just—just wanted to be close to you. Can that be wrong?"

He pushed away from her and rolled from the bed. Then came the yellow flare of a sulphur match and its smell of old eggs and burning pine. Bathed in its yellow glow, Roderic lit the bedside candle in its silver holder, then pinched out the match.

The candle flame wavered, casting searching rays into the dark corners of the room, flickering softly over Mara as she lay raised on one elbow. It made twin points of fire in the darkness of her eyes and outlined the soft curves and hollows of her body through the fine material of her nightgown, gleaming also on the slender turning of her calves and ankles where the hem had worked upward. Roderic stared down at her, aware of an ache deep inside him that had nothing to do with the unappeased fullness of his loins. How proud she looked, with her chin tilted and the standing lace collar framing the purity of her throat and neck, and yet there was something defensive, humiliated, in her eyes. That he had put it there brought the brush of shame to him also. He banished it with a quick shake of his head.

"The question is," he said softly, "can it be right?"

"I would never have taken you for a puritan." She could not seem to look away from the splendid shape of his nakedness above her.

Her mouth was red and swollen from his kiss, in need of soothing. "Nor, I hope, for a fool."

No, he was not that. Mara felt beyond her depth, as if she were floundering in a situation over which she had no control. A shiver ran through her, followed by another, and yet another. Only the thought of Grandmère Helene—so fragile and yet with such joy for living—and of the swift passage of her allotted time forced her to go on.

"You have permitted Sarus to think that I am your mistress, and now everyone assumes it, even the cadre sometimes. What is the difference?"

"The difference is that I know you are not, and you know it." Perhaps he was a fool. The reasons he knew so well in the bright light of day seemed less than convincing here in the shifting light of a single bedside candle. His guard against treachery had never been penetrated, and was unlikely to be now. If she cared nothing for her honor, why should he? And yet it was that lack of caring, combined with her obvious inexperience, that troubled him most, even more than the likelihood of his housing a traitor.

"But I could be, so easily." The words were low-spoken, with a hint of pleading. She held out her hand.

His dark-gold brows drew together in a frown, and he reached to take her fingers, which trembled visibly. "A freezing mistress, all fearful entreaty and icy affection. How can I resist?"

He released her hand and leaned to thrust his arms under her, lifting her against his chest. Swinging about so that her hair swirled around them in a dark curtain, he strode from the bedchamber into his personal salon and through it to the antechamber. There was a light there as Michael, wearing only his uniform trousers, stood in the doorway that led into the rooms of the cadre. Sarus, his Russian Tartar's copper face lined with age and fatigue, his bent form covered by a rough nightshirt, stood beside Roderic's cousin. It was plain that they had heard something of the quarrel, at least enough to awaken them.

Mara closed her eyes, wishing she could vanish, feeling the hurtful rise of tears of despair behind her nose and eyelids. She had thought for one wild moment that Roderic meant to hold her, to warm her in his bed. That hope was gone. She knew, as they moved out of the antechamber and down the corridor of rooms into the rest of the house, that he was returning her to her own bedchamber.

"I can walk," she said, the words stifled.

He did not answer.

It was a long passage. Mara grew slowly aware of the strength of his hold, of the steady thud of his heartbeat. Her skin tingled where she was pressed against him with only the thin cloth of her nightgown separating them. Safe. She felt safe. But also unbearably conscious of him as a man, a prince. Roderic of Ruthenia. They were close, so close. She felt an unnerving impulse to turn, to slide her arms around his neck and press against him. She wanted, in a way that had nothing to do with the instructions she had been given, to make him aware of her, to gain some real response from him for herself as a woman.

As the prospect of physical intimacy receded, it was replaced by chagrin, which was swiftly followed by resentment. Arrogant, overbearing man; his pretense of concern was an insult. How dare he refuse her, and with so little effort? She would like to make him regret it; she really would, if only to restore her damaged self-esteem. But how could she? He seemed invulnerable.

He pushed into her bedchamber and, in the light of a candelabrum left burning on the center table, strode to the bed. He placed her on the high surface and stepped back.

Quickly, Mara rose to her knees and reached out to catch his shoulders. They were warm and firm under her hands, the muscles flexed and, in his surprise, without resistance. She met his cobalt-blue gaze for a brief instant, her own eyes serene, daring. And then she set her lips to his, brushing them on the smooth, well-molded surface, testing with the tip of her tongue the ridged edges, the sensitive line where they came together. He swayed toward her, his lips opening with warm willingness. Light-headed with triumph and something more she would not recognize, she smoothed her hands along his shoulders to lock them behind his neck, deepening the kiss.

Was it calculation that made her draw back or doubts about her temerity? Was it some small movement he made that disturbed her or her own growing need to be nearer? She could not have said, but she did release him, easing away.

"Goodnight," she murmured.

He stared at her, his expression unreadable, for the space of a heartbeat. Then, turning with the smooth and lithe control of limitless strength, he walked from the room.

Mara collapsed on the bed, covering her face with her hands, resting her forehead on her knees. Her hair spilled forward, hiding her face. What was she going to do? She had to face the fact that she might well not be able to win her way into the prince's bed. What was going to happen to her grandmother if she did not? What would de Landes do?

These questions were vital, haunting, but there was one other that circled endlessly in her mind. How was she going to face Roderic in the morning?

She felt scarred and defeated and, yes, exhausted, as if she had been in a desperate battle. Her chest hurt, her lips burned, and her pride was sore. She longed for vengeance and oblivion with equal fervor, for any way to free herself from the humiliation that gripped her. And yet on another level she was relieved. Considering Roderic's manner with his men when they displeased him, she knew that she was lucky to have emerged from the encounter so nearly unscathed. Moreover, she had avoided that final physical surrender. She certainly should be relieved.

The control of the prince was a revelation to her. She had somehow thought, doubtless because of her experience with Dennis, that men lacked that ultimate self-denial, that they were more at the mercy of their desires. Roderic had wanted her. He had not admitted it, but it had been plain enough. Still, he had denied himself. For whatever reason, he had deliberately drawn back from the easy possession of her, had removed her from his bed, his apartment, his vicinity. In spite of her willingness, her touch, even her pleas, regardless of how hard or how easy it might have been, he had summoned the will to evict her.

Mara sat up, flinging her hair back. With a startled look on her face, she considered Roderic's conduct, thinking back to the other time when she had been alone with a man. It became slowly apparent that Dennis Mulholland, on that night in the summerhouse, had lacked self-control. He had shown no more self-discipline than a small boy left alone in a candy shop. He had been presented by accident with an opportunity to gratify his desires, and he had seized it with both hands. He had shown no concern whatever for her, no caring for her predicament, her lack of air; he had simply sought to appease his own appetite at her expense. She had been right to be angry that night, right to refuse to marry him. He had known it. His death had changed nothing.

She felt suddenly as if a great darkness had lifted from her mind. She was not to blame. Dennis Mulholland had not been killed because of her. She was not some seductress who had tempted him beyond his power to resist, thereby causing the degradation that had made him seek death. The weakness had been his, just as the choice to draw back or to violate her chastity with his touch had been his.

Why had she thought otherwise? Was it the urging of marriage by her father and by Dennis, as if in punishment for some sin? Was it her remorse for her thoughtlessness or the attitude of society that seemed to expect her to take some blame upon herself? Or was it the religious teachings of her youth that had, in the tale of Garden of Eden, placed the fault for the failure of will in Adam on the shoulders of Eve?

Whatever the cause, it had taken a Balkan prince to show her the error. For that, at least, she must be grateful to him. It would be much easier to do that if she never had to see Roderic again.

Morning brought Juliana's Prussian. The hour was nearing eleven when Sarus, very correct in his livery, which was not unlike the uniform of the cadre, found Mara in her salon where she was going over the menu for the day with the cook. He gave her a stiff bow and presented a card on a silver tray.

"What is it?" she asked, taking up the card and looking at it in mystification. The name on the card, with a long list of titles, conveyed nothing to her at that moment.

"It is the crown prince, mademoiselle."

"Surely he doesn't wish to see me. You must take this to Prince Roderic."

"The prince has been with Luca this last half hour. His orders were that they were not to be disturbed."

"Then the crown prince will have to wait."

"The Prussian is . . . impatient."

"Prussian—oh!" Mara frowned down at the card, then looked up again. "Perhaps you could inform Princess Juliana of his arrival."

"The princess has not yet left her bed."

"Surely he will wait for her to get up and make ready to see him?"

Sarus hesitated, his lined face knotted with worry. "He is not used to waiting. He may go in search of Princess Juliana, and if he does, she—"

"Yes, I can imagine," Mara said hastily. Juliana would not be pleased and would let everyone know it. A domestic crisis of that kind was to be avoided if at all possible. "Very well. I will be there in a moment."

When she entered the public salon a short time later, the Prussian was standing by the windows staring down at the snow-covered cobbles of the entrance court. He turned as she advanced toward him, bowing with a sharp click of his heels. "Mademoiselle, I apologize for taking you from your tasks."

"Not at all." Mara dropped a slight curtsy, then indicated that he should be seated across from her on a settee. He was tall and well-built, though his chest was as round as a barrel. Perhaps in his late thirties, he had a flowing blond mustache, a luxuriant growth that contrasted sharply with the slick, shaven pate of his head. "Have you had refreshment? Very good. Then how may I assist you?"

He cleared his throat. "It is a matter of some delicacy."

When he did not go on, Mara, in an attempt to help him, said, "It concerns Princess Juliana, I think?"

"Indeed, yes. A fabulous creature. I have her father's permission to pay her my court."

"Yes?" Behind his abrupt manner, he was a most proper man, but calculating with it.

"She is young and frivolous and doesn't know her own mind."

Mara, who was beginning to feel like a maiden aunt, thought privately that the description did not sound like the Juliana she had met. She said nothing, only nodding encouragement.

"In short, she has flown from me. Is she here?"

"Did Sarus not tell you? She is visiting her brother, yes."

"Ah, that is good news. May I see her?"

"In anticipation of your request, Sarus has gone to see if she is in."

"I must see her!"

His vehemence was a little alarming since it was accompanied by the rush of blood to his face. The vessels in his neck appeared ready to burst. What she would do if he jumped up and began to search the house, she did not know.

"Have you known Juliana long?" she asked, hoping to distract him. Where was the girl, or Roderic? Anyone. She could not believe that one of the cadre had not looked in, hoping to meet the bald Prussian. Perhaps they, too, were with Roderic?

"We met in Ruthenia, at the palace. It has been two months since that day."

In the entrance court below the windows, the door knocker sounded. Somewhere Demon was barking, the sound echoed by the sharp yipping of Juliana's Pekingese. Perhaps she was about to be rescued.

"Is that not Juliana's little dog? Surely she is here as she goes nowhere without the animal."

"This is Paris, Your Highness. It isn't always convenient to carry a dog." Where was Sarus? Couldn't he at least learn whether Juliana meant to see her visitor or deny herself? Searching rather desperately for a topic to distract him, she said, "I trust you were not troubled in your journey by the snow?"

"A mere nothing. I was not surprised when it stopped before dawn. I drove through the night without stopping."

At that moment a housemaid opened the door. "The Messieurs Alexandre Dumas, *père et fils*."

Before the new guests could enter, Demon, his tongue lolling out and toenails clicking on the hard floor, galloped into the room with the Pekingese, Sophie, clattering along behind him trailing a gem-studded leash. They circled the settee, then, discovering the crown prince, slid to a halt and gave tongue. Alexandre Dumas the elder advanced into the room, his bonhomie undisturbed by the noise. Behind him came a young man with curling auburn hair and light blue eyes set in features with a faintly melancholy cast.

Dumas shouted, "Mademoiselle Incognito, I give you good morning! Here I have brought my son who wished to meet so fascinating a young lady as yourself. I trust you do not mind?"

Mara presented Dumas *père* to the crown prince, though she was not certain that either caught the other's name over the din of high-pitched yelping and deeper barking from the excited dogs. She spoke to Demon severely, but it did not help, and when she ordered the maidservant to remove the two animals, both mongrel and Pekingese turned the attempt into a new game, playing hide-and-seek among the chairs. During the melee, Estes and Jared appeared in the doorway. They, too, joined the chase. The older Dumas, hugely enjoying the scene, sat down beside Mara and captured her hand.

Distracted, Mara smiled at him, then looked away at once to call, "Be careful of that vase!," as a fine example of Meissen ware teetered on a rocking table. The Pekingese ran between the legs of the younger Dumas, who bent over, trying to catch the dragging leash. At the same time, the crown prince reached for it. The two men butted heads with a sound that could be heard across the room. Young Dumas staggered back and stepped on Sophie. The Pekingese squealed. Dumas shifted, and his foot came down on the dog's leash, which was immediately jerked from under him as the Prussian pulled on it. Dumas floundered, his arms beating the air, then went down on his knees in front of Mara. Demon, rounding the end of the settee with Estes and Jared closing in behind him, made a flying leap and landed on Dumas's back. The young man's head snapped forward, pressing his face into Mara's lap. At once Demon scrambled into the safety of Mara's arms, trying to lick her face.

Mara, choking on suppressed laughter, tried to fend the dog off while Dumas the elder, the crown prince, and Estes all converged upon her.

It was then that Roderic spoke from the doorway, his tones flinty with contempt. "A charming revel, if somewhat vulgar. May anyone join?"

CHAPTER 8

It was a day of visitors, of much coming and going. Juliana, sweeping into the salon behind her brother, was all smiling graciousness toward Arvin, the crown prince of Prussia. Her apparent pleasure in seeing him so dazed his senses, coming as it did on the heels of Roderic's less than cordial greeting, that before he knew it she had carried him off for a drive to see Paris in the snow. The Dumases departed before luncheon, but, pressed by the prince, promised to return for dinner that evening. No sooner had the door closed upon them than it opened to admit a member of the Académie, a politician with virulent republican sentiments, and a scandalous old comtesse who was legitimist to the heart and fierce with it. The trio stayed to luncheon and very nearly came to blows over the *daube glace*. During the afternoon, several ladies and gentlemen from Louis Philippe's court dropped by, complaining of boredom. Life was duller than usual at this season due to the illness of Madame Adelaide, the sister of the king; Ruthenia House was the only place they could be certain of finding entertainment and witty conversation without the aroma of the nostrums prescribed by doctors. Along with the comtesse, the politician, and the academician, who seemed entrenched for the duration, they settled down to tables of cards.

They were joined during the afternoon by Théophile Gautier of *La Presse,* the journalist who was also a poet. He read them a portion of his latest poem, a fragment concerning his travels to a country whose name Mara did not quite catch. It sounded good, however, and was applauded by all. He complained that everyone was traveling and writing about it, or else had plans to do so. Before long there would be books and poems only about foreign places and none about France. Exception was taken to this statement by an older man who strolled into the room. He had been traveling for years over France, he said, looking at its ancient buildings and writing about them.

"Learned articles," Gautier scoffed, "but your most famous short story is about a Spanish lady of the evening named Carmen!"

Roderic, lounging before the fire with a glass of brandy at his elbow, cocked a brow at the pair. "Those learned articles have meant the preservation of many of the architectural glories of France. Appointing Mérimée inspector of monuments was one of the most important decisions of the July Monarchy."

Prosper Mérimée bowed in acknowledgment of the compliment, but one of the court members protested. "You make it sound as if you expect to hear nothing more from Louis Philippe. The man isn't dead yet."

"Very true," Roderic said, picking up his brandy glass and staring into the swirling liquor. "My apologies."

Mara looked up sharply from where she was taking a hand in a game of old-fashioned *brisque.* Through her mind ran the instructions from de Landes: She was to make certain that Roderic was near the king. Where Roderic was, the cadre would be also. Could it have something to do with the fact that his men were known as the Death

Corps? Could there be some plan to assassinate the king? But if there was, and if Roderic was involved, why should it be necessary for her to see that he was in the correct place? And why would a man active in the ministry under Louis Philippe, dependent on the favor of the king, be playing a part? It made no sense. And yet there was some reason. There must be, or else she would not be there in Ruthenia House.

Roderic was the consummate host, seeing to the pleasure of his guests, engaging them in conversation that crackled and sparked like a pyrotechnic display. He had a knack for making people feel welcome, but there was little ease in his presence. There was instead a sense of vivid life, of sharp-edged enjoyment so intense that no one appeared to want to leave for fear they would miss some excitement.

And yet that intensity was fueled, Mara recognized as the day wore on, by his black temper. If she had not noted the signs herself, the soft-stepping attitude of the cadre would have alerted her. The quiet lash of his voice in argument, the brilliance of his logic that annihilated opponents, the gentle tone he used and the solemnity of his features as he encouraged those who had made foolish remarks to enlarge upon them were signals that could not be ignored. So alas was his outrageous gallantry toward the ladies as he smiled upon them with a ferocity that made one hang upon his arm with her breast pressed against him and her eyes bright, while another developed a habit of giggling every time he looked her way.

Juliana, returned from her drive with the Prussian, watched her brother for a moment, then sent Mara a quick glance. "If he isn't careful, he is going to find himself with a sword cane in his back. That, or else under the table from mixing brandy with wine. He never drinks to excess unless he is hurt or enraged. I wonder what can have occurred to put him in such a passion? One would almost swear he had been thwarted in love."

"Hardly that," Mara said, her tone tart.

"No? How interesting."

How much did Juliana know of what had taken place the night before? Her face with its well-defined features gave nothing away. Mara did not think that Sarus or Michael would have spoken of what they had seen, but there was no way of knowing what servants might have been about or who else might have looked out of their rooms. Nor was there any way of guessing what those who had seen might have made of the sight of the prince returning her to her bedchamber. It was an act that could mean anything.

But had Roderic been angry then? Perhaps a little, she had to concede, but not in the same way he was now. Slowly, she said, "It must have been something else."

"Such as?"

"I have no idea."

She had not spoken to Roderic, nor he to her, all that long day. Facing him had not been as bad as she had expected due to the melee with the dogs. Her chagrin at being found surrounded by men and with the younger Dumas's face buried in her lap, plus her anger at Roderic's deliberate misreading of the situation, had carried her over the first moments. His own complete lack of consciousness with her, as if the events of the night before had never taken place, had also helped.

And yet remaining in the same room with him all that long day had been nearly unendurable. She thought that he realized it and cared not at all for her sensibilities. It almost seemed that he stayed on, watching her instead of closeting himself with his affairs as he usually did, as a punishment. She was being fanciful, of course. Her discomfort was real enough, but his reaction to it was surely a figment of her own imagination.

Night fell and dinnertime came at last. Twenty-eight sat down to the table, including the Dumases, father and son. The food was rich in variety and beautifully prepared, the wine bountiful. Mara, pushing a piece of veal about her plate, reminded herself to compliment the cook on her ingenuity in providing so well for a number that had gradually increased as the evening advanced. The voices of the diners were loud, their spirits convivial. Both affected her like the scrape of fingernails on a windowpane. She could feel a headache forming behind her forehead, a sign of the strain of the day. More than anything else, she longed to be alone in the quiet of her room. As soon as it was possible, she was going to slip away.

They were leaving the dining room when Sarus came to touch Roderic on the shoulder. The prince leaned his head to listen to a whispered message, then with a graceful excuse left them, promising to join them in the salon later.

The party became more subdued almost at once, though it was still lively. Almost everyone knew everyone else. People congregated in groups here and there throughout the room, but particularly around Juliana, who sat on the settee in the center of the salon. The Prussian, who had returned for dinner, hovered over her, while the elder Dumas paid her extravagant praise and did his best to convince her that she should give up being a princess to become an actress.

One of the few people who stood apart, alone, in the room was Luca. He leaned against a window embrasure with his shoulders braced against the frame, his dark gaze following every gesture and change of expression on the face of Roderic's sister. There was gypsy blood in Juliana, if Roderic was to be believed, and perhaps it responded to the silent admiration. At any rate the princess was aware of it, for now and then she would look toward Luca and her mouth would curve in a secretive smile.

Mara had thought of herself as being apart also until she was joined where she stood before one of the two fireplaces by the younger Dumas. He placed a hand on the high marble mantel, leaning against it as he brushed back his tailcoat to put the other hand in his pocket. "They are saying, Mademoiselle Incognito, that you have become the mistress of Prince Roderic. Are they correct?"

"What an impertinent question!" she answered, trying for a light tone.

"You don't deny it, so it must be true. I would like to warn you that the life of a courtesan, *la vie galante,* is not as easy or exciting as it may appear."

His manner was serious and no doubt he was sincere; still, she was in no mood for lectures. "You have spoken plainly, so you will not be surprised if I tell you that such advice sounds a little odd coming from one who has, or so gossip has it, shared his father's mistresses for years."

He shrugged. "I was once in the habit of wearing out my father's mistresses and breaking in his new shoes. No longer."

"Indeed," she said politely, and looked around for some means of extricating herself.

"I have no right to speak to you, I know, but you remind me strongly of someone I once knew. She was called Marie Duplessis, but her real name was simply Alphonsine Plessis."

"Was?"

"She died not long ago of a lung ailment. She was twenty-three."

"She was . . . dear to you?"

A shadow of pain crossed his face. "If you mean to ask if she was my mistress, no. We were lovers, but I could not afford to keep her. She drifted away, became the favorite of others, the toast of Paris. But the life of camellias and diamonds and furs doesn't last. As they get older, the women grow grasping and afraid, or else disease claims them. You don't belong any more than Alphonsine did. You should go back where you came from, be a farmer's wife, a nun, a spinster—anything except this."

Mara looked up at him, her gaze dark. "I would," she said, "if I could. Now if you will excuse me?"

She walked away and did not stop until she was out of the room. Still, the things the younger Dumas had said echoed in her mind. She had not needed to hear them to realize the risk she ran; she had known it from the beginning. Outside in the main gallery, she placed her back to the wall beside the door and closed her eyes. What would become of her when her association with the prince became known? Even if she and her grandmother told what had happened, who would believe them? It seemed so unlikely.

She had few illusions. Soon she would be notorious as the mistress of the prince. Once word reached New Orleans, there would be knowing looks and laughter behind fans. They would think that she had made that fatal misstep against which all young women were warned. Inevitably, there would be those who would say that they had expected it all along after the way her father had indulged her and the flighty way she had behaved.

What else would there be for her except to stay on in Paris, to become what everyone thought her already? She had never dreamed when she left Louisiana that she was destined to become a courtesan, a participant in *la vie galante,* the life of pleasing men.

There seemed to be no way out. Through no fault of her own, she had been drawn into this morass of lies and subterfuge. Now she was trapped.

She pushed away from the wall and started toward her rooms. The stair gallery above the entranceway with its double line of windows was cold. She hugged her arms around herself and hurried along. Where the stair gallery met the north-south corridor of rooms that formed the

St. Andrew's cross, she turned left, crossing the three rooms that were seldom used, those leading to the private salon and long gallery favored by the cadre on most days. There were no fires here, and they were also chill and damp. She turned left again to reach the antechamber that contained the servants' back stairs and gave access to her own suite overlooking the west court.

The door to the antechamber was just closing as she neared it. She thought nothing of it, expecting only a house servant on some errand. Pressing down the handle, pushing it open in one smooth movement in her haste, she stepped inside.

Roderic whirled, dropping into a crouch as with a sliding snick he drew a dagger from his belt. She stopped with a smothered cry. He cursed, fluently and long. Behind him a man walked out of the shadows.

"Introduce me, my dear prince. A lady who can face you with a knife in your hand without screaming the house down must be as discreet as she is lovely."

It was Charles Louis Napoleon, Prince Louis Napoleon if he were given his proper title, the nephew of Napoleon I and therefore the Bonaparte pretender to the throne of France. This was the man with whom Roderic had been closeted since dinner.

She gave him her hand, curtsying as he bowed above it. He did not release her fingers, but stood holding them in a gentle grasp as he stared at her. She looked at him just as frankly as she tried to decide what business he could have with Roderic. He was not a prepossessing-looking man, being of no more than medium height with narrow shoulders and thin brown hair with a slight wave in it. His mustache and small beard were neatly trimmed, and he wore a dark brown frock coat and tan waistcoat with charcoal trousers. His best feature was his eyes. Dark and liquid, hooded as if to conceal his thoughts, they held a steady determination.

"Enchanted . . . Chère, is it not?"

"I had no idea you were in France, Your Highness."

"Nor does anyone else. I am still, as I have been for some years, persona non grata here, thus my departure by the back door. It would be flattering, this great fear of me, if it weren't so inconvenient."

From the corner of her eye, she noticed the quick, hard gesture with which Roderic replaced his dagger. He was scowling as he watched the two of them. She said to Louis Napoleon, "You will be in danger then. I must not keep you."

"Yes." He gave a sigh of regret. "I suspect that if you should, it would be worth the risk."

He was a gallant with an eye for a lady; there could be little doubt of that. Still, he was so charmingly diffident about it that he failed to cause alarm. It would be easy, she thought, for a woman to be lulled into a false sense of security by him. She smiled. "Permit me to wish you Godspeed."

"I suppose you must. A pity."

Roderic, watching them, slowly forced himself to loosen his grip on the dagger. It would not do to spill the blood of the Bonaparte pretender all over his own doorstep. He recognized what ailed him with something less than riotous humor. Jealousy. How could it have come upon him so quickly? How could it have happened at all when he was armored against it by cynicism and suspicion? *How* was no longer important. He had allowed a woman without a name to creep under his skin, to burrow toward his heart. She would have to be plucked out because she was nameless no longer.

Mara, he thought, trying out the syllables in his mind against the reality of her before him, and wondered if he had spoken aloud when she sent him a quick, nervous glance. No, they were waiting for him to move, to play the host by showing his guest out through the servants' entrance. Without a word he indicated that Louis Napoleon was to precede him, then followed the other man quickly down the stairs.

Mara did not go to bed. She paced up and down, trying to make some sense of what was happening around her. Roderic was a prince, the heir to a throne, and must be presumed to have a vested interest in seeing that monarchy as a form of government was preserved in Europe. He was also a trained fighter with expertise in the protection of royal heads of state—or else in their removal. Through his house trooped radical republican elements, members of the French court, legitimists who would like to see a Bourbon return to the throne in the person of the comte de Chambord, and now Louis Napoleon, the bright hope of the Bonapartist faction. Roderic seemed to have no loyalties, no purpose, and yet he worked diligently at the gathering of information. Why?

Soon there was to be a ball with King Louis Philippe in attendance. Roderic must be there, must be in a certain place as the king entered. Why?

Why? The question was driving her mad.

If by some miracle she played her appointed part and Roderic was where he was supposed to be at the given time, what happened then would be on her head. She would be the cause. That, too, preyed on her mind.

If he was not there, if nothing happened, then her grandmother would be hurt, perhaps killed. This threat was with her constantly.

It might have been an hour later that Juliana pounded on the door, then opened it and looked in around the edge. "Good, you're still dressed. Come on! Hurry!"

"What is it?"

"They're having a race!"

"Who?"

"The cadre, of course. On the Seine. Bring your cloak!"

Mara came to her feet. "They must be mad."

"Drunk, at least so I think."

The last was muffled as Juliana withdrew her head and pelted away down the corridor. Mara hesitated only a moment. Anything was better than the ceaseless round of her thoughts. Snatching her cloak from the armoire, she ran after Juliana.

The night was cold, the streets slick with dirty, half-melted snow that turned to streaks of black diamonds in the glow of the lanterns. Bundled in furs, buttoned into woolen overcoats, the guests slipped and slid on their way to the carriages lined up outside the house. A few coachmen were exercising their horses, tooling them up and down the streets to prevent damage from standing in the cold, so everyone piled into the few that were available for the short ride to the river's edge. They started out in excitement aided by quantities of wine, but the chill ride along the dark streets, through the Place de la Bastille with its column towering into the night sky to where the Pont d'Austerlitz arched across the Seine, dulled their enthusiasm. They wound up cursing their unpredictable host, though even then they shook their heads in laughing admiration. One never knew what Roderic would be at next: He was a mercurial prince, was he not? So different from the stolid and stiff-rumped bores at court!

There was no clear consensus about the cause of the race. It appeared to have evolved from a discussion of boating on the Elbe in Prussia, but whether it was the result of a wager, a challenge, or sheer high spirits, no one seemed to know. There was no apparent ill-feeling involved, and yet the men were to be divided into two teams, one headed by the prince, one by the Prussian.

The Seine was the lifeblood of Paris, its main roadway. On its green brown waters rode much of the commerce of the city, some of it carried by small luggers and thick-waisted barges, but most by narrow boats with square sterns and sharply pointed prows that could shoot easily back and forth under the arches of the many bridges. These smaller crafts were usually controlled by one man with a sweep oar in the stern, though sometimes another man wielded another oar in the prow. They were individually owned, though the fathers and grandfathers of the boatmen may have plied just such skiffs for generations. These boats were moored at night in small flotillas here and there along the river, but especially near the quays upriver where the incoming ships docked. Roderic and the cadre had gone on ahead of the others to wake the sleeping boatmen and to drive a bargain for the use of four of the crafts.

The boats were waiting under the bridge. Each was double-manned with an oar in both the stern and the prow. The cadre had drawn lots to settle the pairing of the teams. The Prussian and Estes were in the first boat, and Michael and Trude in the second, forming the first team. Roderic would be rowing with Jared, and Luca with Jacques, for the second team. Their course of something less than two miles would take them down a straight stretch of the river to where the waters divided to pass around twin islands in the river, the Île Saint-Louis and Île de la Cité. There the boats would separate, the first team going to the right, the second to the left. They would converge again past the point of the second island for the straight stretch sweeping toward the Pont Royal. The first to emerge from under this last bridge would be declared the winner.

They had gathered a crowd. There was a great deal of banter between the boats and the shore. Underneath the bridge a trio of *grisettes* were tearing the flowers and veiling from their hats, flinging them at Jacques and Jared. The twins were flirting with ready wit, at the same time tucking the makeshift favors here and there about their persons. Estes also joined the fun. The others ignored the pretty seamstresses.

Juliana jumped down from the carriage and ran to the bridge railing. "Roderic!" she called down to the men milling about the bobbing crafts below. "I want to go with you!"

"To risk the damp embrace of the Seine? It is not a consummation to be wished. Our respected father would damn it, and rightly so." His voice floated up, rich and clear and insouciant. His face in the light of the lantern that hung at each prow was pale, but his eyes were bright, too bright. He was not sober.

"He isn't here."

"An unassailable argument. What of the handicap?"

"If it matters that the numbers are uneven, then Chère can go with the other team."

"Fair burdens, both. Shall we see which lady cries quarter first?"

It would not, Mara thought in tight disdain, be her. If it had not been for that slur, she might have refused. The water below the bridge moved black and swift in the night, treacherous with its ripples and wavelets and strings of bubbles whispering of uncertain currents. Here and there along the section of the course that stretched before them was the feeble gleam of lanterns and gaslight street lamps striking across the river's width, but they served only to highlight the windy darkness. From the water rose the sour, oily smell of ancient mud. The boats thudded against the piers of the bridge, oars creaked as the rowers tried to hold them in place. She hoped she did not lack courage, but joining the men in this midnight race did not appeal to her.

"You heard him, we can go. Come on," Juliana cried. Catching Mara's arm, the other girl half dragged her toward the steps that led down to the footpath under the bridge.

The boats were maneuvered to the water's edge. Juliana climbed into her brother's boat, and Mara was taken aboard that of the Prussian. They seated themselves in the middle so that the weight would be evenly distributed. Once more the skiffs took their places under the bridge.

Quiet descended. The boats rose and fell, and the cold wind whistled around the stone piers of the bridge. The water made a chuckling, ruffling sound. The faces of the men were ghostlike in the faint glow of the lanterns. Michael and Trude were dutifully, grimly ready. Estes, with the Prussian, appeared huddled against the chill but willing, while the crown prince was merely impatient. Luca and Jacques were poised now; the twin, like his brother, turning his attention to the task ahead. Roderic spoke a soft order or two, but sat relaxed and competent, replete with concentration that was unimpaired by the least sign of inebriation. They waited.

Above them came a flare of orange light as a torch was lighted. The voice of the elder Dumas rang out in some eloquent speech, the words of which were lost in the windy night. Then, with fine dramatic timing, the torch was tossed from the bridge above. It flared as it fell, smoking, then was extinguished by the water. The boats surged from under the dark shadow of the bridge. The race had begun.

Like whales leaping free, heavily falling, like horses springing out of a farmyard gate into summer's green pastures, the boats, thrust by strong backs and hard, knotting muscles, plowed the waters of the Seine into splashing furrows as they raced with the stream down the course. The oars shrieked and groaned and thudded, digging into the water, throwing spray into the air. The river gurgled and hummed. The men shouted in jubilance and fierce competition as they strained, grunting, into the oars. Behind them on the bridge the cheers of the prince's guests soared, then faded quickly as the crafts swept away.

Neck to neck, the boats held their positions as the

rowers beat the river. Now one, then another, eased forward, fell back, separated by only the lengths of the oars. The wind created by their passage flapped their cloaks and tore at their hair. The outflung droplets fell like rain, splattering onto their heated faces and mingling with the dew of sweat.

The shouting died away. Along the quayside streets on either side appeared the shapes of fast-moving carriages as the guests tried to keep up with the boats. Men hung out of the windows, waving their hats, or else yelled from the coachmen's boxes where they had taken seats to see better.

It settled down to a hard contest. The face of the Prussian in the rear of Mara's boat was set in bulldog grimness. Estes grimaced with each pull, but kept to the same unrelenting pace as the crown prince. Roderic's face, in the light of the boat lantern across the way, was reckless in its gaiety, yet concentrated. He lifted his voice and began to sing, a ribald sea chantey that held a strong and steady rhythm. Jared, Jacques, and Luca, the other members of his team, took it as their mark and pulled together with smooth, hard-bellied strokes.

Within moments the boats began to pull apart, dividing to take the separate channels of the river. Notre Dame with its flying buttresses bulked ahead of them like some ancient squatting stone spider. The boats swept around it, and the night was suddenly quiet as the wind died, blocked by the stone building. The quay on their left was high, a wall of stone brought nearer as the arm of the river narrowed. Above it rose the tall houses of Paris, their windows dark and sightless, the shops on the lower floors closed and with awnings rolled up.

They pulled on in a stone-lined tunnel of dank and black night, the lantern bobbing up and down spreading yellow-orange light on the luminous water ahead of them. The men pulled until the veins stood out in their temples and their breathing grew bellow's deep and gasping, and they had no thought for anything except the next pull, the next breath, the slow-moving turn of the river.

On her seat Mara braced against the regular tugs of the oars and strained her eyes to see ahead. Her thoughts were on the others racing around the opposite side of the islands, nearest to the Right Bank; thoughts harried by distrust. There might be none who could remember how this race had come about, but she would be willing to wager that there was one who knew it well. Roderic, drunk or sober, did nothing without a purpose. If he was racing down the Seine at this moment, it was for a reason. What was it? What was he doing?

Ahead of them appeared gray rags of fog. It drifted on top of the water, swirling, curtsying around them as they struck through it. It grew thicker, and the light of the prow lantern reflected from it, turning it into a dirty and opaque curtain. It hung close, stifling sound, making the world seem distant. When they rounded the point of the Île de la Cité, it lay like a snug coverlet over the width of the river with the Pont des Arts arching above it, an edging of iron lace. And slicing through it, skimming like red-eyed gulls, were the skiffs of Roderic's team, a boat length ahead.

The Prussian cursed, and the boat in which Mara sat leaped forward. It began to close the distance between it and the leaders, but it left behind the boat driven by Michael and Trude. Finally it drew even. For long moments, the three boats held steady, then slowly the other boat of Roderic's team, the one carrying Luca and Jacques, began to fall back. The Pont des Arts swept past overhead. Driven by the river's flow and the heat of the race, the two leading boats moved slowly closer together. The Pont Royal loomed ahead of them, a mass of stone pierced by five fog-filled arches. In a line upon it were the carriages of the guests who had raced ahead to watch the end of the race. The carriage lanterns shone like rubies as the fog wreathed up and around them.

The barge came from the right. It was drifting with the current, rolling low and sluggish in the water, dead in front of them. There was no one on it; it had broken loose from its moorings. Arvin led to the left to pass it by, guiding the boat with his rear oar.

They were going to miss the barge, but Roderic did not have enough room. The Prussian, instead of veering away from the drifting barge enough to allow both boats to pass, was holding to his narrow course. He was going to force Roderic to give way or else collide with the barge, and even so only desperate measures would prevent Roderic's boat from crashing head-on into it.

"Dear Lord, among unpalatable choices," Roderic said, the words coming clear over the water, "I turn like a needle without its magnet. I give it back to you, Arvin."

He made no move to check, but instead bore down harder upon his oar, turning his boat, which was slightly in the lead, toward that of the Prussian. And abruptly it was the choice of Crown Prince Arvin whether to widen the gap to let the prince of Ruthenia's boat through or to ram it.

It was Estes, cursing under his breath in the prow, who chose, overriding the control of Crown Prince Arvin to send the prow of the boat wide with his own oar. Arvin, rage on his heavy features, counteracted with a sweep of his rear oar, but the other boat shot through the opening Estes had made, with Jared and Juliana cheering and Roderic singing a soft song in grunts through his teeth as he lay into his own sweep.

But that vicious counterthrust of the Prussian swung the boat, with Mara crouched in it, across the current. The river caught it, sweeping it around and plunging the stern toward the barge. The wooden hull slammed into the heavier craft. Its planking cracked with a sound like breaking eggshells, and it was sucked half under the barge. The water poured over the side, filling the bottom so that it was dragged down like a leaf in an open sewer. The lantern died, hissing. Mara sprang to her feet with water halfway to her knees, and an instant later she was dumped headfirst into the river.

Cold, cold. The water snatched her breath and turned her cloak and skirts that billowed up around her into a smothering, enveloping shroud. She went down and down, slowly turning, numb to the bone. Her lungs began to burn, her brain shook off the shock with a silent scream, and she kicked upward, fighting to free her arms of the clinging, waterlogged cloth. Her head broke the water and she gasped, choking, opening her eyes to see. She had been carried under the barge to the other side.

She could not swim. She could keep her head above water for a few short minutes by frantically kicking and moving her arms, but she knew that her strength would not last long, especially with the heavy weight of sodden material that was her clothes dragging her down. She was being carried by the river, a piece of human flotsam. She could not see the others and knew that they must be somewhere behind her. She had no strength to look, however, no dependence on them to save her, not when there were Crown Prince Arvin and Estes to be picked up, too.

Ahead of her was the bridge. The guests of the prince were screaming and calling out. Did they see her? She could not tell; it was dark and the river was wide. But there was a supporting pier for one of the arches moving fast toward her.

She struck it with stunning force. Pain flared white-hot along her side, but she reached to catch at the pier's dark solidity. Her numb fingers slid along the stone, which was slick with a vile growth. Her nails broke as she clawed at it, reaching higher. Then she struck clean stone. Her grip caught, held. She clung, coughing, her breath harsh and hollow in her ears.

She could not keep her hold for long. She was so heavy there in the water with the river pulling at her, and her fingertips had no feeling. She had a curious sensation of warmth in her feet and legs and knew with an edge of horror that it meant her body was beginning to freeze from the icy water. It was dark under the bridge, even darker than it had been out there upon the river. In a moment she would loosen her grasp and slip away into even greater darkness. Still she clung obstinately, delaying the moment, hanging by her fingers with her cheek cushioned on slimy stone and her eyes closed.

There was a splash beside her. A finger of fog touched her face, sending a tremor of peculiar feeling like warm pain through her. A corded support passed around her waist, easing the weight on her hands; still she would not let go.

"Rest, lean on me," Roderic said at her ear, his arm tightening about her.

"No."

"Pride or prudence? Listen carefully, *ma chère,* and heed me well: There is no fate worse than death, none. Nor, I swear it, is there one worse for me than that I should lose you without ever knowing you."

They were still, riding there in the bone-chilling water with their numb bodies pressed close. Then Roderic swung away from her. He whistled a sweet, shrill sound.

There came the thump and squeak of oars, and a boat pulled toward them. Strong and hard, the grasp of the prince took Mara's weight, and, sighing, she surrendered. She was held for a brief instant, then sent surging up out of the water. Hard hands reached for her, pulling her with rough competence over the gunwale into the boat. The small craft rocked as Roderic heaved himself over the side, then the two of them were tumbled together in its bottom, lying in a welter of algae and fishy-smelling water under Roderic's uniform jacket as Luca and Jacques pulled for the quay.

A carriage stood waiting as Roderic carried her up the steps. At the door he paused and turned to face his guests, who crowded around, staring, exclaiming, asking questions in wondering voices. His face was shaded with weariness and distaste as he spoke.

"The evening has come to an end. You may go."

CHAPTER

9

The carriage ride back to Ruthenia House was cold and racketing and endless. Mara huddled within her clammy clothes, shuddering with her teeth clenched, trying not to lean too heavily upon Roderic, who held her. It seemed wrong to take his warmth, given in charity, for her own need. Wrong, too, to inflict her nearness upon him when it would not be pleasant for him. She would have clung to him to share her own meager warmth if he had needed it, but he did not. Perhaps because of strong brandy, his exertions at the oar, and his efforts to find her in the water, he came near to steaming with wet heat. The water ran from his hair, oozing from the gold strands he had slicked back with his fingers, dripping from his nose and chin. He seemed not to notice.

"What—what about Estes and Crown Prince Arvin?" she asked.

"They follow with Michael and Trude, who picked them up. Estes, being somewhat excitable, hasn't stopped talking. Arvin does not speak."

"I h-hope you're happy."

He looked down at her. "Should I be?"

"As a bird in May, tra-la. You f-forced the crown prince to expose his weakness, the n-need to win at all costs."

"But, admit it, if there had been no weakness, if he had displayed gallantry by allowing my team a fair and equal chance, he would now be in a position to offer terms as the man who accepted defeat rather than risk the injury of his beloved and her brother."

"Did you arrange the b-barge?"

"What a conniver you make me! Do you think I did?"

"I am trying to d-decide." It was growing harder to prevent her chattering teeth from interfering with her speech. She clasped her arms tighter across her chest.

"What would you prefer, a man who seizes the chance of the moment or one who makes his own?"

"W-what has what I prefer to do with it?"

"You haven't thought. I put you in the boat with Arvin."

She looked at him, straining to see his shadowed face in the dimness lit only by the outside carriage lantern. "Another test, a double one? Enlighten m-me: Did I pass or fail?"

"I am convinced that you are not Arvin's tool."

"Did you think I was?"

"You arrived so close together," he said apologetically.

"I don't believe you thought any such thing!"

"Don't you?"

She did not, but she saw with disturbing clarity that, for all his pretense of wry amusement, he had some concern. She asked, "Do I look like a Prussian?"

"No, and the efficacy of annoyance is such that neither do you now look like a half-drowned kitten or sound like one."

They had drawn up in the entrance court of the house. He stepped down and helped her out. But though his answer had been light, dismissive, she was not deceived.

He had not made his oblique accusation to rouse her to warming anger. That had not been it at all.

She had half expected him to carry her into the house. Instead he went ahead, and the quiet acerbity of his orders could be heard as she slowly mounted the stairs to the entrance gallery with her cloak trailing water over the marble. She started along the gallery toward her suite of rooms, but, at the St. Andrew's cross, found her path blocked.

"There is, of long habit at this time of night, a bath waiting in my dressing room," Roderic said. "Sarus is adding hot water. I make you free of it."

The thought of a hot bath was like balm. She drew herself up. "It's kind of you, but I will wait until one is prepared in my own rooms."

"I cannot permit it. Be sensible."

"I am all sensibility. You don't want me in your apartment, therefore I will not make you suffer my presence."

The others were arriving; there was the sound of wheels on the cobblestones at the entrance and raised voices. His voice light, almost pleasant, Roderic said, "Do you enjoy being carried here and there like a sack of flour from the mill? I am willing to oblige, but it would be helpful if I could know you like it."

"Don't be absurd!"

"Then come into my dressing room now."

There was in his voice that soft edge she had heard before when he addressed the cadre, a promise of sure retribution for denial or challenge. It would be childish to pit her will against his merely for the sake of defiance. She was well aware that if for some reason he wanted her in his rooms, he was capable of placing her there. In any case, though she had no idea whether his motives were anything other than altruistic, it would be foolish of her to miss the opportunity of furthering the task she had been given. Besides, the shuddering of deep chill was returning to rack her body once more.

"V-very w-well," she said, and, holding her head high in spite of that betraying tremor, moved into the antechamber that led to his apartment.

The dressing room was a small chamber adjoining the bedchamber, small so as to be more easily warmed by the fire that leaped and spat in the hearth. The bathtub was of the style known as a hip bath, of porcelain on copper painted with a design of ivy and with a high back for reclining while sitting in it. Thick Turkish toweling was laid out on a rack, with a cake of red brown sandalwood soap in a crystal dish attached to the tub's rim. On a nearby chair lay a robe of deep blue velvet cuffed in white and embroidered with a crown on the pocket. A tall floor candelabrum held six candles, the only illumination in the small room.

Mara turned in a shower of drops from the hem of her cloak, waiting for the prince to leave her alone. He closed the door behind him instead and advanced upon her. He stopped before her, his gaze contemplative. She stared up at him with perplexity in her face and the purple shadows of sleeplessness and exhaustion under her eyes. With steady hands he reached to unfasten her cloak, dropping its sodden weight to the floor, then began to probe the straggling mass of her wet hair for its few remaining pins.

"What are you doing?"

"Performing a service."

"Lila will help me, if you will send for her."

"It will be quicker if I do it."

His voice was beguiling, the warmth of the fire a sap upon her will. Summoning a tart tone, she said, "Not necessarily."

"You doubt my experience?"

"Your motives."

"Oh, they are the purest." He drew his splayed fingers

through the black silk of her hair, spreading it over her shoulders, then put his hands on her upper arms to turn her back to him. She felt his touch at the hooks of her gown.

She should stop him. Or so a part of her insisted. She would if she could find the strength. She did not understand him, did not trust him. He was a complex man, one difficult to become close to and so difficult to know. She had learned only a little and that little made her afraid. Now she was trembling not just from the cold.

His movements were deft and sure upon the hooks. His fingers brushing along her backbone were warm and gentle; still, her skin was so sensitive that each light touch left a stinging sensation in its wake. She stood unmoving, with her head bowed in unconscious grace, until she felt the tug as he began to unlace her corset.

She flinched and tried to step away, but he snaked a hard arm around her waist, quickly loosening the corset strings and releasing the tapes of her petticoats. Only then did he release her. She whirled from him.

Reading the accusation in her eyes, he said, "Inconsistency, thy name is woman. Or did I dream that sweet seduction two nights ago?"

"It had no appeal for you then. Why now?"

"A fallacy. The appeal was there."

Two nights ago there had been something that restrained him. It did so no longer. What had changed in the interval? Horror crept with the rise of gooseflesh over Mara's body as suspicion rose inside her. Was it possible that he knew?

A distant knock sounded on the bedchamber door beyond the dressing room. Roderic glanced in that direction. His voice pleasant but exact, he said, "That will be Sarus. I will be out of the room for a few short minutes while I consult with him. When I return, I expect to find you in the bath, or I will strip you naked and put you there."

He meant it. There was not the least doubt in her mind of that. She stood for an instant balancing against pride and fear her need for warmth and the hard necessity of insinuating herself into the good graces of this man. There was no choice. In haste she slid from her waterlogged clothes, stepping from the oozing pile of them into the steaming water in the hip bath. Shuddering from reaction, she crouched down so that the water rose to her shoulders. Her wet hair spread in the water, fanning out, forming a screen like fine black lace over the pale white globes of her breasts. She wrapped her arms about her body, closing her eyes as she bent her head. She had not known how cold she was until she felt the water's warmth, but, even so, the chill inside her was greater.

"Here, drink this."

She looked up to find Roderic standing above her. Under one arm was a pair of folded blankets, while in his other hand he held a small silver tray. On the tray were two deep silver cups filled with a liquid from which steam rose in small eddies.

"What is it?" It smelled alcoholic.

"God and Sarus know. Drink it."

Even the thought of something warm was reviving. She reached to take a cup from the tray and brought it to her lips. She sipped, then choked on a brew so vilely strong that she could not breathe. He had moved away. There was no place to set the cup down without rising to expose herself.

"It tastes," she said on a gasp, "like every known liquor stirred together with sugar and heated."

"A fairly accurate description of a seaman's punch."

"Take it away." She held the cup out to him.

"Empty only."

She thought of throwing it, then turned her gaze instead to measure the distance to the fire. It should make a merry blaze with so much alcohol.

"There would still be mine," he said as if he had read her mind exactly. "You need it worse than I do."

"If this is yet another attempt to warm my blood with annoyance, then it's succeeding!"

He surveyed her flushed face and the anger sparkling in her gray eyes. "What felicity. I meant only to chase the rheums of winter."

"Did you, indeed? And then?" She took another cautious sip.

"And then take my bath, if of course you can bring yourself to leave it?"

It was no answer. She sipped again as she considered it, lying back against the upswept end of the tub. Warmth was spreading from her stomach along her arms and legs. The tension, hard held, began to leave her. She was tired, so tired. Her brain could not seem to function, refused to come to bear on the problem of Roderic's volte-face. It hardly seemed to matter anymore. He had moved to stand somewhere behind her. From the sound she thought that he was putting more wood on the fire. The flames crackled and sputtered, filling the room with their orange light. The smell of smoke and hot candle wax was heavy on the air, along with the sandalwood scent of the soap that lay in its dish, warmed by the fire.

She put out her hand to pick up the soap, then, after another swallow of her punch, set her cup in the soap dish and began to bathe. She splashed the hot water over her to remove the soap residue, even rinsed the river water from her hair. Mindful of the heat leaving the water, she did not linger, but took up the toweling and got to her feet.

Roderic watched her from where he leaned against the mantelpiece; watched the water cascade, shimmering with the fire's glow, down the slender lines of her back and legs; watched her hair clinging in a dark silken mesh to the pearllike texture of her skin around her hips. He did not think that she had forgotten him, rather that she had accepted his presence as unavoidable and chosen to ignore it. It was not a pleasing conclusion, despite its advantages.

He drained his punch cup and set it aside, then reached to take up a blanket, shaking out the folds and holding it to the fire. As Mara finished towel-drying her hair, he stepped close to wrap the warm blanket around her.

"Thank you," she said, her voice low, and without expression. She did not look at him.

He made no answer, but swung from her and levered off his boots, at the same time unbuttoning his trousers. Mara, staring hard at the fire, heard him step into the water and begin his ablutions. Slowly and carefully, she seated herself in the chair before the fire and began to comb her hair with her fingers, spreading it to dry. She did not turn when after long moments she heard Roderic surge to his feet and dry himself with swift economy on the toweling she had discarded, nor when he leaned over to lift his robe from behind her. She started a little, however, when he went down on one knee beside her chair, reaching to close his fingers on the hanging curtain of her warm hair.

"Dry enough," he said.

"For what?" she asked, her throat tight.

"The purpose."

He came to his feet with easy power, picking her up from her chair with no more effort than he had used to lift the robe he wore. She caught her breath as he swung around with her toward the door and pushed through it into his bedchamber. Here, too, a fire burned, stretching fingers of light into the dark corners, glinting on the gilded crown surmounting the coat of arms high above the bed, dully shining in the white velvet and silk hangings depending from it. The great bed was turned down. Roderic put her, still wrapped in her blanket, on the yielding mattress, then slid in beside her. He stretched his arm out for the thick down coverlet, drawing it up around them, then lay back on one elbow, a detached expression in his dark blue eyes as he looked at her there in his bed.

"Why?" she asked through dry lips, whispering the one question that consumed her.

"I am God's own jester, a creature formed, pure, of curiosity and self-immolation. What other reason could there be?"

"Many, I fear."

"Later there may be, but not tonight. Go to sleep—Chère."

When Mara awoke, the pale sun of winter was edging around the drapes at the windows, lighting the room. The fire under the marble mantel had died to blackened ash and the bedchamber was cold. The bed where she lay was warm, but she was alone in its vast and regal expanse.

She pushed herself up. Her hair was a wild tangle and she flung it back over her shoulder. She reached out to touch the cool linen where Roderic had lain. Her blanket fell away, and abruptly she felt her nakedness, knew it deep inside her with a sense of peculiar abandon. At the same time, she was aware of unease. She had slept the night through in the bed of the prince and nothing had happened. What was the matter with her that she was still untouched? She was grateful naturally; certainly she had no wish to rush upon her fate. Still, she was female enough to be piqued that he could so easily resist her charms.

There came a soft sound from the salon. Mara snatched her blanket into place. An instant later, the door opened. It was Lila who eased into the room. In her hands she held a tray containing a pot of chocolate and a plate of rolls, while over her arm was Mara's underclothing, freshly laundered, and her garnet-red dress. The maid put the tray on Mara's knees, then turned to lay out her garments.

Mara did not question how the woman knew where she was to be found; it was an accepted fact that servants always knew everything. No doubt Roderic, with his usual thorough organization, had ordered breakfast and a change of clothing brought to her.

"Where is the prince?" she asked.

"He has gone out, mademoiselle. I know not where."

There seemed nothing to be done except to drink her chocolate, eat her rolls, and go about her day in the pretense that nothing had changed. In truth, she was not sure that it had.

Dressed, and with her hair in a neat coronet of braids, Mara left the bedchamber. On her way through the salon she paused, noting the remains of Roderic's breakfast and the strewn remnants of his morning post, including three crumpled newspapers and a pile of hand-delivered cards of invitation. Among the latter she caught sight of an envelope of thick, heavy paper. She moved closer, extracting it by a corner from the pile of discards. It was, as she had expected, the invitation from the Vicomtesse Beausire. Roderic, all too obviously, did not expect to attend.

She had to do something. The knowledge remained with her throughout what was left of the morning and into the afternoon. She could not be distracted from it for long. The news that the crown prince of Prussia, sneezing at every breath from a fresh and virulent head cold, had left Paris for good held only momentary interest. Juliana's escapade of going riding in the wilds of the Bois du Boulogne for four hours with only Luca for protection failed to upset her. A crisis in the kitchen brought about by the delivery of a large order of tripe, instead of the expected veal, was an irritant handled without engaging more than the surface of her attention. The arrival of an officious little man with a large bundle who demanded to see Sarus and remained closeted in Roderic's chambers with the majordomo for two hours was only a matter of mild regard. The only thing that exercised her mind as the evening advanced into night was wondering where Roderic had gone and what he would do when he returned.

The first thing he did was to speak to his sister behind closed doors, an interview that Juliana emerged from white-faced and tight-lipped, but with apologies to Luca for expecting him to bear the responsibility of being her sole protector. The second thing he did was to send word to the kitchen that he would dine in his apartment with service for two. The third action was to send for Mara.

Her heart began to pound as she received the summons in her bedchamber. Was this the moment? She was glad that she had bathed early and redone her hair in an upswept style with a waterfall of curls down the back. She wished that she had something else to wear, some of the lovely gowns that were at this moment hanging in the armoire at her cousin's house. The gown she had on was becoming, but it lacked the advantage of novelty since the prince had seen her in it several times.

There was no point in repining. And none in anticipating by thinking of the lovely embroidered underwear she owned, made for her by the nuns in New Orleans. Roderic might well require nothing but a companion for his evening meal.

The food had been placed in the salon on a small table drawn up before the fire with a chair on either side. The firelight danced in the wineglasses and reflected red-gold from the silver. Roderic stood beside the table with his hands clasped behind his back and his feet slightly spread. His uniform coat was speckless, luminously white, slashed by bars of turquoise edged in braiding of gold thread. His hair was damp, falling forward in a glinting curl, as if he had not long come from his bath. His gaze was pensive as he watched her approach.

"I told Sarus that we would serve ourselves," he said as he moved to hold a chair for her. "Do you mind?"

"Not at all."

She sent him a quick upward glance and found herself suddenly conscious of how isolated she was here in this wing of the house with him. The others were in the public dining room some distance away. Even if she called out, it was doubtful that they would come. She was nothing to them, a woman without a name, while the man beside her was their prince. An odd frisson ran along the surface of her skin, and she had a sudden vivid memory of herself, blanket enwrapped, being carried in his arms. She wondered again, as she had so often before, if she had some minor portion of her mother's second sight, some ability to read the thoughts of others. At this moment she did not want to think so.

Roderic saw that small betraying tremor and was satisfied. A guileless innocent this woman might not be, but neither was she accustomed to being alone with a man. His first impulse, very nearly exercised the night before, to take her by force into his bed, keeping her there until she confessed precisely who she was and what she wanted, would not be necessary. It had, he suspected, been driven more by disappointment and rampant desire than considered design. There were other, more subtle ways to achieve the same purpose. They might take longer, but he was in no hurry.

Mara. Marie Angeline Delacroix, a visitor to France, staying with a cousin. On terms of friendship with de Landes, a man with ambition and flexible loyalties. Luca's report, made the day before, had contained that much, but no more. The reason for the alliance was plain; it would be no accident that Mara was his mother's goddaughter. De Landes would wish to make use of the relationship. The purpose of the charade in his house, which had resulted from the alliance, was obscure, as was the reason Mara was lending herself to it. Neither would remain so for long.

Mara ate and drank, but the food she put in her mouth might as well have been the despised tripe and the fine wine mere *vin ordinaire.* She could think of little to say to the man across the table from her. He seemed remote, preoccupied with his own thoughts, and yet she felt that there was nothing she did, no smallest movement she made, that he did not see. It was unnerving.

Roderic finished his meal and tossed his napkin aside. Mara pushed her food about a little longer, then put down her fork. Roderic smiled, a caressing movement of his lips.

"You ate very little."

"I wasn't hungry."

"You feel well? No effects from . . . the accident?"

"No, no, nothing like that."

"Good." He rose, holding out his hand. "Come, I have something to show you."

His clasp was warm and firm. He drew her toward the bedchamber door and pushed it open, guiding her inside. She moved a few paces into the room, then stopped, her eyes widening.

The air in the bedchamber, warm from the effects of a blazing fire, was heavy with the fragrance of Parma violets. The deep blue-purple flowers were everywhere: in small vases on the mantel, nestled among ferns in silver filigree holders lying on a low table; scattered in profusion across the floor. But most of all they were pinned to the new hangings of sheer violet silk that had been hung as under draperies on the royal bed and strewn over the cream silk sheets. On a chair, delicately placed, was a nightgown of white lace as fine as cobwebs and no more concealing, and on the monogrammed case of lace-edged silk that covered the fluffy down pillow on one side of the bed was a blue-velvet-covered box in the shape of a seashell stamped with the emblem of the most exclusive jeweler in Paris, Fossin. The box stood open to reveal a parure of diamonds, including necklace, bracelet, and earrings, on a bed of white velvet.

Mara swung around to face Roderic. "What is this?"

"Naiveté, or even the pretense of it, is not the fashion. It must be obvious to you that this is nothing less than a scene for seduction."

"Mine or yours? I am compelled to ask because of what has passed between us before."

"Whichever you prefer," he answered, his smile guileless and singularly sweet.

She swallowed hard. "I thought you were determined to resist me, for my own good."

"Surrender is such an appealing luxury, one not often afforded me. I changed my mind."

"Inconsistency, thy name is man?"

It was a home thrust, more of one than she realized. Still, her wariness pleased him, for it showed her to be a worthy adversary. It also disturbed him more than he wanted it to. It had been a very long time since he had been uncertain as to the best way to handle a situation or a woman.

"I want you," he said, his gaze steady behind his spiked gold lashes as he spoke that simple truth. "Is there a better reason?"

She wanted him, too, and the pain of that desire was a knife turned against her. And yet the feeling that suffused her was regret. She had honored him for his scruples, for the ruthless self-abnegation of his will. He had put them aside with deliberation. It was a loss.

"I await your decision."

To seduce or be seduced. Was there any other choice? She could not see it. Oh, she might throw herself upon the mercy of the prince, beg his help in saving her grandmother. He would understand, she was sure, but there was no guarantee that he would act. He might well consider the safety of an elderly woman of less importance than swift retaliation against a proven enemy. Roderic was a man of many responsibilities, and there was more to this conspiracy against him than she had been told.

She did not think he would use physical coercion against her if she should decide to retreat even now, but she could not be sure. There was about him a sense of hard purpose that precluded certainty. But even if she had not come too far with him, there was the threat of de Landes to press her onward. The days were growing shorter, the ball coming nearer. She must act.

She had only to move closer to him, to put out her hands to touch him, and the deed would be done. Something held her back. It was not fear or physical reluctance, not embarrassment or even shyness, though she felt all of them. It was the exquisite courtesy of the prince, the end result of that grace and strength and fine control directed by lightning intelligence that she had seen used against others in the last few days. It struck her as being more cerebral than the occasion demanded. She mistrusted it, and him, but most of all she mistrusted her ability to guard herself against it. She recognized fully that though the choice had been left in her hands, he was not as neutral as he wished to appear. He meant to seduce her. The question was, why? And could she prevent him? Could she enthrall him instead?

He did not wait for her answer, but moved to the side of the bed and took up the velvet-covered box. Setting it on the bedstand, he took from it the magnificent necklace with its heavy, glittering diamonds.

She stepped back. "No, please."

"Are you afraid?"

"No." The softly spoken word had an uncertain sound.

He reached to place the diamonds around her neck, fastening the clasp. "Even if you were," he said, his warm breath stirring the silken hair at her temple, "to dare is to deny fear and to live."

"How could I fail to dare then?"

The necklace lay cold and heavy on her breastbone. Was it a bribe? If so, she could not afford to be insulted. He was close, so close. If she turned, she would be in his arms. It was imperative that she should do just that. And yet how could she? He was the prince, and there was about him all the power and burnished perfection of that title. With these things, as well as his stringent control of his men and himself, he did not seem quite mortal. It was unlikely then that he felt normal male desire, normal responses. For all her brave words, she was afraid. It was not simply a fear of the physical intimacy that must come, though that was daunting enough, but of how being so near to him would affect her in mind as well as in body. She could be changed; this she did not doubt. It was even possible that, like some maiden consorting with an unknown ancient god, she would be destroyed.

There was only one way to put that unreasoned fear to the test. Turning with the stiffness of a clockwork figure, she lifted her hands, placing her fingertips on the crisp white cloth of his uniform jacket and sliding them upward. His chest swelled with the sudden depth of his breathing. He cupped her elbows, drawing her nearer. She looked up and was snared in the blue fire of his gaze. Seeing the brightness that burned there, she discovered that, prince though he might be, his desire was intensely human.

He bent his golden head, and his lips, firm and smooth, gently enticing, touched hers. Blindly, she moved closer. His hands slid from her elbows along her upper arms to her back, drawing her nearer still as the kiss deepened. Her heart throbbed against her ribs while the blood ran swift and vibrant in her veins. Her breath was suspended in her throat. Her lips molded to his, infinitesimally clinging, and beneath her bodice and the warming weight of the diamond necklace her breasts swelled tight and full. The taste of his mouth was achingly sweet, endlessly entrancing. She eased her hands higher, clasping them behind his head, sliding her fingers through the short crisp curls that grew low on his neck. In her mind there was no thought except for the rich and unexpected pleasure of the moment.

His fingers at her back found the hooks of her gown. They made soft popping sounds as, one by one, he released them. A small quake of alarm touched her, but she subdued it, concentrating instead on the play of the muscles of his shoulders under his jacket as he worked. She wanted to touch his bare skin. The need was shocking but undeniable. Easing one hand between them, she began with experimental care to unhook the braided and frogged fastenings of his jacket.

Challis and cambric, broadcloth and linen, their clothing fell away, landing on the rug with soft, sighing whispers. Fluttering sleeves and firm folds, gently ruffled, stiffly starched, it piled one piece upon another, intermingling. Finally, they stood naked, bathed in the fire's glow and candlelight, their bodies gleaming, their senses reeling with the fragrance of voilets and their own clean scents, with unappeased lust and strained sensibilities.

"Ah, Chère, you are an unconscious man's dream of loveliness. Pray God I don't wake," he said, and reached to pinch out the candle flames.

Who was seducing whom? And did it matter? It did, of course, but not as much as the pulsating current of desire that held them. Mara turned toward the bed first, placing her knee upon that flower-strewn surface, sinking down among the violets upon the silken sheets that covered the feathered softness of the mattress. He joined her there, supporting himself on one elbow as he placed his hand on her abdomen. He spanned its narrow width easily with his long musician's fingers, which were calloused from swordplay. He studied her face with its suspended composure there in the firelit dimness, then, holding her gaze as long as possible, he leaned to taste the nipple of her breast, circling it with the grainy warmth of his tongue, taking it into the gentle adhesion of his mouth. He trailed kisses around that vibrant, contracted peak, journeying to the other to perform the same ritual. He brushed the valley between them with his lips and pushed aside the tumble of gems at her throat to trace its hollow with his tongue. He tested the pulse that beat hectically in the side of her neck, as if fascinated by its strength, before searing the turn of her jaw with his lips. He captured her mouth once more, exploring its moist inner surfaces, while at the same time, with consummate care, he allowed his hand to settle upon the small mound at the apex of her thighs.

She caught her breath as she felt that first touch there. There was no cause for alarm, however; he remained still except for the most tentative pressure and movement of one finger. A peculiar magic invaded her, spiraling downward to the center of her being. Involuntarily, she moved her hips so that she pressed against his hand, and slowly, gently, he began to caress her.

She was amazed and even a little frightened at the sensations that swept through her. In an instant she was glowing with internal heat and an odd, singing tension, snared in a voluptuous splendor. It did not seem possible that her body was her own, that she could feel so intensely while doing something that must be wrong. With tightly closed eyes and a small, inarticulate sound in her throat, she turned toward him. Still he held her, his fingers tirelessly, gently moving until her stomach muscles contracted in spasms, his mouth teasing her nipples into tight buds of anticipation.

Pleasure rippled through her in waves. She thought

that she could bear no more; still it came. His motions grew firmer, eased deeper between her thighs. She felt an exquisite probing, a slight though burning entry.

He went still. In some far corner of her mind, she realized that he had discovered the barrier of her virginity, or the remnants of it that were left after the rough exploration of Dennis Mulholland. It must not be allowed to make a difference since at this moment it made none to her. Sliding her hand in haste along his arm, she pressed his hand back upon her, at the same time twisting closer to him in an ecstasy of resolve and longing.

"Don't stop," she whispered. "Oh, don't, please."

Her flesh was moist and heated where he touched. He eased deeper, soothing, stretching, applying exquisite pressure until she moaned and turned her head from side to side on the pillow. She was melting, her body and spirit as liquid as hot candle wax. The need to take him inside her was beginning to feel like desperation. She longed to press the hollows and curves of her body upon him, closer and closer still, as if she could make him a part of her in that way.

She felt a tremor pass through the muscles of his arms and recognized the price he was paying in order to extend to her the care, the regard for her responses, the sensitivity to them that he had shown. These things were a part of him, not something he summoned for her alone; still, she was grateful.

Sliding lower in the bed, she reached to place her hand on his lean flank, drawing him toward her in unmistakable invitation.

He entered her by degrees, filling her tightness with the rigid length of himself, holding her close as she drew in her breath at the breaching of that narrow entrance. The instant of fiery pain eased almost before it had begun. As she relaxed, releasing the air pent-up in her lungs, he began to move within her in a rhythm as measureless as it was ancient. She rose against him, clinging, surrendering to the rapture. Boundless, gilded with firelight, it caught them and sent them striving together into the darkness.

The fire had sunk to a bed of black and red coals. The room was growing cool; still, Roderic made no move to reach for the covers. He lay propped against the headboard of the bed watching the woman who slept in exhaustion beside him. He had thought that once he had her in his bed he would be able to understand her. He was wrong. The smell and taste of her was in his nostrils and mouth like some exotic drug, her touch was on his skin like a brand. He had enjoyed her embraces, her astonishing responsiveness again and yet again through the past few hours. Still she eluded him. Still he was not satisfied. He did not like it.

An innocent seductress. Who would have thought it? He still could not quite believe the evidence he had himself discovered. It gave him a peculiar feeling inside to know that he had been the first, to think that she had given him such a gift of her own accord. He was honored, humbled, and exalted at the same time, but also wary. There had to be a reason. There had to be. It made no sense otherwise.

He could see the diamonds of the necklace he had given her shining, catching the faint light in their facets. It was intriguing there upon her nakedness, though it also seemed crude, too hard and glittering. It had been the wrong gift for her. He had been wrong also to seek to sway her with such a display, but he had thought to learn something by it. Instead he was left more disturbed. Why had she taken it? Why hadn't she thrown it back in his face as he had half expected?

He breathed a soft imprecation. He was allowing her to affect him far too much. He must take care.

Mara stirred, opened her eyes. She sat up straight,

staring at his dark shape there beside her in the dimness.

"Virginity is a commodity prized more by some than others; still, I am curious. Why didn't you tell me?"

"I . . . didn't see that it made any difference except to me."

"You thought I would have no interest?"

"Why should you? Unless to keep score?"

"That," he said softly, "was unworthy."

"It seems to me that the question is moot." She swung away from him to reach for the coverlet and draw it up over her.

"It might be less so if there is to be an enraged fiancé or father descending upon me at some time in the future."

"It hardly seems likely." The words were muffled. She thought briefly of her papa, far away in Louisiana. He could not help her, not now.

That elusive answer sent rage tumbling through his veins. He reached for her, catching her upper arms, dragging her warm nakedness against him. "Why?" he damanded through clenched teeth. "Why?"

"I don't know," she cried. "How can I? You're mad to ask!"

His anger faded as quickly as it had come. He eased her down so that she lay across his lap. There was a violet caught in her hair, and he reached to untangle its petals, twirling it in his fingers, brushing it across the tender surfaces of her lips. His voice pensive, he said, "Maybe I am mad, maybe I am, indeed."

Lowering his head, he crushed the violet against her mouth with his own.

CHAPTER 10

The pale winter sunshine falling through the panes of pastel-colored glass spilled circles of soft rose and aqua color over Mara as she paced up and down the main gallery. She was alone. Roderic had been called to a meeting at court. The others had dispersed on odd errands. There were no guests expected. She should have been relieved, happy to have a few moments to herself; instead she felt deserted.

She had need of the time in which to think, however. The plan could go forward now. She had achieved the goal set for her and must take advantage of it. The trouble was that she could not bring herself to concentrate on what must be done.

She had not thought a great deal about how she was going to persuade Roderic to attend the ball of the Vicomtesse Beausire. The problem of how she was to seduce him had loomed so large that she had not been able to see beyond it. Now the difficulties were all too obvious. Despite the glib assurances of de Landes that Roderic would be supremely cooperative once she had gained his bed, she could not believe her influence was any greater than it had been before. The prince found her desirable—

there could be little doubt of that after the night before—but it was ridiculous to think that he would permit her to dictate his movements.

The knowledge that she must in some way persuade Roderic to do her will, using what had passed between them, was distressing. It made her feel like a prostitute. It seemed, in fact, as if the betrayal was not of him, but of her own inner self.

The night she had shared with Roderic had been a revelation. She had not dreamed that she was capable of such abandon, such intense pleasure. The discovery was a gift, one that would be soiled if she used these newly awakened responses to ensure that she had her own way.

And yet she must. She could not escape that fact. Grandmère Helene's continued safety and health depended upon it. She must.

But how was she to bring up the subject of the ball, a ball of which she should be ignorant? What reason could she give the prince to persuade him that he should attend? How could she ensure that he would take her with him when she had no official status, was not included in the invitation? It was all very well for de Landes to speak of social occasions to which a man of position might bring his mistress, but her own impression of French society was that more discretion than that would be expected at any event attended by Louis Philippe, even of an unpredictable prince like Roderic of Ruthenia.

It made her head ache to think of it. What was she supposed to do? Would it be better to wait until some crucial moment, perhaps after making love, and speak wistfully of the brilliant social affairs she had heard of but could not remember having seen? Should she attempt to beg prettily for the honor of being escorted by a prince of the blood?

She could not do it.

Perhaps she might indicate in an oblique fashion that

an outing could result in recognition, a solution to the problem of who she was? Yes, that was a possibility since it was all too true. But could she do it without blushing for the hateful necessity? Without arousing Roderic's suspicions? She doubted it.

The bell pealed at the entrance below. Mara retreated hastily along the gallery to the private rooms at the end as a housemaid hurried past and down the stone stairs to open the door to the visitor. There was a murmur of voices and the tread of feet. A few minutes later the maid came to Mara.

"It is Monsieur Balzac, Mademoiselle Chère. I told him the prince is not at home, but he insists on speaking to you. I put him in the salon."

Mara thanked the girl and, running a hand over her hair, made her way back along the gallery to the public rooms where the writer waited. A footman opened the double doors for her, and she gave him a smile before passing through. Balzac stood at the far end of the room with his back to the small fire that blazed in the fireplace. He had taken an African orange from a bowl that sat on a table nearby and stood eating it out of his hand as one might an apple, rind and all.

"Ah, mademoiselle, forgive me that I do not kiss your hand," he said with a broad gesture and a genial smile, "but I am somewhat sticky with juice."

"Was there no fruit knife? I am sorry. I'll ring for one at once."

"No, no, I beg! There is no need. The good things in life are better for a touch of bitterness with them, a little difficulty in the consuming."

"Oh, but surely—"

"It isn't my theory alone. My friend Hugo sometimes eats the shell of the lobster as well as the meat; I myself have seen him. What jaws the man has, what teeth!

Formidable." He took another ferocious bite of his orange, crushing the seeds with gusto.

"As you like," Mara said, moving to sit on the settee. "I am sure the prince will be sorry to miss your visit."

"A fascinating man, the prince, and a stimulating conversationalist, but you are much more attractive to look upon, mademoiselle."

It was mere politeness, and Mara did not make the mistake of thinking it anything else. She inquired after the work in progress of the author and listened with sympathy to his tales of uncooperative characters, broken nights, and leechlike publishers. Beneath the crude, rough-hewn exterior, he was, she thought, a most sensitive man. She had been reading some of his tales and had been struck by his understanding of women. She told him so.

"How kind of you. How kind. They come to me, these women that I write about, like a vision of passion in the night. Women are ruled by this passion, by love. They are not encompassed by their egos as men are, and so can transform themselves, their lives, their very bodies, with passion. It is not the things man makes that have meaning in this world, but the family that a woman creates out of this enormous love."

"How odd to hear a man say such a thing."

"All men know it, those who can see," he said simply. "What else is marriage, but an attempt by men to harness that love for their own use, their own great need?"

"Yes," she agreed. Then, as an idea struck her, she continued, "Monsieur Balzac, you are a man who knows Paris and its people well. Would you say that it would be permissible for the prince to take his mistress with him, say, to the ball of the Vicomtesse Beausire?"

"Why should you wish to attend such a gathering? It will be altogether boring."

"I am serious."

"Ah." He gave a slow nod and, finishing his orange, wiped his hands on his handkerchief and moved to sit down beside her. "I regret to tell you that this is not my milieu. I have friends among the aristocracy, of course, but I do not move in those circles. You are disappointed?"

She ignored the question. "But you write about them as you have written about the poorest of Paris. You must know what is expected, what is allowed?"

"It is always true that the aristocrats extend to themselves greater freedom of action than do the bourgeoisie, the staid middle class so afraid of what people will think of them."

"That is not an answer," she said, her gaze steady and her voice stern.

He sighed. "You are a difficult woman. Yes, I suppose the prince could take you if he wished to do so. It isn't as if you are a celebrated courtesan. He could always pass you off as a distant relative if the need arose, if it was necessary to present you to the king, for example."

"Heaven forbid," Mara said fervently.

"That is the risk." Balzac shrugged his massive shoulders. "But why come to me with this problem? Why should you not ask the prince?"

"I wished to know if it was possible before I troubled him."

Balzac possessed himself of her hand and raised it to his lips. "I am sure he would not consider anything you asked as a trouble, mademoiselle. How could he?"

"Easily," she answered, her voice dry.

"You fear him?" Balzac asked, looking at her with a frown.

"No, no. But it is sometimes difficult to ask for things, especially when they are important to you. Don't you find it so?" She had said too much; she knew it the moment the words were out of her mouth. Perhaps it would not matter.

"You dislike the appearance of trading your favors for . . . privileges."

"I knew you would understand," she said, trying for an easy tone. Quickly, before he could comment further, she changed the subject.

They spoke of a number of things as the time slipped past. One by one the cadre returned, as did Juliana, looking very dashing in a riding habit that featured a *soubreveste* of black velvet with a gray cross outlined in braid on the chest in the style of the Gray and Black Musketeers of Louis XVIII. It was worn over a red jacket and with a hat made like a plumed helmet. Accompanying her were two poets whose names were lost in the hubbub and a disgruntled comte who followed her about like a dog guarding a particularly juicy bone. A short time later Roderic strolled into the room. He smiled at Mara across the room, saluting her with the glass of wine a servant placed in his hand.

Mara was just as happy that he made no attempt to come to her. She had not seen him since the early morning hours; she had been asleep when he left her. What she would say to him when they were face to face again, she had no idea.

She felt little different inside herself after her night with him. Oh, there was some soreness here and there, but nothing of importance. It had been so natural, so right, while it was happening, not the terrible ordeal she had been led to expect by the whispers and half-overheard remarks she had accumulated since childhood, or after her experience with Dennis's clumsy groping. Regardless, she felt changed, branded in some way. Overnight she had become the mistress of the prince. Many had suspected it; now it was true. Mistress. She had never thought to be that to any man.

More guests arrived until the room scarcely seemed able to hold them all. Mara, mindful of her duties as housekeeper and hostess, saw to the refreshments and circulated through the room. Juliana also moved here and there, talking in an effortless display of royal good manners to first one and then another. Roderic did the same.

Then, as if at some magic signal, the guests began to melt away as the hour for morning visits passed. Balzac took his leave, followed by the poets and the comte. The cadre retreated to the long gallery they had claimed as their own. There was only Juliana left in the salon when Roderic dropped down on the settee beside Mara.

"I am informed," he said, "that you desire above all things to go to the vicomtesse's ball."

She sent him a swift glance as the betraying color rose to her cheekbones. She was not ready for this, not ready at all. "I . . . suppose Monsieur Balzac told you."

"Most obligingly. He seemed to think that I would be delighted to hear how best to please you."

"He was wrong naturally."

"Now why should you think so? Scribes and thieves and braying asses may sometimes speak the truth. As it happens, he was right, though I find it passing strange that I should be read a homily on the delicate nature of women and the obligation of men to see to their dearest wishes, or that I should have to hear of your desires from him." He leaned back, stretching out his long legs and folding his hands upon his chest. "Why could you not have told me?"

"I . . . had no idea if it was even possible."

"So Honoré said. The question is, why does this affair appeal?"

She made a helpless gesture. "It will be a gala event."

Juliana joined them, taking a seat with a sweep of her habit skirt. "Why should it not appeal? The king will be there and everyone else of any consequence. Besides, Chère has done nothing except slave for you since you picked her up out of a ditch on a French hillside. She must be ready for some amusement."

"It is a great pity," Roderic said with a steady look toward his sister, "that Louis Philippe arranged the marriage of the duc de Montpensier to the Infanta Maria Luisa last year; Montpensier would have been about right for you. The comte de Paris is rather young, only seven, but he is the heir apparent, which makes up for other shortcomings. I must speak to our father about a match. Arvin's departure has left you in need of occupation—to keep you from interfering in what doesn't concern you."

Juliana lifted a brow. "I would take care how I mentioned marriage to Father. He might begin to look around him for a suitable princess for you."

"That Damocles sword has a coating of rust. He has had a list of possible alliances made since the day I was first presented, red-faced and squalling, by my nurse."

"You may have avoided the fate of princes, a loveless alliance, until now, but it will come to you. Like the poor little comte de Paris, you are the heir apparent."

"Your concern unmans me. Will you go so that I may speak to Chère in peace?"

"So you can persuade her that the last thing she wants is to attend a ball? No, indeed. I am of a mind for a little gaiety and music myself. You are altogether too dull here!"

"Are we, indeed?" Roderic asked, his voice soft.

Juliana sent him a look of quick alarm. "That was no challenge, I assure you! I believe Chère would benefit from an outing, and who knows? You might find someone who can identify this mystery lady for you."

"An object greatly to be wished," her brother answered, but his voice was without expression.

"That," Juliana said, turning to Mara, "was a capitulation, in case you did not recognize it. Now what are we to wear to this ball? We must decide at once and be off to the modiste if there is to be the least chance of having gowns made up in time."

It has been too easy. Mara had expected that she would have to use every wile that she possessed, to marshal every possible argument, even perhaps to plead. Instead, the compliance of the prince had been gained without effort. It was what she wanted, what she needed; the one thing that she must have. And yet the ease with which it had been gained left her apprehensive.

It was not like Roderic to change his mind so easily. He had not intended to honor the invitation to the ball. She could not think that he had deferred to her wishes purely for the sake of her embraces or because of the rallying comments of his sister. What, then, was his purpose?

She tried to scoff at herself, to tell herself that he had no purpose, that the image she had created of him—that of a man of diabolical mental perceptions—was no more than an illusion. It helped not at all. She could not rid herself of the suspicion that, instead of leading the prince into a trap, she herself was being enticed into yet another one.

The shopping expedition had been a success. Mara had been afraid that Juliana would insist on going to Madame Palmyre. For that reason, she had asked to be set down at Maison Gagelin first, and, once in the draper's shop, had sought out the shop assistant, Worth. She wished to consult him about the materials and colors of her gown, but most of all she wanted to expose Juliana to his views on overornamentation.

Worth had not failed her. He had brought out a sea-blue satin, heavy and stiff, for Juliana that had made her skin look as translucent as the finest china and given her eyes an incredible depth and sparkle. He had also made a hurried sketch of a gown with an elongated bodice that would make the most of her regal height and superb form without weighing her down with pounds of bows and rosettes or ruchings of lace and clumps of silk flowers.

For Mara he had recommended a delicate white silk chiné with a hint of pink in the folds and suggested a cunningly draped bodice that made her waist appear tiny, even less than its normal eighteen inches. He had also suggested a modiste, a former *grisette,* who could be trusted to cut the fine materials correctly and was not so busy that she would not be able to have the gowns ready on time. Since Juliana insisted, he had sold her several egret plumes to be dyed for a headdress to match her gown, but had convinced Mara that all she had need of was one or two pale pink rosebuds to set in her dark hair. When the Englishman with his intriguing accent had bowed them from the store, Juliana had pronounced him utterly charming and vowed to visit him again.

They had returned to the carriage and Juliana had given the order that would take them to a cobbler's shop that was known for its dancing slippers when Roderic's sister said, "You know, we should have brought Trude with us."

"You mean—"

"I mean it's time she stopped playing at being a man. There is a woman's body and heart beneath that uniform she wears. Surely she would like to go to a ball in something other than trousers?"

"She might. It's hard to say with Trude," Mara said.

"She isn't very open, I will admit, and is even less so with you, for obvious reasons."

"You mean because I am now sharing your brother's rooms," Mara said, determined not to spare herself.

"Of course," Juliana said with impatience. "She has followed Roderic about all her life, and he has permitted it because he is too fond of her to hurt her and also—let it be admitted—because she is useful to him. If she would only allow herself to be a woman, however, she might find that there are other men in the world."

"She might, indeed, but would she care?"

"We will never know if we don't do something to help her."

"It will take some persuasion," Mara said.

"I am good at that," Juliana answered in all simplicity.

"Yes. I haven't thanked you for asking Roderic to take you—us—to this ball."

"You think he did it for me?" Juliana shook her head, a bemused smile playing about her mouth. "What a very modest woman you are, Chère."

Mara sent her a quick glance, then looked away again. "Do you mind that I am your brother's woman?"

"Mind? What good would that do? But, no, you have been good for him. I can't remember ever seeing him quite so involved. Everything has always been so easy for him; he has looks, intelligence, strength, limitless ability, good birth, immense resources, a doting mother, a father who cares despite high expectations and the clash of their personalities. He has had a surfeit of women, of the kind who offer a token resistance or none at all; the kind who are so shallow a child can see through them. But you elude him. You have no past, no future, only the present. He cannot know you, cannot explore your mind, and so he is frustrated. It may be a pity for you to ever regain your memory."

Was Juliana suggesting that once he knew who and what she was, Roderic's attraction for her might disappear? It did not matter; she would be leaving him soon anyway, immediately after the ball. Still, the thought gave her a strange ache in the region of her heart.

Trude refused the ball gown. Standing at her full height, which topped Juliana by two full inches, she said, "I am a member of the cadre. What need have I for skirts to hide behind?"

"To hide behind!" Juliana exclaimed, incensed. "They are not for hiding, but to show that you are a woman."

"I am a woman, with or without them."

"Yes, but—"

"Let her be, if you please, Princess Juliana."

It was Estes who spoke. He had come to stand near them where Juliana and Mara had drawn Trude aside at one end of the long gallery.

Juliana turned on the Italian. "Then you speak to her! She has no idea what she is missing by never having danced or flirted or had an assignation at a ball."

"These things have no appeal to me whatever!" Trude said with a stiff gesture.

"Then you have become masculine beyond recognition. My brother has much to answer for."

"It isn't his fault. Not all women want these things. Not all women want admiration and flirtation."

"How can you know what you want if you have never had them!"

"I know. I am happy as I am."

"You don't know—"

"Your pardon, Princess Juliana," Estes tried again, his narrow face serious behind his beard. "It is you who don't know. Some women have other needs than yours, other satisfactions."

"Besides," Trude said, "what good could I do the prince hampered by skirts?"

"If you are doing this for his sake—"

"It is no sacrifice. It's a matter of duty, to Prince Roderic and to the cadre. They depend on me."

This was the source of Trude's pride, Mara thought; she was needed. It seemed to be enough, at least for now. In addition, Trude had gained a champion. For the Valkyrie and the Italian count were standing together, talking in low voices, when she and Juliana left the room.

The days passed with dizzying speed. The weather continued gray and dreary and cold. Rain mixed with sleet sometimes fell. Regardless, the parade of visitors continued: the famous, the infamous, those of importance, and the nonentities. They were always twenty to thirty at the dinner table, and they often stayed late. But when they were gone and the door had been shut upon them, Roderic retired to his apartment and took Mara with him. Slowly, her belongings accumulated in his rooms, and, just as surely, she became used to dressing and undressing before him, to accepting his caresses, to joining him in the great royal bed. She came to believe that it was not mere physical pleasure he sought in her company, but a respite from the duties and obligations that dogged his every waking moment.

By degrees, he told her about himself, and it seemed to Mara as if she could see in her mind the flaxen-haired toddler that he had been; the wild young boy always at odds with his dynamic father, always protected by his mother, the lovely and gracious Angeline. She could picture the mountains and forested valleys of Ruthenia: the swift-running and ice-cold rivers; the small villages and walled towns with their ancient bridges lined with images of what might have been saints, but could as easily have been the effigies of beloved past kings and queens.

Sometimes he would attempt to catch her unaware with questions concerning her past, her own childhood. She had become adept, however, at prevarication, at the use of smiling silence, though in truth it sometimes seemed as if she had no past to remember. It felt as if she had always lived here in Ruthenia House with the prince and his retinue. That she had always slept naked in Roderic's arms and always would. It was dangerous to allow herself to feel that way, she knew, but it was not something she could prevent.

The evening of the ball arrived. The gowns Mara and Juliana had ordered had been delivered the day before, and Mara's hung in the armoire in Roderic's dressing room. Her underclothing had been laid out, along with her silken stockings and her white satin dancing slippers with pearl beading on the toes. She had bathed early so as to give her hair time to dry. Lila had tended her nails, buffing them to a pink glow. She was supposed to be resting, lying down on a chaise longue in Roderic's bedchamber. Instead, she sat staring into the fire with her hands clasped in front of her, trying not to think.

This was the night. It was the evening toward which all her energies had been directed for weeks, the evening of the ball, the evening she would deliver the prince into the hands of de Landes. She had played her part. Her task would be complete when she entered the door of the residence of the vicomtesse on Roderic's arm. What happened after that was not her responsibility. Still, she wished with passionate fervor that she knew what was going to take place. The possibility of public disgrace for Roderic occurred to her, though she had no idea what form it might take. She thought of his assassination or else his arrest and exposure as the leader of the Death Corps, even of his imprisonment and torture.

She tried to make herself think of a more optimistic outcome, of a surprise honor, an award, or perhaps a surreptitious inspection for the purpose of an alliance between France and Ruthenia. The last was unlikely. The daughters of Louis Philippe were married, and his granddaughters were still in their cradles. And as for an award of honor, a simple invitation from the king to the Tuileries would have done as well.

Nothing good seemed to make sense. Her horror of what might happen left her cold inside. She held out her hands to the flames that leaped in the hearth and was not surprised to see that they trembled.

The door opened behind her, and Roderic's soft, even tread advanced into the room. "Moping in the dark? A useless occupation, but enjoyable to some, or so I'm told."

She looked up, glancing at the window. Night had indeed fallen. She got to her feet and turned to face him. "I was waiting for the time to dress for the ball."

"Not happily, it appears. You need not go if you have changed your mind."

The impulse to accept the excuse he offered was strong. If she simply stayed here in the house with him, then nothing could harm him. He would be safe. But her grandmother would not be.

"Juliana would be disappointed," she said, forcing a smile.

"She would survive it."

Would he survive the night? That was the basis of her terrible fears. She must go to the ball, and he with her, but perhaps if he were warned, all would be well. She stepped forward, reaching out her hand to place it on his arm. "Roderic—" she began, then faltered.

"Say what you will," he said, his voice carrying a hint of urging.

She stared up at him, her eyes wide in the pale oval of her face. He was so vital and quick with energy, even as he stood still with his head bent toward her. She could not bear the thought of him going unprepared into that ballroom, and yet how could she warn him? She could not. Once she began to explain why he must take care, there would be nothing left to do except to tell the entire story. It was too great a risk to take. Impossible.

"Nothing," she said, letting her hand fall away from his sleeve, turning away from him.

He watched her, watched the fans of dark silk that were her lowered lashes, watched the firelight gleam in the black and shining waves of her hair that spilled around her waist as she moved away from him. He drew a deep breath, his chest tight with disappointment. For one brief moment he had thought that she meant to trust him, to confide in him. The need had been there; he was sure of it.

It was a signal, however, if he had needed one. Tonight was the night. He had suspected it from the moment the subject of the ball was broached. He could not have said what had alerted him. It might have been some second sense, or it could have been no more than the stiffness that he had noticed in Mara at the time, as if the occasion was of great importance.

So be it. His plans were laid, had been for some time. He had tried to provide for every eventuality and must trust that he had succeeded. He could do no more.

Still, the urge to force her confidence, to attempt in some way to prove his suspicions, was impossible to resist. He moved closer to her, placing his hand on her shoulder. "Are you well, indeed?"

That quiet inquiry, with its threading of genuine concern, was nearly Mara's undoing. She swallowed hard, turning a bright face to him. "Oh, yes. Well, perhaps I'm a little nervous of such grand company as we must meet with at the ball, but I would not miss it."

The gallant courage he saw in her filled him with rage against whatever it was that pushed her. He wanted to take her in his arms and hold her safe. The instant he identified that need, he recognized with a sense of shock that, though he cared for her well-being, his greatest fear was of losing her. He would like to keep her, for himself alone, until that distant and unforeseeable day when the magic between them came to an end. He could do that if he took her away now, tonight. Would she go with him? Would she become his woman, and tramp by his side as the queen of the gypsies? Would she travel with him back to Ruthenia, there to adorn his princely holdings? If she would not, he could always take her by force. By force he could keep her. It would not matter if she never told him of her own accord who she was, if he never knew precisely what she wanted from him. He would forfeit that knowledge if to know meant losing her.

No. He could not take her away, could not go himself. Not yet. There was too much to be done, too much at stake. But he could have her now, once more, before the hour for dressing overtook them. It would be a poor substitute for the closeness he craved, but one that had its own satisfaction.

"You have no need for concern," he said. "You will shine like a pure star among dull planets, will move like a swan passing through a gaggle of geese, with pride and natural grace."

"You flatter me."

"Impossible," he murmured, reaching to take her hand and turning her toward him. He placed her hand on his shoulder and encircled her waist with his arms.

"Not at all, and it has a purpose, I think." She tilted her head back to stare up at him, a challenge in her eyes.

"Will it serve?" he inquired, his gaze upon the enticing curves of her mouth.

One last time. The need to lie beside him, to feel him inside her once more, was a penetrating ache, as if she had only just discovered the source of some deep pain. She swayed against him. With her mouth hovering inches from his, she whispered, "Oh, indeed. Indeed, it will."

By the time Lila and Sarus arrived to dress them for the ball, they were sitting once more before the fire, Mara in her dressing gown, Roderic in his uniform shirt and trousers. There was hilarity in the glance they exchanged as they stood, making ready to allow the servants to remove from them the clothing they had redonned in such scrambling haste moments before.

The smile quickly faded from Mara's face as she moved into the dressing room with the housemaid. The tears were close, but she suppressed them with an effort. It was ridiculous of her to feel this way. She should be happy that this sordid episode would soon be over, that she would be free of her false position here, that she would finally escape from the clutches of de Landes. What had happened with the prince had little meaning. She would return to Louisiana as soon as was humanly possible; that decision had been made in the last few hours. Once there, she would retreat to her father's plantation, if he would allow it, if he would accept a daughter so tarnished. In the slow passage of the days, in that quiet place, the world would forget her, and she would also forget. She would, if it took the rest of her life.

It very well might. She had not known what to expect, had not seriously considered what it would mean to become the prince's mistress. She had not known what it would be like to lie in his arms, to wake up in the morning beside him, to share the generosity, the caring, and the grace of his lovemaking. She would miss those things; this much she recognized even now. She would regret their loss in some deep, unreachable portion of her being.

It was wrong, she knew. She should be relieved that the hateful necessity of submitting to those embraces would soon be over. She should be overjoyed that the strain of her masquerade would be done, that she would be able to return to her former life. But life was never so simple. She had become involved with Roderic and the cadre, had come to care what became of them. It would be painful to part from them, never to know what would become of them. More painful than she would have believed possible.

Finally, her hair was done, piled in glossy curls on her head with ringlets falling from a high chignon in the Greek fashion, and a pair of small, perfect, pink hothouse rosebuds nestling behind her left ear. Silk stockings were rolled up her legs and her slippers placed on her feet. Her gown of pink-tinted white silk was lifted over her head and fastened in the back with a row of tiny pearl buttons, then settled into place over her petticoat, which was stiffened with *crin,* or woven horsehair. Long gloves of fine kid were worked over her hands and up her arms.

"Shall you wear your jewels, mademoiselle?" Lila asked.

They were not needed, Mara could see that, but Roderic had given the diamonds to her and would doubtless expect her to have them on. She nodded her acquiescence. *"Très belle,"* Lila murmured, stepping back to admire her handiwork when the necklace, earrings, and bracelet were in place. "There will not be a lady there who can compare!"

Mara thanked the girl, complimenting her most sincerely on her expertise with hair, then stood back as the housemaid tapped on the bedchamber door and opened it for her to pass into the other room.

Roderic turned from where he had been standing by the fire, staring into the flames. He came toward her at once and, taking her hand, brought it to his lips, inclining his head in a small bow of homage. "Ring the bells and sound the cymbals; she has come."

"Am I late?" Mara inquired in some confusion.

"You are beauty incarnate. Splendid and without blemish."

She smiled, her glance moving over the burnished perfection of his uniform as it was molded to the width of his shoulders and the long, muscled length of his legs; the decorations that glittered on his chest and the smooth, gold waves of his hair. "It's you who are splendid."

He acknowledged her comment with the faintest of smiles and a shake of his head, then went on, "There is only one thing, perhaps two—"

It was Lila who frowned, moving forward in a fashion that might have been called belligerent. "What is it, Your Highness?"

Roderic looked at Sarus, who came forward bearing a velvet-covered box in one hand and a bundle in the other. The elderly manservant flicked open the box to reveal a parure of pearls that were shaded delicately with pink iridescence and had a clasp made of a large baroque pearl, also of an iridescently pale pink. Besides a double-strand necklace, there were earrings and a double-strand bracelet.

"A token of atonement," Roderic said, his voice quiet, "if you will permit it, for my lapse of taste before."

It was a priceless gift. Pearls of so unusual a color, so perfectly matched for size and luster, and with their matched clasp, took years of painstaking care to find and assemble together. They blurred before Mara's eyes, and she swallowed hard before looking up at the prince. "There was no necessity."

"The need was mine."

He made an abrupt gesture to the maid. Lila unclasped the diamonds around Mara's neck and stepped back. Roderic lifted the necklace of pearls from its satin bed and placed it around Mara's throat. Deftly, he removed the earrings from her ears and the bracelet from her gloved wrist, tossing them aside as if they were worthless baubles, before replacing them with the pearls. Without pausing, he then turned and took the bundle that Sarus held, shaking it out to reveal an ermine cloak. This he swung around her shoulders, catching it close at the throat with a hidden clasp.

"You—you are too generous," Mara said, her voice strained. She could not bring herself to look at him, so overwhelming was her sense of guilt and her pain. Instead, she focused her gaze on the blue ribbon of some order that slashed across his chest.

"I am selfishness made whole. It pleases me to see you decked with pearls of my choosing. If I were generous, I would give you the opportunity for refusing to be decorated for my pleasure. If I were generous, I would have let you go long ago, or else—"

He stopped abruptly. There were times when the habit of loquacity was inconvenient. He had very nearly said that if he had been generous, he would have taken from her the burden of her task; forced her to admit her lack of memory loss; wrung from her the reason she was with him so that she need go no farther, need not bear with his demands upon her or suffer the suspense of wondering if she would be found out. That he had not done so was a transgression of his own code. It was too late now to rectify the matter. He had been selfish, indeed.

"Come," he said, taking her hand and placing it on his arm, "the others are waiting."

The cadre milled around the fire in the salon, passing each other as they paced up and down. They were loath to sit out of regard for the unwrinkled perfection of their dress uniforms, which had gold bars across the jacket fronts and cerulean-blue stripes down the trouser legs. Juliana was also there, looking like a goddess in her gown of sea-blue, her height increased by her headdress of plumes and her grandeur enhanced by a small coronet of diamonds and sapphires set among her high-piled curls. The room seemed inordinately crowded with white uniforms, however. It was only an instant before Mara realized why.

"Luca!" she exclaimed. "How handsome you look."

"At last I am one of the cadre," he said, pride in his bearing as he bowed. His uniform fit his lithe form to perfection, and as a token gesture toward the formality of the occasion he had even removed the gold ring from his ear. But there was a shadow in his dark eyes as he looked from her to the prince and back again.

"Just what we need," Estes growled in mock annoyance, "a popinjay with sticky fingers and a talent for the knife."

Luca was unmoved by the insult. "You will appreciate my talents when someday you are starving as you live off the land and it is I who bring you food."

"Stolen chickens? Do you think we would eat them?"

"Every last morsel."

"Including the feet, as we have before," Roderic said. "Shall we go?"

It was an order couched as a pleasant suggestion. Luca held a sable cape for Juliana, and the others shrugged into overcoats, then in high spirits they swept from the house. Mara and Juliana were put into a carriage; the prince and the others mounted horses. The grooms who had been holding the horses stood back, the coachman cracked his whip, then in a body they moved from the courtyard, streaming out into the cobbled street as the great wrought-iron gates were flung wide. Behind them was Ruthenia House, with its lighted windows and torches flaring at the entrance door into the cold north wind. Ahead was the darkness of unlighted streets in this older section of the city. And the ball.

CHAPTER

11

The townhouse of the Vicomtesse Beausire, located on the avenue d'Eylau in the quieter northwestern section of Paris, was an imposing pile in the darkness. Though of massive size, it was far from daring in style, boasting the same mansard roof, Italianate arched windows, golden limestone, and massive front doorway as a thousand others.

Inside was a grand marble entrance hall with great, verd antique columns reaching up from a chessboard floor of black and white squares toward a groined ceiling painted with a classic allegorical scene in the fashionable colors of the season, green, blue, and apricot. A pair of curving white marble staircases led upward to a gallery that ran around the inside of the great foyer. Directly in front of the point where the two flights of stairs met on the upper level were double doors gleaming with gilt, which were thrown open to receive the throng moving up the marble steps.

The members of the Ruthenia party were relieved of their wraps in the entrance hall by a swarm of servants and ushered up the stairs. The vicomtesse, a widow of unlimited means and impressive family connections, greeted them just inside the large open ballroom. The nodding plumes of an unlikely shade of green mixed with an insipid apricot that made up her headdress quite dwarfed those in Juliana's hair. Her gown of the same colors was so bedecked with ribbons and poufs of net in every hue that her shoulders sagged with the weight. Her face was round and heavily powdered to remove every trace of her natural high color for the necessary wan look, but it shone with good nature and enjoyment of her own role as hostess. She welcomed the prince with effusion and waved them all into the room. The king was expected at any moment, she said, and the party could begin then.

The gathering was indeed in a state of hiatus. Music played, but no one was dancing. Though waiters were stationed around the room, and there were numerous tables laden with trays of refreshments of various kinds set around enormous silver epergnes filled with hothouse flowers, no one was yet partaking of the bounty. The air was heated by great blazing fires at each end of the room. The fragrance of more flowers, placed on stands in alcoves, wafted on the warm air, vying with the perfume of the ladies. The guests, for the most part, stood waiting near the doorway to pay the required obeisance to the royal personages who would be attending. In the meantime they talked in voices of varying degrees of stridency and volume so that the room was filled with a dull roaring.

It was a highly fashionable assembly. The evening coats and trousers of the men in their rich black and gray were excellent foils for the lighter gowns of the ladies in silk and crepe de chine, in damask and brocade, in taffeta and satin *broché* and *mousseline de laine.* The colors of the season were much in evidence, along with ecru, pale blue, and the perennial lavender and gray of half-mourning. The skill of Parisian dressmakers was also on display in the current style of the gowns, with tiered skirts heavily embroidered; edged with lace, ribbon, and ruffles; or with alternating bands of color to create an appearance of large horizontal stripes.

The cadre in their sparkling white uniforms, with Mara and Juliana among them in their elegantly simple ensembles, caused a stir. Heads turned as the Prince's name was announced. A concerted whisper ran around the room. Women stared. Men craned their necks. There was a white-haired gentleman with a monocle in one eye standing nearby, and Roderic, as if oblivious of anyone else, moved toward him. Since he held her hand in the crook of his arm, Mara perforce went with him.

The prince introduced the white-haired man as a diplomat representing a small country near Ruthenia, while he presented Mara, with great delicacy, as a friend of his sister. The rush of gratitude she felt for that small but typical courtesy caused her to lose track of the conversation for an instant. She glanced away, surveying the crowd.

Abuptly, her gaze was caught and held by a man among the guests. De Landes stood not a dozen feet away. His gaze was fixed on her, as if by its intensity he could attract and hold her attention, could remind her of what she must do. She had allowed herself to forget for a few brief moments. Now it came back to her with renewed force.

This was not an evening of pleasure. There would be no dancing for her, no flirtation, no carefree enjoyment of the music and food and wine or of the society of the best families of France and the cadre in a festive mood. She was here for a purpose, and she must carry it out. She must hold Roderic beside her near the doorway where soon the king of France would enter.

He showed no inclination to move. It appeared, in fact, that he was established there within a few feet of the entrance. The cadre had spread out as if in some disciplined military maneuver so that there was a cordon of white uniforms in that area. Nearest to Roderic and herself was one of the twins—Jared, she thought—while beyond him Luca stood with Juliana as they both talked to a foppish little man in a lavender waistcoat. The other twin, Jacques, was on their left in conversation with a prelate in a bishop's robe. Michael held a place beyond him. Trude and Estes were on the opposite side of the circle with a short space separating them, Trude talking to an elderly roué and the Italian count paying such absurd gallantries to a matron and her daughter that the girl was smothering giggles with her hand.

For all the ease of their stances, however, there was about them a tingling alertness. The cadre was on guard; there could be no doubt of it. So watchful were they, so evenly spaced around the prince and about the door, that Mara felt her taut nerves tighten still further. She flung a quick glance at Roderic and found his attention upon her. His features were closed-in, his eyes as hard as blue glass.

There was something wrong; she knew it with suffocating certainty. The feeling of being held fast in a snare from which there was no escape was so strong that she could not move.

From outside the ballroom came the faint noise made by the arrival of several carriages. Louis Philippe and his entourage had arrived. A flurry of anticipation swept through the room. The murmur of voices rose, then began to die away. The vicomtesse hurried from the room, and the clatter of her heeled slippers could be heard as she descended the stairs. Then came the sound of the downstairs door opening, of formal greetings exchanged by their hostess, in a tone that was high-pitched with excitement, and the king, in a deeper and slower timbre. There was a pause while the men and women who had accompanied him, members of his household and his guard, were also welcomed; then came the heavy and measured footsteps of the elderly Louis Philippe on the stairs, preceding his hostess and all the others as was his privilege.

The music stopped. There was a slight surge toward the door, a shifting as those gathered made room for the ritual curtsies and bows required of them at the appearance of their sovereign. From the corner of her eye, Mara caught a glimpse of a waiter, a man dressed in white trousers rather than the black that the others of his kind were wearing. He was inching forward as though anxious for a glimpse of royalty, but one hand was hidden under his jacket. He wore no braiding or bars on his jacket, no stripes down his trouser legs, but it struck Mara with the force of a blow that at a glance he looked very much like one of the cadre.

Her chest ached. There was a red haze before her eyes. Each footstep on the marble stairs grated in her ears with the abrasiveness of a grindstone. On they came. She could feel the honed concentration of the man at her side, the poised and balanced intent.

De Landes had moved closer and was within a few feet of where she stood. His attention was not on her, however, but on the door. He stared at the opening with a feral grin baring his teeth as the footsteps sounded, louder, closer, then slowing from the long climb as the king reached the top.

They stopped, became a stride as Louis Philippe crossed the landing, moving toward the wide double doors. De Landes threw a hurried glance behind him, then stared in triumph at the prince. Mara, still watching him, saw that the dark man had looked first toward the waiter, who was now only a few feet away. Within seconds the king would appear. Silence held the room as every eye was turned on the door.

Driven by an uncontrollable impulse, Mara put out her hand to touch the prince's arm. She spoke in an anguished whisper, forcing the words past the constriction in her throat, "Take care, Roderic, oh, take care—"

There was a brief flicker of movement in the doorway.

The chest of the majordomo in charge of announcing guests swelled as he drew breath. "His Majesty, Louis Philippe, king of the French!"

The king, a practiced and genial smile creasing his lined face, his barrel-chested form held with conscious and regal erectness, stepped into the room. Silks and taffetas rustled as the gathering swayed, bending like blown wheat as they paid their respects.

In that instant the white-clad waiter drew a pistol and sprang forward. Roderic, moving like the uncoiling of a cracked whip, was upon him in an instant, flinging up the waiter's arm. The report exploded in the room with a rolling concussion that made the chandelier clash with the tinkling of crystal lusters and brought plaster down from the ceiling.

The crowd surged away from the center of conflict with yells and screams. Cries of "Assassin! Assassin! They've killed the king!" arose in the sudden babble. The cordon of Roderic's *garde du corps* tightened, moving in upon the king, sweeping him back out the door and into the safety of his attendants' arms. As a passage was cleared from the room, men and women poured toward the doorway, surrounding the small struggling group where Roderic and Michael held the waiter.

Suddenly, there was a whispering rush followed by a soft thud, a deadly sound in the din. The waiter stiffened, then slumped with the haft of a knife protruding from his chest. Panic ran through the guests who were nearest. Screaming, babbling, shouting, cursing, they pushed and shoved, trampling each other as they tried to find a way out.

Mara stood still with the shock of comprehension. She saw de Landes backing away from the knot of men around the waiter, saw him turn and run with blank terror on his face.

A strong, hard hand caught her arm. She saw the white uniform and every muscle tensed.

"Don't be afraid," Michael said, his thin, earnest face flushed and his voice breathless as he fought to keep her from being jostled by the crowd. "It's only me. I'm to get you out of here, Roderic's orders."

"No," she cried, "I can't go with you!"

"There's nothing you can do to help. No matter how it looks, I assure you that Roderic has it under control. Come on."

She was half pushed, half dragged through the struggling crowd as Michael, with the ruthless use of elbows and fists, made a path for them both. It seemed useless to protest further. Even if she could make Michael understand, he would still not disobey the orders of his cousin, the prince. There was no one in that maddened gathering to whom she could appeal, no one who would help her. It seemed best to do as she was directed until this upheaval was over. She could think of what she must do later.

They left the room by a side door that led to a back stair. Apparently, the choice of exit was no accident, for at the foot of the narrow staircase they found Luca with Juliana in tow, along with Trude and Estes, who were holding their wraps, which had been left downstairs. Others also knew of this back way out, however, for they could hear them on the stairs behind them.

No words were wasted in greeting or exclaiming. They raced along the dark corridor leading from the stairs and burst out of a door that gave on to a side court. They crossed it. Ahead of them was a small garden with gravel paths and a gate that, in turn, gave on to the front court where their carriage, conveniently turned toward the street, waited. Behind the carriage were the mounts of the cadre. In an instant, Mara and Juliana were handed into the vehicle and the cadre mounted. Michael shouted an order, and they plunged away from the bright lights and confusion of the Beausire townhouse.

The carriage rocked and swayed, rattling over the cobblestones with a force that made Mara's teeth clatter together. She clung to the velvet hanging strap, staring into the darkness, her body shaking not only with the violence of the ride, but also with reaction.

Assassination. The thought had crossed her mind, but she had not really believed it. De Landes had known that the attempt was going to be made; that much was clear. What was not clear was whether he had wanted the prince to be there to prevent it or to be the scapegoat. It seemed the latter, and yet the man prided himself on the twists and turns of his planning. Considering his position in the ministry under Louis Philippe, it made no sense for him to try to depose the king. Had he thought to benefit in some way then, from being on the scene when the plot to kill the king was brought to nothing? Had he seen to it that Roderic and his cadre, famous for the prevention of such crimes, were there to do the dirty work while he stepped in to take the credit?

Bu who would become king if Louis Philippe was killed? The young comte de Paris, grandson of the king, whose father Ferdinand, the duc d'Orléans, had been killed in a carriage accident five years ago, was next in line. Doubtless a regency would be declared if he took the throne, perhaps one controlled by his mother, Helen of Mecklenburg-Schwerin. But other ambitious men might come close to the throne in such a case, men such as de Landes who knew how to think ahead. Could that be it?

Did it matter? The king had not been assassinated. Roderic and his men had intervened to prevent it. The waiter who had made the attempt was almost surely dead, and lost with him was the name of the man or the cause for which he had risked so much.

There had been a moment, when the waiter had been knifed, that she had looked instinctively for the newest member of the cadre, Luca the gypsy. He had been near, though if he had thrown that lethal blade—and, if so, on whose order?—she could not tell and preferred not to guess.

In these things she had no part. The questions that did concern her, and most deeply, were whether de Landes would consider that she had failed, and, if he did, what he meant to do about her grandmother. Another was whether Roderic realized that it was she who had in all deliberation enticed him into the fiasco tonight. She wondered, too, if there was a reason why he had sent Michael to rescue her and return her to Ruthenia House other than concern for her safety. And if there was, what did he intend to do with her? It did nothing toward allaying her fears to discover, as they passed a gaslight street lamp, that Juliana was watching her with compassion.

Mara moistened her dry lips. "Where is Roderic? Why has he remained behind?"

"There will be an official inquiry," the other girl said, her voice calm. "Those directly involved will be expected to give their version of what occurred. Doubtless King Louis Philippe will wish a verbatim report in person also, especially in view of my brother's position here."

"His position?"

"As the official representative of our country."

"I see. Do—do you think that we will be called upon for questioning?"

"It seems unlikely. This is one of the few occasions when it is just as well to be female. In any case," Roderic's sister added in considered tones, "I believe we can depend on Roderic to shield us."

Was the choice of words a deliberate double entendre? Mara could not be certain, and she dared not ask.

Back at Ruthenia House, they settled down to wait, for what it was not quite certain. By unspoken agreement they took up positions in the public salon since it was felt that this was an occasion of a certain formality. Fires were hastily kindled, and trays of wine and of various savories and cakes were brought. There was much heated discussion of what had really happened and when. They spoke also of why, though not of the reason that they had been there to stop it. It was, Mara thought, an exercise in mass diplomacy.

Roderic's cadre was not, either collectively or singly, stupid. They knew their prince had not meant to attend the ball, knew that he had changed his plans for her sake. They had received certain orders concerning the arrival of the king, orders that they knew had been kept from her. It was plain then that they suspected her of involvement in the night's affair. They withheld judgment, pending Roderic's return. There was a general feeling that it was possible the prince had reasons that none could know or guess. Their attitude toward her, however, lacked its usual warmth. At the same time, they treated her with the brusque solicitude usually reserved for those on the eve of their execution.

It was daybreak when Roderic returned at last. His temper was short, his mood perilous, and his words flaying. He had, he said, been suffering the blatherings and slow wits of officials for the past five hours and had nothing more to say on the subject of the assassination attempt. The king was tucked up in his bed sleeping the sleep of the well-served. The waiter had died without speaking. The man who had killed him had not been identified; he had taken himself off posthaste, vanishing in the crowd. It would be as well, the prince of Ruthenia suggested, if his entourage could find in one of those three examples conduct they could emulate. Except for Mara.

Within moments the salon had been cleared and she was left alone with the prince. She sat with her silk skirts spread around her, her ermine cape still about her shoulders, and her hands clasped in her lap. Pride kept her back straight and her gaze steady as she watched Roderic, but inside her was fluttering panic and the leaden depression of guilt.

He stood staring into the fire with one booted foot resting on the massively ornate brass andiron, allowing the endless moments to stretch. At last he turned and placed his hands behind his back. His bearing, regal and military, conferred upon him a towering authority. His fluid yet controlled movements gave an impression of leashed power. In the softness of his tone as he spoke was incalculable menace.

"Who are you?"

"I—"

"Don't!" His voice cut across hers with the slashing force of a sword blade before he went on. "Don't make the mistake of thinking that a new lie will serve."

"No, I won't," she said quietly. "My name is Marie Angeline Delacroix."

"Mara."

She stared at him without surprise. It had come to her that his informaion-gathering system was too well organized for him not to have known who de Landes was, or at least to have discovered his identity after seeing him with her at the Hugo salon. It must have been easy for him to learn who she was. "Why? Why did you let me go on?"

"You seemed to lack the qualities of a true conspirator. Besides, I was curious." The words were curt, tinged with self-derision.

"Were you, indeed? About what?"

"To see how far you would go."

The color drained from her face. He watched it go and felt inexplicably that he had struck an unarmed opponent. His anger was unappeased, but he could at least be fair. He made an abrupt gesture of negation, allowing his gaze to fall. "It was an experience of novelty and enthralling charm. To discover the purpose behind it, it had to continue."

"It must have been an expensive curiosity" she said, lifting a hand to the pearls at her throat.

"Nothing out of the ordinary."

It was amazing, the pain a few words could bring. She swallowed, then went on, "Well, at least it's over now. Whatever you may think, I'm glad that the king is safe."

"That is, of course, an immense relief. Perhaps the next assassination you attempt will be equally unproductive, for the sake of your tender conscience."

"There will not be another."

"Prove it so that we may all sing merrily and shout our great thanksgivings."

She raised her gray gaze to meet the flaring mockery in his eyes. "What do you want of me? Shall I say I'm sorry? Very well. I will always regret my part in what happened last night. Now will you let me go?"

"Go? There is nothing under God's blue bowl of heaven that will make me do that."

"But you must!" She had to get away, had to contact de Landes to find out what he meant to do with Grandmère Helene.

He moved to loom over her. For all its quietness, his voice was inflexible as he came finally to what he wanted to know. "Must I? Screw up your courage, Mara, my own Chère. Scrape your brain pan and rake over the embers of your heart. Make me listen, tell me something I will believe. Give me a reason why I should."

She bit the inside of her lip. "I could tell you, but you would not understand."

"My imagination has a level or two you have not yet explored. I recommend you try."

The bronze planes of his face were angular and hard with determination, but behind the blue glitter of his eyes lay a fathomless stillness. Her answer was important to him. He would not press her further, but he would have an answer, no matter how long the wait. For this moment censure and condemnation were suspended, but in return he required no less than the absolute truth. What he wanted of her, she knew with paralyzing certainty, was total capitulation.

It was not a desire she could afford to disregard, even if it seemed wise to do so.

She drew a deep breath. Her tones strained, she said, "It's my grandmother."

"Your grandmother."

The words were blank. Mara knew a moment of gratification that she had been able to surprise him, but it was short-lived. Haltingly, the story came out, of Dennis Mulholland and his death, of the journey to Paris, of de Landes and Grandmère Helene's addiction to gambling, and of the consequences. Once she began to speak, she could not seem to stop. With tears rising slowly in her eyes, she told him of her fears for the elderly woman and her horror of what de Landes might do to her in revenge for the failure of the evening before.

"You must let me go," she said, her voice near breaking as she put out her hand. "I have to see de Landes to persuade him to let me see Grandmère, to know how she fares. She is old and frail and—and used to having her way. She won't be able to bear being held against her will for long. I've done what he asked of me, and it may be that he will release her or at least let me find some other way of paying the debt."

He turned sharply, moving away from her. "What of your debt to me?"

"What debt?" She looked at his broad back in bewilderment.

"The price of betrayal."

She rose and moved swiftly to stand in front of him. "You don't understand! My grandmother—"

"I understand. And for the sake of a blood tie I am to allow you to prostitute yourself to a traitor? Oh, no, Mara. No."

"I wouldn't!"

"Wouldn't you? If it was required? Your loyalty is an endearing trait, but not one I care to encourage, not at that expense."

She looked away from him, then down at her hands. "What else can I do?"

"You can leave it to me."

The words rang with the promise of concentrated action. She jerked her head up, her eyes wide. "You? What do you mean?"

"I will find your grandmother and return her to you."

It did not occur to her to doubt that he could, or would, do exactly what he said. "Why? Why should you do that?"

"Let us say," he answered, his expression noncommittal, "that my nature is altogether vindictive. I dislike being made to play the fool. If I remove your grandmother, supposing there is a grandmother, I take the advantage now held by de Landes. She becomes my hostage."

"Yours? But for what purpose?"

He smiled, a brief movement of the lips that left his eyes cool. "Oh, for your conduct in and out of my bed. What else?"

Swinging away from her, he moved to the door, where he sent a footman running to fetch the cadre.

It was the gypsies who found Grandmère Helene. Infiltrating every village, stable, and chicken run; seeing, hearing everything while they bought and sold horses, juggled, tumbled, and sold love potion and told fortunes at fairs. They knew every time a foal was dropped, a hen went to nest, or a maiden fell from grace. They certainly knew when a stranger entered their district. The request went out in the *calo* language, traveling as fast as men could ride in relays, for information about an elderly woman of a certain description being held at some gentleman's seat. Back came the answer so quickly that it might have been carried on the wind. There was such a one at a château in the Loire Valley not far from the forests of Chambord. She was well and happy, all amiability in fact, though perhaps a little mad.

By the time the news arrived, the rescue expedition had been organized and was ready to mount. They left Paris in the dark hours before dawn, a group of men on horseback riding at the pace of the fast traveling carriage that swayed along among them. The carriage was low-slung and lean, painted gray black. Inside it Juliana lay back on the cushions, trying to sleep, while Mara sat upright staring out into the darkness. The prince's sister had come because she could not bear to miss the excitement, Mara from a need to see her grandmother—and because Roderic insisted. She thought he did not trust her to remain at Ruthenia House if left alone, though he had said that her presence was to reassure her grandmother when she was confronted by her would-be rescuers.

As a traveling companion, Mara could not have asked for better than Juliana. She did not complain or chatter or exclaim at every alarm and she kept to her side of the carriage seat. On the other hand, her ability to sleep under less than ideal situations limited her use as a distraction.

Mara could not sleep, had hardly closed her eyes in the forty-eight hours since the night of the ball. After Roderic had summoned the cadre to outline his plans, she had gone to her room. She had not left it, though she had waited in momentary expectation of a summons from

Roderic. It had not come. She had been left alone with her thoughts and her fears.

The first of these was that they would fail. She was terrified that de Landes, anticipating an attempt at rescue, would be before them, that he would remove her grandmother, even kill her; or, failing that, would post a guard impossible to defeat. The second was that they would be successful, that Roderic would return triumphant with her grandmother to Paris, where Grandmère Helene would then be forced to witness in intimate detail the degradation of her granddaughter at the hands of the prince and know herself the cause.

There was a third fear. It caused her to return again and again in her mind's eye to the scene at the house of the Vicomtesse Beausire. She pictured the waiter and the men gathered around him, the sighing thud of the thrown knife. Who had killed the man?

It might have been one of the king's guards overzealous in his protection of the monarch. It might have been a guest enraged by the danger to which the waiter had subjected those present. But, most of all, it could have been the prince and his cadre who had killed him, the men who held him in custody. It might have been Roderic, silencing the man who knew the part he had truly played.

Suspicion. It was a dark and dangerous thing, eating away at the mind. Far better to bring it out into the open. But how could she? The greatest threat of suspicion is the fear that it will be confirmed.

What would it mean if it had been Roderic who had ordered the waiter killed? Would it, could it, mean that it had been Roderic who had planned the assassination? Roderic, who had, with his conspicuous protection of the king, thrown up a screen for the actual deed, then, for reasons of his own, stopped it, removed the instrument of it to protect himself?

She could not forget the terror she had seen in de Landes's face. Had it been for his fear of discovery? Or had it been terror of the men he had unwittingly unleashed upon his country?

And what would happen now? Would the prince keep her near him until he tired of her? Would she be released with a generous stipend as payment, a token of his gratitude? Or would she be found some morning in an alley, stripped of identification, a woman who had found favor with an important man, but one who knew too much?

Ruthless, the prince was ruthless. He had taken her with him to Paris as if she were no more than a stray animal he had found. He had scratched Trude's face with his sword to prove a nebulous point. He used men and women to further his own ends, extracting the information they could give, then sending them on their way. He took their homage, their loyalty, as in the case of Luca, and what did he give in return? Bright, flashing words. The honor of his presence. Excitement. Brief moments of being fully alive, of living on the sharp and dangerous edge of pleasure. Nothing that was solid. Nothing that could last.

The carriage jolted onward. They left Paris behind, heading south. The hills rose and fell away. They passed fields lying fallow and orchards where the last leaves clung to trees of peach and pear and apple. They went through villages with the houses built almost upon the crooked streets, crowding close to one another as if for protection. Dogs barked and cattle lowed. Peasants stared with blank curiosity as they swept past in clouds of dust.

They stayed for the night in some such small place, eating beans and ham and drinking a delicious red wine before tumbling into feather-cushioned beds to sleep dreamlessly. Morning saw them far away.

And finally they came to the Loire Valley where the river wound in wide, lazy, leaf-green curves among its sandbars. Here lay dozens of châteaux, monuments to the tastes and amusements of generations of French nobility, from medieval fortresses to fairy-tale palaces, from hunting lodges and monastic retreats to *châteaux de plaisance.* Here were the homes of royal mistresses and the great fortresses where once protestants had been hung by the dozens from the battlements. Here were the places where laughter had rung out and tears had been shed, where all the pageantry and glory of living had been played out and then forgotten when that way of life was ended by the revolution.

They rode along the winding roads, passing the gypsies camped beside the river, entering and leaving forests that had once been called royal. They saw the crumbling aqueducts and the roads that were the legacy of ancient Rome, the towns where gothic cathedrals loomed above the river, beautiful in their indifference to time. And in the dark of night, as a round and yellow moon was setting, they came at last to the château that had been claimed by de Landes.

It was a tumbledown building of stone, the pride of some architect from some distant year but now crumbling and nearly uninhabitable, with bats flying around its moss-grown towers with their blank windows, carved crosses, and vines making a dark tracery on the walls. Woodland, interspersed with fallow fields, grew up to the doors. The cadre settled down in the shadow of the trees to wait.

CHAPTER 12

Dawn, the time when visibility was most uncertain and men slept the soundest, was chosen for the assault on the château. There were a few brief words from the prince before they started out, but they hardly seemed necessary. Each man had his place and his purpose, and knew them well. There was not one among them who did not know that a misstep, a moment of carelessness, could mean death. They were ready, honed by endless training, careful praise, and pithy comments on their few weaknesses. They would not be there if they were not able men eminently suited to the task. This assurance they had in full from their prince, who was not at all easy to please.

Michael had once more been placed in charge of Mara. If it was a duty he found onerous, he did not complain. He guided her as they ghosted through the forest by a touch on the arm, a whispered suggestion. She was grateful for his forebearance, grateful also that it was not Roderic who moved besde her toward the château. In these final moments her mind was filled with doubts as to his purpose and his methods of gaining it. She did not question that these doubts would have communicated themselves to him as surely as the growing light of morning would banish the night.

She did not want that. She saw no need to put him on his guard against her any more than he was already, but, just as important, she did not want to jeopardize in any way his attempt to take her grandmother into his own custody. After a careful weighing of the alternatives, she had found that she preferred to be indebted to the prince rather than to de Landes. If there was any other implication to that discovery, she did not care to think about it.

The walls of the château loomed gray beige and solid ahead of them. A short strip of open field lay between them and the woods. One by one the cadre drifted across it to merge with the shadows of the wall. Somewhere an owl called, a mournful sound. A mouse in the rolls of dried grass squeaked and was still.

Then came Michael and Mara's turn. He took her hand. She picked up her skirts with the other. Bending low, they hurried across the clearing on a track that took advantage of every shifting patch of shadow. They drew up against the wall and stood panting, waiting for the others. Around them they could just make out the crouching forms of those who had gone before them.

"Now, my friends," Estes said softly when they had all gathered beneath the wall. As if at a signal, the cadre moved toward him, grouping, climbing with silent speed one upon the other, forming a human pyramid as effortlessly as if they had been in the long gallery at Ruthenia House.

"Hoopla!" came the suppressed whisper when they stood tall, wavering in the fast-growing dimness.

Roderic, who had been standing to one side, turned. He took a few swift steps, then swarmed up the convenient ladder they made. They were short of the top of the wall. The prince sprang upward the last few inches, catching the edge of the top of the wall with his hands. With the bunching of taut muscles, he levered himself onto the ledge. Seating himself, he made a quick, hard gesture, then waited.

"Now you, mademoiselle," the Italian called in a husky whisper.

"What? Surely the prince will be able to open the gate?"

"If he should not, you must go with him to pacify the old one. Hurry. There is no time to lose."

It was true, there was not. Every moment of delay increased their chances of discovery. Exclaiming in a most unladylike manner under her breath, Mara tucked up her skirts and began to climb up the ladder of bodies. Sheer annoyance gave her strength and will enough to reach the shoulders of those on the top row. Then she slowly stood erect. Roderic reached down to her. She hesitated only a moment, then lifted her arms.

Her wrists were grasped in hard hands as merciless in their strength as steel bracelets. She was hoisted upward. An arm went around her waist, holding her until she gained purchase. For a brief moment she was aware of a hard thigh under her and the sharp nudge of the scabbard of the sword Roderic wore, then she was half swung, half pushed over the wall's edge. Before she could protest, before she could guess what he intended, he let her down the length of his arms, holding her dangling for the fraction of a second it took her to stretch downward toward the ground. Then he dropped her.

She landed in an undignified heap. An instant later she rolled, scrambling, to one side as Roderic leaped down beside her. She opened her mouth to make a sharp complaint about his method of scaling walls, then shut it abruptly as a call rang out.

"Who goes there?"

Roderic's only answer was the scrape of his sword blade as he drew it out with one hand, while with the other he swung Mara behind him. The château guard, shouting for help and dragging out his own sword, backed away. The prince closed with the man in a few swift strides. Their blades clanged with a shower of sparks as they came together. The encounter was violent, but quickly over. The guard gave a strangled gasp as his sword was sprung from his hand to land quivering and upright in a dung heap. Roderic used the hilt of his own to strike a hard blow to the man's chin. The guard dropped and lay unmoving.

Without pausing, Roderic stepped over the fallen man and ran toward the great iron gates of the château. With a single slash of his sword, he cut the rope that held the counterweight. The weight dropped, and slowly the gates swung open. The cadre, with a ringing yell that echoed from the stone walls, poured through.

They were just in time, for a door opened from somewhere, throwing yellow orange light into what appeared to be an entrance court. Men, hastily donning their clothes, clattered out. They saw the cadre and stopped, raising their pistols. The flaring explosions of gunpowder blossomed in the gray dawn like short-lived flowers. The cadre flung themselves aside, drawing their own weapons. The concussions of the exchange of shots roared in the enclosed space, sending pigeons whirling up from their roosts in the dovecote off to one side, rising into the shifting pearl-gray sky. Swords were drawn. The dawn light glinted silver along the blades as they tapped and scraped. Men grunted with effort. Oaths rang out. Feet shuffled and stamped back and forth on the uneven cobbles of the courtyard.

The number of guards was small. Within moments, it was over. The men were trussed up and forced to lie on the ground. There was one, a scarred, tough-looking veteran bleeding from a head wound so that he was half-blinded, who appeared to have an air of authority. Roderic turned his attention to this man, dragging him to a sitting position as he knelt over him.

"Where is your master, de Landes?"

"Who wants to know?" the man growled.

Roderic placed his hand on his sword hilt. "The man who will dispatch you to paradise unheralded should you fail to answer—in your next breath."

Mara waited with every muscle tensed, not only for the answer that would tell them whether de Landes had harmed her grandmother, but because she feared she was about to see a man die. If she who knew the prince had no trouble believing the quiet-voiced threat, it was not surprising that the château's captain of the guard began to perspire in great, beaded drops.

"Your pardon, Monsieur. We—we haven't seen him in weeks."

"You have with you an elderly woman. Where is she?"

"You speak of Madame Helene? Where else should she be but in bed?"

"She is ill?" Mara asked, her voice strained.

The man looked from her to Roderic, his face puzzled. "She is asleep, so far as I know."

Roderic hauled the man to his feet. "Lead the way."

"You won't harm her?"

At that simple question, the tension that held the cadre ebbed. They looked at one another, and wry smiles etched their faces. It was Juliana who stepped forward from among them then. "Imbecile," she said without rancor, "take us to her."

With thudding boots and clanking swords, they entered the door of the château, kicking aside old and warped saddles, tack, and pieces of uniforms as they crossed a large hall. A spiral stair of white limestone curved upward. They mounted it in procession, with Roderic beside the prisoner and Mara following them and the others close behind. Two floors up, they left the stair to cross another hall hung with deer antlers and furnished with ancient settles holding cushions that were threadbare where they were not moth-eaten. There was a door set in the wall beside the great, soaring fireplace of carved white limestone. The captain of the guard stopped in front of it.

Roderic glanced at the man's face, then lifted his hand to knock. The sound was quiet in the lofty room. There was no answer. He knocked again.

"If this was a lie—" Estes began.

"It's no lie. Let me," the captain said, and set up a thunderous banging on the door.

The results was the same. Nothing.

"Stand aside," Roderic said.

"It isn't locked," the captain said.

Roderic stared at him in disbelief before putting out a hand and trying the handle. It gave readily. He stepped back then, nodding to Mara to indicate that she should enter first.

Mara swallowed. Her hand trembled as she placed it on the door handle. Perhaps her grandmother was too weak to rise, to call out. Perhaps her heart had failed her during the long wait for rescue, and she now lay dead in this great drafty stone mausoleum. There was only one way to find the answer.

The door swung open with ponderous slowness. The room was dim, lit only by the faint daylight falling through uncurtained windows. A huge bed beneath a *baldaquin* of embroidered satin that was gray with dust and age could be seen. A painted armoire of the type once called a marriage chest sat against one wall, and there was a settle drawn up near the fireplace. These were the only pieces of furniture. There was, however, a trunk and a pristine white nightgown, convent made, with a high neck and long sleeves that Mara recognized as belonging to her grandmother. The nightgown was thrown over the settle as if the elderly woman might have dressed in haste in front of the small fire that burned under the cavernous mantel.

At Mara's call, the others crowded into the room behind her.

The captain licked his lips as he looked from one grim face of the cadre to the other. "She—she must have stepped outside. She rises early, does the Madame."

They trooped outside once more, leaving the building by a rear door that gave on to a narrow back passageway. This was the passage between the kitchens and the servants' quarters, and led toward the stables and a few other outbuildings, including the privy. They searched the kitchens where a slattern in a greasy apron was just brewing a pot of coffee. The privy was discreetly canvassed. The captain had begun to stammer when Mara, staring at what appeared to be a chicken house, gave a glad cry.

Grandmère Helene came walking toward them. The hood of her cloak was thrown back so that her white hair shone in the light of the rising sun. The hem of her cloak and her gown dragged where they were wet with dew. In her hand she carried a basket piled high with eggs, while behind her like a tame dog walked a white milk goat with a pair of kids gamboling around her. She lifted her hand in a wave, her lined face creasing in a smile of welcome.

"Good morning," she called, her voice gaily lilting as she came near. "You are all in time for a breakfast omelette."

As a good Creole housewife, food was one thing Grandmère Helene knew. Though it had been years since she had prepared a meal with her own hands, she had always supervised her own kitchen personally, and the recipes that appeared on her table were her own, copied out in her elegant, flowing script. She had charmed her guards not only by her gracious manners, but by the quality of the meals she had prepared for them, using the wholesome country items that lay near at hand. The goats and the chickens belonged to the caretakers of the château, a family of peasants descended from a servant of the aristocratic family who had built the place. They had been encamped in the great house since the revolution. Owners came and went with the many changes of government, but they remained.

The captain of the guard was the elder son of the caretakers, the others were distant cousins. Grandmère was not happy about the injuries they had sustained defending the château. They had been good to her, like her own family. She required that they be given medical attention and released for breakfast.

It was kind of Roderic to ride to her rescue, she said; he must not think her ungrateful. He was very like his father, so impetuous, so amazingly able, so handsome. Seeing him brought back such memories. And how thoughtful it had been of him to bring dear Mara; she had worried so about her granddaughter and could now be easy in her mind. He must call her Grandmère, if he pleased. Would he care for a little wild onion and perhaps a bit of goat cheese in his omelette?

Roderic was charmed. He sat in the kitchen talking to the elderly woman as she moved about doing the tasks of cooking. They spoke of his father and the time he had spent in Louisiana, of the things he had done there, and also of Angeline his mother who had been well-known to Helene. By degrees he led the conversation to Mara and her father, and listened, absorbed, to everything the older woman had to say about how they lived and where.

Mara, helping her grandmother when she could, was intensely aware of the growing rapport between the other two. It affected her strangely, for she thought she discerned the glimmering of a purpose on both sides. She was not certain what it was in either case, but feared that she was the cause.

The day wore on. The prince seemed to be in no hurry to leave the bucolic retreat they had found. The cadre gathered in the antler-hung hall and built up an enormous roaring fire, using several tree trunks, in the fireplace. They knocked the dust from the settle cushions and stretched out to rest after their long hours of hard riding. Warm, filled with good food, they soon slept. Even Demon put his head on his paws, sighed, and closed his eyes. He opened them lazily as Juliana's Pekingese, Sophie, came to curl up against his side, then shut them again.

Mara could not seem to relax enough to rest. She had the feeling that it would be best for them to quit the place as soon as possible. De Landes might appear at any moment. What he could do with Roderic and his men in possession, she did not know; still, she had no wish to find out.

She walked to a pair of tall windows that opened out onto a balcony at the front of the château. The windows overlooked one of those distant prospects so admired by French landscape architects. Between an alley of trees stretched a long sweep of ground extending unbroken to a building perhaps a half mile away. Doubtless the vista had once been carpeted with greensward. Now it was made up of plowed fields lying fallow for the winter, though the act of plowing had kept the view open instead of becoming overgrown. On either side the garden had closed in, becoming a tangle of underbrush and dead trees that were the roosts of owls and small falcons. As she watched, a falcon rose from the woods and circled the sky, shrieking its fierce pleasure to the wind.

The falcon was free, and she was not.

"Pensive and forlorn, do you require solace, or would it be an insult?"

Roderic's voice was beguiling. It grated on her nerves, setting up a fluttering in her stomach. Or perhaps that disturbance was caused by his nearness as he moved to stand close beside her with his arm braced on the window frame.

'You have rescued my grandmother, for which I must thank you. I require nothing more."

"I have outstripped my usefulness then? What a blow to my esteem."

"I doubt it will be damaged."

"Do you?" he said, the words suddenly hard and clipped. "I am only a man, Mara, with a man's weaknesses and needs. I have never pretended otherwise."

"You are a prince and expect everyone to bow to your will!"

"To deny my birth would be the act of a fool, but for every privilege that goes with it there is an obligation, for every source of power a danger. And princes are still men."

He pushed away from her. Before she could turn, before she could answer, he was gone.

With the dawn of another day, they were on the road to Paris. The ladies rode in the traveling carriage with the cadre strung out around them. Estes brought up the rear, for he was carrying in a bag on his saddle a goat cheese made by Grandmère Helene that she refused to leave behind. The cheese, in the process of ripening, was extremely aromatic. Demon, wise dog, refused to ride in his basket on his master's saddle, but begged a place inside the carriage with the ladies and Sophie.

Roderic was attentive to Grandmère's comfort, handing her down from the carriage and back into it when they halted, tucking the lap robe around her, using a gentle and hilarious raillery to raise her spirits when they began to flag with fatigue. Once or twice he swung from his saddle into the vehicle to ride with the ladies, entertaining them with a seemingly effortless stream of comments and gossip on the places they passed, most of which was slanderous and so delicately improper that Grandmère

Helene was delightfully scandalized. The result of his efforts was that by the time they reached the city the elderly woman had accepted his invitation to stay with him at Ruthenia House. Her granddaughter would stay with her, of course.

It was so cleverly done that there was never a time when Mara could, with grace, have declined. She might have shouted out a refusal and started a brawling, screaming quarrel there in front of everyone, but the only reason for her objection she might give that her grandmother would accept was so personal that she could not bring herself to do it. She would not stay, however. On this she was determined. As soon as she could see her grandmother alone, she would explain exactly what had happened and that would be the end of it.

It was cowardice, and also an enduring hope that it would not be necessary, that had made her put the explanation off until now. Grandmère Helene had guessed, when she had seen the château and realized that there were to be no other guests, that she was being held to ensure Mara's cooperation in de Landes's scheme. She had taken it for granted, however, that the prince, in coming to her aid, had acted the honorable part, responding nobly to a simple appeal from Mara. She seemed to think that the lapse of time was due to her granddaughter's need to become better acquainted with Roderic before placing her trust in him.

There was no way of knowing how her grandmother would react to the knowledge of the sacrifice that Mara had been forced to make for her sake. She was made of sterner stuff than Mara had known, as had been proven during her recent incarceration. And yet she could not help being hurt. Regardless, she must be told. She would be, as soon as they were alone.

Mara had not counted on how hard it would be to make the elderly woman understand the situation.

"What do you mean you cannot stay, my dear?"

"I will not place myself under Roderic's protection, not be his mistress a moment longer. I am sorry if my plain speaking embarrasses you, but—"

"Embarass me? I am no miss from the English court of Victoria! I assure you we spoke much more plainly even than that when I was a girl. What I want to know is why you feel you cannot abide the man."

"He— Oh, you must know! He has no idea of marriage."

"Has he said so?"

"He is a prince!"

"That was not a bar to the marriage of his father and Angeline. From what you say, you seduced the man, and for a reason that had nothing to do with his attraction to you. You must give him time to come to terms with the idea."

"It wasn't quite like that."

"A promising admission. What was it like?"

"It was— Never mind! Oh, Grandmère, don't you see? We can't stay here. It would be immoral."

"You are afraid you will be hurt. Angeline was like that, running away when she most wanted to stay."

"If you are suggesting that I care for Roderic—"

"Don't you?"

Mara turned quickly away. "Of course not."

It wasn't true, but if she pretended strongly enough that it was, it might be in time.

"You used him, Mara. Think what that means to him."

"He knew what I was doing and permitted me to continue out of mere curiosity." She could not prevent the bitterness from rising in her voice.

"He could guess. Whatever he may have said, he could

not know. The wonder is that he did not murder you or abandon you the instant he discovered the truth. I find it . . . interesting that he did not, that he offered his usefulness as—"

"As a means of taking you hostage."

"As protection."

"He will use you to force me to his will. He said as much. You think him charming, but he can be ruthless. You don't know him as I do."

"You have a different view, which is as it should be."

Mara turned back. Speaking with slow emphasis, she said, "I will not continue as his mistress."

"And a good thing, too! You will naturally sleep in your own rooms, close to mine. But I do not think that I want to remove from Ruthenia House, not at this juncture. In any case, I have already sent for our things. We will stay."

"I can't, you must know I can't!"

Grandmère was not to be moved. "Then you will have to leave alone, and what will you say to our cousin when she asks why?"

The thought of yet more explaining, of the salacious interest and censure she might meet with, was unendurable. Roderic liked her grandmother; it was possible that he would not wish to disillusion her at once. Mara agreed, finally, to stay until morning but no longer.

She did not expect to be able to sleep under the same roof as the prince. She had thought to lie awake, dreading a summons or perhaps even a visit from Roderic. If either came, she did not know it. Exhausted by the journey and her own conflicting emotions, she was still in bed the next day when Lila brought hot chocolate and rolls at noon.

Mara rose and allowed herself to be dressed with reluctance. She had no wish to resume the duties she had made her own here in this house; to do that would be too much like conceding defeat. But neither did she feel like playing the guest, sitting and simpering in the salon. She had no idea what Roderic meant to do now, how he meant to behave toward her. To be forced to continually fend off his advances would be a severe strain; it would be impossible to know what form they might take next. Worse still might be enduring his anger with its outrageous verbal barbs. It was in that guise that he had spoken to her last. She had not enjoyed it. Hardest of all to bear might be in the mien he was most likely to show her, that of his indifference.

She emerged at last, however. It was more of a strain to sit alone wondering how she would be received than it was to come out and see for herself. Lila, with a shy smile, told her that her grandmother was already up and receiving in the public salon, and requested that Mara join her there at her convenience.

The spate of morning callers had slowed. Grandmère Helene and Roderic were just bidding the last of them good-bye. There did not appear to be anyone remaining behind for the noon meal, though whether from luck or the lack of an invitation, it was impossible to tell. Juliana was absent, as was the cadre.

"How delightful you look," Grandmère Helen said, holding out her hand from her chair beside the fireplace as Mara entered. "Don't you think so, Roderic?"

The prince, standing behind her chair, inclined his head. "Delightful, indeed."

"Thank you," Mara said, her voice tight.

His words were so banal, compared to his usual eloquence, that his agreement was mere politeness. It had been a mistake to take such pains with her appearance.

She had done it to make herself feel better, for no other reason. She certainly did not want Roderic to think that it was for his benefit. The gown she wore was her own, however. At some time during the morning a carriage had been sent to the house of their elderly cousin, along with a note from Grandmère requesting that their clothing be packed and given to the driver. Lila had brought the gown she was wearing to her freshly pressed and was even now putting the rest of her things away in the armoire in her bedchamber. The gown was of gray blue challis printed with small gold fleurs-de-lis and had its own matching jacket in gray velvet. Wearing her own things gave Mara confidence since she knew that Roderic had not expended a centime on them.

Roderic moved to place a chair for her before the fire. She sent him a brief upward glance as she murmured the ritual thank you. The bright appreciation she caught reflected in his eyes sent a flush rising to her hairline. He had behaved as he had in order to provoke her, and he was well aware that he had succeeded. Such a man would not hesitate to entice a woman into his bed if she were chaperoned by a phalanx of nuns, much less a mere grandmother. Why Grandmère Helene could not be brought to see it was beyond understanding.

Mara sought in her mind for some topic of conversation that could not be twisted for use against her. Before she could decide on one, the noise in the entrance court of a hard-ridden horse caught her attention. Her grandmother said something she did not quite hear as she was listening to the fast tread of booted feet on the stairs. Glancing at Roderic, she saw that he had heard it, too, and was looking toward the door.

It was Michael who entered. His dark hair was ruffled, and there were spots of angry color on his cheekbones. He strode toward them waving a newssheet printed on cheap yellow stock. Handing it to Roderic, he said, "Read this."

As the prince took the paper, more footsteps could be heard outside. Trude pushed into the room, followed by Jacques and Jared. Close behind them came Estes. Of the four, three had copies of the newssheet clenched in their hands.

"What is it?" Mara asked, looking from one to the other.

Trude, her movements abrupt, handed the paper she held to Mara, then moved to stand near the arm of her chair in a peculiarly protective gesture. Estes, with a shrug, gave his newssheet to Grandmère Helene. The elderly woman looked at the glaring headline, then gasped, falling back in her chair.

PRINCE SEDUCES SISTER! GODDAUGHTER OF QUEEN LOSES INNOCENCE TO HIS HIGHNESS!

Mara stared at the words. For long seconds her brain, in shock, refused to function. Then abruptly she knew. Her lips formed the name without conscious direction.

"De Landes," she said softly.

"De Landes," Roderic repeated, and in his voice was such boundless menace that the soft skin of Grandmère Helene's face, as she lifted her head to stare at him, was suddenly pale with fright.

Mara drew a difficult breath and raised her head to meet the prince's gaze. "It is to be, I think, the Praslin affair all over again."

"The Praslin affair?" Grandmère Helene said, her fear making her querulous. "What are you thinking of? This is nothing like that murderous business."

"It's the scandal among the nobility that is the same and the possible effect upon the present regime."

"Roderic's title isn't French!"

"But he is a public figure, well known in the city and one close to the throne."

"A masterly conclusion, *ma chère,*" the prince said, his voice limpid. "Who pointed it out to you?"

"No one." She was briefly proud of the fact that her voice remained even.

"Not even our incubus, our Machiavellian friend with delusions of evil? Not even de Landes himself?"

"No."

Roderic shook his head, a smile, which did not reach his eyes, curving his mouth. "Remiss of him. He might also have suggested the only proper and holy redress for so obscene an accusation, the only bright and shining sword with which to cut through this Gordian knot of a problem. He might have told you to request marriage."

He waited with pent-up breath for her answer. What he wanted of her was unreasonable: that she should refuse for the right reasons so that he might persuade her to accept for the wrong ones. He held himself erect, his arms at his sides. Not by so much as a gesture would he influence her.

"Never," she said, her eyes dark with disgust. She got to her feet, swinging away from him.

He breathed again. "Why? Have you no desire to be a princess?"

"Not to your prince."

"Though governments clatter down around our ears and kings lose their heads with their crowns? It's a fine thing to place a high value on independence, but you must ask yourself: Am I worth it?"

What was he doing? His voice was too light, too insouciant. He was goading her, or so it seemed, but for what purpose? Her rage would not let her see it. All she knew was an overpowering desire to strike a blow that would force him to answer from the heart instead of from the pure and logical computations of his mind.

She turned to face him, her voice ringing clear. "I am an American. What are titles to me, or the useless trappings of kings? I care not whether governments fall or ancient family escutcheons are stained beyond cleansing. What I require in a husband is a man, not the arrogant son of a king who takes pleasure in manipulating those around him."

"What you require," he said, his voice daunting in its

sudden rich warmth as he moved toward her, "is someone who will make you forget who you are or whether he is or is not your husband."

Swiftly came her answer. "Not you!"

"Me. For reasons we all know and those you have not yet begun to guess, you will be my wife."

"No!" She backed away from him as he advanced.

"Oh, yes. You will. There is nothing and no one who can prevent it."

So intent had they been on the crisis that they did not hear the sound of a new arrival. There came a decided stir at the door. A man stepped inside. He stood straight and tall in the white uniform of the men of Ruthenia, though his hair shone silver-gilt in the pale sunlight shining in through the windows. As he spoke the slashing quiet of his voice reached every corner of the room.

"I can prevent it, and while I breathe I will. If you doubt it, then try me with your threats, my clamorous son, my valiant and most amorous son."

CHAPTER 13

"Your Majesty!"

The exclamation came from Grandmère Helene. She pushed herself from her chair and, with one hand on its arm for support, sank into a deep curtsy. In the sudden silence Roderic executed a curt bow that was echoed with greater reverence by Michael and the other members of the cadre. Mara, lowering her gaze, made her own curtsy.

Rolfe, king of Ruthenia, made a brief gesture of acknowledgment, then moved forward to give his hand to Mara's grandmother. "Madame Helene Delacroix, I believe, whose other name is Mercy."

"You remember that stupid gaffe of mine when first we met!" Helene said, flushing with pleasure. "How extraordinary and how kind."

It was indeed extraordinary since the incident had occurred nearly thirty years before. Mara had heard the tale many times, one Grandmère liked to recount, of how the prince, in thanking her for allowing him and his cadre to come uninvited to her soirée, had said to her in graceful compliment, "your fair name shall be mercy." Her grandmother had replied in some confusion, though with a willingness to please, "as you wish, your Highness, but I have been called Helene from birth."

Mara's grandmother went on, "It's been a long time."

"Many years too long," Rolfe replied. "How fares André?"

"Well. And Angeline?"

"Anxious about what transpires here in Paris. I am her emissary and unofficial minister of justice. It seemed there might be a need for such a dispensation."

In its way it was a question concerning the situation, or at least the part the elderly woman and her granddaughter had in it. The answer of Grandmère Helene was oblique.

"If you have been informed of what has been happening, then you will be aware that the young lady at the center of the controversy is my granddaughter. May I present her to you, sir?"

Rolfe turned and stepped toward Mara with a faint smile curving his mouth and stringent assessment in his eyes. Those eyes were no longer as vividly blue as his son's, and his hair was more silver than gold. His face was weatherbeaten, etched with lines of experience and character, and yet there was in it an implacable strength and insurmountable will that, added to his years, made him seem for the moment even more formidable than his son, if such a thing were possible.

He took her hand as she curtsied once more, raising her with a brief pressure. "Mara. A name from the Greek with yet a lilt of Erin, and allied with it the peat-smoke-colored eyes that see the future in dreams. With your beauty of face, it makes a powerful distraction. I don't wonder that Ruthenian diplomacy in France has lost its delicacy."

"Diplomacy," Roderic said, his tone hard, "is not the issue here."

His father turned a look as set and annihilating as a basilisk upon him. "So I apprehend. The question that rises at once to the reasonable and unclouded mind is: Why not?"

"Petticoat affairs are not, ordinarily, matters of state interest. This one became so only recently, but, barring unwarranted interference, will soon cease to be of interest to anyone other than the lady and myself."

"Would you arm a cannon to kill a gnat? It seems a like extravagance of weaponry to use as valuable a bauble as a crown to mark the end of a mere petticoat affair."

The vicious irony of his father's voice had no visible effect upon Roderic. "It would mark not an end, but a beginning."

"Based solidly on reluctance and hatred overcome by force majeure? It is, of course, a light and frolicsome prospect for the future."

"Would you choose a queen for me, one steeped in duty and stifled hope, all sighs and supine accommodation? There is less prospect of frolic there, I assure you."

Rolfe clasped his hands behind his back, querying at once, "Would you bend to the dictates of bourgeois respectability over a piece of petty gossip? If so, tell me now. It will be as well if the negotiations for the surrender of Ruthenia commence on the instant."

"If the alternative is to surrender, penitent and ash-covered, to uniformed and prejudiced ultimatums, then it may be a kingdom well lost."

In their voices was such suppressed violence that Demon whimpered and slunk under the settee. They were so evenly matched, so nearly the same in appearance and strength of will, that their words rang with the force of a battle of Titans. It seemed as if not one of the others in the room dared move or speak for fear of inviting the verbal blows upon themselves. Mara listened to the enmity in their words with horror and guilt beating in her mind.

King Rolfe stared at his son, his brows drawn together over his eyes. "Ham-handed and minus even the rudiments of guile or manners. If you handled the lady as maladroitly, no wonder she complains."

"This is not a courtly minuet with lace handkerchiefs and flourishes. It is expedient that I marry this woman."

"Expedient for whom?" Rolfe inquired softly.

"For Ruthenia, for France and our relations with this country. For you. For her. For me."

"No such proud immolation is wanted or required. You did not learn such clumsy statecraft at my court."

"No, now," Roderic said in an acid pretense of surprise. "And have all the cunning alliances that have kept our country free of revolution these many years been no more than fortunate coincidences then? Clumsy or cunning, I learned the shifts I use at your knee and no other, my father."

"The lessons, then, are not over. This is no affair for the marriage bed. Harmony in all spheres, the public and the private, requires something more than the exercise of your will." It was deadly wisdom, and meant to be, from father to son.

"I will have Mara."

"Defy your sire, if it pleases you, but defy your king at your own risk. There is a birthright at stake: Yours. Would you place it in jeopardy for this woman?"

"Don't!" Mara cried, the word wrung from her. "Please, don't. There is no question of marriage."

King Rolfe turned on her, his tone lashing. "Why? Have you no taste for crowns?"

"Very little! And none for the brawling that seems to go with them."

Roderic stepped to her side, facing Rolfe. "Leave Mara out of this quarrel. She is not a fit target."

"Thank you," Mara said, rounding on him with anger in the tilt of her chin, "but I need no champion. I am quitting the lists. I am not, nor will I be, a point of contention between you and your father."

"A worthy resolve but useless," the king of Ruthenia said, his tone suddenly, disconcertingly, pensive as his gaze rested upon the two of them.

"Bravo," Juliana said from where she stood, transfixed, in the doorway. "Dare I suppose this display of tempers is caused by the tale spreading through Paris? You might have waited for me since I am concerned in this supposedly incestuous relationship."

"That you are not," her brother told her with a commendable economy of words.

"But you will admit it appears so at first glance? Never have I had such strange looks as were directed at me today. And there are people gathering in the street outside the house. One of them flung filth at my carriage."

"If you were not in Paris," her father said without sympathy, "there would be no occasion for concern, temper, or the contamination of filth. Dare I ask what you have done with the crown prince of Prussia?"

"Arvin? Why, nothing! His manly pursuit has won the day, and we wait only for the bans to be read. Will you wish me happy?"

"Children," Rolfe said softly, "are curses visited upon us by ill-natured gods as punishment for dwelling in their Arcady."

"You aren't pleased?" Juliana asked, all innocence. "Let me understand. You decree that I wed and Roderic remain single? Or is it, perhaps, that your object is the opposite?"

"Tell me the worst. Tell me Arvin sits in the attic drooling and playing with toy soldiers. Or has he, perhaps, escaped you by jumping in the Seine?"

"How clever of you, Father. But he did not jump, he was overturned. A boat race, you see. I regret to grieve you, but I believe he went back to Prussia with a cold in the head and curses on his lips. Roderic arranged it."

"Delicate diplomacy," Roderic murmured.

Mara, watching Rolfe, thought she saw bright pride

rise with a hint of amusement in the king's eyes before it was ruthlessly suppressed.

"It is a great relief to me to know that he can be useful if he so desires," he said, his voice faintly acerbic as he glanced at his son. "I will, of course, require to hear what occurred in detail later."

Roderic bowed. "Of course."

Juliana lifted a brow. "That's all very well, but what of this scandal breaking around us? It promises to be . . . ugly."

Rolfe gave her a look of satirical surprise. "I am here, as is Madame Helene Delacroix. If propriety cannot be served by having as chaperons the lady's grandmother and godfather, then the world may talk as it will."

"Are you my godfather, sir?" Mara asked in surprise.

"As my queen is your godmother."

"I never knew."

"It has been until now, regrettably, an honorary position, a circumstance that can be remedied. Angeline, when she joins us, as I'm sure she will, will also wish to become better acquainted." He smiled with such warm and flashing charm that Mara blinked. Swinging away from her to his daughter, he went on, "But in the midst of these crises, would it be too much to ask for a glass of wine? I have had a tiring journey."

"The fatigues of age," Juliana said in spurious sympathy. "I had better go and see if there is a servant in the house whose nerves have not been wholly shattered from their eavesdropping."

"Direct them to serve it in my quarters, if you please. Roderic, if you will join me there while I remove the dust of travel, we have other matters to discuss. Ladies, I beg you will accept our excuses?"

The two men departed. The cadre drifted away. Juliana did not return from her conference with the staff. Mara was left alone with her grandmother. She seated herself in a chair on the opposite side of the fireplace. A footman came into the room to mend the fire and went away again. They were left alone.

When the door had closed behind the servant Grandmère said, "Well, my dear?"

Mara lifted a troubled gaze to her grandmother. "Yes?"

"Do you still wish to leave?"

"It would be best."

"Possibly, but is it what you want?"

"I'm so confused," she cried, her voice low. "I don't know whether I'm being protected or merely prevented from becoming a nuisance. Or both. I can't tell whether Roderic indeed wishes to marry me or whether it's duty and responsibility that drives him."

"Or defiance?"

"Yes, that, too."

"You could stay here, and wait and see."

"I don't want to wait!"

But even if she discovered that Roderic's desire to make her his wife was real, it would change little. Her appeal for him was based on some fantasy woman he had created in his mind. He thought her a creature of duplicity and caprice, and that image held an errant fascination that fueled his desire. He loved her not at all; he didn't even like her. When he came to know her, when he had solved the mystery of her to his satisfaction, it was all too likely that he would lose interest.

Grandmère sighed. "The impatience of the young. There are some things that require time."

Mara hardly heard the words. Looking steadily at her grandmother, she said, "Why is King Rolfe so set against me? He didn't want a Prussian prince for Juliana either, so it isn't necessarily a matter of bloodlines. What will it take to satisfy him?"

"You might ask him—strictly out of curiosity—if you stayed."

"Do you think it might be that he suspects, in spite of your being held by de Landes, that I might—might have some political reason for helping the man?"

Grandmère Helene pursed her lips. "It's possible, I suppose."

"I would not like to leave with him thinking such a thing of me."

"No. That would not be good."

"There is something else. If we quit Ruthenia House now, so soon after the appearance of this terrible story, it may look as if we are running away. Surely it would be better for everyone concerned if that impression were avoided."

"Yes, indeed!" the elderly woman said, a martial look in her eyes.

"Then there is my godmother. I have heard so much about her, and I long to see and talk to her. It may seem strange if, having stayed one night here, we leave before she arrives, and I would not hurt her for the world."

"I would very much like to see her myself."

"Yes, I'm sure."

There was yet another reason, though Mara could not bring herself to speak of it to her grandmother. As she had watched Roderic with his father, she had been assailed by a strong need to find out what kind of man he really was, whether there was anything behind the hard façade he wore, if any shadow of real emotion lay beneath the sharp and convoluted processes of his mind. She refused to conjecture what caused this need within her; she only recognized its presence.

"It is decided then? We stay?" Grandmère asked.

"Yes, it is decided," Mara answered. The capitulation, though firmly made, was without joy.

The ensuing days gradually took on some semblance of normalcy. After a visit by Rolfe to the editor of the newssheet that had printed the scandalous story, a retraction was published. The gathering of rabble outside Ruthenia House melted away, not the least reason being the guard mounted, of their own accord, by the cadre. Whether because of the demands on Roderic's time or the presence of Rolfe, Mara's nights were uninterrupted.

The king and his son remained estranged, but they managed to function together as hosts for the horde of visitors who descended the instant it was learned that Rolfe was in residence. Grandmère Helene was accorded the role of unofficial hostess and presided over most gatherings from her seat at the foot of the table or her chair beside the fire. Mara was treated as a daughter of the house, patronized by the king and alternately teased and ignored by Roderic. There were a number of speculative glances cast in their direction at first, but so solid was the air of respectability that had been cast around her that interest soon waned. The nightly gatherings in the salon continued, but many of those attending were of an older generation. The conversational tone became correspondingly less racy and exciting and more staidly boring. Attendance, not unnaturally, began to decline.

There were advantages, Mara discovered, to discarding her pose of amnesia. There was no longer a need to guard every word so that she could speak and act in her own natural manner. She could talk of Louisiana and of the way things were done there without reserve. All the questions she had longed to ask the different members of the cadre could now be expressed.

Michael's father, Leopold, she discovered, had married one of Angeline's ladies-in-waiting, a dark and merry woman who had given him nine children. They lived in a great, drafty castle perched high above a valley with a winding stream where the indestructible stone halls rang with shrieks and laughter. Michael's one ambition, when his soldiering with Roderic was done, was to find a wife and join his brothers and sisters in that vast keep, to grow wine grapes to rival those of France, and to perpetuate his line.

The twins, Jared and Jacques, were the sons of another of Rolfe's original cadre, Oswald. Their father had had a twin also, but that brother had died in Louisiana. At the moment they were both courting a seamstress, a desperate flirt who kept them both dangling. Their loyalty was given to Roderic, however, and they were content to follow where he led for as long as he cared to lead them.

Estes, the Count Ciano, told her so many tales of events he had witnessed and deeds he had done that the two became confused in her mind. He was an indefatigable talker, a gifted raconteur who always wove a thread of mirth thought his stories. When not on duty for Roderic, he was writing a book based on his life that would rival anything, so he declared, penned by Monsieur Dumas. Filled with dungeons and deserted castles, with endangered maidens rescued by the dark and passionate rogue of a hero, it had all the elements that would make it certain to pour gold into his pockets. It might be a trifle ribald, but not to excess.

"It will be banned," Trude told him, "placed on the pope's list of dangerous literature."

"Only because I contend that the hero should always be properly rewarded for his rescue efforts? What's wrong with that?"

"Your hero looks like you."

"Well?" the Italian inquired, preening as he smoothed his thick mustache.

Trude tipped her head toward the count, speaking to Mara. "He thinks he is the Eros of the nineteenth century."

He leered at her. "You think I am not?"

The blond amazon actually grinned at him. "Eros Estes."

Estes shook his head, his dark gaze mournful as he looked at Mara. "She doesn't understand literature. She thinks it's a joke. I had to fall madly in love with a big, blond amazon who laughs at me in her ignorance."

Estes got to his feet and wandered away with his head hanging. Trude chuckled. "He is a funny one. This love he has for me is the biggest joke, I think. At least—isn't it?"

It was the gypsy, Luca, who was the hardest to know. He seemed to fit no pattern. He was of the cadre and dressed in their uniform, but it always looked different on him, more rakish, less militarily correct though it was difficult to say just how the impression was gained. He performed the maneuvers expected, trained for strength and agility and quickness of reflexes in the various galleries and courts of the house as assiduously as any, and yet there was in his movements a hint of the unpredictable.

Something else not readily evident was why he had wished to join the cadre. The reason was not loyalty to a man. He respected Roderic and followed his orders without complaint, but there was nothing of devotion in his manner. It was not to belong to a company of his fellows. He mixed with them, laughed with them, drank with them on an equal footing, but he often slipped away by himself. It was not the military trappings, for though he was proud of his uniform and accouterments, he wore them only when occasion demanded. When it did not, he put on his gypsy clothes and was content. Usually he slept in one of the bedchambers occupied by the men of the cadre, but sometimes he still left the house to sleep in the courtyard, in the open.

Mara sometimes thought that though he had been drawn by many things, it was Juliana who held him. He leaped to be the first to perform a service for the princess and was always ready to act as her escort. Often, when she was not looking, he watched her, and once Mara had seen him pick up a glove the girl had dropped and slip it into his pocket. But he made no excuse to be with her and, when in her company, had little to say. He was an enigma, darkly handsome, a little wild, but steadfast and protective.

It was Luca who invited the household to the gypsy encampment. The band was growing restless with the inactivity of the restraint Roderic had imposed upon them. They had heard that the *boyar* was in Paris, and they wished to have their master, and also his son, among them once more. There would be feasting and music and singing, and they would dance the night away. Would they come?

They smelled the roasting pork and poultry before they reached the caravan, the rich aromas mingling with the tang of woodsmoke and the scents of hay and horses. The caravans stood in a circle, acting as a break against the cold, blustery wind. Inside the ring, cook fires burned bright red with coals, while another fire for warmth and light leaped high with orange tongues of flame licking toward the dark sky. Rugs were piled around the edges, and upon them men and women lounged. Children were rolled in the smaller rugs for warmth, or else raced here and there, playing with the dogs that ran in packs. Music throbbed, an undercurrent to the chatter and laughter and high-pitched yelling of children that rose inside the enclosure.

The dogs discovered their arrival first and hurtled down upon them, furiously barking. Roderic and Luca quieted them with a harsh command, but could not subdue the shouts and screams of welcome as the presence of Rolfe, the *boyar,* hereditary ruler, was discovered. The gypsies crowded around, trying to touch him. He accepted their homage with every sign of pleasure and enjoyment, slapping the men on the back and kissing the women who flung themselves into his arms.

With scant ceremony but much affection, he was led to the place of honor on the richest of the rugs before the fire. Roderic was placed at his right and Mara was pressed down beside the prince. The man who led the band in Roderic's absence, a rough fellow with a craggy face and straight black hair covered by a kerchief, was seated on the *boyar*'s left so that they might consult together. Juliana was welcomed and seated beyond the gypsy leader. Luca took the place beside her. Michael procured a chair from a nearby caravan for Grandmère Helene, setting it down next to Mara and dropping down beside it; the others found seats where they could.

Wine was poured and handed around. A mandolin was put into Roderic's hands. The music of gypsy violins began softly, rising into the night. Wild and sweet, it spoke of life and love and freedom of the spirit. Roderic picked up the counterpoint, the notes falling mellow and pure from his fingers.

Mara had thought to be diverted, perhaps amused. She found instead that she was content. Above her was the open sky with its tiny pinpricks of stars. The night and the winter wind were held at bay by the caravans and the roaring fire. The wine was raw and new but good, warming her inside. The music was soothing and, at the same time, exciting in an unexpected fashion. But it was the gypsies themselves who affected her most. They might be curious, but they did not intrude. They accepted her as she was, without question, without judgment. She was there. It was enough.

Around her, the others were also leaning back, smiling, drinking. It was only as the tension slipped away that she realized how tightly strung they all had been. It was as if beneath the careful masks they displayed they were in grim anticipation of some further cataclysm. For tonight they could relax, could believe as the gypsies did that life was life, and no matter how it was lived, it was far better than death. It was this that Roderic had tried to tell her that night he had found her in the Seine. His words had hardly registered then in her distress, but now they echoed clearly in her mind.

Listen carefully, ma chère, *and heed me well: There is no fate worse than death . . .*

There had been something more, but she could not quite bring it to mind. No matter. The words held a certain power, and she cherished them.

Into their circle toddled a small girl not much more than a year old. Her hair grew in soft, feathery, dark curls over her head, and her eyes were deep black and laughing. Behind her came an older girl of five or six scolding like a mother as she tried to head the child off.

The little girl, hardly more than a baby, stumbled on the edge of the piled rugs, falling toward the fire. Roderic thrust out a hand to catch her, clutching a handful of skirt by which he swept her, one-handed, into the curve of his arm. He put his mandolin aside and tossed the child up so that her startled whimper turned into a radiant chortle of joy.

"A tender morsel, but too precious for roasting," Roderic said.

The baby grabbed at his hair, tangling sticky fingers in its gold strands while placing a very wet kiss on his nose. He discovered the damp condition of the gown he held and heaved a resigned sigh.

"Drooling and encroaching, incontinent and inconveniently affectionate. It's a mystery how the human race has survived."

Mara, watching him patiently disentangle the small hands and cuddle the child, nuzzling her tender neck, felt a foolish smile curve her mouth at this unexpected insight into the prince of Ruthenia. Why she should be happy or surprised, she could not tell. They had spoken of babies, she and Roderic, on the night they met, but there had been little to indicate that he liked them. Or was good with them.

When it was ready, the food was delicious, seasoned with herbs and garlic, the fat crisp, brown and crackling, the meat succulently tender. The bread, baked in the coals, was crunchy and tasted faintly of smoke, a perfect accompaniment. It was all washed down with more wine, after which they, at least those who were guests, wiped their greasy fingers on rough toweling that had been dipped in water scented with vetiver.

They were still eating when a troop of horsemen approached. Silence fell as the uniforms they wore were identified. It was the gendarmes. The gypsy leader cast aside the turkey leg he held and rose to his feet. With Roderic, who was already standing, he walked to where the mounted police had stopped.

It was a matter of a stolen horse, or so ran the whisper around the caravan. The gendarmes wished to search for the animal and the thief. The gypsies had nothing to hide, of course they did not. Let the police enter. Give them food and drink. Play, dance, sing.

Roderic, as courteous as if in his own salon, directed the men to places on the rugs. Wine and roast pork were brought and put before them. The music rang out loud and gay. A young woman carrying a bright red scarf embroidered in gold ran from the edge of the circle and began to whirl, scarf flying, around the main fire. The cadence of the dance was picked up by the gypsies as they began to clap in time to it. The dancer's eyes gleamed and her smile flashed as she turned and stamped and undulated. The coins strung in a necklace about her neck clashed. Faster and faster she danced until with a crashing discord she flung herself down before the gendarmes and Roderic. There was a burst of applause that quickly died away as the music began once more. It was a slow and sensual melody in a minor key, and the movements of the dancer as she rose were smooth and controlled, timeless in their seductive power. She danced for the gendarmes, trailing her scarf across their faces and over their shoulders, but, most of all, she danced for Roderic.

The prince's smile remained polite, but there was appreciation in his eyes. Watching him, Mara felt her stomach knot inside her. She looked away. Demon sat begging at her feet, his eyes anxious. She handed him the pork rib she held and wiped her fingers, then picked up her cup and drank deep. The race of the wine in her blood was half pleasurable and half painful. Her contentment was gone. It was not hard to find the reason. She was jealous.

She had been forced to seduce a prince and had made the mistake of falling in love with him. It was a stupid thing to do, stupid and useless and humiliating. He was from a different world, a world of privilege and power and careful alliances. Even if they had met under normal circumstances, because of the slight family connection, it would have been unlikely that they could overcome the differences in their stations. After her betrayal of him and the scandal that she had brought upon them both, it was impossible. The best that she could hope for was to prevent him from learning how she felt and so salve her pride.

She looked away from Roderic and her gaze fell on Luca. The gypsy sat with his arm resting on the top of a drawn-up knee and his attention upon the face of Princess Juliana. The firelight flickered over his dark features, limning in orange yellow gleams the naked emotions that hovered there. Because Mara felt the same longing that she saw reflected in the gypsy's eyes, she recognized it at once. The newest member of the cadre was in love with Roderic's sister.

The dance continued. Now a gypsy man signaled for slower music and began to move to its rhythm. With majestic sureness, he posed and strutted, circling the crowd gathered around. At last he chose a woman, beckoning, his smile enticing. She joined him, and together they glided, turning back to back with arms extended, whirling suddenly to be face to face, coming close, springing apart, holding perfectly to the heartbeat pulse of the music. With their hands on each other's hips and passion in their eyes, they moved in a ritual of suggestive courtship, advancing, retreating. The music quickened; faster they danced, and faster still. Until, abruptly, the man pulled his chosen woman into his arms and swept her through the crowd and into the darkness beyond.

The night progressed. The gendarmes, growing maudlin on strong wine, began to sing, and the gypsies joined in. They sang old peasant songs and the lyrics from the most popular operettas; arias from the operas of Donizetti and Bellini; and risqué ditties from Left Bank cabarets. By the time they had run out of songs, the horse thief had been forgotten. In any case, so great was their feeling of comradeship that when the gypsies offered once more to let them search, the gendarmes declined with fervor. Shortly thereafter they rode away to make their report to their superior.

The children were put to bed. Grandmère Helene nodded off in her chair. Roderic took up his mandolin once more and began to play a soft and haunting tune. The violins picked it up, the sounds blending, rising, falling, passionately pleading, heart-stopping in its sweetness.

The music seemed to reach inside Mara, to touch the ache in the center of her chest. Driven by an urgent need to escape it, she drained the last of her wine and rose to her feet. She pushed away from the circle about Rolfe, skirting a cook fire and following the enclosing line of caravans. She came to an opening between them and eased through it. Beyond was windswept darkness, lit here and there by a scattering of fires where more gypsies were encamped. It was cold away from the fire. She drew her cloak around her, shivering.

From the caravan just beside her came the sweet smell of hay. Though it had solid sides and the same curved top as the others, it had no back. Wisps of the hay, apparently fodder for the horses raised by the band, spilled on to the ground. It would make a soft seat and the caravan's walls would offer some protection from the wind.

She had been seated for no more than a few minutes when the music that had so disturbed her died away. The relief was intense. Allowing her muscles to relax, she leaned back upon the hay piled up behind her. She closed her eyes, willing herself not to think, trying to recapture some of the careless philosophy of the gypsies. Life is life. Each moment is a gift. Enjoy.

The bed of the caravan creaked at a shift of weight. The hay rustled. Mara opened her eyes to see the shape of a man outlined at the end of the caravan. With a smothered cry, she threw herself to one side, ready to slide past him.

"Don't be frightened. It's only me," Roderic said.

Slowly, she subsided, though her heart was jarring in her chest. "What do you want?"

"You should not wander away alone. Some lusty gypsy might take it as an invitation."

"He would be wrong."

"But the discovery could come too late."

She could not quite make out his face in the dimness, though she could see the faint white shimmer of his uniform as he moved to let himself down beside her. His form bulked large, making her acutely aware of him as a man and of their isolation.

"I must rejoin the others," she said quickly.

"There's no hurry since you are no longer alone. Of course, if it's fear that impels you—"

"I'm not afraid of you." Wary, distrusting, but not afraid.

"Then why do you avoid me?"

"I don't!"

"You have left my bed—"

"You could hardly expect me to stay!"

"Why? Because my usefulness to you was at an end? Because there was no one to force you? Because propriety has been restored? Because King Rolfe might frown? Or is it because I used fear as a weapon to gain your cooperation, and you cannot forgive it."

"All those things," she answered in defiance.

"Then take them in order and tell me why they have validity."

"You know why!"

"I only know that the memory of you burns in my mind, violet blue and shimmering with the iridescence of pearls. I know that I want you, that there is no kingdom that will suffice if you are not in it. I long to touch and to hold you, to taste the honeyed essence of you . . ."

To stop the flow of his words, she said, "You want a woman. The gypsy dancer will undoubtedly please you just as well."

"You noticed." There was satisfaction in his tone.

"How could I not when you were positively doting on the command performance? How could anyone?"

"You were jealous."

"I was not!" She pushed away from him, trying to get out of the caravan. He caught her arm, hauling her toward him with such quickness that she landed on her back in the hay.

"You were," he said softly as he leaned above her, pinning her arms beside her. "You want me."

"No!"

"Yes. You remember as I do the silken nights and the mornings that came too soon."

"No," she whispered, but it was a lie.

He did not bother to answer, leaning instead to press

his lips to hers. He molded their smooth and tender surfaces to his own, gently trying the sensitive line where they came together until they parted to permit him entry. He took that permission unhesitatingly, exploring in sensual wonder the fragile inner surfaces. Warm and flavored with wine, their mouths clung, then slowly she raised her arms to lock them behind his head.

Life was life and must be lived. Yesterday was gone and tomorrow was no more than a shadow. Tonight was the only certainty, the present moment all that was guaranteed. It could not be wrong to take the pleasure it offered and make of it a bright memory for the future, if there was a future. She loved this man. No matter what he might have done, she could not deny the quickening of her blood or the aching fullness of her heart that only he could bring. Drowning in languor and fatalism, Mara pressed closer to Roderic's hard length.

Their bodies sank into the thick hay. Its fragrance surrounded them with the intimations of summer and warm sun. It rustled quietly as they moved, a soft but prickly bed. The wind made a soughing sound around the edge of the caravan's curved top and touched their skin with chill fingers so that they burrowed deeper into the hay.

Roderic's lips burned along the curve of her cheek, the turn of her jaw, the tender arch of her neck. He reached to gather her skirts, drawing them higher until his hand touched her knee. He pushed the mass of skirts and petticoats higher, and she made a soft sound in her throat as she felt the warmth of his hand through the thin material of her pantalettes. He spread his fingers over her abdomen, spanning its flat width, then in a swift movement leaned to press his face into that firm softness. Gently, insidiously, he parted her thighs, searching for and finding the slitted crotch opening of her pantalettes.

She felt the slight roughness of his fingertips at the most sensitive point of her body, and then the warm exhalation of his breath, the heat of his mouth.

Pleasure, a vital and perilous rapture, swept in upon her with such force that it took her breath. Awareness receded and yet, at the same time, expanded until she was not sure she could bear it. Never had she felt so alive, so vital. She was a part of the night and the music and the wild freedom of the gypsy camp, of the chill winter wind, and also of the man who held her. The blood raced in her veins and her heart swelled to bursting, jarring as it beat against her ribs.

She gripped his shoulder with her hand, clasping tight, kneading, stroking. Her lower limbs felt heavy, the muscles taut. Her skin glowed with heat. Inside her was a quickening, burgeoning sensation. She wanted, needed, to feel his strength against her, within her. She want to encompass him, to take him deeper and deeper still, until he was a part of her and she a part of him, without differences of rank and station, female and male. Without end.

She pushed her hand between them, slipping the frogs of his uniform jacket from their clasps. He shifted to help her. They opened their clothing, drawing the edges aside, lowering those garments that were most constricting. They came together then with the shuddering inevitability of magnet and iron, face to face in the whispering, sweet-scented hay. Their limbs entwined, they pressed close.

"Mara," he said, an entreaty and a benediction, then with a powerful twist of his hips he entered her, plunging deep.

Caught in the passionate compulsion of the joining, Mara moved with him, against him. Together they strove with the blood pounding in their veins and their breathing deep and hard. Their skins were moist, burning to the touch. Their lips met in a kiss devouring in its ecstasy.

The tumult stretched, gathered, flowed, swept in sudden grandeur toward the inevitable explosion.

It burst upon them, silent and glorious, seductive in its magic. They let it take them, close-held, into grateful beatitude. With entwined limbs and soft caresses, they drifted and came, slowly, to rest.

It was some time later that a cold wind touched them. With reluctance, they eased apart, sitting up, adjusting clothing. Finished, Roderic reached to help Mara, doing up the tiny buttons of her bodice as she smoothed her hair. Halfway through his task, he bent his head to press his lips to the deep valley between her breasts.

It was at that moment that Rolfe stepped into view. He placed one foot on the footboard of the caravan, speaking in dulcet tones with an undercurrent of steel.

"What crude pastoral joy, tumbling in the hay. It lacks polish, finesse, and even common sense, but can be sublime in a scratchy fashion. I trust the experience was memorable, for it will be the last."

CHAPTER 14

Revolution was in the air. Not in nearly sixty years had the mood of the people been so angry, their dissatisfaction with the present government so vocal. They were also, and most overwhelmingly, bored. They looked back on the days of the empire under Napoleon and sighed for the past glory of France, forgetting the blood of the flower of French youth that had been spilled to secure it and the enormous sums it had cost. The heads of the aristocrats of the Old Regime had been loped off in the Place de la Concorde and good riddance, but, ah, what days those had been when the Sun King had ruled from Versailles and all the world had journeyed there to pay homage to La Belle France!

And how different was the court of Louis Philippe. There was no glory and no grandeur there. There was only pompous respectability, lean times, and, as one sage put it, "a chicken-hearted monarchy which allows France to be humiliated." Their country, which had once stretched from the English Channel to the Rhine River, from the North Sea to the Ottoman Empire, had been reduced to less than the original boundaries before Napoleon. Stirring events, important revolutions, and alterations in the governments of other countries had taken place while France stood idly by. People were starving in the winter cold while nothing was being done to help. They were being ruled by a corrupt and vulgar middle class and a ridiculous usurping king, a cause for shame. A change would have to be better; it could not be worse.

The poet-politician Lamartine's book, *Histoire des Girondins,* with its idealistic presentation of the revolution and excuses for the excesses of the Terror, was being read and quoted everywhere. Lamartine was much in demand as a speaker at the series of reformist banquets that were being given all over the country. At these banquets people were being fed great helpings of oratory concerning universal suffrage, the rule of the common man. It went down well. The king and his advisers watched the unusual feasts with mounting alarm.

At the gatherings in the public salon at Ruthenia House, there was unimpaired complacency among the increasingly staid visitors. Louis Philippe was a decent and moderate man. His reign had been the most stable since the revolution. No one would be mad enough to resort once again to violent change with all its attendant dangers, no matter how much romantics such as Lamartine ranted about individual freedom.

But as company in the public salon grew thinner and more middle class in complexion, the visitors to the private quarters of the prince not only increased in number, but became more rabidly opposed to the present government. Here came the writers and artists, sculptors and composers who had been in the vanguard of the romantic movement; Hugo, Balzac, Madame Dudevant, and Lamartine, with a dozen others. They talked, argued, drank, and sometimes smoked small Turkish cigars or the exotic hookah with pellets of opium. How seriously they took what they had to say, how much they truly desired the reforms that would bring about the rule by the common man they so avidly espoused, was difficult to say.

The stream of merchants, modistes, doctors, lawyers, maids, hairdressers, and drivers of drays continued to flow through the house. The cadre came and went on mysterious missions. Mara would have expected that such activity would slow with the defeat of the assassination plot; instead it seemed to increase. The information gathered was seldom mentioned among the ladies, but from an occasional reference was assumed to be less than reassuring.

Late one evening a fast, lightweight traveling carriage pulled into the courtyard. Its gilt-work was bright, its turquoise paint gleaming, and the arms on the door royal. Two liveried footmen stood up behind it, and outriders surrounded it. The door was opened and the steps let down. From it descended a lady dressed in green velvet trimmed with mink, with a plumed hat tilted forward on auburn hair only slightly fading into silver at the temples.

By the time her elegantly shod foot had touched the cobbles, Roderic had clattered down the stairs to the courtyard while behind him Rolfe descended with more dignity. It was Rolfe, however, who stepped forward to take the lady's hand and raise it to his lips before dragging her into his arms.

When they could speak, he said, "Angeline, wretched female, all curiosity and meddlesome instincts—who is minding my kingdom?"

"A bevy of people from chamberlain to ministers, all more qualified than I," she replied, blithely unrepentant. "You could not have thought that I would spend Christmas alone when you are all in Paris? Confess, you have been expecting my arrival for days."

"And marveling at your restraint."

"Odious man," she said, her smile caressing. Straightening her hat, she turned to her son. "Well, then, where is your seductress?"

"Outrageous, Maman; you might consider her feelings," he said, laughing as he gave her a vigorous hug that once more required attention to her hat.

"Now, why? If either of you has shown that much forebearance, I shall be extremely shocked."

Mara had been waiting on the steps. She came forward, and Roderic stepped over to take her hand, presenting her in form. Angeline, a smile curving her generous mouth and rising to the soft gray green of her eyes, enveloped her in a warm embrace.

"What a delightful surprise to meet my goddaughter at last and to discover her to be something quite out of the ordinary. I see your father in you, a little. I understand Helene is with you? Let us go inside and all have a long talk."

The arrival of Roderic's mother brought a greater lightness to the atmosphere of Ruthenia House, and crowded the public salon once more with her friends, acquaintances, and those who thought it proper to welcome her formally to the city. The days whirled past in a round of visits, soirées, balls, and performances at the theater and the opera; of shopping for gifts to be exchanged at the new year; and of carriage rides about the city. Angeline, after that first evening when she had heard the full tale of the relationship between Mara and Roderic, said little more about it. She treated Mara with a certain familiar fondness, but did not take sides in any way in the quarrel between Roderic and his father.

There was one incident to disturb the smooth tenor of the days. At the Comédie Française one evening, Mara lifted her opera glasses to the box across from the one occupied by the Ruthenian party and saw de Landes. The man had the temerity to smile and bow. He was not pleased, not at all, when Mara allowed her gaze to pass over him without a sign of recognition.

The Yuletide season came and went. They attended midnight mass on Christmas Eve, a beautiful ceremony celebrated by the light of thousands of candles. On Christmas Day, they carried several carriageloads of food baskets to orphanages and hospitals, baskets personally packed by Angeline, with the help of Juliana and Mara. The principal day for the giving of gifts, the first day of the new year, was clouded, however, by the death the evening before of Madame Adelaide, sister to King Louis Philippe.

The city was thrown into gloom. The court went at once into deepest mourning. Entertainments were canceled. Black draped the windows of houses and shops. Draper's shops were inundated with the demand for cloth in the mourning colors of black and purple, gray and lavender. Modistes and the seamstresses who labored for them in the ill-lighted back rooms of Paris worked through the night for weeks to supply the demand for garments. Because Angeline was related in the most distant of fashions to the royal family, black arm bands were ordered for the men at Ruthenia House and a pair of gowns in somber, black-trimmed gray for each of the ladies, one for day and one for evening.

With the sudden decline in amusements, those at Ruthenia House were thrown back upon themselves. Mara spent one evening writing to her father, a task she had been putting off for some time. She began and then tore up so many drafts that she very nearly exhausted her stock of writing paper. There seemed to be no delicate way of setting down what had taken place, no way of explaining without sounding either as if she were making excuses for her conduct or blaming what had happened on her grandmother. At last she had written down the sorry tale as simply and completely as she could, then sealed it before she could change her mind yet again.

Roderic came upon her as she was setting the letter out for Sarus to carry to the sending office. He strolled with her to the salon. The situation between them was fresh in her mind after having just written of it. She had managed in the round of daily events to distance herself from it somewhat, but now it troubled her once more.

"The world is spinning toward destruction and France toward anarchy, but the fault isn't yours. Why then the scowl?"

"I'm not scowling," she said, and ruined the effect of a ferocious frown by allowing the corners of her mouth to twitch into a smile. She sobered at once. "No, I was thinking of your father. He doesn't seem overly concerned with the trappings of royalty; certainly he doesn't stand on ceremony. Your mother, despite a connection to the Bourbons, disclaims all pretense of being a blue blood. What then is it that King Rolfe objects to in me? Is it my character? My appearance? Or is it the part I played in involving you in the attempt on the life of Louis Philippe? It can make no real difference, but I would like to understand it."

Roderic, watching the play of emotions across her face, recognized her quiet courage in her search for the truth. She was not the fiery type of woman, quick to anger, flamboyant in her passions, and yet there burned inside her a steady and unquenchable flame. He saluted it by offering her what she needed to know.

"You need not trouble yourself. It's much more likely that it's my defects that stir his wrath. You assume he protects me, a grave error. He is much more likely to be protecting you."

She stopped still. "It cannot be."

"He is a loving parent and a devious one, but it would not, I think, occur to him that I stood in need of his defense."

"But why guard me?"

"Being of such a devious turn of mind, he suspects me of planning your seduction and foiling a coup in a single operation."

She stared at him. "You mean he thinks that you might have sent de Landes with instructions to embroil Grandmère Helene in illegal gambling, in order to persuade me to do his bidding? Why would de Landes do that?"

She was very quick, something to remember. Or else the possibility had occurred to her before. "For the sake of my aid in assassinating Louis Philippe."

"But you didn't aid him. You protected the king."

"A fine double cross, in that case."

She put her hand to her forehead, trying to think clearly. What he was saying made sense in a terrible kind of way. Abruptly, her face cleared. "No. You had no idea I existed until that night at the gypsy camp."

"You had been in Paris some weeks. Perhaps I had seen you somewhere, on the street, at the theater? Perhaps I knew you had arrived due to some communication between my mother and your grandmother and made discreet inquiries. Once I had seen you, I might have decided to make you my mistress, an impossibility if we had met in the respectable family circle."

"Surely you would have known that our—that the association would become known, with the attendant scandal?"

"Perhaps I never intended it to last beyond a few nights. Perhaps once I had held you in my arms I was content to let matters take their course, content to accept the consequences that would tie me to you."

It was no more than a game of words and ideas. That was all it was. "How could your father believe such a thing of his own son?"

"Easily," he answered, his eyes shadowed in the echoing dimness of the great corridor. "Why should he not since you half believe it yourself?"

"That I do not!"

"Don't you, *chère*? Don't you?"

She gave him a cold look. "It might help to clarify my feelings if you could tell me why it is that de Landes is still free, still going about his duties at the ministry?"

"How is it," he inquired softly, "that you know what he is doing and where?"

"What are you suggesting?" she asked, her spine stiffening. Her face paled with a fearful anger.

"It was a civil question."

"In whose opinion? But you need not exercise your mind upon the problem; there is no mystery, no subterfuge. I saw him at the theater, as you might have if you had not been occupied with your reformist friends."

His gaze was opaque behind the gold spies of his lashes as he studied her. Finally, he said, "There is a saying, hackneyed but expressive: 'Better the devil you know . . .' "

"Meaning you are watching him?"

"Something like that."

"Why?"

The question was bald, but she thought he would respond to it as well as to any attempt as subtlety.

"To see what may be seen."

If she had thought to learn what manner of man he was by direct methods, she must accept defeat. Her face tightened. "Very well. Be secretive if it pleases you."

"You suspect me of evasion?"

"Do you deny it?"

"Do you think," he asked, his tone pensive, "that if I wished I could not find a more pleasing lie?"

"I think that for you simplicity may pass admirably for a devious ruse."

It was not fair that he should stand so straight and tall, the embodiment, in his perfection of form and masculine beauty, of all that was proud and honorable.

He answered, unsmiling, "Then you will have to decide for yourself which it is, won't you?"

The weather moderated, becoming almost mild. The sun shone so bright that it hurt the eyes, and there was a feeling of spring in the air though it was only late January. The poor of Paris stirred from their dank rooms, coming into the streets to lift their faces to the sun; women with thin, silent children, beggars in their rags. Men gathered on the corners, talking, arguing, sometimes marching and shouting until dispersed by gendarmes on horseback armed with sticks and swords.

The ladies of Ruthenia House, drawn out by the warmth, went for a walk, down to the rue de Faubourg St. Antoine and along it to the Place de la Bastille, then to the right over the Pont d'Austerlitz to the Jardin des Plantes. The gardens were extensive, with thousands of botanical specimens collected from the far reaches of the world and methodically cultivated within its precincts. There were huge conservatories with arched glass roofs shining in the winter sun, and also a collection of exotic animals, including lions and giraffes from Africa.

They strolled along the gravel paths between the rectangular flower beds with their layers of mulch. They nodded at the nurses with young charges in prams and the elderly gentlemen who tipped their hats as they sat sunning on the benches beneath the bare-limbed trees. By degrees, Juliana and Mara drew ahead of Angeline and Grandmère Helene, who were walking at the pace of the older woman.

Demon, who had attached himself to Mara for the day, raced up and down inspecting this new territory. Juliana's Sophie trotted on her leash with her head up, sniffing the air, starting and darting momentarily under Juliana's skirts as a lion roared. Pigeons swooped here and there in flocks, descending en masse to strut about the walks, scratching in the gravel. Sparrows fluttered about like dry leaves. Children ran up and down, some bowling hoops along, all happily scattering the pigeons.

The Pekingese, being a dog with a superior pedigree, took exception to the looks of a common poodle, barking in pitched excitement. Demon joined in for support. The poodle, not to be intimidated, spread its forelegs and stood its ground beside its mistress.

"For shame, Sophie!" Julia exclaimed. "What conduct is this for a dog who is in a delicate condition. You have no more manners than morals." She turned on Demon. "As for you, you Casanova, quiet!"

The poodle's owner, a lady in an expensive toilette of varying shades of apricot beginning with the darkest color at the hem of her gown and gradually lightening to the palest at the silk flowers on her extremely fashionable bonnet, laughed and scolded her pet.

The poodle looked away in disdain. Incensed, the other two dogs increased their protests at its presence. In annoyance, Juliana commanded her Pekingese to be quiet in such quelling tones that Sophie flattened herself on the ground with a final, deep-throated growl. Demon, his assistance no longer needed, sat down with his tongue lolling out and awaited developments.

When she could make herself heard, Juliana apologized for her dog, and Mara added her own excuses for Demon.

"Please do not concern yourselves! It's only natural." The woman glanced over their gray costumes. "You are, I think, the ladies from Ruthenia House?"

"Have we met?" Juliana inquired, her tone a little distant. There was a dashing veil attached to the lady's apricot bonnet, and on closer inspection it could be seen that the jacket of her ensemble was cut with pronounced fidelity to the curves of her breasts.

"Oh, no. It would not be very likely. You were pointed out to me at the opera."

"I . . . see."

"Yes, you are quite right. I am indeed one of those 'dangerous and wonderful' women of the world, as we have been called. I prefer that to other names less complimentary. You need not fear, however, Your Highness, that I will claim an acquaintance when next we meet; I know my place better than that."

The words were spoken with such dignity and obvious sincerity that Juliana relaxed. She turned away. "Well, we are sorry to have inconvenienced you."

"Don't go, please! I would not speak ordinarily, but since the opportunity has come, I would like a few words with the other young lady."

"With me?" Mara inquired.

"If you will permit? You have been called in the gossip sheets an adventuress, one who has allowed herself to become involved with a most unstable prince. I would like to warn you, *ma chère,* of the danger you run."

"You know Prince Roderic?"

"Only by reputation. But though you have advantages of birth that have not been given to other women he has known, there can be no future for you there. He will have told you so himself; it's his way, or so I'm told. Believe him. Believe me."

"Spite and fatalism make a poisonous combination. Don't listen to her," Juliana said, catching Mara's arm.

"His affections are violent, compulsive, but are quickly over. You will be left to make your own way, and that way will lead you to this half-life that I live. Be warned."

There was, as Juliana had said, an undertone of defeat in the woman's words. Moreover, the things she said had occurred to Mara a hundred times over. She thanked the woman with a few stiff words and walked away with the princess. Still, the things that had been said would not leave her mind. Adventuress. Was that how Paris saw her? Was that how King Rolfe and Queen Angeline saw her? It did not bear thinking about.

There was only one aspect of the situation for which she could be grateful. Unlike poor little Sophie, she was not *enceinte.* There would be no consequences of that nature from her sojourn in Roderic's bed. It was a relief, and yet she could not be entirely happy. The complications that would have arisen were not something she cared to contemplate; still, the thought of carrying Roderic's child had an insidious and warming appeal.

There was an opportunity a few days later to discover what Roderic's father thought of her. Mara, with a footman behind her to carry her purchases, had been shopping for fresh vegetables for the house in the early-morning market at Les Halles. It was a job usually left to the cook, but now and then she liked to do it to keep current with what was available. She had thought that the queen might prefer to oversee it herself, but found that Angeline was no more inclined to usurp the place Roderic had given her than Juliana. Angeline had, in fact, been loud in her praise of the transformation in the house since her last visit. She herself had always been a little in awe of Sarus, she said, and fearful of offending him. She might have ventured it if she had spent much time in the house in Paris, but she and Rolfe had always missed Ruthenia too much to make an extended stay. It was brave of Mara to risk the dirt and thievery of Les Halles for the sake of a better table, but surely it wasn't necessary?

Mara had been returning from the market when an open carriage pulled up beside her. The door panel carried the crest of Ruthenia, and lounging on the seat behind the coachman was Rolfe. He inclined his head and reached to swing open the door. "Angeline sent me to find you. Get in, if you please."

Mara instructed the footman to return with his basket

to the kitchens without dallying for flirtation or political speeches. That taken care of, she stepped into the vehicle. The order to proceed was given at once.

"It is kind of the queen to be concerned about me," Mara said, "but there was no need."

"Martyrdom is not necessary either, whether for the reputation of the table at Ruthenia House or for the benefit of my scapegrace son. From now on you will send a servant."

"I don't mind at all, and even enjoy it at times."

"Bliss among the broccoli? That is a pleasure you may easily forego."

Mara recognized the command in his tone. "As you wish, sir."

He sent her a long glance. She stared back just as frankly. He was a distinguished man, with his silver-gilt hair and the laugh lines at the corners of eyes that gleamed with intelligence and calculated daring. This was the way Roderic would look in thirty years, she knew, and the thought caused a spasm of pain in the center of her chest.

"Tell me, mademoiselle, has Roderic been annoying you since the gypsy feast?"

"Not at all, sir."

They understood each other very well. Roderic had not been to her rooms, had made no overtures of a clandestine nature since that night in the hay wagon. Mara hardly knew whether to be glad or sorry, nor did she have any idea if the omission was due to the man beside her or to Roderic's peculiar set of principles.

"It seems unlikely."

"Perhaps you don't know your son as well as you think."

"I know he is a silver-tongued devil drunk with the delusion that he stands at the center of God's universe and has use of the four corners of the pellucid sky for his handkerchief."

"He is," she remarked demurely, "a great deal like his father."

"He is power mad and graceless with it, dense of mind for those things he has no wish to understand, but as cunning as a Gascony peasant at plotting degrees of treason and confusion to his enemies. He is agreeable to any piddling or dangerous mischief and resists common sense as if it were a disease."

There was heat in the tirade, though no virulence. Mara smiled at the man beside her. "And you would not have it any other way."

"He would not thank you for comparing us or for defending him."

"Then it's a good thing it isn't required."

There was in the look the king gave her a peculiar kind of approval. She had the fleeting impression, brief but definite, that she had passed some kind of trial. It gave her an unpleasant sensation, reminding her of those first days with his son when she had been forced to watch her every word, every gesture. The king had been more subtle, or perhaps she had just had less reason to be on her guard. Either way, she was grateful that she had not known.

The coachman appeared to have been given his instructions in advance. Instead of turning toward home, a short drive, he swung his horses in the direction of the center of town. They had threaded their way through the back streets, inhaling the smells of Paris compounded of roasting coffee and wine dregs; the aromas of tobacco from the shops and of ancient stone, ancient furniture, and ancient sewer drains.

Now they were turning into the Champs-Elysées. The boulevardiers, gentlemen who made a habit of promenading up and down the long, straight thoroughfare for the purpose of ogling ladies in passing carriages, raised their silk hats to her. A number of the glossy vehicles, known as victorias since they had found favor with England's queen, glided past with their tops down so that the ladies sheltering from the sun's rays under fringed parasols, whether comtesses or courtesans, could be seen while enjoying the mild weather. Under the bare limbs of the trees that lined the avenue were gypsy fortune-tellers, an organ grinder with his monkey, a man with a trained dog, and a trio of musicians with an upturned hat placed hopefully in front of them.

So long as she was alone with King Rolfe and temporarily in his good graces, however, it seemed as good an opportunity as she was likely to have to ask a question that troubled her.

Taking a deep breath, she said, "Can you tell me, sir, why Roderic is in Paris?"

"Easily. He is the bulwark of my information system, its strongest and most dependable link."

"Yours?"

"It began that way, and continues, though for some years he has delved into the affairs of Europe for his own reasons."

"If that's so, then—then you were not estranged before he came here?"

"Estranged, no, but that does not imply agreement between us."

She considered that for a long moment. "May I ask for what purpose you are gathering information in France?"

He gave her an appraising glance as if debating the wisdom of answering. His mind was made up quickly. "The stability of any country in Europe is affected by instability in any other. It's as well to know where the underpinnings are weakest."

"You would not—intervene—to increase, or to prevent, that instability?"

He lifted a brow, saying softly, "Would I not?"

"You must have known then what Roderic was doing

while he was here, you must have other sources of information, otherwise you would not have known about me and so would not be here now. That being so, why are you so incensed with him?"

Rather than answering her question, he said, "It is kind of you to be concerned under the circumstances."

"It . . . isn't kindness." She looked away into the street.

"What felicity. And brains as well. I have, perhaps, been a fool, but I did mean well."

"What?"

His expression abstracted, the king did not answer.

The days turned gray once more, and cold rain fell. Week after week, the chill dankness continued. The long gallery echoed with the snick and clang of sword blades as the cadre worked off their fidgets. Queen Angeline, in the best tradition of royal ladies, started a tapestry, a scene of hunters on horseback with a gypsy camp in the background and around the edges a thousand tree leaves depicting a vast forest. She sat stitching for long hours in the private salon in the royal apartments. Sometimes Mara helped, taking a part of the large canvas on her own lap. Juliana often plied a needle also, but seldom for long. She was too restless to sit still for any length of time.

It was on a particularly gray morning that Mara, moving from her own rooms toward the royal apartments, stopped to listen to the sound of a bout with swords coming from the long gallery. There was something different about it, something wrong, too slow and uncertain, in the beat of the blades. Michael and Estes, she knew, had been sent on some commission by Roderic, while the twins had discovered a new object for their affections. They were, with single-minded charm that seemed unlikely to fail, pursuing her maid Lila. Several members of the cadre were, she knew, out on errands. Swinging around, she moved to look into the matter.

Inside the double doors of the gallery entrance she paused. Before her was a sight she had never expected to see. Alone in the long room were Trude and Juliana. The female member of the cadre and the princess faced each other with buttoned épées.

Trude wore her trousers and a shirt. Juliana had put on a loose smock over what appeared to be an old habit skirt tucked up in front in order to give herself more freedom of movement. Roderic's sister looked up as Mara entered.

"Do come and join us, for pity's sake. Trude is determined to teach someone to fence, and my arm muscles are numb!"

"It is good to be able to defend oneself," the other girl said as she stepped back, disengaging. The scratch on her face had healed, fading without a scar. She still wore her trousers and took Roderic's orders with the others, but her braided hairstyle was softer, with deep waves at the temples.

"Yes, I know, particularly if one is a princess in these trying times." Juliana put the point of her épée on the floor and leaned the hilt on her hip as she wiped her perspiring face with the tail of her skirt.

"Any woman should be able to protect her person."

"My person is tired," Juliana complained. "I think it would be easier to surrender."

"But cowardly. Besides, surrendering to the mob can be dangerous."

"All right, I won't surrender, but I demand reinforcements. Mara, please!"

"I have another épée," Trude said with the brightening of her austere expression that was as close as she ever came to enthusiasm. "We shall be female musketeers."

And so began the lessons. They took place on the mornings when the long gallery was empty since neither

Juliana nor Mara felt any inclination to listen to the strictures and advice, or suffer the overzealous demonstrations, of the men.

The lessons included not only instruction in swordplay, but also in hand-to-hand fighting, in the handling of a knife, both in close combat and throwing it, and also proficiency with a pistol. For practice with the last weapon, they drove out to the edge of town, telling anyone who asked, most mendaciously, that they were going to visit a silk warehouse.

Sometimes Angeline came to watch and offer encouragements, but always firmly disclaimed any desire to try the weapons for herself. Mara and Juliana had cause to wonder if they were wise; their muscles were so cramped and sore at first that they were hard put to find excuses for their involuntary expressions of pain. With the passage of time, their strength grew and they became quite adept at the various skills. Their confidence increased with the strength and suppleness of their bodies, and, though they did not make the mistake of thinking that they could hold their own in every situation, they had the satisfaction of knowing that they could defend themselves.

It was on a night perhaps a week after the lessons had begun that Mara came wide awake. She lay listening, trying to identify what had roused her. At last she caught the murmur of voices coming from the antechamber where the back stairs descended. Easing out of bed, she picked up her épée, which lay on a chaise longue, and crept toward the open door of her dressing room. On the far side of that small cabinet of a room was the door into the antechamber. Crossing to it, she placed her hand on the handle.

She jerked it back at once. Directly on the other side of the door, the voice of King Rolfe could be heard. Its tones rang mellifluous and freighted with heavy irony through the heavy panel. Almost before he finished speaking, Roderic's voice began, the timbre of his words the same, though it carried an undercurrent of rage.

She could not tell what they were saying. It was frustrating beyond endurance not to know what was happening. It appeared that Rolfe was barring his son's entrance to her apartment, but why and with what means she could not tell. Before she could make up her mind to open the door and find out, the king issued what sounded like an ultimatum. Roderic answered, then their voices began to fade away.

Had Roderic been on his way to visit her bedchamber?

She leaned her forehead against the door, a little weak at the thought. More disturbing still, however, was the next question that occurred. How many other times had he tried and been turned away?

She would not have admitted him in any case. Or would she? Desire was a strange thing, a destroyer of resolve and moral sense. She had learned far too much of her own responses of late to say with certainty what she would and would not do.

She felt sheltered, safe. The protective mantle of a king was a privileged thing. At the same time, she was instinctively wary.

Why? Why was he interfering? Was it as Roderic said? Was his father guarding her against his attentions because he thought Roderic unworthy? Or was it at some request of Angeline's, made out of motherly concern and a sense of responsibility for the daughter of her former suitor? It was more likely because her position was so equivocal; as a goddaughter she could not be thrown from the house, but as an adventuress who had embroiled their son in a political and social fiasco, she must be prevented from entangling him further in her net.

She was sure of only one thing. It was not mere propriety. Rolfe had disposed of that motive when he had refused their marriage.

Nothing she could think of satisified her. She had the feeling that there was something more she could not see. It might be something simple, but she doubted it; both Roderic and his father were too fond of the devious for that to be so.

Like a rat in the wainscoting, she worried at the question for the rest of the night, but came no closer to the answer.

The affairs of others in the house proceeded with less complication. On the following evening as Mara made ready to dress for dinner, she decided on a hot bath to ease some of the soreness from her muscles. She rang for Lila and began to take down her hair.

The girl was slow in coming. When she finally arrived, she lingered outside the dressing room. The sound of her quiet giggles and comments could be heard, along with the rumble of bass voices. It took Mara only a moment to identify Jared and Jacques.

The dressing-room door gave inward and Lila whisked inside, turning back to speak through the cracked opening. "No, no. Not now, I have work to do. Later, I promise!"

The maid pushed at a protesting twin with one hand before slamming the door shut upon them both. She turned, then, seeing Mara standing in the bedchamber doorway, dropped a quick curtsy. "Forgive me, mademoiselle. They are so persistent, those two."

Mara smiled at the girl's flushed excitement. "Which do you like best?"

"I cannot say. They are two beautiful men."

"It would be hard to choose, I will agree."

"But yes, very hard, and so I will have both."

"Both?"

"A double pleasure, yes?"

"I suppose so," Mara said doubtfully.

"You think it unfair? Perhaps it would be, if it were a question of marriage, but I know, me, that it is not. Some day they will each marry a lady very different from that chosen by the other. For now they amuse themselves, first here, first there. I also."

"You must be careful not to get hurt."

"It is kind of you to be concerned, and I will try," Lila answered, the look in her dark eyes roguish, but also wise beyond her years. "But it is necessary, sometimes, to pay in pain for our pleasures."

It was too true to be denied. Mara turned away, a drawn look about her features.

Lila came forward to touch her arm. "Why so sad, mademoiselle? If it is because the prince no longer sends for you, then take heart. He does not because he cannot."

Mara swung sharply around. "What are you saying?"

"The old one, Sarus, he gives the order that no servant is to bring such a summons to you on pain of dismissal. The instructions, he says, come from the king."

"A . . . very thorough man, King Rolfe."

"Just so, mademoiselle. I do not think, me, that the prince would embarrass you by sending anyone other than his trusted valet, but the order was given as I have said."

Anger at the interference and relief that she was spared the final rejection warred inside Mara, along with a peculiar and most reluctant gratitude. Whatever the reasons for the ban on intimacy between Roderic and herself, it seemed that the results would be to prevent her from slipping into the role of perpetual mistress to which she had begun to fear her own desires might lead her.

And yet, in the empty nights that followed, when she lay alone in her bed with the fire dying and the cold creeping into the bedchamber, she was not sure that she should be grateful.

Toward the middle of February, the weather turned warm once more, becoming almost balmy. Over breakfast a few days after the change, Grandmère Helene mentioned that Mara had not seen Versailles. Immediately, Roderic and the cadre, grasping at any excuse for activity, mounted an excursion to the famous estate outside of Paris. Once the most grand, and most copied, royal residence in the civilized world, the magnificent buildings had been stripped of their furnishings and vandalized during the revolution. Early in his reign, Louis Philippe had begun restoration of the place and its gardens, creating a museum there dedicated "To all the Glories of France." Many of the priceless antiquities and works of art had been returned. A vast amount of work had been done, and the place was now well worth seeing.

They planned to make a day of it. The carriage carrying Angeline and Helene, followed by that with Juliana and Mara inside, was on the road early. It was a distance of some twelve miles to Versailles, and it had to be covered in good time to allow them to see everything. It was decided to take two vehicles in order not to crush the wide gowns of the ladies, and also to give the different generations freedom to speak as they pleased.

They traveled through the city to the Place de la Concorde and down the Champs-Elysées past the Arc de Triomphe. They left Paris by the old Port Dauphin gateway, proceeding through the Bois de Boulogne with its chestnuts, acacias, and sycamores that had replaced the venerable oaks cut by the English and Russians during the occupation in 1815. Passing St. Cloud, they came at last to the spreading complex of buildings that had become known simply as Versailles.

It was fascinating to Mara, used to the young and uncomplicated history of America, to think that the kings and queens of France, their relatives, advisers, mistresses, and lovers, the nobility and the quasinobility, had for two hundred and fifty years been traveling back and forth between Paris and this place along the same road she had taken. In this great pile of golden limestone and brick the men and women who had ruled this country had been born, lived, and died. They had known pleasure and pain, joy and sorrow, passion and heartache; the exaltation of art, drama, and music; and the sighs of ennui. Here the Sun King, Louis XIV, had held court in such splendor that he had awed the world; and here the rabble, the sansculottes, had poured in on a fine day a century and a half later to take Louis XVI and Marie Antoinette prisoner, and to insult the royal princesses in their chambers.

Decoration, decoration, it was everywhere: in enormous ceiling frescos with vivid figures far larger than life; in carved and gilded cornices, moldings, door panels, and door and window facings; in intricately inlaid marble floors, wall panels, and marble staircases in colors of veined green, copper, pink, white, gray, black, and golden yellow. There were arched and vaulted and groined ceilings; walls hung with damask, brocade, velvet, and silk that was embroidered in colors and also in gold and silver thread, or with tapestries from the looms of Gobelin and Savonnerie. There were carvings of leaves and flowers, palm branches, fruit and ferns; of garlands and swags and rosettes of ribbons; of stags, chimeras, dolphins, lions, and peacocks; of lyres and violins, bugles and harps; of crowns and urns and shields and swords and bows and arrows; of goddesses and cherubs, angels and cupids; and everywhere the Rhodian sun that was the symbol of the Sun King. Most, if not all, of the ornamentation was covered with gold leaf.

So much carving, such tons of gilding and acres of rich fabrics, so many miles of marble and suites with fine and delicate inlaid furniture, gave an impression of incredible richness. What was even more amazing was that it could still impress when so much was gone: so many gold and silver pieces, balusters, railings, and objets d'art that had been melted down; so many paintings and pieces of furniture that had been sold out of the country by a rapacious and careless revolutionary government.

And yet it was hard to blame them. There was such a terrible contrast between the opulent lives of the former French royalty and the hovels of the country and the dirty back alleys of La Marais, where the common people had lived at the time of the revolution, and still lived now in the nineteenth century. It was no wonder that the French throne was still shaky.

At this season, the Ruthenia group had the great château very nearly to themselves, except for a bored guard or two and an old crone who flipped a dusting cloth here and there with scant interest and less effect. They saw the famous Hall of Mirrors, that great vaulted corridor once hung with chandeliers and laid with enormous Savonnerie carpets to match the ceiling paintings by Le Brun, the passageway leading from the king's apartments to those of the queen. The parquet floor was intact, as were, miraculously, the mirrors that lined the walls opposite the seventeen arched windows, but the carpets and chandeliers were gone. This open expanse of flooring where Marie Antoinette had been married seemed to invite dancing. Juliana and Michael whirled down it in an impromptu waltz, in imitation of the revels that had once been held on its shining length. The others followed suit, whirling until they were giddy and Grandmère scolded them for their lack of reverence.

The cadre fought a mock battle up the Queen's Staircase with its inlays of marble in green and copper-pink, cream and white, and made up ribald stories about the dignitaries who must have trod up and down it. They crowded into the Hall of Battles, a corridor as long as eight large rooms, which Louis Philippe had created out of apartments once occupied by various royal relatives. Here could be seen scores of paintings on a grand scale depicting the great military events of French history. Though many were quite old, most had been specially commissioned. Of particular interest was one by Delacroix, the flamboyant painter Mara had seen wearing a burnous at the Hugo salon. Entitled *The Battle of Taillebourg*, it was a romanticized view of Saint Louis defeating the English at the bridge over the Charente in the thirteenth century, a canvas filled with vigor and grace and spilled blood, with flying flags and fury under a lowering sky. Predictably, the cadre voted it splendid.

In the Queen's Bedchamber, where nineteen royal children of France had been born, Roderic pointed out the ceiling medallions by Boucher illustrating the virtues of Charity, Plenty, Fidelity, and Prudence.

"Queenly virtues, all," he said. His face was grave, but the light in his eyes was teasing. "The lady who occupies the seat beside the throne must be compassionate to the poor among her people, overseeing the dispensing of charity; plentiful with the production of heirs, for obvious reasons; faithful to her liege lord so that their offsprings' legitimacy will not be in doubt; and prudent in her demands upon the treasury."

"Nonsense," Angeline said briskly. "If she has a good head on her shoulders and an iron constitution, she will need nothing else."

"Not even the affection of the king?" her son murmured, his gaze on Mara's face as she stared up at the orante monochromatic ceiling with its loops and curves of molding and heavy carving of arms and cherubs covered with gold leaf.

"That is certainly helpful with the production of heirs!"

Mara smiled at Angeline's quick rejoinder, but there was no lightness inside her.

It was while they were walking through the parterres of the garden that the rain began. The balustraded terraces with their finely graveled walks and clipped hedges in intricate designs were not at their best in the winter season, and were even less hospitable with the cold rain spattering in the fountains and dripping from the naked limbs of the statues. They bolted for the carriages and sat huddled inside.

The rain showed no signs of stopping. The hour for luncheon had passed while they were viewing the Hall of Mirrors. Driven by hunger, they removed to a café in the village at the gates of the château. It took some time for the flustered owner to prepare a meal, and when it was finished, the rain was still streaming down the windows. Grand'mère Helene's feet hurt from walking the long marble corridors; in fact, she ached from her head to her toes, she said. The cadre yawned at the thought of returning to view more French glory. Mara had seen enough. They gathered up Jacques and Jared, who were in the kitchen flirting with one of the maids, and set out once more for Paris.

As she stared out the carriage window through the streaming rain, Mara's spirits were as leaden as the sky. The golden rococo richness of Versailles had shown her, if she had ever doubted it, how impossible her unacknowledged dreams were. She was only an American girl of ordinary birth. Between herself and those who could claim a right to live in such splendor stretched a vast gulf. Never would she reign over a palace. Never would she become a queen filled with virtues, or even the princess consort of the future king. She had been the mistress of the prince, if her brief sojourn in Roderic's bed could be honored by so grand a title. It was all she would ever be. All she would ever know of love and loving.

CHAPTER 15

It was time to go home. She did not belong at Ruthenia House. Paris with its glamor and gaiety had not been the cure her father had expected it to be. The money he had spent to send her here, money he could ill afford, had been wasted. It would have been better if she had never seen the crooked streets and fine old houses of Paris, the theaters and cafés and book stalls and pastry shops; and far better if she had never met a volatile prince by the light of a gypsy fire. She would put aside her vain hopes, packing them away as most young women did their dance programs and split slippers and faded flowers when a memorable ball was over. She would return to Louisiana, to take care of her father's house on Bayou Teche near St. Martinville. In time she would forget the pain, but she would remember the pleasure and the joy.

To make the decision was fine; to act on it, another thing entirely.

Mara went to Grandmère Helene's bedchamber to inform her of what she meant to do early the next morning. Her grandmother was still in bed with a cloth soaked in violet water on her forehead and down-stuffed comforters piled two feet high over her thin body.

"Don't come in," she croaked. "I have a chill from our outing yesterday. You mustn't catch it."

Mara ignored the warning, coming to stand at the side of the bed and place her hand on her grandmother's forehead. It was burning hot. "Shall I bring you some tea or broth?"

"No, no, nothing. I feel like the crone of death, and all I want to do is lie here."

"I think I had better send for the doctor."

"Not if you want to please me," the older woman said with asperity. "French doctors always want to prescribe for the liver, no matter what ails a body, and there's nothing wrong with my l-liver."

The words ended with a violent shiver that sent a spasm of pain across the lined face on the pillow. Mara said, "Perhaps a few drops of laudanum then, to help you sleep?"

"If it will make you happy."

Mara ordered the fire built up, despite the mildness of the day, and sat beside Grandmère Helene until she dropped off to sleep. Only then did she get up and leave the room, going in search of Angeline.

A doctor was sent for, and he came within the hour. The elderly lady was ill, but not desperately so. It was imperative at her age, however, that she be kept quiet and warm and out of the slightest draft. On no account must the windows in her chamber be opened, and she must not touch so much as one foot to the cold floor. If these instructions were followed, and should the functioning of her liver remain normal, she would most likely not develop the dreaded pneumonia. If she did, he refused to be responsible for the consequences.

"Pompous charlatan, full of wind and noise," Roderic

said dispassionately as the doctor's frock-coated figure disappeared down the stairs.

Mara shook her head. "It's my fault for insisting he come. Grandmère said how it would be."

"We are at the mercy of our fears when we love."

She could only agree. "I must go and sit with her."

"It won't help, and may disturb her. If you will settle for the small salon beside her chamber, I will bear you company."

She looked at him, startled. "Surely you have more important things to do?"

"Nothing," he said simply, and, placing her hand on his arm, strolled with her back to the salon that separated her own bedchamber from that of her grandmother.

"You have grown thin, too thin," he said when they were seated in that small, oval-shaped room. He sat with one leg drawn up and his elbow resting on the back of the small settee, supporting his head.

"A condition caused by lack of appetite."

He ignored her attempt at lightness. "Travail and sorrow and a shameful deflowering; it has not been a halcyon interlude for you."

She looked down at her hands, which were clasped in her lap. "Not shameful."

"Generous. But, then, you have been that from the first. You offered me half of your apple."

She lifted her head to look at him, and her gray eyes were steady and very clear. "I told you once that I was sorry for—for what happened. I don't think you believed me. It was the truth, I swear it."

"You had cooperation, even collaboration."

"That doesn't alter the fact that it was wrong to use you."

"Wrong to try, perhaps. I could have stopped it at any time with a single word. I chose instead, not in cold blood but in full knowledge of the consequences, to accept the gift you had to give, yourself. For that I hereby beg your forgiveness."

"There is no reason that you should."

"Only self-respect and honor and honesty—and uncertainty."

She blinked in surprise, then lifted a brow. "You have never been uncertain in your life."

"No? You caught the edge of my temper after the attempt on Louis Philippe. Unfairly. There are many emotions I would arouse in you, but fear is not one of them."

A faint haze of color appeared on her cheekbones. She refused to acknowlege it or the words that had caused it. "Why unfairly?"

"I wanted the confidence you could not give. Instead of seeking the cause, I staged a spectacular of damaged pride and rage. It was not helpful and may now be a hindrance."

"A hindrance? To what?"

"To earning your trust. Ever."

His face was composed in lines of suspended concern. The fine gold waves of his hair fell forward on his forehead, and she had to clench her hands in her lap to prevent herself from brushing them back. She could smell the fresh-starched scent of his linen shirt and the faint hint of sandalwood from the soap he used, and it seemed that the heat of his body reached her across the width of the brocade seat that lay between them. She felt a little dizzy with the things he was saying and his nearness, as if someone had turned her in circles and then let her go. She could think of only one reason why he should have concluded that she did not trust him, and though it was difficult for her to put into words, she wanted to reassure him.

"If you think that—that I have been afraid to answer your summons these last weeks, afraid to come, you should know that—"

"Dear Mara, there have been no summonses. Not because of my colossus of a father or his colossal impudence, but because, with the exception of one night of weakness, I felt you deserved something better."

"One?" she murmured.

"What are you smiling at, like Circe on the shore?"

"A night when I heard you and your father having words in the antechamber of the back stairs."

"To have us both prowling the corridors in the dark hours of the morning is, I will grant, amusing, but not, quid pro quo, a sign of guilt for either."

"My apologies. And what, in your considered and superior opinion, do I deserve?"

"Oh, a prince charming, of course, all languishing airs and manly graces, executing a courtship dance of slow and purest delight."

Why could he not say in plain words what he meant? There was no chance to delve into the matter, however, for Grandmère called out then and she had to go to her. Mara was left to wonder if Roderic referred to himself or to a prince charming in the abstract, some man who would court her in the approved fashion with marriage as the end result. Was he, in effect, renouncing her? She could not believe that he meant to ignore what had been between them, to start over, and so it must be the last. He had gone to great pains to indicate that he shared the responsibility for his own seduction; that he understood what had forced her to an act so unnatural for her; that, in fact, he bore her no grudge and wished her well. That was all. The knowledge was no consolation.

The banquets of the reformists continued. The speeches that accompanied these political meals grew more inflammatory. It became obvious that only radical change would satisfy the rabble-rousers. They wanted an immediate end to the absolute power of the monarchy and a vote for every citizen. There was a great outcry against Louis Philippe's conservative minister, Guizot, seen as holding the country to its present humiliating course. The English government, upset by what it considered to be the treacherous alliance of France and Spain by marriage the year before, did its best to increase the furor. The legitimists added fuel to the fire, as did the Bonapartists, in the hope that in the confusion of a change there might occur an opportunity to snatch the crown for their own candidates.

France seethed with unease like wine fermenting in a barrel. The yellow newspaper journals printed scurrilous cartoons of the king and his minister and lauded the sayings of Lamartine. There were food riots in the provinces and sullen gatherings ending in marches under a red flag in the back streets of Paris. The carriage of a rich merchant was overturned by a mob and the man severely beaten. Another round of marchers, after breaking into the warehouse of a wine merchant, went on a rampage, looting several shops and breaking windows in one of the elite districts near the Faubourg Saint-Germain.

At Ruthenia House, in the public salon, the growing seriousness of the situation became the main topic of conversation when more than two people gathered. Some blamed it on the king of the French, a man they admitted had done nothing wrong, but also nothing right. Others blamed it on the unseasonable warmth that allowed the proletariat to crawl out of their hovels and think of something beside keeping alive in the winter cold and damp. Some frowned and shook their heads. Some smiled.

It was difficult, if not impossible, to know the attitude of Roderic and his father, King Rolfe. They could speak as well for one side as for the other, and often did. They continued to entertain everyone and anyone. If Roderic bowed with a sharp click of his heels over the hands of comtesses and duchesses at the receptions given by his father, then in return Rolfe argued and drank rough red wine at meetings in his son's rooms with Lamartine, the moderate scientist Arago, the socialist Louis Blanc, and with men in rags who carried pistols in their belts and left by the back stairs.

To Mara, the crosscurrents and questions were disturbing. She pitied the people she saw huddling and begging in the streets and tried to give the children centimes when she could. She could see the justice in the call of the people for some voice in the manner in which they were governed, for some concern for their need for jobs and fair pay for their work. At the same time, it appeared that Louis Philippe was doing the best he could for his country and his subjects. People were suffering everywhere, not just in France.

Despite the unrest, it seemed impossible that violence could erupt and barricades be installed once more in the streets of Paris while the mob ruled. Until one sunny afternoon.

Mara had gone with Juliana and Trude to visit a *parfumerie* in the back streets of La Marais. She had heard that she could get a scent there called Creole Garden, which combined the scents of a New Orleans garden: gardenia, sweet olive, and honeysuckle, all lightened with a fern undertone. Beyond the fact that the perfume sounded interesting, she wanted it as a gift for Grandmère. The eldely woman was doing well enough, but she needed something to lighten the days she was forced to spend in bed. Besides, it would make a most suitable opening for a discussion of their return to Louisiana.

The distance to the shop was not far, perhaps a ten-minute walk. It had been so long since they had been out that they decided not to take the carriage. The cadre was out, as were Roderic and Rolfe, so they decided not to wait for an escort. It would be safe enough if the three of them went together, especially since it was a short excursion.

The walk there was uneventful and pleasant in the fresh air. On their return, Mara carried the small glass vial of perfume in her reticule, and all three walked in a delicious aura of the many scents they had been encouraged to apply on their persons by way of trial. The streets were narrow and twisting, with uneven cobbles underfoot that did not make for the easiest of walking. The sun did not quite reach here, only catching the tops of the buildings. Refuse littered the doorways, windows were broken, and shutters hung askew.

When they had left the *parfumerie,* there had been children running here and there, cats scratching on doorsills, and women hanging out the windows to shout across at their neighbors. They rounded a corner, and suddenly the street was empty. Somewhere a child cried and was hushed. A shutter banged shut and a bolt was slammed into place over it.

Mara turned her head to exchange a look with Juliana. Then they both looked at Trude.

"We had best make speed," the blond woman said, her face grim. With one hand on the hilt of her sword, she looked around her, her cool gaze comprehensive, missing nothing.

They walked on more quickly. Their footsteps echoed among the stone buildings, making it sound as if they were being followed. The sun dimmed as it went behind a veil of cloud. A small wind funneled between the buildings, raising gritty dust that stung their eyes.

Ahead of them they heard the sound of voices raised in a chant or marching song. Closer they came until the song could be identified as "La Marseillaise." Male and female, there was anger and raw exultation in the shouted words.

"It's a mob. Quick, back the other way," Trude said.

But it was too late. The crowd of men and women, perhaps thirty strong, armed with clubs and other crude weapons, emerged from a cross street ahead of them. Their clothes were shapeless and faded to a dingy gray brown, while on their heads they wore flat caps or, for the women, colorless kerchiefs. Their faces were gray, and their teeth were bad as they opened their mouths to sing. They caught sight of the two women in their telltale mourning for the dead sister of the king and what they took to be a young man with a black arm band.

The mob surged toward them as if with a single mind. "Aristos! Oppressors of the people! After them! After them!"

The blade of Trude's sword rasped as she drew it. She gave Mara and Juliana a shove. "Run! I'll hold them."

"Dear God," Juliana breathed, "I would give my diamonds to have my épée here now."

"You can't hold them; there're too many!" Mara shouted, grasping Trude's arm and pulling her with them. "Come on!"

Trude was far from being a coward, but she had been taught to calculate the odds and to know the value of strategic retreat. She backed a few steps, then whirled and ran. Yelling, screaming, with the mindless instinct of hounds on a trail, the rabble pounded after them.

The direction the three women were heading in would take them deeper into the La Marais. They needed to work back toward the river and Ruthenia House. Trude pointed to an alley, and they dived into it. It was piled with refuse heaps, slimy with slops and garbage, and above them sagged lines of gray washing strung from the balconies on either side. As they ducked and twisted through the shortcut, Trude leaped to slash at the wash lines so that they dragged down into the alley behind them to impede their pursuers.

They gained a little time, but not much. When they burst from the alley, the mob was close behind them. Juliana, clutching her skirts above her knees, sprinted toward a *pâtisserie*. "In here!"

The proprietor saw them coming and tried to close the door. Trude hit it with her shoulder, flinging the man backward. They dashed through the shop, pushing over tables of cakes and pies and a display case of bonbons as they went. They pushed into the kitchen and, ignoring the screams of the fat and blowsy woman who turned from stirring a custard with her spoon dripping spots of yellow on her massive bosom, crashed through the back door into yet another alley.

Trude, cursing with a virulence that did not seem in the least surprising under the circumstances, overturned a vat of rancid grease that stood beside the door. Farther down the alley, they joined forces to upend a barrel of pig and sheep entrails behind a *boucherie*. Choking from the smell, each breath a jagged ache in their chests, they ran on, but had the felicity of hearing the hoarse yells as the first of the mob out of the pastry shop went sprawling in the grease, sliding into the entrails.

They emerged from the alley and swung back to their left. Their feet pounded on the cobbles. Juliana's hair was coming down, her skirts were lifted above her knees, and her face was pale with hectic color on her cheekbones. There was an ache in Mara's side and a red mist before her eyes. She could not keep this pace much longer. Hearing Juliana gasping beside her, she thought the other girl was in the same condition, though Trude hardly seemed winded.

Their one hope was to gain enough time to find shelter, to hide, Mara thought. They were closer to Ruthenia House, but still some five or six blocks away. The street was wider here, lined with a better variety of shops, though every door was closed against them. Outside the establishments stood the merchandise that had been left when the shutters had been slammed and the bolts shot home. There was no place to hide, no refuge. Behind them the howls of the mob were coming closer.

Then, ahead of her, she saw it. She laughed out loud. When the other two looked at her, she could only point with a shaking hand and redouble her speed.

The shop with its line of men's accessories was tightly shuttered, but outside was a rack holding men's hats: derbies and stovepipes and opera hats, alpine hats, hats of silk and beaver fur and woven wool. There was a case of heavy waistcoat chains with fobs and seals to be attached. Hanging from the awning were canes: canes with gold and silver handles, canes with carved-ivory and amber handles, and canes carved from blackthorn, brilliantly polished. And in a stand were canes with knobs instead of handles, canes extra thin and limber and also extra thick: sword canes.

Mara and Juliana fell upon the canes, twisting the knobs, throwing aside those that did not open until, with cries of triumph, they each drew a sharp and slender blade from its hard sheath.

They spun around. "In the street," Trude said tersely. "There's more room."

The pack sighted its prey and bore down on them. Mara, standing shoulder to shoulder with Juliana and Trude, realized suddenly that she still had her beaded reticule on her wrist. She shook the strings down and, catching the top, flung it aside. It landed near a doorway. The door opened and a young boy of ten or eleven peered out. A voice called out sharply, but the boy darted out to pick up the reticule.

"What's in it is yours," Mara said, her voice ringing, "if you will carry a message to Ruthenia House. Tell them to come."

"Tell them, *A moi! A moi!*" Trude called.

It was the ancient battlefield call for assistance. To me. Rally around me. Help me. The cadre would come without fail. If the boy took the message. If he was allowed inside. If the men had returned.

In the meantime, there was only themselves.

The rabble poured down the street toward them. Nearer they came. Nearer. Their mouths were wide open, and the tendons in their necks corded as they screamed. Their eyes glared with hatred and blood lust. In their clenched fists they brandished their crude weapons. Their rough shoes clattered like thunder on the cobblestones. Nearer. Nearer.

"En garde," Trude said softly.

The three blades swept up, then down, steadying. Balanced, poised, they stood ready.

The sight that met the gaze of those in the front of the mob was so unexpected that they checked their progress. They were pressed forward by those behind them so that they skidded, stumbling and staggering on the cobbles. They came within inches of those glittering, gently rotating sword points, then flung themselves back against their fellows, cursing and yelling. There was a moment of milling confusion.

Abruptly, the mob broke, a half-dozen men charging from the crowd. They came at the women with their cudgels raised, their teeth bared. Mara had no time for the others, only for the two who were bearing down upon her. She ducked the first swiping blow and, leaning in that same crouch, thrust low at the legs of the first man. He yelped, hobbling out of reach. Mara recovered, whirled, slashing the wicked blade in her hand at the belly of the second man. He jumped back and the stick he was bringing down scraped her shoulder. Ignoring the numbness, seeing only the winking shaft of the knife he held in his other hand, she immediately reversed, slicing at his arms. He caught his wrist with a hoarse cry, dropping the knife as blood welled between his fingers. His place was taken by a woman swinging a hatchet. Mara met the harridan with whirling, incipient death in her hand. The woman screamed in rage and threw the hatchet. It tore at the thick material of Mara's skirt before clattering harmlessly to the cobblestones. A man with a poker advanced, holding it at full length like a sword. Mara parried it in the same way, knocking it aside again and again until, with a swift riposte, she circled it with her blade and plunged through the man's guard, piercing his shoulder.

The mob was closing in, surrounding them. Trude, her eyes alight with the fire of battle, called out, "Back to back! We can hold them!"

In a smooth movement, Mara and Juliana turned, and the three of them formed a triangle with their backs together, guarding each other from attack from the rear.

There was another charge, and another. Again and yet again, they fought the rabble back. Two men lay dead or dying at their feet. Another had crawled to one side where he twitched and moaned, holding a hole in his neck. The attack slowed, fell away.

The mood of the mob that crowded around them on all sides had gone past the mass ill will that had exploded into an urge to chastise three well-dressed aristocratic women, to frighten them into some respect for the precariousness of life by stripping them and applying a few blows with sticks. It was now uglier by far, murderous with the need for revenge for blood spilled, for being made to look small by mere women. In it was the same vicious hysteria that had, less than a hundred years before, caused such a mob to cut literally to pieces the Princess Lamballe, confidante of Marie Antoinette.

"Stone them!" a woman cried. "Let's see if they can fight stones with their swords!"

The cobbles of the street were easily prized up. Heavy cubes of stone, denser and larger than bricks, they were of a size that could be quickly piled into a strong barricade or flung by a man. If thrown with only reasonable force, they could break bones; with rage and hatred behind them, they had stood off armies and routed squadrons. They were the weapons of the proletariat.

If the women stood where they were, they would be battered to their knees in a matter of seconds. If they tried to run, they would be chased down and mangled like hapless vixens caught by the hounds. There was only one defense.

"Charge?" Mara asked quietly.

"Charge," Trude said.

They looked at each other, the three of them, their eyes filled with rage and resolve and terror. Perspiration trickled from their hairlines due to their exertions, and their legs trembled. There was blood matting Juliana's streaming tresses, and Trude's uniform sleeve was torn away at the shoulder seam. The hems of Mara's and Juliana's skirts and Trude's trousers were soaked with grease and unspeakable filth. Their swords were bloodied, disgusting, and the muscles of their shoulders and arms so cramped they might never again move in smooth answer to the commands of their brains.

Suddenly, they grinned and, as abruptly as released springs, leaped, screaming, into a dead run straight at the thickest group of their attackers.

The men and women scattered, wild-eyed, scrambling, dropping their weapons and spreading out as they ran. But behind the trio came the thud of running feet, closing in, gathering for the kill. They whirled.

The men behind them skidded to a stop, recoiling, flinging up their hands, which held the lethal lengths of swords. Their uniforms, white and unsullied, glinted platinum bright in the sunlight.

Estes, who had Trude's blade touching between his eyes, bleated an oath.

Luca, his gaze upon Juliana hungry and searching, shook his head in admiration.

"A moi?" Roderic said and, after one comprehensive look at the stunned, almost angry faces of the three of them, burst out laughing.

CHAPTER 16

"They were magnificent, invincible! A trio of amazons," Estes declared, holding forth that evening before the rest of the cadre, along with Rolfe and Angeline.

"All for one, and one for all," Juliana quipped.

"So well in hand did they have the situation, they hardly needed our help at all."

Mara, a wry smile of remembrance curving her mouth, shook her head. "I wouldn't say that."

"Never will I forget the absolute horror of the moment that vile-smelling urchin came running up to us holding your beaded purse, Mademoiselle Mara, and shouting *'A moi! A moi!'* at the top of street-crier lungs as we rode into the courtyard. I thought my heart would stop."

"Vile-smelling?"

"He reeked to the rooftops of the most abominable scent."

"Grandmère's perfume! It must have broken when I threw down the reticule. I forgot all about it."

"How could you?" Roderic, standing behind Mara's chair, murmured.

Trude, nearby, looked at him with stern displeasure in her light-blue eyes. "With good reason."

"Swift as the wind, we raced to the aid of Mademoiselle Mara, without stopping to ask why or how or who might be with her," Estes went on. "Imagine our dismay to find all three ladies beleaguered, surrounded by dead men but in deadly peril. Before we could make our presence known, the ladies charged straight at the enemy. Never have I seen anything so gallant, so stirring, so—"

"So foolhardy?" Roderic suggested.

"What would you have us do?" his sister demanded. "Stand and be stoned? Kneel and pray? There was no other choice."

"I would have had you remain safe within these walls."

"So you would not have to be worried," his sister replied with a flounce in her seat.

"It was my fault," Mara said. "I had no idea it would be so dangerous."

"Nor I," Juliana agreed.

Trude lifted her chin. "Nor I."

" 'All for one—' " Roderic quoted softly.

There was a moment of silence. Estes filled it. "And then when we had dismounted and joined our force to theirs to rout the crazed ones drunk on looted wine and liberty, they turned on us, these viragoes, as if they would slice out our hearts for ending their sport."

"And you laughed," Trude accused.

The Italian count looked offended. "Roderic laughed. Luca and I merely joined him for politeness."

"It was the relief that they were unharmed." Luca, unexpectedly, joined the discussion.

"Don't anyone believe it," Juliana said with a sound suspiciously like a snort. "It was the bedraggled appearance we presented."

"Bedraggled, beleaguered, and infinitely dear."

Juliana, turning in surprise to look at the gypsy, flushed

suddenly at something she saw in the depths of his dark eyes.

Jacques and Jared looked at each other and sighed. "Why is it," Jacques said to his brother, "that we never get to rescue the maidens in distress?"

"You're always too busy distressing them yourselves," Michael told them with brutal frankness.

Roderic quelled such comments with a single opaque glance. "I did not," he said quietly, "speak in jest or to hear the clattering in my windpipe. Henceforth, no woman will leave this house without an adequate escort of at least two, preferably three, of the cadre, and even then only in a carriage. Members of the cadre will ride out in twos only. No exceptions."

Angeline leaned forward, a frown between her eyes. "Is this really necessary, all for a few street riots?"

Her son turned to her, but his face did not soften. "Last night the Comédie Française closed its doors."

The Comédie Française, the official and leading theater of Paris, closed down for nothing short of disaster. Paris had learned to keep an eye on it in the past decades of political upheaval as a reliable gauge. When the theater shut, the citizens of the city battened down the hatches and waited for the storm.

"And I, my son?"

The query came from Rolfe. He sat in a high-backed chair with one booted foot thrust out and his elbow resting on the chair arm, supporting his chin on one knuckle. If there was a challenge in the words he spoke, Roderic declined to rise to it.

"You, sir, will, of course, do as best pleases you. But I would like to consider you as one of the cadre, available for escort if necessary and for any other duty."

Mara expected an explosion. She had underestimated both the king of Ruthenia and the understanding of his son. Rolfe's question had not, apparently, been made out of concern for his dignity, but from a determination to participate in the crises. That he was satisfied was obvious from his ironic nod.

It was Juliana who next sought Roderic's attention. "What of Mara's perfume? Even if we scrape the galleries and beg for chaperons, I'm not certain an outing to replace it has any appeal."

"Is she sure she wants it?" Estes exclaimed in pretended disbelief.

Roderic disregarded the count. "I'll get it for her."

"That isn't necessary," Mara said hastily. "I can go myself, if someone, perhaps Jared and Jacques, will bear me company."

"I will get it."

So steely was Roderic's voice as he repeated the words that she subsided. Let him go then! Pigheaded man. She certainly had no wish to make the excursion; the very thought of it made the muscles of her stomach clench. He could not know that, naturally. Could he?

She sent him a swift glance from under her lashes. He was watching her, his gaze resting on the thin line of her lips, and the expression in his dark blue eyes was armored with tender humor.

Trude, observing the byplay, shifted in her seat before averting her eyes with a fierce frown. Estes sighed.

It was dinnertime when Roderic, true to his word, brought the perfume to Mara. She was sitting with Grand-mère Helene. He tapped on the door of the salon, then let himself in and turned to usher in a cavalcade of servants. The first of these bore on a pillow of blue velvet a large, frosted-glass flacon with a hand-blown stopper shaped like a gardenia containing over a pint of perfume. The second carried an enormous bouquet of hothouse flowers, yellow jonquils and white Narcissus and pink quince, in a crystal vase. The third held a guitar in a polished wooden case. The fourth was burdened with a silver wine stand in which a long-necked bottle of champagne cooled. The remaining servants were weighed down with trays containing covered silver dishes, stands, compotes, and a variety of china, crystal, and silverware.

"You have come to cheer the invalid. How splendid!" Grandmère Helene called through the open bedchamber door.

He moved at once to the bedside to bow over her hand and raise it to his lips. His smile enigmatic, he answered, "Among other things."

Grandmère Helene, her fine old eyes keen, gave him a quick, hard glance. "If you are thinking I may fall asleep early after a glass or two of champagne, I may fool you."

"I hope you may," he returned.

She gave a short laugh. "Prevaricator."

"How can you think it?"

"You forget, I knew your father. It gives me an advantage."

"Something you have never needed, surely?"

She pulled her hand away, slapping at his, but there was no displeasure in her smile.

The food was wonderfully prepared and beautifully presented, delicate enough to tempt an invalid, but substantial enough to sate the most voracious appetite. The servants laid everything out, checked it for completeness, then went away.

Grandmère opened the perfume and applied it lavishly so that the air in the room was heavy with its scent combined with that of the flowers. While they ate, she had to hear once more the tale of the first small bottle and what had become of it, of the part Mara had played and the last-minute rescue. Mara tried to warn Roderic with a shake of her head, but he seemed to pay no attention. Still, listening to the tale he spun as she helped her grandmother eat her meal, she hardly recognized the sugarcoated events. She gave him a grateful smile above Grandmère Helene's head, but to that, too, he made no response.

He set himself out to please, however, presenting Grandmère with an only slightly embroidered version of the political situation, spicing it with snatches of gossip, wit, and drollery. He also kept her wineglass refilled. When they had finished the last bite of their dessert, a creme custard with almond sauce, and the remains of the feast had been taken away, he picked up his guitar. He played the clear and complicated melodies that had been fashionable in Grandmère's youth and the old, faintly risqué love songs of the *ancien régime*. His supple fingers wandered from Mozart to a Spanish bolero, trailed into a Norman serenade that dated from the time of the Crusades, and ended with the stately and softly fading measures of Haydn's "Farewell."

He lifted his hands from the strings. The sweet vibrations died away. Mara looked at her grandmother. The elderly woman lay with her eyes closed, gently snoring. Together Mara and Roderic rose and eased from the room, drawing the door between the bedchamber and the salon closed behind them.

"You are a devil," Mara said, her voice low.

"Because I lulled a lady with wine and music, and sent her dreaming?"

"You did it on purpose!"

"What purpose, Mara? To make love to you on that desperately uncomfortable settee? To steal you away to my seraglio, supposing I had a seraglio? To use the ancient wisdom that the way to a girl's heart is through that of her grandmother?"

"Don't be ridiculous."

"Not I, *chère*. If I were to woo you, it would not be with perfidy. Nor would it be with heavy perfume or serenades or bunches of indiscriminate flowers." He reached out to touch her cheek with one knuckle. "It would be rather with something rare and fragile and without blemish."

It took fully as much courage to meet his gaze as it had taken to face the mob. She expected to find derision there, or perhaps irritation; instead, there was translucent patience.

"Then I must thank you for entertaining Grandmère this evening and for—for all the lovely gifts, not the least of them your music. It was kind of you to give us so much of your time, and I'm truly grateful."

"A charming speech, *chère*, or it would be if your gratitude was what I wanted."

He paused, expectant. Her wariness, the stiff control he sensed inside her, hurt him in some inexplicable way, as did the dark shadows under her eyes and the blue stain of a bruise on her neck. He wished he knew what she was thinking.

The obvious question echoed in her mind: *What is it you want then?* But she could not force it to her lips. The answer was not one she was sure she wished to hear.

A grim smile touched his mouth. He took her hand and raised it to his lips, then, with a soft good night, left her.

Mara stood where she was for a long moment. With a turn so swift it sent her skirt belling out around her, she moved back toward her grandmother's room. She banked the fire and set the screen in place, then turned down the lamp that burned behind a frosted rose globe on the bedstand. Tucking the covers close around the sleeping woman, she leaned to kiss her forehead, then moved into her own bedchamber that lay on the other side of her grandmother's.

Lila rose from beside the fireplace and came forward.

As Mara summoned a smile for her, the girl said, "You are tired, mademoiselle, and no wonder. Let me help you."

She was more than weary; she was stiff and sore, and on her body there were great livid bruises in places where she had no memory of being hit. A hot bath earlier had helped, but suddenly she ached for her bed.

Lila eased her clothing from her, clucking in quiet sympathy over the bruises, and slipped her nightgown over her head. Mara sat down in a slipper chair, and the maid removed her stockings and shoes. As Lila put her things away, Mara, yawning, rose and turned toward her bed.

There was something lying on her pillow. It was a single flower, a pale pink camellia. Each small petal was perfect, gently overlapping, and so delicate that the faintest touch would leave a brown spot of bruising upon it. The pair of leaves that framed it were a dark and glossy green, equally unmarred. The plants from which such flowers came had been imported from Asia not so many years before. Due to their beauty and scarcity, they commanded high prices.

" . . . *rare and fragile and without blemish* . . ."

Mara turned toward the maid. "Where did this come from?"

The maid gave a helpless shrug. "I don't know, mademoiselle. It was here when I came."

Roderic. There could be no other explanation—unless it was one of the cadre? No, it did not seem likely. It must be Roderic.

Was this, then, a sign of his wooing? Could it be that he was paying her court? But for what purpose? He himself had said that his marriage, a political alliance, had been in his father's plans since his birth. He had congratulated himself on escaping it so far, but seemed resigned to eventual capitulation. Did he hope to persuade her to a permanent position as his mistress then? Did he really think she would accept it, or that if she did, she could be happy?

Did she think so herself?

It sometimes seemed that she would do anything, be anything, in order to regain the closeness they had shared, to feel his touch, to be lost in the overwhelming power of his presence. But would it be enough? Would she not come to resent her dependence upon him? Could she live with the knowledge that his need for her was based on desire rather than love?

He had asked her to marry him. The reason had been propriety and expediency, with a leavening of desire. Was it possible that he still contemplated such a union regardless of his father's edict against it? Or even because of it? It would not be a flattering proposition in either case.

And yet the more she saw Roderic and his father together, the less she believed that Roderic was influenced by the king, despite his respect for his father's authority. They might disagree on issues major and minor, might flay each other with words, but each stood tall during and after the fray. And sometimes, as over the protection of the occupants of Ruthenia House, the king deferred, with stiff magnanimity, to his son.

What, then, was she to make of the enmity of Rolfe's remarks concerning his son's character? Had they been made for a purpose, to elicit from her the response the king wanted? Or was the plain fact simply that Rolfe did not trust his son? And if his father could not place his confidence in Roderic, how could she?

How could she?

In spite of what had been said concerning the need for staying indoors, when dinner was announced the next evening, Juliana could not be found, nor could anyone say where she had gone. She was not in her bedchamber or the salon that adjoined it; she was not in the long gallery, the apartments of her parents or brother, or any of the public rooms. No one had seen her since midafternoon when she had been walking in the main gallery with Luca. It was only when the cadre was assembled, making ready to search the streets near the house, that it was noticed that the gypsy was also missing.

They searched anyway, sending Jacques and Jared as far as the Bois de Boulogne and the gypsy encampment, and Michael and Trude with Rolfe to canvass the shops along the rue de Rivoli and the rue de Richelieu before plunging into the rabbit warren of La Marais. They rode up and down until their horses were lathered and half the canine population of Paris barked at their heels, but glimpsed not so much as her bonnet plumes.

Juliana was headstrong and independent, but far from unintelligent. Mara could not believe that she would flout Roderic's instructions, either deliberately or out of thoughtlessness. There had to be an explanation.

"Wasted loyalty," Roderic said with a rasp in his voice when she put her thoughts into words. "Never was there a female more flighty or ripe for trouble, though how she escaped the surveillance I don't pretend to understand."

"Surveilliance?"

"Just a precaution," he said with a dismissive gesture.

Mara, her mind on more important things, said, "Juliana was frightened yesterday morning. She would not run into danger again, not so soon."

"You don't know her as I do. The danger was forgotten the instant it was over. She will tell us, blithely, merrily, when she deigns to return, that she counts herself as one of the cadre now that she has proven her skill with a rapier. And I, in my lack of foresight, specified only a single companion for those of that status."

She sent him a quick glance, noting the lines of strain

about his eyes. He held himself responsible. That he did so stemmed partially from his training, but also from his nature. To comment, to tell him that he could not be held accountable for the indiscretions of the world, would do no good. Juliana was his sister, and though he might grossly condemn her, he cared for her in equal proportions.

Still, Mara could not make herself accept Juliana's foolhardiness. There had to be some reason for her to slip away, with or without Luca. That the cause might be clandestine she had trouble making herself believe also. In many ways Juliana might be a law unto herself, but Luca's respect for the *boyar,* and by inference for his daughter, could not be denied. The heated gypsy blood ran in his veins, but, though he might yearn, he was unlikely to overstep the bounds of race and class and position that separated them. Unless, of course, Juliana so commanded. Then, being a servant of the *boyar,* how could he refuse?

There was someone else missing from the house. It was some time after Roderic and the cadre, joined by Rolfe, had gone out to search once more that Mara noticed the absence. Demon was gone.

It seemed natural to check for the whereabouts of Juliana's Pekingese, Sophie. The little dog had grown increasingly plump and heavy lately, and had taken to lying much of the time in her basket in her mistress's bedchamber or else curled with Demon before the fire in the long gallery. She was in neither of those two places.

Once more the house servants were marshaled and instructed to search for the dogs. They were to leave no room unopened, no cabinet or armoire uninvestigated. They were to quarter the courtyards and take a lamp into every storeroom, tack room, and darkest corners of the stables. They were not to return empty-handed.

In the end, it was ludicrously easy. Juliana and Luca were found sitting on a bench in a corner of the north court. They were wrapped in a horse blanket against the night chill as they rested from their labors as midwives, and the gypsy was pointing out the constellations overhead. In the gardener's storeroom nearby, on a pile of canvas that had once played a part as an awning for an outdoor entertainment, lay Sophie with four husky pups. Demon sat on guard beside her, grinning from ear to ear and giving his tail an occasional proud but ridiculously weary thump.

By the time the search party returned, the new mother and her progeny had been moved to the private salon. Juliana and Luca had removed the odors of mildewed canvas, horse, and canine midwifery from their persons and returned, repentant, to where the others hovered over the small bundles of wavy fur that squirmed beside Sophie in her basket near the fire.

The wide door was flung open. Roderic and Rolfe, shoulders abreast, tramped into the room, with Estes, Michael, Trude, and the twins marching behind. The faces of the prince and his father were etched with exhaustion and hours of worry that had turned in an instant to rage. Those of the cadre were carefully noncommittal.

Luca got to his feet with color surging into his dark and handsome face. Juliana rose to stand beside him, lifting her chin. It was the gypsy who spoke first, however.

"There is no excuse for the disturbance we have caused. We make none."

"A fine tactic; I congratulate you," Rolfe said with heavy irony. "Still, I trust there is an explanation."

Juliana answered, "We didn't hear anyone calling, not where we were in the house."

"Stygian darkness is a daily phenomenon, but are you certain it did not attract your notice?"

"It was dark anyway in the storeroom, and in the excitement of the birthing we lost track of the time."

"The birthing?"

"Of Sophie's pups."

Her father looked down at the dogs at his feet. Deliberately, he raised his blue gaze to the man at Juliana's side. "Mongrels," he said softly, "the bastard results of the coupling of a purebred bitch with a male of no breeding whatever."

Mara saw Roderic send his father a swift, frowning look. Beside her, Angeline drew in her breath in an audible gasp. Juliana took a step forward.

"An infusion of healthy mongrel blood is sometimes beneficial to a line of effete purebreds."

"And sometimes fatal," Rolfe countered.

Luca put his hand on Juliana's arm when she would have spoken again. "Your daughter is beautiful and warm and wise, sir," he said, "but I well know she is not for me. There is no need for you to tell me. Or for me to stay to hear it."

He stepped away from Juliana and the others, striding toward the door.

"Wait," Roderic said, his voice carrying. "You are of the cadre. Those who are accepted cannot leave it without permission. That you do not have."

The gypsy turned and, with nimble fingers, opened the frogs of his jacket and stripped it off, tossing it onto a table. "Perhaps they can't, not with honor. But what has honor to do with a mongrel gypsy?"

"Luca!" Juliana called, but he did not answer. Whirling, he opened the door and went from the room.

Angeline got to her feet, and there was queenly grace in her carriage and anger in her eyes as she faced her husband. "That is a loss. It will be felt."

Rolfe turned to her, speaking as if they were alone. "It was needful. He must choose between the moon for his *baldaquin* or one of dusty damask."

Mara, watching Angeline digest that cryptic explanation, forced herself to remember that few things Rolfe or his son did were obvious.

"You injured his pride," Angeline said more tentatively, "the most dangerous wound."

"It is his gypsy pride that will have to be subdued."

Roderic spoke in tones heavy with irony. "But did it have to be subdued during the present and more transcendent crisis?"

"Crisis?" Angeline asked quickly, turning to him.

"King Louis Philippe and Guizot, in their collective wisdom, have forbidden attendance at the reformist banquet to be held tomorrow night in the Place de la Concorde. Lamartine is swearing to go and speak even if there is no one there except himself and his shadow. The working-class districts are now up in arms."

"What can we do?"

"We can entertain the reformists on Friday night as planned in order to keep abreast of their intentions. Otherwise, we wait and hope that Louis Philippe can act enough like a king to mend matters."

What Louis-Philippe did, however, was nothing.

The following day was one of constant demonstrations and marching in the streets, of chanting and cheers and the singing of "La Marseillaise." Roderic and the cadre left the house early and did not return. Rolfe was called to the Tuileries, supposedly to consult with Louis Philippe on a course of action. The women were left alone.

The afternoon was overcast, but still unusually warm, though there was a feeling of change in the air. After luncheon, Grand mère took a nap, and most of the others retired to their apartments. Mara looked in on her grandmother, then sat for a time before the fire, flipping through a copy of the fashion periodical, *Le Follet*. She was restless, on edge, worried against all reason by the thought of Roderic and the others being out in the streets. She longed to know what was happening to them, where they were and what they were doing, and if they were involved in the shouting and outcries that could sometimes be heard.

She jumped as a knock came on the door. At her call, a maidservant entered. "Your pardon, mademoiselle. You have a visitor."

"Who is it?"

"He would not say, only that his business concerns a sum of money owed by your grandmother. I put him in the antechamber downstairs as he seemed to be a tradesman. I hope I did right?"

Mara, her face stiff, nodded at the girl. De Landes. It could be no other. He had no power any longer to harm her, and yet it might be as well that he did not enter the main rooms of the house. She had no idea what he might want after all these weeks, but certainly she had no thought of introducing him to the others as if he were an honored acquaintance. She wished she dared to refuse to see him. It would give her great pleasure to send such a message and have him thrown out by the footmen. She could not risk it. No. She would have to hear him out.

She moved along the corridors to the main gallery and descended the staircase. The antechamber to which the maid referred was a small room opening almost beneath the stairs, a chill and barren cubicle where tradesmen and other supplicants, those who could not be classed as guests or intimates, were left to wait. There was no fireplace, no refreshments, no footmen on call here, only a bench, a threadbare rug, and a view through a leaded-glass window of the shrubbery of the west court.

De Landes rose from the bench as she entered, as did a large young man with a vacant smile who was his companion.

"How charming," he said, touching his pointed beard with one long, slim hand. "You seem to be well established here with the prince."

"That need not concern you. Why you are here?"

"There is still a matter of money owed to me by Madame Delacroix, your grandmother. I hear she has been ill. I did not wish to disturb her, and I'm sure there will be no need. You and I have come to terms before and can again."

"My grandmother's debt has been paid in full. It's unfortunate that the outcome of the attempt on the king's life was not what you wanted, but I did as you asked. More you cannot expect."

"You place a high value on yourself, do you not?" he said, his tone ugly beneath its surface smoothness. "There was nothing said about the paltry service you rendered canceling the debt."

She ignored his slighting reference to what she had done. "That was the impression I received."

"Then it was erroneous."

She swung away from him to stare out the window as an idea struck her. It might be as well to know what he had in mind. Here also was an opportunity to discover precisely what had occurred during the assassination attempt, to learn once and for all what Roderic's part had been in it. Over her shoulder she said, "You have your revolt, or so it appears. What more do you want?"

"This is a minor upheaval only, a mere opportunity to bring about a major revolution."

"I see no way that I can be of use to you for such grandiose plans."

"You may leave that to me."

As he spoke the last words, his voice was nearer, rich with satisfaction. A shafting realization of her isolation there with the two men in that small room struck her. She started to turn. A sickly sweet smell caught in her nostrils. Hard hands wrenched at her arms and shoulders, and a wet cloth was clamped to her face. She drew in her breath to scream and choked, coughing, nearly retching.

Dizzily, she felt herself lifted, half dragged, and half carried from the room. There was a space of darkness, then she was thrown upon a hard surface with the smell and feel of a leather carriage seat. It jolted into motion, swaying, lurching sickeningly. Gray darkness descended, blotting out the light, the afternoon, everything.

CHAPTER 17

The cold was in her bones, curling in the joints so that they ached. Her feet were numb, and she could not feel her fingers. A violent shudder took her. She made a soft sound of distress deep in her throat. The low moan filtered through her mind like liquid straining through layers of gauze. She opened her eyes.

She closed them again immediately, swallowing on a wave of nausea. Another shudder gripped her.

She was more cautious when the nausea passed, this time barely lifting her lashes. She was lying on her stomach in a bed alcove. The mattress under her was lumpy and covered with a coverlet gray with grime and smelling of sour feathers and unwashed bodies. The bedchamber was in a garret, for the ceiling sloped at an angle. It was small and bare, with only a broken-down chair and a scarred wooden table under a set of high windows. The windows themselves were warped in their frames so that the wind whistled around them. Beyond the glass was the gray of twilight. With the approach of night, the air was growing colder, especially in the dank room where the sun never reached.

She tried to move, to turn over, and gasped as pain flooded through her hands and feet. She was bound, the ropes cutting into her flesh, cutting off the circulation of blood. She gritted her teeth and, by slow degrees, raised herself, turning, easing to her back.

For long moments she lay panting with the effort, holding sickness at bay. As it receded at last, and her breathing eased, memory returned. De Landes. The evil smell of some drug. The carriage.

Where was she? There was no way of telling from the barren room with its gray, water-streaked plaster walls. The only thing to be seen through the dirty windows was a portion of rooftop and a stretch of sky the purple gray of mourning. She closed her eyes, listening. At first she could not hear a sound, then slowly she became aware of a child crying. A door closed somewhere in the building and the crying stopped. There was a distant murmur that slowly evolved into the shouting of a group of men in the streets below. The voices were fervent, yet without the mad rage of the mob she and Trude and Juliana had faced. Mingled with the voices was the tramp of feet. The sound grew louder, passing under the window, then faded into the distance.

She was still in Paris then. From the looks of the room, it was in one of the poorer districts. The voices in the street might belong to students, in which case it was possible that she was on the Left Bank, near the Latin Quarter. It was only a guess; she could not be certain. Certainly there was no reason she could think of why she should be there.

Nor could she know why she had been taken. Floating through her mind was every whispered tale she had ever heard about young women stolen from their homes or the streets to be forced into houses of ill-repute, sold into a degrading slavery of the senses, shipped to foreign lands. As quickly as they came, she dismissed them. She had been abducted by de Landes, not some person unknown to her. There would be a deeper reason.

Was she to be held as ransom for her grandmother's debt then? Or had that been merely a ruse, some means of approaching her and of distracting her long enough to place her in his power?

Revenge was a possibility. She had, in his view, failed him. Perhaps he suspected that she had in some way alerted Roderic to the danger before the ball so that he was prepared to deal with the attempt on Louis Philippe's life. De Landes had been bitterly disappointed; she had seen it on his face that night as well as this afternoon. There was one other possibility. De Landes had suggested more than once that he found her attractive. Her lip curled at the thought, and she closed her fingers into fists, straining at the rope on her wrists.

Her bonds were of jute. It was stiff and prickly, the knots hard and intricately coiled. She lifted her hands to her mouth, pulling at the knots with her teeth, but it did no good.

Across the surface of her thoughts drifted a story Grand-mère had told her of how in New Orleans Angeline had once been taken and held as bait to capture Rolfe. He had walked into the trap for her sake, a knowing sacrifice. Surely such a thing could not happen again?

It was doubtful that she would be such a successful lure; Rolfe had loved Angeline, while Roderic no longer even desired her. De Landes would be disappointed once again.

Whether from the drug she had breathed, her long stillness, or the chill in the room, she was deathly cold. She had lost the shawl she had been wearing and had only the sleeves of her gown to protect her from the damp, penetrating coolness. She rolled, trying to catch the edge of the coverlet to pull it over her. Her feet thumped the wall and she gave a cry of pain as the blow radiated through her ankles, which were swollen from their binding.

Footsteps sounded beyond the room. A door opened somewhere out of sight. There was a scuffling noise, then a woman waddled into view. She was nearly as wide as she was tall, with frizzy gray hair springing from under the kerchief on her head and a greasy apron over her protruding stomach. She bore a remarkable resemblance to the loutish youth who had helped de Landes abduct Mara, his mother perhaps. The woman grunted as she saw that Mara was awake, then heaved herself around and started out.

"Wait!" Mara cried. "Don't go."

She might as well not have spoken. The door closed and the woman's heavy footsteps passed out of hearing.

Mara closed her eyes, assailed by sudden despair. She thought of Ruthenia House, of the consternation there would be when it was discovered she was missing. There might not be quite the uproar that had broken out over the disappearance of Princess Juliana; still, they would be worried. There was fondness for her among the servants and the cadre, and Rolfe and Angeline would be upset for Grandmère's sake, if not out of affection. Her grandmother would be aghast, if she was told. Even Roderic would be concerned, would use every means at his command to find her; she knew this once she considered it. She was, or so he regarded it, his responsibility. She enjoyed his protection so long as she was under his roof, domiciled as his guest.

How long would it take before the alarm was given? Only the maid knew that she had spoken to de Landes, and even she did not know his name. There had been no footman, no one to see her taken away unless it was by accident. Hours would pass before she was missed. Even then it was likely that the search would be delayed. There had been too many alarms of late. After the uselessness of the panic concerning Juliana and Luca, it would not be surprising if everyone sat back for a time and waited for her to reappear of her own accord.

She thought of de Landes and his henchmen invading Ruthenia House, carrying her off like some parcel they had come to collect, and slow anger began to gather inside her. Roderic's arrogance was a natural and healthy thing beside the overweening conceit of de Landes. The Frenchman thought he could do as he pleased with people, manipulate them for his own purposes, force them to do his bidding. He felt free to interfere in their lives, to destroy them as a child might destroy a toy it no longer valued. He should be stopped. He must be stopped. She did not have the power to do it, but she could control what she herself did. She need fear him no longer. Grand-mère Helene was safe at Ruthenia House and could not be harmed. Whatever de Landes wanted of her, he would get little satisfaction.

So deep was her concentration that she did not hear the returning footsteps. The abrupt opening of the door brought her head around. The sight of de Landes, with the fat woman behind him, did not surprise her. She returned his gaze with a stare as insolent as she could make it.

"So you are awake. Your powers of recuperation are amazing but welcome."

She would not lie supine, trussed, before him. She slid across the mattress and pushed her bound feet over the side, struggling up by pressing her hands together to brace herself. She swayed, swallowing convulsively, as she came to a sitting position, but it was worth the effort.

"I can't think why," she said, speaking with slow control.

"Because I have a use for you, of course."

"Which is?"

"Why, to induce Prince Roderic to come to terms. He will if he values your safety."

"Your ideas of how to gain what you want seem to be limited."

His mouth tightened at the slur upon his inventiveness. "Why abandon a means so effective? You did what I wanted for the sake of your grandmother. Your prince will do the same for your sake."

The thought of Roderic being forced to bow to the dictates of this posturing, self-satisfied creature filled her with repugnance. "What makes you think he will? What makes you think he cares in the least what becomes of me?"

"You shared his bed."

"For a few days only. The association did not last."

"How very distressing for you."

"Not at all. I was happy to be free of the obligation."

De Landes stared at her, frowning, then gave an abrupt laugh. "I think you protest too much. Did innocence pall for him? What a blow for your pride! No doubt you expected to hold his attention longer than the average courtesan. Why, I can't imagine; a courtesan has at least some skill in her trade."

He was a despicable man. She was on the right track, however. She gave him a blazing look. "I told you, I was glad when it ended!"

"A woman scorned. How affecting. Then you will not mind if I use him a bit . . . roughly."

She shrugged. "As you wish, but he won't come."

"He is one of the noble ones who have been taught from birth that duty is supreme. They take responsibility with the utmost seriousness. Because you are a pawn in this game, at risk for him, he will feel the weight of it. He would come if you were no more than a foot soldier under his command. He would come if you were a gypsy maiden with whom he had whiled away a chance hour. He would come if you were the lowest servant. Instead, you are a guest under his roof, the goddaughter of his mother, and a woman who once claimed his affections. You are entitled to his protection three times over. He will come."

"Why you should want him to is more than I can see. Isn't it a little like Jack inviting the giant to dinner?"

"I am no Jack," de Landes said, a flush of annoyance rising to his face. "I can handle Prince Roderic."

"Can you? Still, what is the purpose? If it's revenge, you are a trifle late."

"It's never too late for vengeance. Being a patient man, I preferred to wait until the time was ripe."

"What makes now any different? If you think you can injure Roderic with impunity, I fear you underestimate him."

"Injure? *Ma chère,* I mean to kill him."

She had suspected as much, but to hear it put into words sent a chill down her spine. It might be done. A foreign prince found beaten to death, an apparent victim of one of the demonstrating mobs that prowled the city, would be an incident as regrettable as it was unfortunate. Apologies would be tendered to Ruthenia, promises of a full investigation would be made, and that would be the end of it. If the threatened revolution actually occurred, the matter might not receive even that much attention.

"Will that suffice for you?" she asked, keeping her voice light with an extreme effort. "I would have thought a public humiliation would be more satisfactory."

"So it might. This much I will give him, however: He is too wily by far to lend himself to any situation that might be suitably compromising."

She gave him a small, tight smile. "Is he, indeed?"

The idea that was burgeoning in her brain was vague but daring. Could she do it? Would it work, or would it rebound on her and Roderic, making matters a thousand times worse than they were now?

He took a step closer. "What do you mean?"

"Why should I tell you while I am trussed up like this and freezing? Why should I talk at all when my mouth is as dry as cotton?"

The Frenchman stared at her, his black eyes hard and shining in the dim room. Finally he nodded to the heavy-set woman. "Release her. Bring some wine, whatever you have."

The instructions were obeyed. Mara rubbed her wrists with her hands and flexed her feet as they prickled and burned with the return of circulation. She pulled the coverlet up around her shoulders as a cloak, then shifted to sit with her back to the side wall of the bed alcove before taking the greasy glass of wine. She sipped at the thin, sour liquid, grateful for the warmth it brought to her stomach.

"Get out," de Landes said to the other woman, "leave the ropes."

He did not trust her entirely and wished that knowledge to serve as a warning to her. It would, indeed.

"Now," he said when the door had closed upon the woman's bulk, "let us hear this charming scheme of betrayal."

"Certainly, but should you not be making preparations for the arrival of the prince?"

"Presently, you will send him a message. Until then he need not trouble us."

"How clever."

He sent her a sardonic glance, but at the same time smoothed his mustache with is fingers in a preening gesture. She looked down at her hands, trying to be certain that what she was doing was correct. There was no way to be sure. She must trust to instinct. One thing she knew. She could not bear it if Roderic was hurt because of her, because he came when she was in need. She would die inside if that happened. But it would not. She would prevent that immolation, no matter what the cost.

"Come, what good are second thoughts? Unless you have discovered within yourself an unwillingness to do to him what he has done to you."

"I was only thinking," she said slowly, "that if you acted quickly and well, it might mean execution for him."

"Execution?"

"As a spy."

"Indeed?" he answered, but so significant was that single word that it compressed within it intense gratification.

"Of course it depends on your own loyalties."

"My loyalties?"

"I am assuming that on the night of the assassination attempt you did not, in fact, wish it to be prevented?"

"Brilliant," he drawled.

"Roderic was to have been the scapegoat—" She paused for confirmation, but it was not forthcoming. She went on hardily since it was too late to stop, but abandoned a line that did not appear to be productive at the moment. "It follows then that you are not a supporter of the Orleanist party. I cannot think that you are a reformist, for you have never been involved in that circle. That leaves either the Bonapartists or the legitimists."

"I congratulate you, mademoiselle, on your grasp of the situation. Which, do you think?"

She looked down into her wine, pretending to consider. "Those who clamor for Louis Napoleon Bonaparte seem to be chiefly concerned with the glory of France, while those who support the Bourbon heir Henri, comte de Chambord, are anxious for personal gain. I do not think you are a Bonapartist."

"Take care, Mademoiselle Mara," he said, his dark eyes

cold. "My interest in your proposal is not so great that I will tolerate insults."

The satisfaction it had given her was great, but not enough to jeopardize everything for it. She refused to acknowledge his threat, however. As if he had not spoken, she went on. "The present unstable situation seems to have been caused by the reformists, some of whom are republicans and some merely frustrated monarchists who would like to persuade Louis Philippe to be more like the constitutional monarchs of Great Britain. That is only the surface. I suspect that many people are secretly stoking the fire under this particular *pot-au-feu.* Among them would naturally be the legitimists. When the pot boils over, they hope to seize power in the ensuing panic."

"Come, come, hearing a recital of the obvious grows tedious. What is your point?"

"It would greatly enhance your personal consequence and strengthen the legitimist position if you could capture the leaders of the reformist faction before they are able to move to overset Louis Philippe. Is this not so?"

He merely inclined his head, but there was a stillness in his face that told her she had his complete attention. There was, she saw quite clearly, more than one kind of seduction. Whether the appeal was to passion or to greed, however, the approach was the same, through the mind, the imagination.

"Of course, you could engage the cooperation of your fellow conspirators for this coup, but they would share in the honor. Then there is always the chance that the present situation will come to nothing. If that should happen, it might be better if you alone had the traitors under lock and key—to exhibit as proof of your loyalty to the regime?"

"And where might I lay hands on these reformists?" he asked softly.

Trust. Trust was the cornerstone of what she was doing. Trust that she could persuade de Landes to let her go once the die was cast, trust that Roderic would be able to turn what she was doing to advantage, trust that if he was the manipulator of events that he appeared to be that he had good reason. She had thought she could never place her dependence in him; she had been wrong. The knowledge gave her courage.

"They will be meeting three nights from now at Ruthenia House."

A slow smile curved the thin lips of the Frenchman. He came to his feet. "Excellent. I said some time ago that we worked well together. If I had known quite how well, I might have handled matters differently."

Mara watched his approach with uneasiness. "How so?"

"I could have taken you into my confidence, shared with you the problems so that your understanding would have been greater. Our arrangement might have been much . . . closer."

She forced an arch smile to her lips. "You don't strike me as a man who would place much confidence in a woman, much less make her free of your secrets."

"Very true, but for you I might have made an exception."

Could she force herself to endure any intimacy this man might force upon her? She did not know, but as he reached to touch her cheek with his hot, dry hand, she thought it unlikely. It would have pleased her to think that his advances were a means of testing her, but the increasing heat that she saw in his eyes dispelled that illusion.

"You—you could do so now, concerning plans for taking Roderic at this meeting."

"That is something we may indeed discuss, but only after this night."

He reached out to cup her face, thrusting his fingers into her loosened hair. She knocked his hand aside.

"Just as I have no liking for the embraces of the prince, I have none for yours."

"You'll learn to like them, my dear Mara," he said, towering over her, then placing a knee on the bed. "Oh, yes, you'll learn."

She flung up her hand to fend him off. He caught it, twisting it so that she gasped with pain as the bones ground together. A cruel smile on his face, he forced her backward on the bed, his other hand closing on the soft mound of her breast, kneading it, slowly tightening.

Hard on the soft sound she made, the door crashed open. Roderic surged through with a pistol in his hand, coming to a halt with his heavy cloak swirling about his wide-set, booted legs and his face a hard mask. Behind him was Michael, who leaped to one side in a half-crouch, also leveling a pistol.

"Cozy as two peasant women gossiping over a churn," Roderic drawled. "Is it any wonder that the milk of human kindness is sour?"

Cursing, de Landes sprang away from Mara. She came slowly to her feet with the color draining from her face and then flooding back again. How much had he heard? It was impossible that he could understand, and yet in a daze of distress she willed him to make the effort.

He glanced from de Landes to her. His cobalt gaze held on the soft, entreating darkness of her eyes. The frown that drew his brows together lessened imperceptibly. There was an easing inside him, and it seemed that in the shadowy dimness of that dingy room, Mara reached out and placed her cool fingers on the sensitive surface of his mind. He accepted that touch, assimilated its strangeness, its limitless acceptance and tentative dependence, and turned on her in cold suspicion.

"You were saying before our crass interruption?"

"Why, nothing, just commonplaces," she answered, summoning a bright smile. "How did you ever find me?"

"The house has been under surveillance as a precautionary measure for days. The sentries saw you taken, followed to discover where, and sent for me."

"But when Juliana disappeared—"

"I did not trust them sufficiently when they said she had not left the house. My mistake. Enough. Let's get out of here. Unless you plan to stay?"

Beneath his impatience ran a steely determination to take her away. There was no hint in his manner or words of concern for her or pleasure at finding her. He could not have made it plainer that nothing more than doubt of her discretion, coupled with duty, had brought him. His attitude was like a blow, but at the same time she was well aware that no better ploy to convince de Landes that what she said was true could have been found.

Mara started toward the door. Michael, giving her a brief smile, backed out into the hall. As she passed through the door opening, Roderic moved to follow her without talking his eyes from de Landes. When they were out, the prince reached to slam the door shut and turn the key that stood in the lock. Down the hall, another door was cracked open, and through the slitted opening could be seen the stout woman. Roderic, with a brief glance in that direction, pocketed the key.

They swept along the hall to a rickety set of stairs, clattering down them to the landing, then circling around to the next. Behind them, de Landes set up a shout, pounding on the locked door. They ignored the noise. As they ran, Roderic swung his cloak from his shoulders and draped it around Mara, putting a hard arm about her waist to urge her forward. Another landing, and another, and then they were out in the cold, fresh air and the fast-approaching night.

"Can you walk?" Roderic inquired. "A carriage or horses seemed conspicuous tonight with so many abroad on foot."

"I can now," she answered shortly, and set off beside

the two men as they walked with long strides away from the house where she had been held.

"Now?" Michael asked, directing a quick, inquiring glance at her.

"I was bound. The ropes were too tight."

"And you talked de Landes into removing them? What nerve; I'm all amazement. And pride. Aren't you, Roderic?"

"Both, immeasurably." Roderic, scanning the street ahead of them, did not look at her.

His distant manner was an affront. She took a deliberate breath, saying, "There is something I must tell you."

"Not now. We aren't out of this yet," Roderic answered over his shoulder.

"It's important!"

"Staying in one piece also has a certain value as well as persistent charm."

He had heard what Mara and Michael had missed as they spoke, the deep murmuring of a distant crowd. Coming in waves like a dark sea, the sound drew nearer. The street was narrow and lined with trees. The light of the torches and lanterns held by the demonstrators was thrown ahead of them along the twisting length, illuminating the fronts of the shops with rooms for let above them and shining on the bare branches of the trees. It was only as Mara saw those piercing gleams that she realized night had dropped down upon them like a smothering woolen blanket.

"Michael, you will join this group, see who they are and where they are going."

There were times when the cadre left their uniforms behind as they moved about the city and the countryside at Roderic's bidding. That day must have been one of those times for Michael, for he was wearing a nondescript coat and pair of trousers with a faded waistcoat under his cloak. As he received the instructions of his prince, he tossed back the cloak, handing it to Roderic, and pulled a cap from his pocket. Settling the cap on the back of his head, he pushed his hands into his pockets and set off along the street as if he had not a care in the world.

Roderic whipped Michael's cloak around him to cover the shining white of his dress uniform, then, with a hand on Mara's arm, faded back into the deep shadows of a doorway.

The crowd came nearer. A few red banners waved over them, crude, hand-made strips of cloth. Although a few were students from the university and the École Militaire, most seemed to be craftsmen and artisans still wearing their leather vests and aprons and carrying hammers and other tools in their fists. Among the men were a few women, their faces alight and determined in the torchlight. Shouts and laughter rang out as they came, and now and then they broke into song. They did not seem to be unruly or violent, and yet there was defiance in the rumble of their voices. They kept to the center of the street, relentlessly marching.

They filed past where Mara and Roderic stood, their tramping over the cobbles taking on a muffled, hollow sound between the buildings. They overtook Michael, and with a joke and a quick question, he joined them. They took him with them like a river gathering flotsam into its current.

When the noise had ebbed and the night was quiet, Roderic stepped out into the street and Mara joined him. They turned in the opposite direction from that taken by Michael and the crowd. They had not gone more than a hundred yards when, nearing a cross street, they heard yet another group of men coming toward them. There was anger in the yells and curses they flung into the night sky. Though their numbers were much smaller, they seemed more vicious.

"The garden," Roderic said. "Over there."

They ghosted beside a building constructed of the omnipresent soot-streaked stone and down the wrought-iron fence beyond it, then slipped through a pair of tall gates. Inside the garden were head-high evergreens and a series of paths. Mara, moving in front of Roderic, turned a corner and stopped, gasping, reaching out to prevent Roderic from moving forward. Ahead of her stood a tall man, a dark shape outlined against the lighter darkness, one hand upraised. A moment later, she gave a shuddering sigh. The man wore Roman draperies that did not move in the faint night wind. It was a marble statue.

They stood still where they were until it was safe to emerge. As he stepped from the dark garden, Roderic stood staring after the receding group of men. Reaching for her hand, he started after them with only a single word. "Come."

The were retracing their footsteps, going the wrong way.

"What are you doing?" she asked, breathless from the pace he had set.

"I sent Michael on an errand I should have taken myself."

"He was dressed for it; you aren't." There was no heat in her words, however. She herself wanted to know what was taking place. The crowds, all of them, seemed to be heading for the river. If she had her bearings, they would, after a time, cross the Seine by the Pont Royal near the Place de la Concorde. It was there that Lamartine had been scheduled to speak at the reformist banquet that had been canceled by the king.

The wind was rising, turning colder. It tugged at their cloaks, flapping them about their bodies, and brought the sting of tears to Mara's eyes. Without a lantern to light the way, they stumbled on the uneven cobbles. Mara's slippers of soft leather were for wearing inside the house; they had never been meant for extended walking, particularly on the sharp-edged stones. She refused to complain. She was free, not bound hand and foot and shut up in a sour-smelling room. She was with Roderic in the fresh night air. And if there were other shadows hanging over her, what better way was there to escape them than to outrun them?

The streets near the bridge were more congested. The atmosphere was almost like a carnival with people hanging out of windows and calling back and forth. Street vendors were out selling roasted chestnuts and hot meat pies, candied fruits and bunches of violets, and the organ man with his monkey played on a corner. Still, above it all could be heard the shouts of *"Vive la réforme!,"* "Down with Guizot!," and that old one from another revolution, *"Liberté, égalité, et fraternité!"*

From the bridge they could see the gathering in the Place de la Concorde, the torches and lanterns glinting like fireflies, casting eerie reflections upon the great stone shaft of the obelisk that had been presented to Louis Philippe by the viceroy of Egypt, Mohammed Ali. The crowd numbered several hundred strong, and the sound of their voices was a distant roaring.

"What are they doing?" Mara asked as they drew nearer. She could not see above the throng, but there was a dense cloud of black smoke roiling into the air that appeared to have nothing to do with the scattered torches.

"Lamartine is trying to speak. A few are listening. The rest are making a bonfire of the chairs from the Tuileries."

"What? But why?"

"No doubt they were cold."

The crowd parted then, and she could see off to the right the façade of the Tuileries palace. Men were coming from that direction carrying chairs above their heads like prizes of war. As she watched, a window in an upstairs room shattered into glittering fragments and the throne of Louis Philippe came crashing through. A great shout arose, and the throne chair was seized and thrown onto the fire. That the throne and the chairs that had, many of them, survived the revolution and all that had followed should be wantonly destroyed here on this night seemed like a sacrilege.

"France should be grateful that beds and armoires are heavier," she commented.

There came the atonal tinkling of more breaking glass from the direction of one of the side streets lined with shops. Roderic turned his head swiftly toward that sound. "I believe they have found something else for their attention. I've seen enough. Let's go."

"What about Michael?"

"He can take care of himself."

They threaded their way through the Tuileries gardens, away from the wrenching, tearing noise of shop doors being forced and the yells of the looters. People still milled under the leafless trees and around the clipped shrubbery, but with less purpose. A pickpocket, caught at his trade, was chased past them. Here and there were lovers, taking advantage of the general unrest to kiss in the evergreen bowers.

The street between the Seine and the Louvre was dark and deserted. Roderic walked with one hand on his pistol and every sense alert. The ancient pile of masonry loomed above them on the left, stretching endlessly with its myriad windows and doorways. It was once the home of French kings where sovereigns strode in splendor along the majestic rooms that smelled of the privy because of the habit of impatient courtiers of relieiving themselves in the gilded corners and behind the carved doors. To the right, the Seine wound its way with a soft, rushing sigh, channeling the night wind along its length so that it blew damper and stronger.

Mara was footsore and weary with reaction, her spirits lowering as the sense of danger lessened. She noticed they were nearing the end of the palace wing, coming close to another of the Seine's many bridges, the Pont Neuf, and the cross street that led onto it, though these things made little impression.

The mob seemed to rise up out of the ground, boiling up out of a stairwell that led down into a shop's cellar. Small in number, not more than a dozen, it was the most bizarre group they had seen. The faces of its members were painted like red Indians, and they brandished hatchets and knives and whirled torches in the air as they whooped and yelled. Hanging about them were articles of women's clothing, petticoats and pantalettes, and at their belts hung silver vases and coffeepots.

There was no way to avoid them, no hope of outrunning them. Armed as they were, it would be suicidal for Roderic to think of fighting their way free, though he might have attempted it if he had been alone. Roderic stopped, shielding Mara with his body.

And then as the looting mob came bearing down upon them, the wind lifted his cloak, exposing his white trousers with their cerulean stripes and his polished boots. For an instant the braiding and bars on his coat gleamed, richly royal.

As swift and as precise as a parade drill, Roderic whirled away from the mob, catching Mara in his right arm. With his left, he imprisoned her chin and lifted it higher. His mouth came down to crush her soft, open lips. For a moment she was stunned, then her heart throbbed against the wall of her chest and comprehension flared inside her. She forced a low moan and reached up to push her fingers through his hair, twining them in the silky golden strands as she strained against him.

A coarse jest or two was thrown in their direction. They were jostled as a few men on the edge of the crowd stopped and stared. They paid no heed.

"Lean on me," Roderic whispered, and moving with the slow footsteps of those entranced by desire, they turned down the path that led under the span of the bridge. Paris had from time immemorial respected the privacy of lovers. The looters let them go.

In the darkness Roderic stopped and stood listening, staring upward. The main body of the men was moving over the bridge. After a moment there were a few curses and more shouted crudities, then thudding footsteps as the laggards ran to catch up. Silence.

Mara turned blindly to Roderic, twisting her hands in his cloak and burying her face against his chest. She was trembling deep inside, and those hidden tremors hurt worse than the most violent shivering. His arms closed warm and firm around her. Silently, he held her there in the darkness, his legs firmly planted as he gave generously of his great strength. In his touch was acceptance and welcome, without a trace of the unyielding hardness of anger.

A sob rose in her throat. She drew back. "I must tell you what I've done."

"Never mind. I overheard a little and the rest I know." He paused, then went on. "I'm not sure how I know, but I could not be more certain if you had been, for a brief moment there with de Landes, a part of me, your thoughts my own."

Her mother had had strange gifts, the sight. She could not depend on having them herself. "No, let me—"

"Later," he whispered, and lowered his mouth to take her lips, this time with the gentleness of a benediction.

CHAPTER 18

Here was security and warmth and sheltering darkness. The danger of the moment was past. They were alive and their senses quickened with the glory of it. Mara pressed against the man whose arms enclosed her with a dissolving feeling inside. That he was a prince, Roderic of Ruthenia, no longer had meaning. What kind of man he was, what he had done or might do in the future, could not concern her. She accepted and trusted what she knew of him. The quickness of his mind, his strength and instinct for command, evoked her respect. His flashing humor, his concern for those around him and understanding of their needs, and his willingness to expose the softer side of his nature touched her to the heart. The time they would have together might not be long, but for now it was theirs.

He parted the edges of her cloak and slid his hand inside to cup the tender globe of one breast. "Sweet Mara," he whispered, his voice rich and warm against the silken waves of her hair, "I meant to hold you unassailable, a precious thing, to prove your worth by returning to you the privilege of denial. I did not know that to keep the vow would shrivel the edges of my soul and make the inside of my skull fit for no more than a drinking cup."

"I absolve you of it—gladly."

"And if I said you are free to choose, that no one and nothing will coerce you to the joining of my desire, will you deny me?"

His touch made her weak, and her words were low, unsteady. "If I had the wiles of a courtesan, I would entreat you or, if need be, seduce you all over again."

"You need no such wiles; all that is required to bind me is a smile with promise."

"Something you cannot see at this moment."

"I have seen it a thousand times, enjoyed a thousand embraces in my dreams. Tell me it is there, and I will conjure it up."

"From layers of imagination? But will it be mine?"

He understood her fears and answered them without hesitation. "None other will suffice, not now, not ever."

She wanted to believe it, and so she lifted her mouth to his, her lips trembling into a gentle curve.

There was a promise of another sort in the infinite care with which he took her mouth, melding it to his, tasting its sweetness. He smoothed its delicate surfaces with his tongue, awakening the exquisite sensitivity that dwelled there before probing, easing deeper. She surrendered to that soft ravishment, touching the fine-grained tip of his tongue with her own, twining, inviting greater penetration, daring her own exploration.

With close-held breath, she traced the even line of his teeth, the resilient inner lining of his mouth, the firmly cut edges of his lips and faint roughness of the beard stubble where lip and chin met. Inside her grew a deep and wracking need to learn his body inch by inch, every muscle and plane and angle. She wanted to impress his shape and size and form upon her own body, to take him into her to forge a memory past forgetting. Lifting her hand to his chest, she pushed aside his cloak, spreading her fingers over the hard-muscled surface of his chest.

He shrugged from the cloak, letting it fall, and stripped the fastenings of his uniform coat free with hard fingers, guiding her hand to the buttons of his shirt. The warmth of his body, the heavy thudding of his heart under the fine linen of his shirt, the warm male scent of him, caused the muscles of her abdomen to contract with longing. She needed no urging to kneel with him, to spread the cloak he had dropped, to yield to the sure touch of his fingers as he untied her own cape and slipped the tiny buttons of her gown from their holes.

He was not content with loosening their clothing, but lowered her to the soft wool on the ground and rid her of petticoats and camisole and pantalettes. He removed his own stiff garments, then drew her naked against his hard, unclothed length as if he divined her harbored need to press close and shared it.

Vital, glowing with the heat of passion long suppressed, they paid no heed to the cool breath of the night, the damp ground, or such minor annoyances as twigs and stones under them. The blood in their veins ran as swift and full as the river that murmured in their ears. The smell of the earth on which they lay, musty and rich, was natural, and so went unnoticed. Lost in the sensations that flooded them as with heightened senses their two bodies touched, glided one skin surface upon the other, they did not hear the footsteps of the strangers who passed overhead.

His hands cupped the rounded curves of her hips, gently squeezing. She could feel his springing, pulsating firmness against the small mound at the juncture of her thighs. Bending his head, he brushed his warm lips along the curve of her neck, her shoulder. He traced sweeping circles around the swollen mound of her breast that jarred with the thudding of her heart before capturing the tightly budded nipple with the soft adhesion of his mouth. With one hand, he smoothed from her hip down across the flat plane of her abdomen, slipping it between her thighs, questing, finding the sensitive source of her femininity. He followed a similar trail with his mouth, gliding from breast to slender waist, to hip, and lower still.

It was pleasure nearly beyond endurance, spiraling, lifting until her every muscle was tense and full with its flow, until her being vanished into nothingness, floating, then was suddenly, violently reborn, made whole and new once more.

With trembling hands and a vibrant need to return the wondrous gift she had been given, she caressed him with open palms and soft, searching lips. He gave himself up to her, touching her hair, her face with tender fingertips. At last he sighed with the ghost of laughter threading his voice. "It is now, darling Mara, sweet temptress, or else I will become flame to your tinder."

Together they forged the link that made them one as he drew her beneath him with firm urgency and plunged deep into the moist and welcoming warmth of her. She took him deeper still, rising, opening, leaving nothing in reserve.

Turbulent and beautiful, the fury took them. They moved to its ageless measure, caught in the violence and glory of time's most primitive dance, attuned with every fiber to its necessity, its labor, its boundless promise. There was, for those who felt its music, also a reward. It came to them in full bounty: the enthrallment, wild and without end, the stupendous eternity that marks the moment when humankind is most alone and yet comes closest to transcending their basic loneliness.

And in its aftermath they held each other, staring into the darkness, comforting, being comforted.

Roderic and Mara made their way back toward Ruthenia House some time later. They were met halfway there by Michael, Trude, and Estes. When Roderic's cousin had returned to discover that the prince and Mara were still missing, he, with Rolfe and the rest of the cadre, had launched a full-scale search. Hilarity sprang into Roderic's eyes as he saw his followers, but it was quickly extinguished. With every commendation for their swift action and gratitude for their concern, he gave them an expurgated account of what had happened. If his explanation of how the dirt and grime came to be decorating his and Mara's clothing was rather glib, no one seemed to notice.

Grandmère Helene, driven from her bed by her fears for Mara's safety, waited in the salon with Angeline. Roderic and Mara were scolded and hugged in equal measure. The story had to be told again, from the beginning, and yet again as other search parties returned. Finally, Angeline took pity upon them and sent them away to bathe and change before dinner.

The meal turned into a celebration, with three kinds of wine accompanying the courses, Mara's favorite *tartelettes aux fraises* for dessert as an offering of thanksgiving for her return from Madame Cook and the staff, and champagne served in the salon afterward.

Due to the unrest in the streets, they were not disturbed by visitors, which was felt to be a blessing by all. The discussion of the political situation was lively. Rolfe felt that Louis Philippe could weather the crisis if he just held firm. Roderic disagreed. Some gesture was needed, he thought, to show the king was not intransigent, that he was aware of the march of progress and the changes in French society of the past forty years. Grandmère Helene, who seemed to have been rejuvenated by being once more in company, sided with Rolfe, as did Juliana. Angeline, however, was of the same opinion as her son, and Mara herself saw the logic of his reasoning. The cadre were equally divided in their opinions and equally vociferous. Despite the differences of opinion, and regardless of the gravity of the situation, everyone seemed to feel that the matter could be resolved so long as there was no violent confrontation between the crown and the reformists.

Roderic excused himself early in order to see to what he described as a problem that demanded his attention. Mara discovered soon after that weariness from her adventures, combined with the wine she had drunk, was making her so drowsy that she could hardly hold her eyes open. Kissing her grandmother, she said her good-nights and left them also.

She expected to find Lila waiting for her in her dressing room. The girl was not there. Mara swept into the bedchamber, thinking that she might be laying out her nightgown or mending the fire. As she went, she pulled from her hair the pins that were pressing into her scalp, letting the heavy skein slide down to uncoil over her shoulder. Her head was bent as she searched for stray pins in the shining swath. She glanced up and came to an abrupt halt.

Roderic reclined in a slipper chair before the fire, his legs outstretched and crossed at the ankles, his hands clasped behind his head. There was a kindling deep in his eyes as he watched her, surveying the dark veiling of her hair, her red lips parted in surprise, and the rounded curves of her breasts, which were emphasized by the lift of her arms.

Her mouth closed with a snap. "So this is the problem that required your attention?"

"A very important one. You might call it a problem of strategy, a flanking movement." He lowered his hands, coming to his feet in a fluid gathering of muscles and moving toward her.

"I see, to outmaneuver your father."

"It seemed more filial than defying him. He likes to think he is omnipotent, all in the best interests of those concerned. Sometimes he is, of course, and it's an endearing trait, but not now."

"You love him very much." There was no reason to be surprised at the knowledge; still, she was.

"He is my sire twice over," Roderic said simply, "and my father."

Her weariness had vanished. She turned from him slightly, saying over her shoulder, "To avoid him, you may now have to stay here the night through."

"I may," he answered gravely as he reached to lift a soft, curling strand of her hair, rubbing it gently against her cheek. "Does it trouble you?"

"Not if I can be released from this prison of clothes. What have you done with Lila?"

"I? Why, nothing. But she went away when she saw I meant to stay."

"Did she, indeed?" Mara said in derisive suspicion.

He settled his hand upon her shoulder, turning her back to him. He bent his head to touch her tender nape with his lips, punctuating his words with soft kisses upon the smooth skin of her back as he released her buttons. "Autocrat that I sometimes am . . . I may have given her reason . . . to think . . . that you would not be needing . . . a maid . . ."

Luca returned the following evening. Roderic received him in the salon with everyone present. Every inch the prince, he stood before the fireplace with his legs spread and his hands loosely clasped behind him while the gypsy walked down the room toward him. Luca saluted, and

Roderic acknowledged it, but there were no glad greetings.

Neither was there condemnation. Roderic, his voice softly incisive, asked, "Why are you here?"

"I am of the cadre," Luca said, his head high, his shoulders squared with gypsy pride. He wore his uniform, and it was pristine.

"You left us once. What reason do you have for returning?"

"You know what is happening in the city: the marches, the barricades of cobblestones in the streets. The word that reached us at the camp is that the National Guardsmen were called out to quell the riots, but instead of standing steady, they threw down their guns and joined the reformists. More, it has come to us that a man you have cause to distrust, de Landes, is gathering men. He buys toughs, riffraff, the kind who will do anything for a price. He jokes of needing an army to attack a palace. You are my prince, son of the *boyar*. You may have need of me. I am here."

A wry smile twisted Roderic's lips. "It's been said, and truly, that there is no gratitude in princes. I cannot promise you the hand of my sister in return for your allegiance."

"I don't expect it." The gaze of the gypsy flickered briefly to Juliana's face, then away again. His expression was impassive, without hope, but also without resignation.

"If I place you to guard my back, how can I know that you will not desert that post for the sake of the tents of the *Tziganes*?"

"I have grown used, with you, to life lived at a faster pace, to thoughts that fly more swiftly and days that have purpose. I am addicted to these things as surely as the opium-eater is to the juice of the poppy. For them, and for your sake, I will cease to be a *Tzigane*."

Roderic stared at him, weighing his words and the steady light in his eyes. Finally he said, "You will always be a gypsy—and that is as it should be. Welcome, Luca."

He put out his hand and the gypsy took it. The cadre, with a volley of yells, closed in around them, slapping them on the back and buffeting them on the shoulders. Juliana, watching, made a sound of distress under her breath. Her blue eyes icy with contempt, she jumped to her feet and left the room. Luca saw her go, followed her progress with a somber look, but made no move to go after her.

It was the next day, the twenty-third day of February, 1848, that King Louis Philippe, bowing to the will of the crowds in the streets of Paris, if not of his people, dismissed his foreign minister and most trusted advisor, François Guizot. In his place, the king appointed a man with reformist sympathies, Comte Molé.

The news was slow in reaching the rampaging mobs. Later that evening they gathered in force outside Guizot's house on the boulevard des Capucines, chanting their slogans and brandishing torches. The military had been called in to protect the former minister and his property. They stood nervously fingering their rifles while the crowd grew larger and louder. Insults were hurled, along with a few stones and a great deal of rotten fruit and eggs. A man in the yelling multitude waved a pistol. Whether accidentally or with a purpose, the pistol went off. The soldiers fired a salvo directly into the crowd. People scattered, screaming, helping the injured to stagger away. On the ground, among the dropped torches, were left the bodies of twenty men and women.

The reformist called them martyrs; the Bonapartist labeled them fools; the legitimist hailed them as pawns, but the Orleanist wept with rage as five of the corpses were trundled through the street, recognizing them for the symbols of the end that they were.

Within twenty-four hours, Louis Philippe, king of the French, under pressure from the mobs in the streets and his own sons, abdicated the throne. As his successor, he named his grandson, the comte de Paris, with his daughter-in-law, the duchesse d'Orléans, as regent. Having learned well the harsh lesson posed by the executions of the Louis XVI and Marie Antoinette, the bourgeois king did not tarry for heroic gestures, but fled Paris with his queen in a hired carriage. Possessed of little more than what they could carry in their hands, they crossed the channel to England and exile.

The reformists were in disarray. Their accomplishment had far exceeded their hopes. They had expected to force change down the king's throat; instead, they had toppled the government. Among them were many who, like Victor Hugo, now looked for great things from the regency of the young duchesse, Helen of Mecklenburg-Shwerin, who was considered a liberal and intelligent lady. There were just as many reformists who suddenly wanted to have done with royalty, to establish a government of the people based on a constitution like that of the United States. The reformist meeting at Ruthenia House had been planned originally to discuss further means of bringing about the desired changes. It became instead a forum to discuss and reconcile their differences.

They congregated in the long gallery. Chairs of various sorts had been brought in from other parts of the house. Tall candelabrums of brass were ranged down both sides of the hall. The candles that filled them burned bright, their flames wavering in the drafts that eddied in the enormous open space, sending smoke curling up to the vaulted and frescoed ceiling. The light was reflected, multiplying, in the tall, arched windows that faced each other along the length of the gallery. The men, perhaps fifteen in number in addition to the cadre, gravitated toward the fire since the night had turned bitterly cold.

The conduct of the meeting had, so far, been vocal and yet sober. It was as if those gathered there felt the weight of what they were doing and of the changes they were making in the course of history. They had been calling for months for reform, for a revolt of the people; until that moment, it had not seemed like treason.

Perhaps it was the sense of responsibility, the feeling of emerging on to a wider, more public stage, that made them accept the audience that gathered to watch. Grand-mère, fascinated at being so close to this political process, had demanded to be allowed to attend, and Angeline, no less interested, had supported her. Juliana and Mara had added their requests—Juliana out of curiosity, Mara from a feverish need to be present, to see what would take place concerning de Landes.

Would the Frenchman come? Did he mean to carry through the suggestion she had made, or had her rescue by Roderic caused him to abandon it? It seemed that he might be still determined from the news Luca had brought; surely he was the man hiring thugs about which the gypsy had spoken? If he was, and if that information was put together with the plan they had discussed, it seemed ominous.

Was Roderic prepared? Mara did not know. She had tried to speak to him about it. Her choice of time and place had not, perhaps, been the best. He had nodded his comprehension of what she was saying and continued making love to her. If he accepted the seriousness of the situation, if he had made plans to counter whatever de Landes might do, he had given no sign of it. His preparations, like his mental processes, were seldom overt, and yet it would have given her more confidence to see some show of force on the part of the cadre or at least some indication that they were armed. Roderic himself, and Rolfe beside him, did not appear to have so much as a penknife between them as they lounged in chairs near the great marble fireplace.

Roderic's *garde du corps* stood near the edges of the gathering: Michael, Trude, and Estes on one side; Jacques and Jared on the other. Mara looked around for Luca, but he was nowhere in sight. She had seen him earlier in the corridor outside, however. Perhaps he was standing guard? It was good to think that someone was on alert.

The man who had become the leader of the reformists, Lamartine, was on his feet addressing the group. He stood tall before them, his thin face ennobled with the force of his belief in the cause he had worked for with such fervor for so long. "My friends, the time is now. The king and the Orleanists have fallen, not in blood but caught in their own trap. In the past we have had the revolution of freedom and the counterrevolution of glory. Now we have the revolution of the public conscience and the revolution of contempt!"

There was an outcry of agreement. When it died away, Lamartine went on. "We must grasp this opportunity that we have been given, for its like will never come again. We can rally to the duchesse d'Orléans and the comte de Paris, hoping to use influence to gain the goals we seek, or we can form a provisional government, a second republic. The choice is ours. But we must decide, we must move. Already the legitimist followers of the comte de Chambord gather like vultures. Already the radicals and socialists are meeting at the Hôtel de Ville to form their own government. We cannot endure another bloodbath, another round of fraternal wars between the aristocracy and the assembly, or between the assembly and the commune. It is for us to prevent Paris, and France itself, from being plunged once more into chaos. It is for us to place our influence behind the force for greater good, and with our weight provide stability. We alone can do it!"

"Not so, poet!"

The shout came from de Landes. He stood inside the doorway with a pistol in his hand. Behind him, armed men poured into the room. They were a vicious group, bearded and scarred, with blank, unfeeling eyes. They had extra pistols and daggers thrust into the waistbands of their trousers. They fanned out to cover the men in the room, enclosing them like rats caught in a barrel. The reformists leaped from their chairs, cursing, exclaiming as they spun to face the men who hemmed them in the room.

Mara came to her feet with horror in her eyes. Why had there been no alarm? Where was Luca? Was he dead, killed before he could give the warning? Or was the failure his revenge, an act of treachery in retaliation for the slur cast upon his birth? She looked at Juliana and saw the same fears mirrored in the eyes of Roderic's sister.

Or were they the same? Juliana was looking at Roderic and her father. The faces of the two men were grim, but showed no surprise. It was natural, of course, since they had known the attack might come; still, there was something here that she did not understand.

Abruptly, a thought struck her. It was so blighting that she felt the blood leave her face and congeal, aching, in her heart. Was it possible that Roderic stood unarmed, unafraid, because he was a part of this attack? Was he making no move toward defense because he had manipulated this entire diabolical betrayal?

What if she had been drawn into the affair with Roderic in the beginning not to persuade him to become a scapegoat for de Landes, but to provide the prince with an excuse to be at the ball and so be on hand to prevent the assassination. Had not Roderic once suggested that it was he himself who had seen her, desired her, and ultimately arranged his own seduction? What if the assassination plot had been a sham, a means of gaining the trust of

King Louis Philippe and, at the same time, disassociating Roderic and his men from the legitimists who were responsible?

It could not be. Roderic had mounted the rescue of her grandmother that had nullified de Landes's control of her.

But he had done that only after the attempt on Louis Philippe had been foiled, when her usefulness was done. Immediately afterward King Rolfe had arrived. Was it possible that Roderic had known his father was en route to Paris, had known the king would not permit the game he was playing with her? He had offered her marriage when the scandal of his supposed seduction of her, his mother's goddaughter, had broken, but he must have known this was also something Rolfe would not allow.

Was it possible that Roderic had spoken nothing more than the truth when he had said that the reason Rolfe had denied his approval was because the king thought her too good for his son?

And what if, once Roderic's identity was established as a liberal prince, one who had foiled a legitimist plot, he had then ingratiated himself with the reformists in order to betray them? What could be more natural? As a hereditary prince, he would have great sympathy for the Bourbon heir, the comte de Chambord whose throne had been stolen by Louis Philippe; after all, he was related, if distantly, through his mother. He would be ready to aid the reformists in their aim to overthrow the usurper. But once the deed was done, he would be just as ready to use the knowledge he had gained, the trust he had engendered, to lead them into this snare.

But, in that case, why had she been kidnapped by de Landes? Why the elaborate pretense of revenge against Roderic? Could it be that de Landes had not been made privy to the plans of the prince? Was it possible that until the afternoon she was taken, the Frenchman had not known of the deep game Roderic was playing? Had Roderic used the man's much-vaunted love of manipulation to manipulate de Landes himself?

The Frenchman was here and Roderic faced him without the least indication of disturbance. If she was right, then it was plain that the differences between the two men had been set aside, that they were now ready to collaborate in returning a Bourbon to the throne of France.

But while these thoughts burned like wildfire through her mind, Lamartine was speaking. His face dark with fury, he demanded, "What is the meaning of this?"

"It means we have you, my friend," de Landes answered. "It means that Henry V, our rightful king, will rule France, and you and this den of traitors will not interfere."

"Bourbon dog, you cannot hold us here forever!"

"Perhaps not, but my men and I can imprison you until Madame Guillotine is made ready once more in the Place de la Concorde."

"This is madness! Would you have the Terror all over again?"

"Now, what is this? Is the proletariat the only ones who may claim that means of annihilating enemies?"

Roderic took an easy step forward, but so dynamic was his presence that the attention of everyone in the room swung to fasten upon him. The candlelight gleamed bronze across his face, turned his hair to gold, and lay like a yellow stain upon the barred breast of his uniform. "Ambition is a hard taskmaster and a poor protector. Who will save you if you fail?"

"I will need no protection, especially from you," de Landes said with intense satisfaction. "You thought you had won, didn't you? You thought I could be safely ignored. You were wrong."

This was not going as it should. Had de Landes opted for revenge after all, betraying the betrayer? The need to hear every nuance of what was being said drew Mara forward. She took a step, and another, easing between the two men to stand beside Trude. Attracted by the movement, de Landes's gaze flickered to her, then back to the prince.

"I may have underestimated you," Roderic answered, his tone pensive.

His imperturbability seemed to add to the other man's annoyance. "Do you think you are immune to the threat of execution? You are a foreigner on French soil who has been engaged in gathering information. That makes you a spy and liable to the most severe penalty."

"Does diplomatic immunity no longer hold? The officials of the French embassies scattered over the world will be dismayed to hear it."

"You claim to be the official representative of your country? Perhaps. But it is not a matter for concern. Your credentials will, I am sure, disappear. Or perhaps an apology may be extended to Ruthenia for this . . . unfortunate mistake."

"With condolences?" inquired Rolfe, king of Ruthenia, moving also to the forefront. "To whom do you intend to deliver them?"

De Landes gave Roderic's father a cold smile. "Why, to the Ruthenian reformists who are no doubt panting to overrun your country, and will if you and your lovely wife and daughter fail to return due to another mistake."

"No," Mara whispered. "No."

De Landes turned to her and stretched out his free hand while holding his pistol trained on Roderic with the other. "Come, my dear Mara. You should share this triumph. It would have been impossible without you."

"You can't do this," she said, her voice throbbing with appeal as she took a step toward him.

"Mara, stay back," Roderic said, a deep note of concern in the warning.

De Landes raised his voice. "What, you object to my plans, *ma chère?* Have you grown squeamish then?"

"I never meant this to happen."

She looked at Roderic, her soft gray gaze dull with pain and the burden of the things she had discovered. He stared at her, and his eyes narrowed.

"Poor Mara," de Landes said with an acid laugh. "You have been used—again."

There was a blur of white on her right. It was Trude in her uniform, her sword dangling uselessly at her left side, the scabbard brushing Mara's skirts. "Don't listen to him," the young woman said, her voice cold.

Trude, who was of Roderic's cadre. Trude, who was in love with her prince. What force could her words have? What trust could be placed in them? And yet she and the blond amazon, with Juliana, had once stood off a mob together.

Roderic spoke then, capturing her attention, the look in his eyes burning, incisive. "Stay, Mara, and hear me swear by the leaf-green rivers, the sun burned meadows, and the high, blue mountains of Ruthenia: *It isn't what you think.*"

She heard the rage and pain in his words, and the conviction, and she knew. She had been a fool to doubt him. Roderic was no traitor. What he had done had been undertaken for the good of Ruthenia, and perhaps of France. She could not let him die. She would not. That he was threatened was her fault. If his last breath was drawn under the sharp and shining blade of a guillotine, if his last lilting word was spoken on a scaffold, the anguish of it would eat at her heart for all her days, or for as long as she could bear to live. It could not happen, it would not if she had to die to prevent it. She must do something, but what? What?

De Landes thought her Roderic's foe and had little fear that she would cross him since she had never been in a position to do so before. She had the best chance of creating a diversion, of doing something to distract the others and allowing the cadre to act. But what weapon could she use?

She felt the brush of Trude's sword against her skirts once more. She did not stop to think, but swung to draw the blade, scraping, from its scabbard. There was no time to close with de Landes. Bringing the sword up, she flung it with all the skill that had been drilled into her by the blond amazon during the gray days of the winter, with all her strength, with all her perverse and scalding rage for the way he had used her.

Roderic saw her intent in disbelief. That she would risk so much for his sake twisted his heart with terror and remorse. Breathing a soft imprecation, he whistled, a sharp, clear signal. At that same moment he launched himself with a hard surge, his hands reaching for the Frenchman's gun hand.

Behind de Landes's cutthroats the doorway filled with dark, springing forms. Armed with pistols and knives, their teeth flashing white in their fierce grins and gold rings in their ears, were the gypsies. Leading them was Luca in his white uniform of the cadre. With ferocity they fell upon the hirelings of de Landes.

The sword Mara had thrown flew across the room, spinning, singing, its aim sure, perfect. De Landes glimpsed it and turned his pistol by instinct. His eyes widened, and his mouth opened in a scream.

The pistol exploded with the roaring boom of a cannon. Black smoke spurted with yellow fire from the barrel. Roderic ripped the pistol from de Landes's hand, flinging him backward. The Frenchman crashed to the floor and lay still, the vibrating blade of the sword standing upright in his chest.

Roderic swung around. Mara lay crumpled on the floor with a crimson splotch, slowly widening, on the basque of her gown. He was beside her in an instant, thrusting Trude and Michael aside, kneeling to lift her head with hands that were suddenly as gentle as a woman handling a newborn.

Her lashes fluttered upward. She saw the face of the man bending over her, saw the anger that shone like blue fire in his eyes.

"I'm sorry," she said, the words no more than a flutter of sound in the room that had grown suddenly quiet. "I'm sorry."

CHAPTER 19

Pain. Gray waves of pain. Voices advancing, receding. Tearing sounds. Lights glowing, glowing. Movement. Darkness. Pain, swirling, building, bursting. A warm grip on her hand, anchoring, protecting. Darkness. Cold, so cold.

For Mara there were moments that stood out, razor-edged and intensely colored in their clarity. Roderic gathering her into his arms so that her blood stained the white of his uniform coat. The infinite care with which he placed her upon her bed. His refusal, flat and uncompromising, to leave the room while the basque of her gown was cut from her and the rest of her clothing stripped away. Grand-mère, her face twisted with weeping, telling her beads. Angeline bending over the bed. The bustling doctor with his black coat, goatee, and sharp, shining lancet.

Time had no meaning. Night and day were one, an endless grayness. An enormous fire, continually replenished, burned on the hearth; still she was cold. She knew her wound was fevered, but could not find the strength to care.

There was a night, or perhaps it was day, she could not tell, when the doctor had come, felt her forehead, and looked into her eyes, muttering. He had stretched her arm out over a basin, then picked up his lancet while he felt with his thumb for the vein under the fragile skin at the turn of her elbow. He located it, then tightened the skin to ready it for the incision.

Abruptly, Roderic was there, his fingers lashing out to catch the doctor's arm in a grasp so crushing that the man buckled at the knees. The prince's voice rasped with weariness and tried patience. "Pretentious, posturing quack! I have told you she cannot stand bleeding. Spill a single drop of her life's fluid and I will draw yours as a peasant drains a wine skin."

"Her fever is too high. I will not be responsible if she is not bled."

"Will you guarantee the outcome if she is?"

"As to that, these things are in God's hands."

"Ah, I had thought you had taken that role for yourself."

The doctor wrenched free and began to cast his instruments back into his case. "Upon your head be it, then!"

Roderic, his gaze opaque, said softly, "That is where it has always been."

There had been a great weight of blankets then, and the smell of hot stone wrapped in flannel. Water had dripped upon her parched lips. She had drifted, and she sometimes heard herself trying to reason with those who lifted and turned her and placed cool cloths on her forehead.

Then came a night when her body was on fire, and her mind, and the world. She seemed to be floating, like a bird riding a warm updraft on a hot summer's day, and yet she was tethered, held fast by one hand.

Her eyelids were weighted, nearly sealed; still, she lifted them by slow application of effort. Roderic sat beside the bed, her hand in his strong grasp. His hair was tousled as if he had been running his fingers through it and damp from the heat of the fire that burned on the hearth. The stubble of a growth of beard glinted gold in the lamplight. His eyes were red-rimmed with sleeplessness and there were dark shadows in the hollows beneath them.

He raised her fingers to his mouth, brushing them with his lips. "Don't leave me," he whispered. "Mara love, if my love can hold you, I won't let you leave me."

Mara closed her eyes. Peace. Stillness. The crackling fire. A candle flame sputtered. Her chest lifted and fell in a silent sigh. She was motionless.

Roderic watched her, hardly breathing. After a time, he got to his feet and gently placed her hand upon the mattress. He lifted the coverlet and drew it over the thin fingers. With a hand that had a distinct tremor, he brushed the fine black strands of her hair back from her face. He closed his eyes, tensing the muscles of his shoulders and then releasing them with a shuddering ripple and hard shake. Moisture gathered under his eyelids. He wiped it away, then turned from the bed.

Her hand had grown slippery with perspiration. She must not become chilled by having it outside the covers. The fever had broken.

A week later, Mara lay in bed propped up on pillows. She wore a bedjacket of pink lace. A wide band of pink ribbon held her hair back from her face. Beside her on the bed was a turned-down book, while on the bedstand sat a box lined with silver paper holding bonbons. The room was warm and heavy with the smell of flowers, violets and daffodils and narcissus and hothouse roses that sat on the mantel and on tables. Trude and Estes were playing a vicious game of vingt-et-un at a small table near the fire. Michael lay stretched out on the carpet with his chin in his hand trying to read a newspaper. Jacques and Jared, lying nearby, were pretending to be taking naps, though Jared had a puppy staggering around on his chest and Jacques had one licking his ear. The parents of the pups were curled together with their other two offspring not far away, both studiously ignoring the antics of the missing pair. It was the first time that Mara had been allowed visitors, and it gave her pleasure to see them all so at ease in her bedchamber.

Roderic sat on the end of the bed with his back against the footboard and one leg trailing over the side. On his drawn-up knee rested his mandolin. His strong fingers brought forth a soft and beguiling melody, though his gaze rested on Mara.

She was lovely this morning, the pink thing she was wearing reflecting color into her face. Still, there was an ethereal quality about her, and an elusiveness that troubled him. She was not as thin as she had been, however, or as pale. Her spirit was returning, too; last night when he had insisted that she drink her red wine to build her blood, she had waited until his back was turned and poured it into her flower vase. The daffodils had promptly wilted, but he had allowed her that small victory. He had grown so used to bullying her for her own good that he had not realized he might seem overbearing. It had been such a delight to see that small secret smile of triumph on her mouth, instead of listless acceptance, that it had been all he could do not to snatch her up in his arms and smother her with kisses. She was not ready for that. Not yet. He could wait until she was. And he would.

Mara shifted on her pillows, grimacing a little. Roderic sat up and put aside the mandolin. "Would you like to lie down? Shall I move the pillows?"

"No, no, I'm fine," she answered, holding out a hand as if to ward him off. The pistol ball had torn across her ribs, breaking one and lodging just behind it. The wound might have been more serious if the ball had not been deflected and slowed by her corset stay. The doctor's probing for it had caused the most damage, adding to the scar she would always carry.

Roderic studied her face, then, satisfied, sank back and picked up his mandolin once more.

Mara sent him a quick look from under her lashes. He was always there, always ready with water, a pillow, a gentle rub for her back, soothing music; divining her need almost before she knew it herself. Nothing disturbed him, nothing made him uncomfortable. Whatever she asked, he did it at once, understanding with a frightening perception exactly what she required so that she needed to use only a minimum of words. So acute was he that she had come to rely on him before the others, even Grand-mère Helene. She did not like that.

She remembered very well the words he had said when she was so ill, and she honored him for them. But she would not depend upon them. He was a complex man with an enormous sense of responsibility that caused him, she was afraid, to blame himself for what had happened. He was compassionate, with a great capacity for understanding the working of the hearts and minds of men and women. Those qualities could lead him to say, not what was true or right, but what he felt a person most needed to hear at that particular moment. It was not that he lied; it was merely that his moral code put the welfare of the individual first. That code was flexible enough to allow that a half-truth told in the name of good was not wrong. But his code, though his own, was strict. Once a vow was given, he would not draw back from it. That was her greatest fear.

If my love can hold you . . . It could, of course, and always would, though he would never know it if she could help it.

She closed her eyes, thinking. After a few minutes, the music died away. She felt the bed give as Roderic slid from it, heard him give a quiet order. The others in the room gathered themselves and went quietly away. She thought of protesting, but realized that the visit had tired her.

Still, when the prince approached the bed, stood looking at her, and then turned away, she spoke. "Roderic?"

"Rest, he said, "I'll return later."

"What happened to de Landes?"

She waited for his answer. When it was not forthcoming, she opened her eyes. "I killed him, didn't I?"

"He was a traitor to his king and a murderer who died of his own greed for power."

"But I killed him."

"There are some men who require killing, who will petition fate and their fellow men until someone relieves them of their miserable lives."

"He wasn't even of the nobility, and he had gained so much already, an office in the ministry, a degree of power, and hope, surely, of more. Why should he risk everything to install a Bourbon king?"

"Nobility can be conferred with the tap of a sword, the stroke of a pen. It is a potent promise for some." He moved away from the bed, reaching to close the bonbon box, to straighten the vase of flowers.

"Who made that promise?"

"The same people who paid him to hire an assassin and to kill the man whether he succeeded or failed. The same people who suggested that, with my reputation for involvement in the overthrow of other rulers, I would make a good scapegoat; men who could with authority promise him a title and wealth if their needs were met."

"The legitimist circle around the comte de Chambord?"

"We can guess but never know. In any case, it doesn't matter. The revolution is over."

"The young comte de Paris is king?"

"Unfortunately not, or fortunately, as your politics dictate. The duchesse d'Orléans went with her son to the Palais Bourbon to meet with the assembly and claim the crown for the young comte. The assembly was in agreement until they were overrun by a rabble, perhaps paid by the legitimists, perhaps instigated by the socialists. To save the situation, Lamartine declared a provisional government controlled by the reformists, along with a number of the socialists from the Hotel de Ville. France has now entered into the Second Republic with Lamartine at its head."

"Will it endure?"

"I have my doubts. The guiding of a country requires a hard head and a farseeing eye; there's little room for idealism. In this struggle we saw almost nothing of the Bonapartists. They are waiting in the wings, watching to see if Lamartine stumbles or misses his cue. When he does, they will pounce."

"And Louis Napoleon will become king."

"Or emperor, in imitation of his uncle."

She frowned. "You think he would dare?"

"Quiet men are often the most ambitious and daring."

"Like de Landes."

He faced her. "No, not like de Landes. Louis Napoleon's ambition is to build, to stabilize, to restore the pride of France, not to destroy everything in the hope of gaining some small selfish concession. I understand what you feel, Mara, and I honor you for it. To care is what makes us human. The current of life flows through all of us, and to stop it, even in a mad dog, is to diminish its force. But mad dogs must be stopped. My only regret is that I didn't do it when I had the chance."

"So you could take the blame?"

"It would have been my privilege."

She gave him a level look. "The responsibility is mine, and the privilege."

"Because," he said, a smile curving his lips and rising into his eyes, "you saved my worthless skin?"

"Call it reparation."

His smile died away. His words abrupt, he asked, "For what?"

"For the betrayal."

"As to that," he drawled, "I took my own reparation long ago."

"And the night of the meeting?"

"Overconfidence, mine. Lack of trust, mine. Too great a dependence on . . . a form of communication that has limitations."

"What do you mean?"

"I thought I could read your thoughts. But all the time what I was reading may have been my own wistful impulses."

"No!" She sat up suddenly, then fell back with a cry, breathing in short, shallow gasps.

Roderic sprang forward with a curse. He held her as he threw her pillows aside and eased her flat on the bed. Brushing aside her bedjacket, he stripped open the buttons of her nightgown and pulled it aside without the least hesitation or regard for her modesty. He had done it many times before, she knew, but she had not been so aware then. Now she was.

There was an ache in her chest that had nothing to do with the wound in her side as his hand brushed over her, searching for renewed bleeding, some sign that she had opened her wound. She saw the tension leave his features, the easing of the lines about his eyes, and had to swallow a hard lump in her throat. It was easier to be angry than to allow herself to be touched by his concern or meltingly affected by the mere sight of him so near, bending over her. For an instant his knuckles rested against the swell of her breast as he tested the bandaging just beneath it. She slapped his hand away.

"I'm perfectly all right!"

"Yes," he agreed, a faint smile playing about his mouth, "I think you are."

He reached to refasten her nightgown. Once again she pushed his hand aside. "I'll do it."

"I couldn't permit you to overtax your strength," he said gravely as he returned to his task.

"There's little danger of that with you hovering." She caught his wrists this time, realizing too late that though she had prevented his access to her buttons, she had also prevented her own.

"I am at your beck and call, a perfect slavey. Doesn't that make you happy?"

"Oh, ecstatic, except that though you may come when I call, you don't go when you're not needed." Under her fingers the pulse that beat in his wrists was hard and not quite even, a fascinating discovery.

"I begin to understand. Shy, delicate blossom that you are, your modesty is offended," he said, his tone caressing in its mock sympathy though there was wicked delight in the glance he lowered to her bared breasts. "How can you ever forgive me?"

He could have broken her grip with laughable ease, and they both knew it. That he was content with the display she made, lying with her hair like a dark and shimmering background for her nakedness, her cheeks flushed with irritation and a belated awareness masquerading as embarrassment, they also knew. And yet beneath his enjoyment was such tenderness that she caught her breath.

He saw that sudden, questioning vulnerability. It required an answer. Drawn irresistibly by the soft contours of her mouth, he leaned over her.

There came a tap on the door. It was opened hard upon that brief knock, and a man stepped inside. Distinguished in appearance, of medium height, he was perhaps in his midfifties. His mustache and small, neat beard were sprinkled with gray, and his hair was thinning on top: His skin was olive and burned by a Southern sun to a deep brown. His eyes were dark and the deep lines around them indicated basic good humor, but now there was wrath building in them as he absorbed the sight before him.

"What is the meaning of this?" he demanded.

"I might ask the same — " Roderic began.

"Papa!" Mara cried.

" — except," Roderic finished smoothly, "it appears redundant."

As Mara, in shock, released his hands, he straightened and turned with smooth grace, placing his body in front of her as a screen. Behind him, she refastened her nightgown with trembling haste and flipped the edges of her bedjacket back into place.

"You, sir, must be Monsieur André Delacroix," Roderic went on, his bow a model of politeness. "I assume you have been welcomed in form to Ruthenia House, but I will add my own."

Beyond Mara's father, Angeline stood in the doorway, her green gaze filled with rueful amusement overlaid by concern.

"You also need no introduction," André said in grating tones. "I would recognize you as Rolfe's spawn anywhere. You have the same look, not to mention the same damnable and undiluted gall!"

"I thank you, sir."

"It wasn't a compliment! Would you care to explain what you were doing with my daughter?"

"No."

That simple, unadorned syllable seemed to fuel André's temper as no flowery speech could. "Don't you, indeed? I receive a shocking letter from my daughter concerning events I can only describe as incredible. After weeks of travel to discover the full story, I arrive to learn that she has been shot, and then to see with my own eyes you forcing your attentions upon her while she is abed! As her father, I demand a full accounting of her presence under your roof."

"An accounting that would not be necessary if you had escorted her to Paris as was your place."

André gave him a fulminating stare. "Are you presuming to lecture me on my duty, sir?"

"It seems someone should." Roderic, his face grim, was unperturbed by the older man's ire.

Angeline moved forward to step between her son and her former fiancé. "Please, I don't think — "

"I require to see my daughter alone," André said, his tone flat.

"That is impossible."

"See here, young man, you may be a prince, you may command where there are those who will obey, but you have no control over me or my daughter."

Mara saw the muscle that stood out in the prince's jaw, saw his hands clench into fists. She tried to sit up, saying imploringly, "Roderic — "

He heard the appeal, and his features relaxed. He glanced down at her, then, seeing her struggles, moved swiftly to raise her. His arm was an iron band of support across her back as he drew her pillows behind her, placing them with a practiced hand.

"My son, as you can see," Angeline said quietly to André, "has been caring for Mara since her injury. He has become quite adept."

"Men do not ordinarily frequent the sickroom of a lady."

"Some men," she corrected gently. "There are also those who have no fear of infirmity, men who are equal to any task."

André refused to be mollified. "I still wish to speak to my daughter. I must ask to be left alone with her."

Roderic faced him. "Mara is in no condition for a long discussion of events that she has already explained once to you in writing."

"But she is in a condition to receive the kind of rough addresses you were pressing upon her? I should call you out!"

A duel. The prospect filled Mara with horror. "Papa, no! Roderic—"

"I am at your disposal, sir. However, it might be more to the point if you will come with me to my apartment where I will undertake to answer whatever you may wish to ask."

"Very fine, but I prefer the truth."

There was a close silence in the room. The tension vibrated in the scented, overheated air. It was a grievous insult, one for which any other man, at any other time, might well have answered with his life. Mara reached out to touch Roderic's arm with tears of distress in her eyes.

He did not disappoint her. His tone even and deliberate, he said, "I will naturally adjust the facts only so much as is necessary to enhance the good opinion you hold of me, sir."

Mara looked at her father. "What he is more likely to do by far is to shade the truth to protect me, leaving himself exposed. Otherwise, if you will listen, there is none who can better explain what has taken place."

"Oh, I know," André said, flinging up his hands in querulous defeat. "An explanation couched in high-flown words and phrases so that the meat of it has to be searched out like picking a dragon's teeth. But if he can overlook an insult gratuitously given in his own house, I suppose I can at least hear him out."

Her father stepped to the bed and, with awkward care for her injuries, gave her a hug and pressed a kiss to her forehead. Promising, with a defiant glance at Roderic, to return later, he went with the prince from the room.

Mara watched them go, one straight and tall and golden-haired, the other thick of waist, graying, and infinitely dear. The tears spilled over her lashes.

Angeline stayed behind, moving to straighten the bedclothes, setting Roderic's mandolin aside and rescuing Mara's book from under an extra pillow. Her busyness was an act of tact. Mara wiped her eyes on a corner of the sheet, impatient with her own weakness, as she turned to the older woman.

"Do you think they will come to blows?"

"They will try each other, but should not become dangerously at odds so long as Roderic maintains a degree of control."

"But can he do that against such provocation?"

Angeline paused to give her a warm smile. "You should know as well as any. No one else, I would venture to guess, has tried him quite so completely."

"I would have thought his father—" Mara began, then stopped since the comment was hardly complimentary.

"Well, yes, but you have attributes—for provocation, you understand—that Rolfe lacks."

Mara gave her a faint smile, then turned her attention to a piece of nonexistent fuzz on the bedclothes. "Where is the king?"

"Being a man of some discretion, and a most frustrating instinct for trouble, he left me to greet your father alone."

"He didn't mind, that he is here, I mean?"

"As to that, he may, but I will never know it unless he should judge that I am unhappy with his lack of jealousy."

Mara leaned her head back on her pillows, looking up into the canopy of her bed. "Is nothing ever simple and straightforward with him, or with his son?"

"Oh, yes, often, usually when ordinary people would use a certain delicate circumlocution."

Mara made a wry face. "In those difficult moments of embarrassment or—"

"Or desire?"

"Yes."

"Forgive me, I seem to have caught the habit from them," Angeline said with a shake of her head. "Is there anything you need?"

How easy it would be to keep Roderic's mother there talking, merely for the pleasure of saying his name, of learning more about him. It would do no good, and was painful in its way.

She summoned a smile. "No, thank you."

"Then I must go and see to having a room prepared for André. I would send Juliana to you, or Trude, but I expect it would be best if you tried to rest, perhaps napped a little."

Mara nodded. After a moment she heard the door click shut behind the older woman. She had never felt farther from sleep. What were Roderic and her father saying to each other? She did not dare think. She could not remember ever seeing her father so upset. Not the least reason, she thought, being because Roderic's accusation had struck home; her father had felt some stirring of guilt for allowing her and her grandmother to jaunt to Europe unprotected. It had been the grinding season when they left Louisiana, the season when the sweet juice of the cane from plantation fields was made into sugar. The process required close supervision, particularly this year when the yield was important to repair their fortunes affected by the panic. Still, André's worry left him open to the charge.

What did her father think of what she had done? Did he feel differently toward her? It did not seem so. The way it looked, he had instead transferred the entire blame to Roderic. She could not allow that. She must make certain as soon as possible that he understood her own part.

It was, perhaps, a good thing that de Landes was dead. In his present humor, André might well have decided to horsewhip him, or to call the man out also. The duello was banned in Paris, as in most of the world, but gentlemen incensed because of slights to their names or their persons could circumvent the regulations easily enough. In New Orleans it was not at all uncommon for men to be killed on what they were pleased to call the field of honor.

Pray God that Roderic did not quarrel with her father. With pistol or sword, it was impossible that he should be bested by the older man. Unless, of course, Roderic permitted it out of misguided conscientiousness.

It was not his fault. The blame was hers entirely. He might claim otherwise, might suggest that he had planned her seduction in order to relieve her of the guilt, but she knew better. Just as she knew that the blood of Nicholas de Landes was on her hands. She had killed a man, and nothing that Roderic could say would alter that fact. It was something she was going to have to live with for the rest of her life.

The door swung open and Juliana swept into the room. "Are you asleep? I thought not. Maman said I must let you rest, but I suspected you were in here alone fretting yourself to tatters. You must not, you know."

"Mustn't I?" Mara asked with a wry smile, though she was willing enough to be beguiled.

"What's done is done; nothing can change it. You must turn your thoughts toward tomorrow, and the day after. Life is life, and you must live it."

The gypsy influence. Mara wondered if Juliana realized it. "That's easy to say."

"But difficult to do? You begin by forgetting. And then you interest yourself in something else. My problems, for instance. Did you think you were the only one who had any?"

"What I think is that you are a great deal like your brother."

"You've only just noticed? But I was telling you about Luca."

"Were you?"

"Pay attention, Mara. Do you know what that earringed scoundrel has had the impudence to do? He has had himself appointed as my official bodyguard. As if I needed one!"

"By Roderic?"

"Who else? And the king will not rescind it." Juliana took a turn about the room that sent her skirts flying in a wide sweep.

Watching her, Mara said, "I can see why Luca did it; he is obviously besotted with you."

"Oh, yes, to the point that he publicly repudiated all claim to my hand!"

"He was forced to it."

Juliana's face took on a look of scorn. "He could have defied the cadre and my brother, as well as my father."

"Could he and retain his principles, his worth as a man?"

"He didn't have to come crawling back."

"He came to bring information Roderic needed and his help. What I don't understand is why he was sent away in the first place, why your father insulted him so. It doesn't seem like King Rolfe to harbor such prejudice. Could it be that it was a trial by fire?"

"Naturally, and he passed it to my father's satisfaction, but what of mine?"

Troubled, Mara was silent until the other girl stopped striding about and turned to look at her inquiringly. Then she said, "What of Luca? To appoint him your bodyguard is to encourage him, or so it seems to me, though it may be the same as with Crown Prince Arvin, a means of throwing you together so that you conceive a disgust for one another. Still, if it has the opposite effect, what will be the outcome? You are a princess, he is a gypsy."

"There is nothing in the laws of Ruthenia that forbids marriage between royalty and a commoner. It has happened before."

"Perhaps, but the need for alliances, for protective agreements between countries, usually means a marriage of state to cement them."

"Such alliances mean nothing; they are as easily broken as any other. The world is changing. That sort of diplomacy is hopelessly outdated."

"Would you become a gypsy woman, then, and roam Europe in a caravan?"

"I might, but Luca, if he wished, could make a place for himself with my brother, become someone of importance in the government of my country."

"It seems he wishes to do so. And now what of you? What do you want?"

Juliana gave a toss of her head, then the irritation left her face to be replaced by a somber shadow. She made a helpless gesture with one hand. "If I knew, I would attempt to get it. But I don't."

Juliana had succeeded in her aim, which had been distraction. When she had gone, Mara lay staring at the fire across the room, thinking. The world might be changing. Alliances between royal houses might be a thing of the past. One thing remained the same, however. Princes did not wed their mistresses or the women who tricked their way into the royal bed. Pride must refuse that choice, even if common sense did not. But if, because of a vow given in a moment of self-blame, Roderic should seek to wed her, she trusted she would have the strength to refuse.

CHAPTER 20

"I would like to go home as soon as possible."

Mara had meant the words to be a firm statement of fact. Instead they had a tight, defensive sound.

"Why, *chère?*"

André, sitting in an armchair before the fire in her bedchamber, looked up from his newssheet to peer over his spectacles at her where she sat in a chair across from him. It seemed everyone spent half their time reading the columns of print these days, trying to discover what was happening with the new republic and its leaders.

"It isn't a sudden decision. I wanted to go before, weeks ago."

"But I've been here such a short time—what is it, eight, nine days?—not nearly enough time to reacquaint myself with the city. The theaters are opening, the opera houses, the restaurants. It's been twenty years since I sampled these pleasures in Paris itself, and I look forward to them."

Her father, after that first explosive quarrel, had come to terms with Roderic. They seemed to understand each other on some entirely masculine level. Within a day or two André had become accustomed to the peculiar household and had fitted himself into it with remarkable ease, exchanging tales with the cadre and joining them on some of their visits to the upper rooms of the restaurants, making himself agreeable to the guests who had begun to come and go again. With Angeline he was part gallant and part childhood friend. They often sat reminiscing, and sometimes he served as her escort about the city. Rolfe accepted his presence with equanimity, without effusiveness, but also without a trace of jealousy.

Mara forced a smile. "It's springtime in Louisiana, my favorite season. The fruit trees will be blooming, and the honeysuckle and rambling roses. The clover will be high. It will be planting time, and you know you don't want to miss that."

"My overseer is a good man. I gave him his instructions before I left as I had no idea how long I would be gone. In any case, I'm not sure you are fit yet for the return journey."

"I will be before long, perhaps another week."

He put down his newssheet and took off his spectacles, folding them and attaching them to the watch chain that looped across his waistcoat. "Mara, *ma chère,* are you certain you know your own mind? I thought—that is, I had assumed you and Roderic—"

"No."

"What do you mean, no?"

"The prince has not asked me to marry him, and, in any case, I don't wish it."

"You don't wish it." He stared at her, a frown gathering between his brows before he repeated, "You don't wish it. You didn't want to marry Dennis Mulholland when he had compromised you in the summerhouse. Now Roderic has done much more, but you don't care to be wed to him either. What, may I ask, will it take to please you in a husband?"

"I don't know, Papa," she said, leaning her head back

on the chair cushions, closing her eyes. "I only know I have no need of a man who will marry me out of a feeling of obligation."

"Such scruples do you credit, but are they wise?"

"That doesn't matter."

"It matters to me. I'm your father, and it's my duty to see that you don't ruin your life over this unfortunate affair."

She turned her head to look at him. "You forced me to become engaged to one man out of that fear. I will not allow you to do the same thing again. Please don't interfere, Papa. Just take me home soon."

Long seconds ticked past before he spoke, and even then he avoided her gaze. "You are more like your mother than I supposed. I married her because—who can say precisely why? I was lonely. She was beautiful and as different as possible from Angeline, and most of all she loved me. She discovered soon enough that my affection was not deep. She knew that I would never dishonor our wedding vows, that as my wife she would always grace my table and share my bed, and that we would be comfortable together. It wasn't enough. I suppose it isn't enough for you either. When you are strong again, in a week or two, I will make the arrangements for our departure."

"Thank you, Papa." The victory had been easier than she had expected. She should have been glad. Instead, she felt numb, and in her eyes was gray bleakness.

Her father's well-meaning interference was not all she had to face. The cadre, for no reason that she could see, began to treat her as though it were an accepted fact that she would be with them always. They solicited her opinions on a thousand things and listened as if the answers had the weight of authority behind them. She could see no reason for it, unless it was Roderic's constant presence at her side, his air of possession. It made her uncomfortable, yet at the same time it gave her such a warm feeling of belonging that she was reluctant to discourage it. It would end soon enough.

She had progressed from sitting up in a chair in her room to taking her meals with the others and joining them in the salon. She put aside her dressing gown for ordinary clothing. She had thought she would have to leave off her corset, but discovered that the whalebone-stiffened garment, so long as it was not too tight, supported her mending ribs. The knowledge gave her hope that she would be able to leave sooner than she had expected.

In Louisiana it would be spring, but in Paris winter lingered. Despite the swelling of the buds on the trees and bright displays of primroses on windowsills, the days continued gray, often with chill, drizzling rain. It was on such a day that Trude approached Mara in the salon.

Mara had been trying to embroider. She lay on a settee under one of the tall windows opening onto the entrance court, trying to find light to see the faint pattern she was following. As the other woman drew up a chair, she tucked her needle into the stretched linen in her hoop and thankfully flung it aside.

"There is something I have wanted to say to you," Trude said, her face solemn.

"This sounds serious, indeed," Mara teased her. "What is it?"

"Once I thought—I thought I loved Roderic. I know now it was only because he is my prince, my leader, and a handsome man."

The humor died from Mara's eyes. "And now?"

"Now I know something more is needed. I will honor him, I will follow him, perhaps I will love him a little. No more."

"It . . . will be his loss." Mara could think of nothing else to say to such a simple declaration.

"I think not. I love you also. I will be content."

"Trude, you must not think—"

"I don't think, I know. You have his love. I want to tell you that you take nothing from me. I also have my love."

Diverted, Mara asked, "Estes?"

A faint blush stained the amazon's cheeks. "The count. He is droll, is he not? He makes me laugh. I like that. And he has knowledge of women. That I also like."

Mara tried to picture the Italian and the tall, blond woman in a moment of passion, and failed. Perhaps Trude had not meant that Estes was experienced with women, but that he understood their needs. She would never know, and it was not important that she should. She reached out to press the other woman's hand. "I wish you joy."

Trude smiled, returning the clasp. "And you."

A few days later, Angeline arranged for a *musicale soirée*. The music would be provided by a trio of gypsies, great musicians all. Much of the music of Europe, Mara had been informed, had been taken from the ancient melodies and rhythms of the *Tziganes,* and many of the greatest violinists had gypsy blood in their veins. It was to be a rare treat.

Many of the people she had met in Paris were on hand: Aurore Dudevant, known as George Sand; the Dumas, father and son; Honoré de Balzac; Victor and Adele Hugo. Conspicuously absent were Lamartine and the other deputies; they were much too busy for frivolous entertainments.

The music was superb, the sounds brought forth from the common stringed instruments were exciting in their complexity, yet achingly pure and sweet, like a pain in the heart. The hardened experts that were gathered applauded with tears in their eyes and shouted for encore after encore.

The conversation afterward was witty and sharp-edged.

A great deal of it centered, not unnaturally, on politics. There was already a feeling of disenchantment, or so it seemed to Mara, with the new regime. The compromises necessary to govern a diverse people and the lack of firm proposals to deal with the worsening economical situation were viewed with disdain by the literary elite. The ideals of reform appeared to be lost. The only surprise in that, according to Roderic, was why the French, usually such realists, were so surprised.

Mara wore a gown of pale yellow satin for the soirée. She was feeling much better, and had even persuaded Lila to draw her corset strings a bit tighter for the occasion. Still, even when the music ended she kept to the settee where she was ensconced. Michael brought her refreshments and, deputized by Roderic, who was performing his social duties, stayed to keep her company. He was relieved a short time later by the twins. When they deserted her to chase after an actress from the Comédie Française, they were replaced by Luca.

The gypsy talked easily enough of the music they had heard and of great composers who had been influenced by his people, but his mood was morose. He seldom took his gaze from Juliana as she moved about the room. The princess never looked in his direction. That very omission seemed suggestive to Mara, but the man standing behind her was not encouraged by it.

There was a long period of quiet while Luca watched Juliana flirting with extreme vivacity with a French nobleman. His hand gripped the carved rosewood back of the settee until the knuckles were white. He said a soft word in the *calo* of the gypsies that sounded far from complimentary.

"What does she want of me, the Princess Juliana? I have given her my love, my heart, all that I am. I have suffered insult to gain her father's favor. I have left the tents of my people for her. What more can I do?"

Mara, watching the willful set of Juliana's head on her shoulders, said on impulse, "You have given so much, perhaps too much. What have you asked of her?"

"Only her love."

"But don't you want to know her, to discover what she thinks and dreams, what makes her laugh and cry, what strengths she has to complement yours?"

"More than the world, but how can I learn these things if she will not let me near her?"

It was, indeed, a problem. Finally, Mara asked, "What would you do if she were a gypsy woman and treated you this way?"

He smiled so that his teeth flashed white in his face. "That would be easy."

"Well, then? She is a princess, but also a woman."

He looked skeptical, then, as he continued to watch Juliana with the light of the chandeliers gleaming on her white shoulders and in the gold of her hair, his gaze became thoughtful. "Yes," he said slowly. "Yes. And if she still despises me, it can be no worse."

That might be so, and again it might not. In some trepidation, Mara asked, "Luca, what are you going to do?"

He did not answer. "Ah, Mara, what would we do without you? You must hurry and be well so that you and Roderic may be wrist-joined as man and wife."

He left her then, moving with the smoothness of the excellent muscle control of a man who has danced as well as fought for most of his life. He bowed before Juliana, speaking to her. Juliana said something sharp, turning away. Luca caught her arm so that she was pulled off balance, stumbling against him. In an instant, he bent and swung her into his arms, striding with her toward the door that led into an antechamber not far away. After the first moment of stunned incredulity, Juliana struggled, pushing against his chest, but she did not scream or call out for help. So quietly and quickly was it done that only a few people turned to stare.

Mara had swung her feet from the settee to rise, to go after them, when Roderic stepped in front of her. He put a hand on her shoulder, detaining her. "What, may one ask, did you say to Luca to turn him into a brigand carrying off the spoils?"

She looked up at him with a worried frown. "I only recommended that he treat Juliana as he would a woman of his own people. I had no idea that was what he would do."

"So simple," he murmured. "Why didn't I think of it?"

"Aren't you going to stop him?"

"I don't expect he will go far; Juliana will see to that."

"But what if he harms her?"

He shook his head. "He is still her bodyguard, not an assignment he takes lightly. Luca is the one in danger, or so I would have said until a few minutes ago."

What Luca had said to her still rang in her ears. She took a deep breath. "Then if you have a few moments, could I speak to you?"

"Darling Mara, you have been speaking to me."

The facetious answer was, she saw, a barrier designed to give him time to assess her request. "I mean, seriously."

He searched her face, the smile dying out of his eyes. Inclining his head, he said, "As you wish."

He helped her to her feet and gave her his arm for support as he led her from the room and along the main gallery to his own apartment. A fire burned in the private salon, and he put her in a chair in front of it. He offered her wine and she refused. He moved to stand in front of the fireplace with his back to the glow until he saw the way she was forced to look up at him. He stepped then to the companion chair to her own, dropping into it, relaxing with his elbow propped on the arm. His face pensive, he waited without the least sign of impatience for her to begin.

She could not think of what to say. All the many things she wanted to make plain to him tumbled together in her mind without form. She wished futilely that she had planned better for this meeting instead of bringing it about on the spur of the moment. It was so important that he understand and accept the decision she had made.

She looked down at her hands, moistening her lips with the tip of her tongue. "It seems we have been at cross-purposes since we met, always doing what was required of us, but for a different reason than the obvious. I am deeply ashamed of the way I used you. You have dealt with me better than I deserve. I—I did what I could to right the great wrong I had done, to repair the damage. And now I must leave."

She glanced up at him, at the arrested look on his features, then transferred her gaze to the fire. "There seems to be a feeling among your cadre that you—that we will be wed. I don't know where it came from, but I wanted to tell you that it isn't required. I am grateful beyond measure for your support while I have been ill. I know—I remember some of the things you said. They helped at the time, immensely, as they were meant to do. But I would not hold you to the letter of them. I will be returning to Louisiana soon with my father. You will be free of me, I give you my word."

His answer was soft. "That has the sound of pious renunciation."

She should have remembered how acute he could be. She sent him an earnest look. "There is no reason it should. It was an accident that two people such as you and me, from different sides of the world, ever met. That we should go our separate ways again is normal."

"Sacrifice. Ritualistic and complete. I cannot allow it."

"I won't marry you." She could not put it more baldly than that.

He got to his feet, regaining the dominance he had willingly set aside before. Clasping his hands behind his back, he gazed in some bemusement at the oval of her face framed by the upswept curls of her hair, at the gentle curves of her breasts revealed by the low décolletage of her gown and the swift rise and fall of her breathing under the yellow satin. How lovely she was, and how stubbornly determined. Unlike Luca with Juliana, he could not sweep her up and shake some sense into her head or kiss her until she yielded because of her injured condition. The only weapons he had against her denial were words.

"Do you know why I came to Paris? It was not to occupy the official residence of Ruthenia or to sample the entertainments at which the French excel. I came because the events taking place here threatened the stability of Europe and my own country, because there were rumors flying of yet another attempt to assassinate Louis Philippe, one that showed signs of a greater chance of success than most—and because violent death among crowned heads is like a spreading disease; one often leading to another. My task was to prevent the assassination and to minimize the effects of the attempt."

Mara, aware that few ever received an explanation of his actions from Roderic, listened closely. When he paused, she said, "I would have thought the prevention of the revolution would have been your goal?"

Real humor lit his eyes. "I appreciate your confidence in my ability to control the political factions of France, but I confess it is beyond me—as it has been beyond several French kings to date. I did try. I took what steps I could to learn what the different groups were doing, but my first concern was to protect Louis Philippe since it appeared that he would be able to keep his middle-class support and therefore had the chance of holding France together."

"Juliana told me about your cadre and your role in preventing other assassinations."

"We were called the Death Corps, not what we would have chosen ourselves, but apt since assassins are usually driven men who must be permanently stopped if they are to be deflected from their objects. In Paris, the *garde de corps* and I set about testing the wind, collecting information. And then I saw you."

"You saw me."

She repeated the words with dull acceptance. Until that moment she had not really believed him capable of the duplicity of enticing her into his orbit, had not wanted to believe it. The knowledge hurt.

A grim smile touched his mouth, then he went on. "One of the many things we learned through the channels we encouraged was news of the presence in Paris of Madame Helene Delacroix and her granddaughter. The names were familiar to me, of course, since I had heard much from my mother about Louisiana. The social requirements having been impressed upon me since childhood, I set out to pay a duty call. I saw you and your grandmother getting into a carriage with de Landes. That's how close we came to a properly dull introduction. I left my card with a servant where you were staying and went away again. That night I left Paris to visit the gypsy camp, and before midnight you dropped into my lap like a gift from the gods."

"And that was all?"

She did not know whether to be relieved or incensed that the thing she had thought was not true. "But you let me believe—"

"You so obviously saw me as capable of any villainy.

I could not resist. In any case, the part I played was base enough."

"Because you recognized me?"

"I thought I did," he answered, a troubled look passing across his features, "but I had seen you so briefly, and not at close range. I knew something of de Landes and could guess that there was a purpose in your arrival, but it seemed incredible that someone like you would do his bidding. I could not rule out the possibility that you had simply been fooled by him and persuaded into a carriage ride in the countryside, that you had been discarded there or perhaps had escaped him by jumping from the carriage at that spot. Your loss of memory could have been real. The more I saw of you, learned of you, the less I could imagine anything else. You were a most convincing actress. And yet the coincidence was too great to swallow."

"So you took me with you to Paris."

"The situation required pursuing. What I discovered was that you and Madame Helene were supposedly out of the city at some property belonging to de Landes, another unlikely coincidence. And then when you left this house, he contacted you."

"You set Luca to spy on me. I thought he was a protector."

"Could he not be both? But after that day I nearly went mad trying to decipher the riddle you presented, to find some excuse, any excuse, for what you were doing. You came to me as such an innocent temptress, but a thousand times more effective because of it."

"You were able to resist me easily enough," she said with some tartness.

"Easily? How can you think it? No Hades conceived by a monk made mad with celibacy could have been more wracking. You were my mother's goddaughter; how could I despoil you? Yet how could I not when it seemed the best way of coming close enough to you to discover what de Landes intended, the best way of carrying out my duty, would be to cease to resist."

"Duty?" she exclaimed with loathing.

"But in the end it was not duty that made me succumb." He waited, his narrowed gaze upon her face.

"What was it then? You need not tell me it was an uncontrollable passion, for I remember all the preparations for the seduction, the violets and the diamonds—everything but gypsy violins!"

He smiled, satisfied. "Oh, I would have brought those, too, if I had thought of it. And there was desire, a white-hot and consuming obsession of it. But the final seduction was a thing of sheer cunning, the ultimate trap."

That he could talk of it so easily gave her the courage to do the same. "Trap? You mean it was the proof you needed that I was the accomplice of de Landes?"

"Ah, no, because by then, willing or not, you had become mine. I knew you, on some deep level, by some instinct I could not begin to analyze. Allied to my other sources, I was certain I would be aware of when and where de Landes expected to use me from your reactions. No, it was more perfidious than that. I saw that your presence with me must become known—in fact, I took you with me to various public events so that it could not be missed. This course was chosen because it was plain that the masquerade would have to end, and when the unmasking came, when you were exposed as my mother's goddaughter, I must naturally be called upon to do the honorable thing. The greater our intimacy, the more imperative it would be."

Words, their shadings of meaning, were his stock-in-trade, as was the careful manipulation of people in order to achieve the results he wanted. She must remember that. She must.

"You are saying that you *wished* to marry me?"

"To bind you to me beyond sundering."

"But you did not."

"My father, in his ineluctable wisdom and crass fashion, pointed out the unfair advantage I had taken. He was right."

"And all that about bourgeois respectability was—"

"Mere bombast. But he is magnificent, isn't he?"

So was his son. If only she could believe what he was saying with such relish. No, it was too unlikely to be true. He was not an ordinary prince concerned with proper behavior; he made his own rules that had little to do with the conventions. And yet there were some he could not ignore, those that touched upon his family, his country, his duty. To these he was bound more than most, precisely because he was above the crowd and therefore highly visible. He would not have deliberately flouted the unwritten laws of decent conduct. It was a lie. A munificent one, but a lie. She looked down at her hands clasped in her lap to hide the rise of tears.

When she failed to comment, he went on, though there was a heaviness inside him. "I had the best of intentions. I meant to retreat, to give you breathing room. It was not always possible to hold to such high resolve. The political situation required my attention. And every time I took my eye from you, you ran straight into danger." He lifted a hand to rub his eyes. "God, to see you facing that mob with a sword in your hand: I was bloated with pride and, at the same time, shriveled like a sun-dried date with unadultered terror."

"My safety was not your problem."

He shook his head as if he did not hear. "And that afternoon when I found you in that Left Bank garret with de Landes. I have never felt anything quite . . . It was as if we were one, two parts of a whole, and sharing for an interminable instant a single beating heart and transcendent mind. I knew what you were doing. I knew."

He turned his back to her, staring down into the flames of the fire. "I suppose I expected that oneness to last. I expected you to understand that I would act on the snare you had laid so carefully for de Landes. You didn't. My failure to see that you didn't nearly cost you your life."

"The failure was mine," she said through the tightness in her throat. "You trusted me. It was a trust I didn't, couldn't, return."

"How could you? I gave you no reason."

"Oh, I could have, if I had listened to my heart instead of my head."

He whipped around, held out a square, brown hand. "Then listen to it now!"

"Please. Don't." She pushed herself to her feet, moving away from him. "You are very convincing, but I can't forget that you have been forced to this."

"Forced? By what? By whom? I could have stopped it at any time."

"You didn't, and the reason lies in what you said: It was the best way to carry out what you had to do."

"Tripped by my own logic," he said with a hollow laugh, "the penalty of being too articulate."

He watched her as she turned away, and he ached with the need of her and the necessity of releasing her from the prison of doubt that she had built around herself. It was a protection, he thought. She was afraid he would hurt her. Rather than that, he would withdraw into his own confinement, leaving her free to make the escape she thought she needed. There should, however, be some compensation.

"Mara, do you love me?"

She sent him a quick glance, then looked away again. "If I did, it would change nothing."

"Even so, do you?"

The love she felt for him had been a gnawing pain inside her since—she hardly knew how long, perhaps since she had seen him playing a mandolin by the firelight in the midst of a gypsy camp. To deny it now seemed pointless, another needless betrayal.

"Yes, I love you."

The urge for violent action was nearly overpowering. To stand where he was, set like some item of the salon's decor, was the most difficult thing he had ever asked of himself. His impulse was to cover the distance that separated them in a single stride, to take her to the settee and—He couldn't. For the thousandth time, and the most bitter one, he wished that her injury was his. In its way it was, and might prove to be mortal.

What reaction she had expected, Mara could not have said; still, his frozen acceptance was deflating. She lowered her lashes, moving toward the door. "My father and I will be going home as soon as possible."

"Wait."

She paused to look at him. His gaze was hooded, considering, and yet behind the gold-tipped screen of his lashes was a flash of cobalt brilliance.

"There will be a gypsy wedding for Luca and Juliana if I am any judge. It will be something to see. Will you stay for it?"

The request sounded in her ears like a reprieve. She knew she should be wary. But to refuse this small thing would be graceless and ungrateful under the circumstances. Besides, Juliana had grown to be very like a sister to her.

"I will do that much, yes," she said quietly.

"Thank you," he answered, his tone just as grave. "Juliana will be pleased."

He moved not a muscle, not an eyelid, as she left the room and closed the door gently behind her.

The month before Juliana's gypsy wedding was the longest period of Mara's life. The delay was caused in part by a concern for appearances, but primarily by the necessity of visits to the modistes and milliners to order a wedding gown and trousseau for the Catholic wedding that would follow in Ruthenia. Mara said nothing more to her father or the others about leaving. It seemed best to wait until the celebration was over. They could then slip away at the same time the others were leaving Paris for the journey to their homeland. There would be fewer explanations to make, fewer recriminations to be heard. It might be cowardly, but she excused it by telling herself that she did not want to draw attention away from the bride and groom.

For the gypsy ceremony, Juliana had ordered a gown cut on simple lines, rather like the blouses and wide, flowing skirts of the *Tzigane* women, though it was made of layers of white tissue silk banded on the many hems with cloth of gold. She insisted that Mara should have something similar instead of wearing her stiff, unwieldly skirts that made it so difficult and inconvenient to sit gypsy fashion on the rugs.

Mara was reluctant, due to the unnecessary expense, but Angeline added her weight to the argument in favor of it. Juliana would be more comfortable in her own rather conspicuous costume if she was not the only one wearing such a thing, and since Mara would be lending the bride support, it would be a gift from her godmother. Angeline, like her son, was difficult to circumvent. It was finally agreed that Mara would wear pale blue silk banded with cloth of silver.

The gypsy camp was much the same, loud with laughter and music and bright with the light of fires that made a gray cloud of smoke above the caravans. The smell of roasting meat hung in the air. Women, their festive clothing like bright splashes of an artist's oils in red, blue, green, and yellow, turned food on spits over glowing red coals or stirred pots. Children chased each other, yelling, calling, with unabashed vigor. Dogs barked, chickens cackled, horses whinnied. And yet there was an air of impermanence about the gathered caravans. They were tightly packed, with everything stowed away or hanging neatly here and there. The encampment would be breaking up that night when the feast was over. The gypsies would also be leaving for Ruthenia to join in the festivities that would take place there after the official wedding of the *boyar*'s daughter to one of their own.

The ceremony was not elaborate. The gypsies ceased what they were doing and gathered around the main fire. Violinists, who had been regaling the guests already, played a spritely and flirtatious march to bring the couple from the caravans where they had been secluded. From separate directions, they approached the *boyar,* Rolfe, who stood waiting. Mara walked with Juliana and Roderic with Luca until the couple were side by side, then they stepped back into the crowd. Rolfe took the right hand of Juliana and joined it with Luca's right hand, bidding them hold fast to each other while they exchanged their vows.

Luca, darkly handsome in a full-sleeved shirt of red, with his gold ring in his ear, spoke in firm, clear tones. "I, Luca, take this woman to wife and give her my oath that I will leave her free to seek happiness elsewhere as soon as love has left my heart."

Juliana stood tall and proud, gazing into the eyes of her groom as she repeated the same vow. Then Roderic stepped forward to hand his father a knife with a jeweled handle. Rolfe took Luca's wrist and slashed an incision perhaps an inch long. Juliana offered her wrist, and a similar incision was made in it. The two cuts were placed together and their wrists bound. Thus they stood with their blood mingling, facing each other as the night wind lifted the edges of their hair and stirred Juliana's silk skirts against Luca's boots. Around them were their friends and family, above them nothing but the dark, star-filled sky.

A shout went up, ringing into the night. Music burst forth wild and full of passion. Wine flowed. Food was snatched hot and crackling from the fire. People talked and laughed and shouted in a rich, communal joy.

Mara stood alone. She could see Grandmère and her father with the others, gathered around the bride and groom. She felt outside that circle of happiness, bereft, cold inside.

. . . as soon as love has left my heart.

There was nothing permanent in such a vow, and yet what good was permanence without love? The words suggested that to feel love inside oneself was the important thing, not being loved. To give love as long as it lasted, not to take it. In that case it was a vow that she could make, given the chance.

The chance had been there, and she had let it go. She had let it go out of—what? Pride? Distrust? The fear that she was not loved in return?

But she loved. She loved a golden prince, and to leave him to go across the ocean thousands of miles away, perhaps never to see him again, would be to maim some tender portion of her being.

For the gypsies, to love was enough. The happiness of the moment was what mattered, and each person was responsible for his or her own happiness, none other. Life was life. Love was love. Neither could be measured or bartered or hoarded away. They required use. Living. Loving.

The music had slowed, becoming sweet and vibrant with desire. The feasting was over. Soon the bridal couple would leave to be alone in Luca's caravan. Not long after, the caravans would begin to roll. The wedding would be over.

But not yet. Luca, his arms held out from his sides,

began to move to the music. The crowd spread, forming a circle, giving him room. Advancing, retreating, the dance he wove before Juliana was as old as time, a courtship ritual as natural as it was obvious. As if enticed, Juliana joined him, circling, whirling, moving with him as if mesmerized, and yet with elegance and a rising emotion that matched that of her new husband. The music rose; faster and faster the violins played until they reached a crescendo. Suddenly, Luca swept Juliana up and the two of them broke through the crowd, vanishing into the dark line of the caravans.

But the sweet, high note of the violins did not end. It held, stretching in audible tension, seeking, demanding. A sigh swept through the crowd as Roderic stepped into the circle. He had removed his uniform coat and wore his shirt open at the neck and tucked into his trousers with a sash of blood-red about his waist. His hair gleamed with the dark luster of old gold coins in the firelight, and his expression was self-contained as he moved with lithe and muscular grace, slowly turning as if searching. The crowd retreated, jostling, widening its circle until Mara was included where she stood. Roderic's gaze touched her, lingered, held.

She watched him advance upon her as the music throbbed into its sensual melody once more. Her heart began to pound, and she felt a flush mounting to her hairline. There was such distress racing with the blood in her veins that her body ached as if she had been poisoned. And yet there rose within her such excitement that she could not breathe, could not think.

He held out his hand. She raised her gray eyes to his and saw reflected there an infinite and implacable will, a perilous challenge, and an aching need.

She loved him, and it was enough for now. But once she had seduced him. She had made him desire her in spite of all his talk of duty and traps and causes. It was possible that she could do it again. She could try, beginning here with the wine and the music and the night as her aids. And so she allowed a smile, sweet and gently enticing, to curve her mouth and placed her hand in his as if the touch would burn.

Together they moved, their bodies attuned, gliding as one. Now locked together, now apart, they whirled in splendid unison. With spirit and tender longing, they courted each other, Roderic guiding Mara's movement, Mara drawing him, entranced, toward her. Their faces were absorbed, secretive. The silver banding on Mara's skirts flickered like lightning around them. The white of Roderic's clothing glowed incandescent. They were burnished by the firelight, enwrapped in magic and a tremulous, soaring desire.

And the music of the violins rose, building, straining, reaching for that fervent, sustained note. Higher and higher, faster and faster, describing violent joy, wild ecstasy, teetering on the fine edge of a dissonant scream. It came.

Roderic spun Mara into his arms. He lifted her, pushing, forcing his way through the crowd. Behind them was sudden, crashing silence. Then came the roaring cheer. The sound wafted them toward a caravan, long remembered, of white and blue. It loomed before them and then they were inside. The door slammed shut behind them, closing out the noise. They were alone.

He put her on her feet, retaining a light grasp on her arms. In the light of the single candle that burned beside a bed strewn with violets, he searched her face. "Ah, Mara," he said, the words strained, a husk of sound, "if you don't mean to stay, then go now, before it's too late."

"It's already too late."

"I swear I love you. You hold my heart by steel ribbons, and you are the tether that anchors my soul. If you leave me, I will be a rattling husk of a man, fit for nothing more than to frighten ravens."

"I won't leave."

His hold tightened. "Tell me how I can prove it and that will become my grail, my golden fleece, my hope of heaven and dream of paradise. Let me show you—"

She raised her hand, placing it across his lips. It was possible that she believed him, but for now it did not matter. Her eyes clear gray and bottomless with trust, she said, "Roderic, princely love, tell me what I am thinking."

He met her gaze, his own suspended, infinitely receptive. A moment passed. The corners of his mouth twitched, began to curve upward. The light of a fine amusement rose in his eyes, growing, shining bright. His grasp tightened and he drew her against him, crossing his arms behind her back, burying his face in her hair and inhaling its fragrance as he drew a deep breath. There was laughter and warm relief and pulsing longing in his voice when he spoke.

"Sweet temptress, light of my days and solace of my nights, you might have spared my blushes."

She drew back to give him a skeptical look, saying, "I would have if you had—"

She was not allowed to finish.

ABOUT THE AUTHOR

Jennifer Blake was born near Goldonna, Louisiana, in her grandparents' one-hundred-twenty-year-old hand-built cottage. It was her grandmother, a local midwife, who delivered her. She grew up on an eighty-acre farm in the rolling hills of north Louisiana and got married at the age of fifteen. Five years and three children later, she had become a voracious reader, consuming seven or eight books a week. Disillusioned with the books she was reading, she set out to write one of her own. It was a Gothic—*Secret of Mirror House*—and Fawcett was the publisher. Since that time she has written twenty-eight books, with more than eight million copies in print, and has become one of the bestselling romance writers of our time. Her recent Fawcett books are *Royal Seduction, Surrender in Moonlight, Midnight Waltz*, and *Fierce Eden*. Jennifer, her husband, and their four children are currently enjoying their house near Quitman, Louisiana—styled after old southern planters' cottages.